A Reluctant Courtship

Books by Laurie Alice Eakes

THE MIDWIVES

Lady in the Mist

Heart's Safe Passage

Choices of the Heart

THE DAUGHTERS OF BAINBRIDGE HOUSE

A Necessary Deception

A Flight of Fancy

A Reluctant Courtship

The Daughters of Bainbridge House, Book 3

A Reluctant Courtship

Laurie Alice Eakes

A Novel

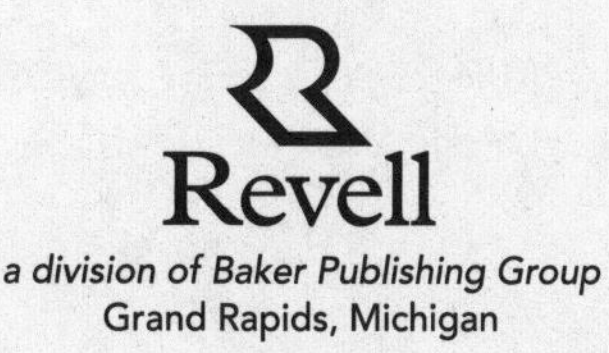

a division of Baker Publishing Group
Grand Rapids, Michigan

Published by Revell
a division of Baker Publishing Group
P.O. Box 6287, Grand Rapids, MI 49516-6287
www.revellbooks.com

Printed in the United States of America

Library of Congress Cataloging-in-Publication Data
Eakes, Laurie Alice.
A reluctant courtship : a novel / Laurie Alice Eakes.
pages cm. — (The Daughters of Bainbridge House ; book 3)
ISBN 978-0-8007-3468-8 (pbk.)
1. Man-woman relationships—Fiction. 2. England—Social life and customs—19th century—Fiction. I. Title.
PS3605.A377R45 2013
813′.6—dc23 2013018739

Scripture quotations are from the King James Version of the Bible.

This book is a work of fiction. Names, characters, places, and incidents are the product of the author's imagination or are used fictitiously. Any resemblance to actual events, locales, or persons, living or dead, is coincidental.

Published in association with the Hartline Literary Agency, LLC.

13 14 15 16 17 18 19 7 6 5 4 3 2 1

In memory of another author
who profoundly impacted my writing,
though she was gone before I ever heard her name—
the incomparable Georgette Heyer.

The Spirit of the Lord GOD is upon me; because the LORD hath anointed me to preach good tidings unto the meek; he hath sent me to bind up the brokenhearted, to proclaim liberty to the captives, and the opening of the prison to them that are bound.

Isaiah 61:1

September 1813

Miss Honore Bainbridge was about to fall off a cliff. One minute she stood examining a fissure in the stratified rock, and the next, the crack turned into a gaping hole, ready, able, and apparently eager to swallow her whole. Her feet plunged off solid ground. Her pinwheeling arms grasped a spindly shrub struggling for life above the sea, and she clung to it with about as much hope of survival as the infant bush.

She did not scream. She had opened her mouth to do so, but her middle slammed into the rock, driving the breath from her lungs in an ignominious squeak.

And there she dangled with her arms around a sapling, her feet swinging two hundred feet over the sea, and a hawk circling above as though trying to decide if her feathered hat was some kind of new small bird.

"I am not your dinner," she gasped out to the hawk.

More like supper for several schools of fish.

At least Papa would never know that his youngest daughter had culminated her disastrous penchant for falling in love unwisely by falling off a cliff.

"I suppose this is one catastrophe you can't get me out of, Lord?" Through gasps for air from her constricted lungs, she managed the kind of cynical prayer that had become her usual way of communicating with God of late. "I suppose you can, but it looks like—"

The shrub began to loosen from its precarious hold on the thin soil.

This time Honore screamed.

"Hold on." A male voice sped past Honore's ears.

She gritted her teeth. "I am . . . holding."

A pity the bush to which she clung was not. Half its roots, connected to the earth shallowly at best, now waved in the constant wind from the sea.

Like someone saying goodbye.

Honore kicked her legs, seeking the side of the cliff, seeking a toehold. No good. Empty space met her flailing limbs. A jagged edge of broken limestone scraped along her side. Inch by inch, her torso slid toward the abyss into water foaming and roaring over a tumble of serrated rock.

"If you get . . . me out of this . . . Lord . . ." No, she was not supposed to bargain with God. She made herself stop staring at the tearing bush between her hands and gazed into a sky made of the kind of clear blue that her beaux had described as dull compared to her eyes. "Please, God?"

The shrub tore a little further. Only Honore's arms and hands clung to the earth. Only two thready roots still clung to the thin soil.

So, apparently God did not please.

She doubted she could even make the heroine of her novel in progress endure such an incident.

Honore closed her eyes. "Will I see you in heaven, Papa?"

He would not wish to see her if she died without doing something of which he could be proud.

Hands like iron bands grasped her wrists. "I've got you," an unfamiliar voice with a peculiar accent pronounced.

Honore's eyes popped open, closed, opened even wider the second time. She was not hallucinating. A being was indeed crouched in front of her and gripping her wrists.

"Angel," she murmured.

If angels possessed medium-dark hair and eyes, and skin too bronzed to belong to a gentleman. Perhaps angels were not gentlemen.

A giggle bubbled into Honore's throat. She swallowed it down so as not to sound mad—laughing while she dangled off a crumbling cliff.

"No, ma'am, I'm not an angel," the stranger said. "I'm just a flesh-and-blood man who heard you scream. Now, if you'll—"

The cliff trembled. The rough-edged rock digging into Honore's collarbone broke away. She wanted to scream, but tin-tasting lint seemed to have replaced the moisture in her mouth, keeping her silent.

The man flattened himself along the ground. "Let go of the bush and grip my wrists." His voice was deep, slow, even. "I'm less likely to lose my grip that way."

"I ca-cannot."

"And I can't let you go, so we'll both go tumbling into the sea."

She could not be responsible for another death. Nor could she get her hands to loosen their grip on the shrub.

The man's hold tightened on her wrists. "So one of the Bainbridge daughters is a coward."

"Yes, me. I." Another chunk of limestone broke away, slamming her diaphragm against the striated wall of rock. "Ooph!"

The man laughed. The gall of him.

She could not let him get away with laughing at her, this—this peasant. She would show him.

She kicked her legs as though the air was water and the motion would propel her forward. The motion set the cliff face trembling.

"Don't move." He yanked her hands apart, tearing her gloved fingers from their tenuous clutch on the sapling. "Now hold on to me."

"I do not think—"

He narrowed his eyes and flashes of gold speared into hers. "I would rather live another thirty years or more. If you wouldn't, tell me so I can let go and save my own neck."

"Why, you heartless, unfeeling—"

A slab of cliff large enough to form a table for King Arthur and his knights broke off not a foot away. Chalky dust misted the air. Honore cried out and lunged for her rescuer. Her fingers scrabbled at his shirtsleeves, tore through fabric, held.

Muttering something unintelligible above the thunder of falling rock and crashing waves, he started to rise. His body reared up from the ground. Honore slid over the edge of the cliff. What was left of her pelisse tore down the front. Muscles bulged against the sleeves of the man's shirt. Her muscles strained, ached, surely were tearing away from her bones. Hiccuping sobs shredded her throat. Her fingertips shredded his shirtsleeves. The wristbands ripped away and she lost her hold.

But he gave a mighty heave. She slammed onto the ground. Air whooshed from her lungs.

And the earth tilted beneath her.

"Move!" He surged to his feet, dragging her up after him.

He sprinted inland. Honore followed, limping, skipping,

hopping to keep up with him. Beneath them, the cliff side shivered like a giant with the ague. Behind them, veined stone tore free and boomed into the sea. Ahead of them, a low stone wall that had graced the Devonshire coastline for centuries promised stability and safety.

Honore collapsed upon it and doubled over, gasping for breath. Her hat had vanished. One shoe likely provided a home for the fish, and even a rag picker would reject her gloves and stockings as too damaged, not to mention her skirt, pelisse, and petticoat sliced to muslin ribbons.

"You'll be wanting this." Soft wool settled around her shoulders.

She glanced up at him through a spill of hair freed of its pins, took in his torn shirt, and shook her head. "You look as though you need it more than I do." She curled her fingers around the coat's collar, intending to hand it back to him.

He stayed her fingers against the fabric. "No, Miss Bainbridge, you keep it. You, er . . ." He looked away, his ears turning a fiery shade of red beneath shining waves of auburn hair.

"But you have done enough, and—" Honore glanced down at her ruined garments and gulped.

No wonder he had given her his coat. No wonder his ears looked about to catch fire. Only her lace fichu, snagged and frayed but still in place, lay between her stays and the view of the world.

She grabbed the lapels of the coat and wrapped it across her chest. Her own ears, along with her cheeks, throat, and everything below her fichu, burned. "Th-thank you." She kept her head bowed. "Thank you for everything. If I can repay you in any way, just give me the word."

From the quality of his coat, his shirt—even if it was in tatters—and his buckskin breeches and Hessian boots, he did not look in need of money. But he did not talk like a gentleman. His voice was pleasant, kind of smooth and rich like Devonshire cream. Yet he sounded like no Englishman she had ever heard, so he was likely not a gentleman. Perhaps a merchant from the provinces or one of the Channel Islands.

"I am a Bainbridge."

"Yes, ma'am, I know."

"Of course you do." She twisted one of the brass buttons on his coat between her thumb and forefinger. "Then you know I have considerable influence in the county."

And money at her disposal, since she had been left in charge of the estate by default.

He coughed. "Thank you. I don't need any thanks or favors. I didn't do anything any man wouldn't have done had he been near enough to help."

And strong enough to lift her.

"I-I think you were an answer to prayer," she admitted.

The first one of those since Papa had died during a debate with his friends over the war with the Yankees, leaving them all shocked and devastated a month after her sister Cassandra's wedding.

Cassandra's elopement, the minx.

The stranger laughed. "I don't think anyone's ever accused me of being an answer to prayer before." He still did not look at Honore. "Except maybe your father, God rest his soul."

"You knew Papa?" Honore sprang to her feet, forgetting her missing shoe. The sole of her foot landed on a sharp stone and she squeaked.

He glanced at her then. "What's—ah, a shoe is a casualty of the rock fall."

"Yes, and I liked the pair. They fit so well and exactly matched this gown." Honore stared at her ragged skirt and started to laugh. Mirth bubbled up inside her chest and burst out like sea foam in a high wind, flying about without purpose or control. She tried to stop, but her chest continued to heave until tears trickled down her cheeks and the giggles metamorphosed into sobs. Covering her face with her hands, she sobbed like a babe missing its mama, deep, rasping hiccups clawing at her chest and lungs.

"There now." The man cleared his throat, and several sheep baaed in the field beyond the wall.

Honore shook her head, tried to breathe slowly to stop the weeping, and only cried harder.

"Miss Bainbridge, you're really all right, you know." His big, strong hand touched her shoulder.

Honore sobbed harder, eyes squeezed shut in an attempt to stop the flow of tears, hands fisted around the ends of the too-long coat sleeves.

The coat's owner patted her shoulder. "Hush, please. Miss Bainbridge, you're all right now. No need to cry."

"I-I-I know." Honore hiccuped the words and sniffled. "I ca-cannot . . . s-stop."

"Hmm. Well then. Um, there's a handkerchief in the pocket of that coat."

She fumbled through every pocket without finding anything more than the crackle of paper folded into an inside pocket. Her face grew wetter. What was left of her fichu grew wet. Finally, she drew the lapels of the man's coat up to her face and sobbed into the soft wool smelling of sunshine and bracken and coffee, familiar, comforting aromas that reminded her of home as it had been only two years ago, before she insisted on a London Season and made amok of her debut into Society, before Papa died.

"I want my papa," she wailed into the stranger's coat. "Nothing bad happened to me when he was alive."

"Nothing bad happened to you today." The stranger smoothed a strand of her hair away from her cheek. "Not in the end. You're safe now."

"Without Papa, I will never be safe."

"That's rather illogical." He moved a step away from her. "You scarcely ever saw him."

"I know. I know." Honore nodded too many times. "But nothing bad happened to me when he was alive."

"Ha! That's not what I've heard."

Her gasp of indignation interrupted her next sob, and she jerked her head up to glare at him. "What have you heard?"

"A great deal." He pressed a cambric handkerchief into her hand with a muttered, "Apologies. This was in my breeches pocket."

"Indeed." Her face hot from crying, from him mentioning his unmentionables to her, and, most of all, from his knowledge of something unsavory about her, Honore snatched the handkerchief from him and dashed it across her eyes and cheeks. Hiccuping sobs still disrupted her breathing, and she dared not speak.

"Good girl." The stranger smiled at her. "His lordship would be ashamed of such a display from one of his daughters, wouldn't he?"

Most definitely. But then, Papa had been ashamed of most everything she had done those last months before he died.

With one last heaving sob, her breathing returned to normal. She wiped her eyes a final time and shoved the handkerchief into the pocket of the man's coat. "I wish those sheep were horses so I could ride home."

And get away from this bold, kind, and rather rude stranger.

"Unfortunately, they are just sheep." The man's tone was abrupt. "I'll have to carry you."

"Sir, you cannot." She stared up at him, her eyes wide.

He met her gaze full on, and for the first time, his eyes' true color reached her brain. *Colors* was more accurate—brown and gold and green swirled together like paint on her sister Lydia's pallet. The longer he looked at Honore, the more the gold stood out like sunshine breaking through a cloud bank.

She swallowed against that lint dryness in her mouth.

He swallowed too and grinned. "I can carry you. You can't weigh more than a calf."

"A calf?" Honore narrowed her eyes. "You just compared me to a cow."

"A young one, small as you are."

The corners of her mouth tightened. "I will manage to walk, thank you."

"You'll cut your foot to ribbons." And without a by-your-leave, he scooped her into his arms and started along the wall toward Bainbridge Hall.

"Put me down," Honore commanded.

Lord, please do not let anyone see me.

With her gown in tatters, her person swathed in the coat of a man whose shirt also hung in little more than ribbons, she would be ruined if someone caught sight of them and drew terrible conclusions, as people were wont to do about her of late. Ruined worse than her two disastrous courtships the previous year had left her. At least those men were gentlemen. Villainous, but gentlemen. This man was—

"I don't even know who you are," she blurted out.

"I beg your pardon." He stopped and set her on her feet with the gentleness a body showed a Sèvres vase, then he granted her a somewhat stiff but proper bow. "Allow me to present myself, since no one else is here to do the honors. I am the sixth earl of Ashmoor."

"You—you are Lord Ashmoor?" The ground beneath her feet took on the consistency of the quaking edge of the cliff. She swayed. She pressed her fingers to her lips to cover her gaping mouth. She could not call a peer of the realm a liar. Then again, if he was a liar, he was not a peer of the realm.

"Speechless, Miss Bainbridge?" Gold sparkled in his multicolored eyes. He crossed his arms over his chest and propped one foot on the low stone wall. "Let me see if I can help. Local gossip says I'm too ashamed of my father's past to show my face in Devonshire, so I'm hiding out on one of the lesser estates. Or maybe you heard that I was locked up in Newgate or Dartmoor or a hulk in the Nore the instant I set foot on these hallowed shores. Is one of those stories close to the gossip you've heard about why the new owner of the title hasn't yet shown his face in Devonshire?"

His wool coat grew too warm for the crisp autumn day. The heat spread all the way to her hairline, and she turned her face into the wind blowing straight from the Bristol Channel. "I, um, yes, I've heard all of that."

"And it's all true." He let out a humorless laugh. "Don't look so shocked. I arrived from New York after the war started and was immediately suspect."

Honore jumped. "You are an American?"

"That, my dear, is debatable now, since I wasn't born in the United States or England and have been invested with the title, thanks to your father."

"Papa?" Honore stared at him. "Papa helped you accede to the title?"

"Our fathers were friends long ago, so I appealed to Lord Bainbridge when I found myself taken up for a spy the instant I arrived here."

"And your jailers listened to you?" Honore barely suppressed a skeptical snort. "You expect me to believe they contacted a peer of the realm for a foreigner?"

He shrugged. "I was carrying a letter with a royal seal. I expect the local magistrate didn't want to risk being wrong about my claim of who I was—er, who I am."

"And just like that my father got you freed and accepted by the Royal College of Arms?"

If she were not missing a shoe, she would have set off across the field for home at a trot. She had spent quite enough time alone with this odd stranger with his claim of a connection to her father. More like a claim to a physician at Bedlam.

"If three months is 'just like that,'" he responded to her with the ease of the self-assured—or someone so insane he thought he spoke the truth—"then yes, he helped me 'just like that.'"

Honore gazed at him through narrowed eyes. "When?"

"A year ago."

"Aha!" She backed away a step, prepared to climb over the low wall around the pasture, one shoe or not. "Papa was not in London or Devonshire a year ago."

"He was until the end of September and again from the end of November until his passing." He held his hand out to her without touching her. "I was with him that night, you know."

"You were?" Honore halted her retreat. "You knew him that well?"

"By then, yes. Well enough to attend a private meeting in Cavendish Square regarding a marriage settlement."

"A marriage settlement?" A distant bell of memory rang in

Honore's head, and she started to feel queasy. "You wanted my father to find you a wife?"

"It was his idea." He set his foot on the ground and straightened to more than a head taller than she stood. "He considered the earl of Ashmoor a suitable match for his youngest daughter."

"But I'm his youngest daughter." Miss Honore Bainbridge's face turned the same whitish green as the froth atop the waves a hundred yards away. "Papa would never have—he could not have—" She set her hands on her hips and shot him a glare from eyes as blue as the September sky. "You must be lying. Papa would never have signed a marriage contract on my behalf without consulting me first."

The earl of Ashmoor swallowed the impulse to tell the honorable Miss Bainbridge that not only was he telling the truth, but she would have gotten a good bargain in him. A young lady with her dubious reputation rarely deserved courtship from a peer of the realm with an income of twenty thousand pounds a year. But she would have gotten Lord Ashmoor, né Americus Poole—called Meric by family and friends—on a ship somewhere between Plymouth and New York if he had signed those papers. He had not signed them, a fact for which he gave thanks whenever her name arose in conversation during the past nine months.

"I have the papers with me," he told her instead. "That's why I was looking for you this afternoon. I thought you might like to have them."

"You took them from my father's house the night he—he—" She dropped onto the low wall around the pasture.

He shrugged. "Would you have wanted me to leave them and allow someone else to find them?"

"No. No, I would not have." She gazed at him, her lips parted as though she intended to say more but couldn't form the words.

Even pale and tearstained, her face presented an image of artistic perfection in a wash of gold from the afternoon sun. The perfect oval, the wide eyes, the curve of cheekbones and chin formed the stuff about which poets had written for hundreds of years. Her beauty—added to the courage she demonstrated that afternoon, clinging to that spindly shrub of a sapling while most of her dangled above certain death if either she or he let go—sent a line or two of verse running through Meric's head.

Such a pity she had blotted her copybook with not one but two regrettable attachments during the first six months after her debut into Society. Had he known about those connections to unsavory, even criminal, men, Meric never would have so much as discussed marriage to Bainbridge's youngest daughter, let alone let him go so far as to draw up a settlement. Meric needed a wife to cement his new role in life. With a cloud of suspicion still dangling over his head like the Sword of Damocles, not to mention the lingering gossip about his late father, that wife could never be Miss Honore Bainbridge. He could not clear his father's name unless he made only impeccable alliances with a daughter of the local landowners, one or two of which looked promising.

Meric filled in the silence. "The papers are in the inside pocket of that coat you're wearing."

"You could have simply destroyed them." She fumbled with his coat until she drew out a sheaf of vellum.

"I could have."

"Why did you not?"

"I thought you might enjoy the privilege since Lord Bainbridge signed them."

She gasped and flipped through the pages until she reached the last one. Lord Bainbridge's signature ran in bold strokes near the bottom and ended in a circle of wax affixed with his seal. Beneath it, just enough space remained for Meric's signature to make the document valid.

Her hands shaking hard enough to rattle the paper more than did the sea wind, Miss Bainbridge folded the pages and then sat rubbing her fingertips back and forth across the creases. She kept her eyes downcast.

Meric followed her gaze to the toes peeking from beneath her tattered gown. One foot remained shod in a creamy slipper wholly inadequate for walking along the cliffs, and the other showed the pink tips of toes poking through a torn silk stocking.

"Now that you know I had your father's approval," Meric said, "why don't you let me carry you home."

"I would rather walk on my own, thank you." Head still bowed, she swung her legs over the wall in one graceful motion, rose, and headed across the pasture on a well-worn path through the grass.

A handful of sheep ceased their munching and stared at her.

Meric vaulted after her, and the sheep scattered.

"You can't walk home alone," he said.

She shouldn't have been walking at all with only one shoe.

"I walked here alone. I can walk home alone."

"So you did, and so you can. And I will still do the gentlemanly thing and accompany you."

She stopped and glared back at him through a tangle of gold

hair. "The gentlemanly thing for you to do would be to leave me alone as I wish to be, as I am quite capable of being."

"Yes," he said, "you did so well on that cliff."

"I—well, I—" She ducked her head. "Thank you for that. I expect there is some way I can repay you."

She looked so dejected, so shaken, his heart softened. Had she been one of his sisters, or even one of their friends whom he had known all their lives, he would have slipped an arm around her shoulders in a reassuring embrace. Unfortunately, she was a stranger for all practical purposes—and a young lady with a less-than-stellar reputation that could too easily tar his.

He settled for stepping closer to her, close enough to catch a whiff of something sweet like honeysuckle drifting from her wildly disarranged curls, and gave her his gentlest smile. "I don't need repayment, Miss Bainbridge. I wanted our first meeting to be without the scrutiny of the rest of Devonshire society because of your father's notions regarding us, and that plan brought me to find you on the cliff, by the grace of God." He couldn't stop himself from raising one hand and brushing a tendril of hair away from where it clung to the tips of ridiculously long eyelashes. "It's the Lord you should be thanking, not me. I nearly went home when I learned you were out."

"Yes. Yes, of course I thank the Lord." She clutched the marriage settlement so tightly it ripped in half.

She jumped as though stung and cried out.

"Step on something?" Meric stooped and retrieved a bit of metal from the path. No, not a bit of metal—a broken button, smooth on one side, etched on the other, rough where it had snapped free of the thread holding it to its garment.

Rough and now specked with bright red drops of blood.

He shoved the half of a button into his pocket. "You cut yourself."

"It is nothing more than a scratch." She started walking again, limping really, placing weight on only the toes of her right foot.

"You shouldn't walk on even a scratch without protection," Meric persisted. "It's really nothing for me to carry you."

"Even though I'm the size of a calf?"

Meric grinned. "Only at birth."

She shot him a look that should have withered him to a husk, but one corner of her mouth twitched.

"I'd offer to bind it up for you," he said, "but that's probably more indelicate than me carrying you."

"Truly, my lord, it scarcely hurts, and I doubt it's still bleeding." She turned her foot sideways and leaned forward to look.

So did Meric. The sole of her foot was bleeding. A slow trickle of blood oozed from her heel.

"It—it is still nothing." Her voice quavered.

"It's enough."

Meric gauged the distance between their location and the house. A quarter mile away, the laden branches of apple trees poked their heads above a high stone wall. Somewhere beyond the orchard stood the house. He guessed half a mile to go. He should offer to carry her again. On the other hand, she was right—it would do neither of their reputations any good if someone saw them in such an intimate position, whatever the reason for it. He could leave her in the pasture and go to fetch help, but he didn't like what he thought he recognized on that half of a button—the word *égalité*. French for "equality," as in the Revolutionaries' cry of "*Liberté, égalité, fraternité*."

No French buttons should lie in the Bainbridge pasture unless someone with a connection to the French had cut across it on his way to the sea. Despite the war between America and England, France was still Great Britain's greater enemy. Nearby Dartmoor held many more French prisoners than American ones thus far, and some of those had escaped right out from the guards' noses—not in broad daylight, but still . . .

He curved his hand around Miss Bainbridge's elbow, halting her. "I'll carry you as far as the edge of that orchard. No one will see us from there."

"I suppose not." She kept her head bent. Swaths of hair hid her expression. "All right then."

Meric picked her up. She weighed more than he recalled from those moments he'd hauled her off the crumbling cliff, but she was still a little bit of a girl, the size of his middle sister Sarah, who was sixteen and the smallest of the eight of them. Sarah wouldn't have reposed in his arms without moving, as did Miss Bainbridge. The latter would have been easier to carry if her stillness didn't verge on stiffness, and if she had wound one arm around his neck. As it was, she clutched the lapels of his coat together around the now torn marriage contract, and kept her head lowered as though reading something from the plain brass buttons on his coat.

"So," he began, seeking ordinary conversation to maybe set her at ease, "do you make a habit of walking on the cliffs?"

"It is the first place I go when I come home, but yesterday was too wet for cliff walking." She turned her face away from him, and strands of her hair blew across his cheek. "When I was younger, I played daring games here with some of the tenant farmers' children. It is a good thing no children were playing here today. It looks like we have all neglected the cliff and other things, being gone so much this past year and a half. Look at those apples. They are falling off the trees for want of picking."

"Do you have the labor? I believe the Ashmoor harvest is done. I could send over—"

"I can manage." If the stiffness of her body came from the kind of cold conveyed in her tone, his arms would soon suffer from frostbite.

"Then it's a good thing you came back," he murmured.

"Someone needed to. My brother has decided that country comes before f-family at present." A hint of a fissure in the iceberg of Miss Bainbridge.

Meric probed at it. "England is in the middle of two wars. She needs the guidance of Parliament."

Miss Bainbridge looked at him for the first time since he'd picked her up. "You are not sitting in the House of Lords."

"I'm needed here to ensure the estates remain profitable and pay lots of taxes to support these wars." Hearing his own cynical tone, he hastened to add, "The estates have been neglected by all but their stewards for the past three years. I am blessed that they are fine and apparently honest stewards."

"Ours too, but nothing truly substitutes for the presence of the owner."

"Ah, at last, Miss Bainbridge, we are in accord with something." He put her down in front of an iron gate set into the orchard wall. "Is your foot well enough to walk through?"

"It is well enough to walk, my lord." She performed the rather remarkable feat of standing on one foot while holding the other up at an angle so she could inspect it. "See, it is no longer bleeding."

"No, it isn't, but your chances of stepping on sticks and such are rather high, don't you think?"

The spreading acreage of laden trees, sharp-scented with the juices of windfalls fermenting on the ground, harbored a chill not apparent in the sunlit pasture—discounting Miss Bainbridge's tone, of course.

"I suppose you are right." She heaved a sigh that Meric half expected to produce frosty vapor. "Very well. If you prefer it."

"I prefer it." He picked her up again.

She resumed studying his unremarkable buttons.

"I expect we'll meet at church Sunday," he said.

"I doubt as much. My parish is Clovelly, not Ashmoor."

"I'm staying in the Poole house in Clovelly."

Her head shot up. "But the Clovelly house is nothing more than a cottage."

Meric snorted. "I hardly call twelve rooms a cottage, Miss Bainbridge. Ten of us lived in a house not half that size and never considered ourselves cramped for space."

Not with miles of Crystal Lake and pristine forest around them, they hadn't. Not like he felt in this orchard with its regimented trees inside walls to protect the fruit from the sea winds, and the endless pastures and moorlands beyond. If not for the miles of coastland, he might have gone mad with everything so close together.

"The Poole house is more comfortable than that drafty manor at Ashmoor," he added. "And I like being by the sea."

Miss Bainbridge grew the slightest bit less rigid against him. "So do I. I did not like either Shropshire or Lancashire. That is where my sisters live now. And Bath, where Mama is staying? Too, too dull."

"I should think you'd find Devonshire dull." He ducked to avoid a low-hanging branch across the path and caught her honeysuckle sweetness through the apple smell. It reminded him of home, the vines winding around the fence that never quite kept the wild animals out and the domesticated ones in.

An ache started in his heart—a longing for his loved ones, for people who knew and trusted his integrity, for the pretty young woman he intended to offer for but told not to wait for him when he received word of the inheritance. Too much hope had shone in Mama's face for Meric to say no to the title, the income, the excuse to return his father's branch of the family to Devonshire.

Miss Bainbridge suddenly grew too heavy in his arms, and he welcomed the sight of the orchard's end. He set her beside the wicket of another barrier, this one a white-painted fence with a lawn stretching in manicured perfection to the nearest wing of a sprawling, asymmetrical house.

"Will you be all right from here?" he asked.

"I would have been all right from the pasture." She dropped a slight curtsy. "But I thank you for your chivalry, my lord. I shall have your coat returned to you as soon as it is brushed and pressed."

She spun on the heel of her one slipper and tiptoed across the lawn just beginning to show signs of browning up for the winter. Despite the uneven gait and tattered dress beneath his overly large coat, despite her missing hat and tumbled hair, she held her head high, her back straight in graceful dignity. Such a pity she had forgotten her dignity on two occasions since her debut into Society and had thrown herself at wholly unsuitable men. Worse than unsuitable men—a traitor and a murderer.

Meric turned his back on her. His American upbringing made him suspect to some—unfortunately, some in high places. To matchmaking mamas, however, his title and income swept concerns about his loyalties right out the door. An alliance through marriage with a solidly English family would even further clear him of suspicions of disloyalty to the Crown. Once he was fully accepted in his new country, he could amply provide for his siblings and grant his mother her two greatest wishes—to clear his father's name and reunite her with her parents. All he had to do until then was keep himself and his younger brother out of another English prison, and maybe marry a suitable young lady whose pristine reputation would enhance his consequence—such as the Devenish chit, who reminded him of the girl left behind.

Despite the pain in her heel, Honore took the circuitous route along the orchard fence and garden wall to the terrace and long window leading into the library, from which she had exited the house what must have been a lifetime ago. To avoid the footman who perpetually stood in the main hall, she ducked down a side passage and up a narrow servants' staircase leading to the family bedchambers. All of them overlooked the walled orchard and pasture and sea beyond, but if the hand of the Lord that had brought Lord Ashmoor along in time to save her from the cliff kept her companion Miss Lavinia Morrow in another part of the house, Honore just might manage not to disclose how close to death she had come. If she could avoid talking about the near fatal accident, she could avoid revealing her thoroughly humiliating encounter with Lord Ashmoor.

"Marriage settlement indeed." She flung open her bedchamber door.

Miss Morrow, as straight and flat as a boy in her dove-gray round gown, emerged from the dressing room with an armful of Honore's gowns from her London Season. "There you are. I was thinking, now that it is time you can start wearing colors again, that we could refurbish these, perhaps set in a colored overskirt or two, and not be rid of them altogether. What do you—" She stopped on a gasp, her soft blue-gray eyes widening. "What . . . happened to you? Why are you wearing a man's coat?"

"It is a terribly long story." Honore threw herself onto a wingback chair by the cold grate. "All I've worn for the past nine months since I came out of blacks for Papa is white and gray, and I am thoroughly weary of both. Go ahead and tell me your thoughts on those gowns."

"Oh, I think not now." Miss Morrow laid the gowns on the stool to the dressing table and crossed the room with her gliding walk to stand over Honore. "What scrape have you gotten yourself into this time? Do I need to send for Lady Whittaker or Madame de Meuse?"

"You are leaving out my brother and Mama," Honore said with more than a hint of asperity.

"Not at all." Miss Morrow, related to Honore and the Bainbridges distantly through the marriage of the middle Bainbridge daughter, Cassandra, perched on the edge of another wingback chair and fixed her deceptively gentle gaze on Honore. "I know as well as you that your brother is more interested in his seat in Parliament than he is in his sisters, and Lady Bainbridge is unwell."

Indeed, for all she was never quite well, Mama seemed genuinely in a dangerous state of poor health since Papa's death from apoplexy. She had collapsed upon learning of her husband's demise, and deteriorated from there until two different doctors recommended the waters at Bath as a possible cure. She and her companion, Barbara, had resided in Bath ever since, one reason why Honore was now in Devonshire instead of enjoying the less frenetic entertainments of the Little Season in London.

A legitimate reason, but one as distant as Miss Morrow's

relationship to her. The other reasons were just too humiliating to consider.

Honore tucked her head against one of the chair's wings and closed her eyes. "My sisters cannot come here any more than I could stay with them. Well, I could have stayed, but they thought I should not."

Of course they had. Lydia, married just over a year, was expecting her first child any day now, and she did not want her unmarried sister nearby without her to manage her social engagements in the neighborhood, no matter that Lydia's mother-in-law was perfectly capable of doing so, or so Honore believed. Lydia thought not, citing something about her husband's younger sister being unmanageable.

Farther north in Lancashire, Honore's middle sister, Cassandra, after barely ten months of marriage, was also expecting her confinement any day. Considering what had happened on the Whittaker estate the previous autumn, Honore did not wish to go there even if she were welcome, which she was certain she was not. Someone needed to manage Bainbridge, so she took it upon herself to return to Devonshire with one of her brother-in-law's spinster cousins for a chaperone and companion. Nothing horrible would happen to her in the splendid isolation of the main seat of Lord Bainbridge.

Except it had. She had nearly died from a terrible fall. She had nearly died from mortification over Lord Ashmoor's claim that Papa had come within moments of signing a marriage contract for her with an American. Whatever his claim to the Ashmoor title and fortune, he was the enemy. Worse, perhaps, his father had fled the country under a cloud of scandal. Given the choice between her father's near contract for her marriage to a Yankee and dangling off the cliff, she would dangle off the cliff.

Except Papa had wanted the man for her.

"It's too, too awful." Honore's eyes burned. She squeezed them shut. She would not—would absolutely not—weep again that day.

"Would you like me to ring for tea?" Miss Morrow asked.

As if tea could help anything.

"Yes," Honore said on a sigh. "And hot water for a bath."

"In the middle of the afternoon?"

"In the middle of the afternoon. I am beginning to ache all over and have several cuts and scrapes and—never you mind. I simply need a hot bath and perhaps some macaroons before I can even think about talking."

And she needed to think before talking.

"All right, but I insist on a full explanation as to why you look like you do and—" Miss Morrow halted on her way to the bell pull. "You are only wearing one shoe."

"I am."

"Where is the other one?"

"Halfway to Wales on the ebb tide, I expect." Honore managed a tight smile. "Along with my hat and my pride."

No, her pride had blown across the moor on the sea wind the instant the man calling himself Lord Ashmoor announced her father's intentions for her.

"Papa, Papa, Papa, how could you?" She pressed the heels of her hands to her eyes.

A Yankee. The son of a criminal. A man who had himself been in prison under suspicion of spying. Papa wanted him for her husband?

The urge to wail like an abandoned infant rose inside her so profoundly she sprang from the chair and tried to pace around the room. Her cut heel throbbed. Her shoulders tensed as though her arms weighed tenfold their unsubstantial weight. Her heart . . . it ached worst of all.

Papa had betrayed her.

She buried her face in her hands, but she had apparently wept out all her tears near the pasture wall. That was one more humiliation of the day. She had howled like a bawling calf in front of that Yankee stranger.

"He compared me to a calf." She yanked off her scarred and lone slipper and tossed it into the grate.

Miss Morrow retrieved it and smoothed down the once pretty cream satin ankle ribbons, as though all the shoe needed to repair it was a little ironing. "Who called you a calf, Miss Bainbridge?"

Honore jumped. "I, um, did not mean to say anything about it."

"Perhaps you should say a great deal more." Miss Morrow held her gaze.

Honore shook her head. "Not now. Not yet."

Not ever.

She liked Miss Morrow's calm practicality and knew the spinster, aging at somewhere around thirty, appreciated the work. At the same time, Honore had known her for only a few weeks. Miss Morrow had come to Shropshire to be Honore's companion when Lydia grew too advanced in her condition to entertain—look after—her youngest sister. Gentle nudges from Lydia's oh-so-kind and diplomatic husband, along with their brother's announcement that he intended to remain in London where he had been since their father's death, sent Honore back to Devonshire. She, apparently, was the only Bainbridge who cared about managing the estate.

Miss Morrow suited well enough as a companion. She played chess, loved the same Gothic novels Honore adored, and, despite her plain, invariably dove-gray or walnut-brown gowns, possessed a fine eye for fashion. But she was still a stranger. Honore wanted one of her sisters. They would scold her about walking alone even on the estate. They would reprimand her for being rude to a stranger. They would let her cry on their shoulders and remind her that Papa had always held the best interests of his daughters in his mind and heart, even if he tended to be high-handed about it.

Honore shot to her feet. "If you do not plan to order that bath and tea, I shall. I am feeling worse by the mome—" She took a step and came down hard on her cut heel. A squeaking gasp burst from her lips.

"You are injured." Miss Morrow reached Honore's side in a flash and slipped her arm around the younger lady's waist. "Come sit down again. I'll fetch tea and macaroons myself and order up the bath. When you wish to talk"—she offered Honore a shy smile—"if you wish to talk, you can tell me what happened."

Of course she would talk. Of course she would tell her paid companion about the near tumble into the sea. Of course she would confide about the new Lord Ashmoor and his outrageous claims.

Except they were not outrageous.

While Miss Morrow departed to fetch tea and cakes and order up a bath, Honore spread the two halves of the marriage papers on her dressing table and read them through. Most of the language made little sense to her, especially the Latin bits. Dead languages were Cassandra's forte. The message came through loud and clear anyway—Lord Bainbridge would pay Lord Ashmoor ten thousand pounds to marry his youngest daughter.

"Ten thousand?" Honore stared at the number printed in the precise hand of her father's secretary.

Despite the jagged tear between the words *ten* and *thousand*, they were still legible, clear, nauseating in the clarity of their message. Papa had felt the need to offer even a suspicious stranger three thousand pounds more to marry Honore than he had granted as a dowry to Lord Whittaker when he married Cassandra, even though they had eloped to the Scottish border in order to marry before Advent.

"And Ashmoor does not need the money." Honore started to close her hands around the papers, crumpling them more than she had already done.

She smoothed them out instead. She must keep these. She could even repair them, glue them onto another sheet of paper to put the halves back together. They would encourage her to continue writing her Gothic novel so she could acquire her own income as a famous authoress. No man would buy and sell her like—like—

"A calf." She snatched up a brush and began to yank it through her hair.

She was attempting to disentangle the boar's bristles from a hopeless knot in her tresses when Miss Morrow returned. She bore a tray complete with a teapot, steam billowing from its spout, a jug of warm milk, and a plate of macaroons bristly with slivered almonds. She passed Honore on her way to the low table before the grate, and the tannic sharpness of the Bohea teased Honore's nostrils.

She cast the brush onto the dressing table and rose. "I believe I am thirsty."

"I expect you are, after your ordeal." Miss Morrow poured tea into a delicate china cup, added a dash of milk, and gave the drink to Honore.

Honore gave her a smiled thank-you and sipped before asking, "What makes you believe I have had an ordeal?"

"At our level of society, Miss Bainbridge, one rarely keeps a secret for long." Miss Morrow smiled as she seated herself with a cup of tea. "And a young man named Philemon Poole came seeking his brother."

Honore jumped, spilling tea onto her already ruined gown. She said nothing. She dared not. She simply stared at her companion.

"Seems like his brother—Meric, I believe he called him?—intended to call here," Miss Morrow continued in her quiet, placid voice. "The young Mr. Poole was quite agitated because he knew his brother was coming along the cliff path, and he saw a fresh scar where that path had broken away. He is afraid his brother has fallen into the sea. I took the liberty of giving him and Mr. Chilcott, his steward, permission to use the Bainbridge boat to search on the seaward side if they feel the need. But I expect they'll find him safe and sound on land, if he is missing his coat."

That missing coat still wrapped around her, Honore grew hot from hem to hairline. She stared into the swirling amber depths of her tea. "I suppose it is no use to dissemble, is it?"

"You can, but I do not know why you would want to. If . . . hmm, there is reason for the man to be brought to justice . . ."

"Brought to justice?" Honore stared at her companion. "Why would he need that?"

Miss Morrow turned the delicate pink of sea foam at dawn. "He, um, did not harm you in any way, did he?"

"How would he have—oh, gracious, no." Honore felt lightheaded.

Miss Morrow heaved a gusty sigh. "That's all right then. You did not act like a young lady who had had her virtue insulted, but I am concerned about your reluctance to tell me why you are in such *déshabillé*."

"That is because—because it is all too awful. And humiliating and—"

A knock sounded on the door.

Miss Morrow rose to answer it, and Honore tiptoed her way into the dressing room. She peeked through the door at the arrivals. Two footmen, identical in their crimson livery and old-fashioned powdered wigs, entered bearing cans of steaming water. A third followed with the bath. No one spoke while the footmen set up the tub before the hearth, and a maid scurried in to light a fire. Once screens stood around the tub for modesty and to keep the heat around the bath, Honore emerged from her hiding place and moved toward the steaming water smelling of woodbine and lavender. The lavender oil would soothe her bruises and scrapes. The woodbine would soothe her senses.

"Perhaps now that there is a screen between us," Miss Morrow said from somewhere in the room, "you will tell me how you came to be wearing Lord Ashmoor's coat."

How long could a body hold her breath under water and not drown? Probably not long enough for Miss Morrow to grow bored and go away.

Honore rubbed lavender oil into her scraped knees as though it took all her concentration. "He saved my life and then dealt me an insult too great to be forgiven." Her conscience pricked her, and she added, "Well, to be forgiven without the grace of God."

Miss Morrow said nothing. A gust of wind rattled the window in its frame, portending rain in the near future. From the grate, a puff of smoke burned Honore's nostrils, and the flames bowed from a downdraft. Otherwise, the room lay too quiet and too still.

"Are you still there?" she asked in a small voice.

"I am. Simply waiting for your tale of adventure."

"Scarcely an adventure I would like to repeat." Though she could do something of the like to her heroine.

Miss Morrow said nothing yet again.

Honore sighed, laid her head against the rim of the bath, and began to talk. The silence grew so heavy she might have been speaking to an empty room. Not so much as a chair creak, the sharpness of an indrawn breath, or the rustle of fabric indicated that the companion remained present.

"And worst of all, I blubbered like a baby once I was safe," Honore completed in a small voice. "If you can believe I did such a thing."

"Of course I can believe it," Miss Morrow said. And then she sniffed.

Honore stood in the bath and peered over the top of the screen. "Miss Morrow, are you weeping too?"

"You are such a brave child." Miss Morrow mopped her streaming eyes. "And to have a handsome and strong young man come along to save your life—why, it is better than any novel I have read."

"Who says he's handsome?" Honore plopped down into the water again, found it was not quite warm anymore, and decided she needed to emerge and dress for the evening in the event that someone like the vicar called. "Or young?"

"His brother is both. Such beautiful eyes."

"Humph."

"And fine thick hair."

"Humph."

"And those shoulders."

"Miss Morrow."

"Did I say something improper?" The companion sounded too innocent.

Honore giggled and wrapped her dressing gown around herself. "All right, yes, he is a passable-looking gentleman with impressive shoulders. But if I never see him again, it will be too soon."

Miss Morrow clucked her tongue. "Even after he saved your life? I should think you would have an entire plot of love and marriage written out in your head."

"Perhaps under other circumstances I would have." Honore emerged from behind the screen and snatched up the torn pieces of the marriage contract. "This is the rest of my mortification." She waved the scraps of paper in the air. "Papa wanted me to marry this man so badly he was willing to pay three thousand pounds more to be rid of me than he was willing to pay for my sisters' dowries. Ten thousand pounds altogether, and this—this Yankee Lord Ashmoor gave me back the contract because he has no intention of carrying through."

"Indeed?" Miss Morrow straightened her already erect posture even further, and a gleam shone in her blue-gray eyes.

"Papa thought enough of this Yankee—"

"I beg your pardon, Miss Bainbridge, but if he is a peer of the realm, he is not an American, is he?"

"He talks like it, and he has not lived anywhere else." Honore picked up her hairbrush and dragged it through her hair.

Miss Morrow took it from her and nudged her toward the dressing table stool. "You are making amok of it. Do, please, continue with your impressions of Lord Ashmoor."

"I think . . . I think . . ." Honore closed her eyes so she could not see the grief in the face of the young lady in the mirror. "Papa told me he had found a husband for me, and I thought it all right considering I have done worse at choosing suitors than I have at brushing my hair. But this man is surely not up to snuff for a Bainbridge."

"A Poole of Ashmoor and a substantial income? I think that makes up for a number of faults in the area of manners. After all, manners can be taught. Titles and incomes cannot."

"True, but he was scarcely out of prison for three months when Papa suggested the contract. And he offered to pay him more." Honore opened her eyes and twisted up her face as though smelling something terrible. She drew a handkerchief from her dressing gown pocket and began to shred the lace edging the fine cambric. "He does not wish to wed me even with ten thousand. You know my brother would have honored the contract, especially with Papa's signature on these papers. But this man does not think I am good enough for him."

"Hmm." Miss Morrow tapped the hairbrush against her chin and held Honore's gaze in the mirror. "So what distresses you most? Is it that he is an American or that he does not wish to marry you even for ten thousand pounds in a dowry?"

Honore stiffened. "That he is an American, of course."

"But did not Lady Whittaker—your sister, that is—say your father had chosen a husband for you and you were more than willing after . . . everything that went wrong last year?"

"Yes, but . . ." Honore deflated like one of Cassandra's balloons robbed of hydrogen. She propped her chin in her hand and shifted her gaze to the jars and boxes upon her dressing table. "I did agree to marry Papa's choice for me when I thought it would be a suitable match."

"You know most would consider an alliance with even an American-raised Lord Ashmoor a suitable match. Far better than . . . well, better than your previous suitors."

"You mean the one who was a traitor or the one who was a murderer?"

Miss Morrow laughed. "Either. You could do far worse."

"What, a cit?"

"Remain single for the sake of your pride." Miss Morrow's voice held such sorrow Honore jerked her head up and stared at the older lady.

"Did you do that?"

Miss Morrow shrugged. "It was long ago when I was young and above myself."

"Are you saying I am being above myself to think Lord Ashmoor is not good enough for me?"

Miss Morrow did not answer.

Honore glared at her reflection for several moments, then inclined her head in surrender to the truth. "I am here instead of in London with my brother because I have blotted my copybook beyond recognition."

"It's not quite that bad, my dear child, but you may not attract the best of the crop of eligible young men for another year or two, and then you will be climbing the age ladder toward being on the shelf. A pity for such a pretty and charming girl."

"With unwise choices in her past." Honore massaged her suddenly aching temples. "All right, yes, had Papa presented Lord Ashmoor to me last December instead of—of dying on us, I likely would have gone along with the plan. But it does not matter. His lordship returned these papers to me because he has no wish for an alliance."

"No, *he* does not."

"Miss Morrow, what are you saying?" Honore spun on the stool to face her companion head-on.

She smiled. "You have such a competent steward here that I doubt the estate will take up much of your time."

"I will see that it does. I must do something useful." Honore's voice dropped to a tone just above a whisper. "I have to do something Papa and the rest of the family would have approved of."

"Lord Bainbridge, cousin Whittaker told me, only wanted his daughters to wed well. And the rest of your family loves you as you are."

"Humph." Honore shook her head. "They banished me here when none of them could take the time for me."

Miss Morrow smoothed Honore's hair over her shoulder. "No, my dear, they wanted what is best for you right now."

"And I shall die of boredom unless I can do something with the estate."

"Unless you catch yourself a husband." Miss Morrow smiled, making her only passably pretty face lovely. "The sort of husband your father thought you should have."

"You mean a Yankee traitor?" Honore curled her upper lip.

"No, child, an earl with twenty thousand a year."

After Miss Bainbridge had slipped along the orchard wall and vanished into the house, Meric plucked an apple from one of the trees and bit down on the glossy red fruit. The juice ran sweet and tangy across his tongue, refreshing after his ordeal, but probably an offense that would get him transported if anyone caught him stealing the Bainbridge harvest.

He took another large bite in an effort to dispel the image of Miss Bainbridge dangling off the cliff, clinging to the spindly sapling. His mouth went dry. Not even the juice from the rest of the apple removed the tinny taste of fear from his mouth. She was such a little thing, nicely rounded, and fortunately, quite a pocket Venus even bedraggled and dirty. Had she been much larger, he doubted he could have lifted her off that cliff. For weeks, no doubt, he would have nightmares about losing his hold on her, and her going over to break upon the rocks like a discarded wooden doll.

He shuddered, tossed the core of the apple atop a mound of windfalls, and disturbed a swarm of wasps dining on the fallen fruit. They rose into the air in a menacing cloud.

Meric ran, ducking under laden branches, climbing over a low wall separating apples from peaches, and ended up scaling the seawall to elude the angry insects. Most of them anyway. Two managed to sting him through the thin linen of his shirt.

"You'd think I'd know better." He leaned against the wall and rubbed the one wound he could reach on the back of his right arm. "It's not as though we didn't have wasps dining on fallen fruit in New York."

Sometimes, by the middle of the harsh winters prevalent in the upper end of New York, the fallen fruit, wild berries, and grapes they had hunted all summer and dried were all they had to eat, especially in the years since Father had gone through the ice while fishing on Lake Champlain. But not last winter. Last winter, his title and inheritance firmly under his control, Meric had managed, through a series of smugglers and privateers, to send a small fortune home. Doing so had brought him under the scrutiny of the excise men or horse guards, or some such organization of Britain's military might. They had waylaid him twice upon his travels between a Poole estate and London and questioned his activities on specific nights without giving him any information at all.

"You were seen talking to a fisherman who is a known smuggler," they had said on the second occasion, all but accusing him outright.

"Then arrest him, if he's known to be a smuggler," Meric had responded.

One of the officers had dropped his hand to a horse pistol at his waist, convincing Meric he would soon find himself back in a prison. But his companion had caught hold of his friend's arm, muttered something like, "That is all, my lord," and dragged the first officer away.

"The privilege of a title," Meric murmured. "And falling under suspicion again was worth it." He smiled in satisfaction.

A tearstained letter from Mother had found its way back to him. Because of the war and fear of attack, they had moved back to Albany. His middle brother was working, the two younger were still in school, and his eldest sister was able to get married.

Ensuring the continued comfort of his family back in America, ridiculous war or not, was why he found himself without a coat and with his shirt shredded to rags as he retraced his path back to Clovelly, to the twelve-room house he called a mansion and the English called a cottage. He had needed to settle the marriage agreement with Miss Honore Bainbridge.

Settle it so she knew he wouldn't marry her.

Nine months of contemplation on the issue assured him that he was not acting dishonorably. He hadn't signed the papers. No announcements had been made. Apparently Lord Bainbridge hadn't so much as told his daughter of his plans, let alone how far they had gone. The way he had secured the settlement papers upon Lord Bainbridge's demise kept even rumors of an alliance out of the mouths of the gossipmongers.

He had acted wisely. With the cloud of suspicion still hanging over his head, he needed a wife above the kind of rumors and even facts surrounding Miss Honore Bainbridge. One beau a traitor and the other a murderer did not fine spousal material make, not with what people thought of his own father still rife in the county.

But he couldn't avoid her. They would attend the same church. They would attend the same social gatherings. In just three days' time, he would attend some sort of musical evening at the home of a local squire and his wife, and if Miss Bainbridge's name was not already added to the guest list—for the sake of her family's social standing, if not hers—then Meric had learned nothing in the past year regarding the socially ambitious. The

Devenishes' eldest son was of marriageable age for a girl barely out of the schoolroom like Miss Bainbridge. And their second eldest daughter was old enough to make her debut into Society the following spring.

"She is not an heiress, my lord," his steward, Chilcott, had informed him, "but she is of a quiet, good nature, is better than passably pretty, and will bring some kind of dowry to the union. Not that you need concern yourself with that, if you will forgive me for being so vulgar."

"If I can't discuss money with my steward, who can I discuss it with?"

A pained look on the steward's fine-drawn features had Meric racing back through his words to figure out how he had offended the man. "Who can I . . ." he murmured.

"With whom, my lord." Chilcott removed his spectacles and rubbed them on his sleeve.

Meric laughed. "Thank you for keeping me on the grammatical straight and narrow."

"Yes, my lord." Chilcott had bowed, his body as stiff as his voice, and withdrawn behind his ledgers. He didn't withdraw so far that his little smile went unnoticed.

Chilcott was once a schoolmaster. With four younger brothers, Meric didn't need to ask why the man had chosen to be an estate steward and secretary to the late Lord Ashmoor instead.

As though his thoughts of the steward and the Poole offspring conjured them from the earth, two figures in the distance began racing toward Meric, one tall and slightly built, the other as big as Meric. The latter waved his arms and hollered something unintelligible until he drew within a dozen yards.

"We thought you went over the cliff, you addlepate, and I was afraid I'd have to be an English earl." Philemon Poole, aged four and twenty, flung a brawny arm around his eldest brother's shoulders. "I expect a spare is good, but I don't like the role."

"It's worse for you than being a spare, lad." Meric punched his brother's shoulder. "You are now the heir until I beget my own."

"Then get married and do so soon. I want to go home."

"One can't rush these matters. But what brings you all after me?" Meric glanced at Chilcott.

"Some news, my lord." Chilcott drew his coat collar up around his ears. "But we are in for rain soon, and with you in such a state of undress, we should get you home."

"Agreed," Meric said. "But tell me your news while we walk."

"It can wait, my lord," Chilcott said.

"Not if you felt the need to chase after me." Meric glanced from steward to brother. Both avoided his eyes.

"Looks like you have something more important to tell us," Philo said. "You look like you lost a boxing match."

"A boxing match with a bit of granite." Meric glanced back. The coastline had curved enough so he couldn't see the scarred bits of the cliff where a brave and beautiful young lady had clung for life. "The true hand of God manifested in my life today. But if your news brought you out here . . ."

"We needed to know where you were." Philo shot a glance at Chilcott, who nodded.

"We still do, my lord," the steward added. "I can explain why afterward."

"If you like."

Meric didn't like. Something in the exchanged glances, even more their very presence in chasing after him, gave him the same sickening jolt to his middle that seeing Miss Bainbridge hanging off the cliff had done. Since both of the other men remained stubbornly silent, Meric gave in. As they hastened along the cliffs, racing the rain clouds blowing in from the Bristol Channel, he told his brother and his steward about the incident on the cliff. Neither of the other men spoke. A burst of raindrops sent them dashing for the "cottage" perched at the top of the village that tumbled down the cliff side to the sea.

"You really should start riding, my lord," Chilcott admonished Meric. "This walking through the rain is beneath your touch."

"I like to walk, and riding . . ."

Meric wouldn't admit that he hadn't ridden a horse until a year ago. Handled a team of six horses pulling a wagon, yes. Ridden a high-stepping English horse, never—until Lord Bainbridge insisted he learn. He had. He could manage without embarrassing himself unless someone required him to jump fences, but he preferred the propulsion of his own two feet to trusting in four hooves.

"I wanted the walk along the cliffs," Meric did admit.

"But if you went to call on Miss Bainbridge," Philo pointed out, "you need to arrive by the road."

Meric frowned at his brother. "Is Chilcott civilizing you?"

"I hope not. I'm going back to America as soon as this war is over or you have an heir."

"Miss Bainbridge," Chilcott said, "was not at home, according to her companion."

Meric took the steps to his house in one bound and banged the brass knocker like a guest, as he still believed he was. Then he turned back to his comrades. "You called at Bainbridge?"

"We wanted to ask for their boat to hunt for your broken body." Philo grinned, but tightness around his Poole hazel eyes betrayed the strain he'd suffered in fearing his eldest brother had gone down with a chunk of cliff.

Meric started to respond. The opening door stopped him. Even more, the lugubrious face of his butler, who had been dragged practically kicking and screaming from Ashmoor, stopped him.

"The maid just mopped the entryway, my lord," Wooland announced as though informing his master that the young woman had just died.

"And we will get it muddy." Meric gave the butler a thoughtful glance. "We shall remove our shoes here on the stoop."

"No, no, my lord. That is unnecessary, I am sure." Chilcott sounded appalled.

Wooland pursed his lips, and Philo laughed aloud.

Meric simply held up one foot. "Perhaps you will do the honors and pull off my boot, Wooland?"

Wooland backed away. "No, my lord. No. I will have the girl return to mop up after you."

Still laughing, trailing muddy footprints behind him, Philo led the way into the library, where a fire always burned on wet days. Meric started to follow, but Chilcott held up a staying hand.

"Perhaps you should change, my lord. You cannot afford to catch a chill."

Meric started to point out that he had never caught a chill in his life after getting wet, read the genuine concern on the steward's face, and nodded. A chill had carried off Chilcott's uncle a mere week after his two sons had died while salmon fishing in Scotland. Gross misfortune likely plagued the gentle-natured steward.

"Send my brother up to do the same, if you will, and don't forget yourself. I want to hear what was so important that you came out to find me." Meric took the steps to his room two at a time.

He had hired a valet at Lord Bainbridge's insistence. Huntley stood barely more than five feet tall and possibly weighed less than Miss Bainbridge. His hair, eyes, and skin held no color, merely reflected shades of white, gray, and grayer from his perpetual white cravats and black coats. But those coats and cravats fit him to such perfection that Meric hired him to put refinement on the "Yankee Earl," the epithet with which the newspapers had christened the new Lord Ashmoor. He had learned a great deal about proper garb from the valet, who spoke in a deep, decisive voice.

"Your coat, my lord, what has happened to your beautiful coat?"

"No longer beautiful, I'm afraid. And it's a long story for which I haven't the time or patience at the moment. Chilcott and Philo are holding something back, and I want to hurry down and make them talk." Meric gave his valet a narrow-eyed glare. "Unless you can enlighten me?"

"I would not presume to do so, my lord."

"Ha, you presume to do a great deal, man."

Huntley began to remove garments from the dressing room clothespress. "Mr. Philo told me not to tell."

"And if I tell you that you should tell me, who do you—" An image of Chilcott's disapproval flashed into Meric's mind, and he cleared his throat. "To whom do you listen?"

"You, my lord, unless I use my discretion."

"At risk of dismissal?"

Huntley merely produced an impeccable pile of what passed for comfortable clothes in England. Their perfection of tailoring and ironing was his answer—who else was capable of and willing to guide his lordship through the murky waters of male sartorial excellence? Perhaps a few gentlemen's gentlemen in London, but no one in the wilds of the West Country.

Meric sighed over the knowledge that his servants seemed to manage him more than he managed them, and changed into the dry clothing. As Huntley folded the breeches over his arm, something fell out of the pocket and rang on the stone edge of the hearth. He stooped to pick it up.

Meric waved him off. "Just a button I found in a pasture today."

"A broken one, I see."

"Yes, but it has an interesting embossing on it, and I wanted to study it further." Meric tucked the button into his pocket.

Huntley wrinkled his high-bridged nose. "Embossed buttons are too dandified for you, my lord. I am afraid I could not dress a gentleman who wore that much fancywork on his buttons."

Meric gritted his teeth. He needed to start giving a few orders instead of hearing ultimatums. If only he knew how to order servants. The past year hadn't really taught him, apparently.

A refrain sounded in his head: *You need a wife to run your life.*

Miss Honore Bainbridge's face, lovely even dirty and tearstained—presenting the sort of delicate sculptured bones that would make her beautiful at any age—floated before his mind's eye. Such beauty and courage shouldn't be connected with a morally suspect character.

"The Lord will provide for you," Mother had assured him before he and Philo sailed for England by way of France, then a Channel Island, and then a smuggler's vessel. "See how He is providing for us?"

She was right, of course—the Lord had provided for him and then some. But Miss Bainbridge as marriage material was not amidst the provisions of the Lord. The Lord would provide another female, maybe already had.

Heart rather heavy, Meric descended to the library, a fire, and blessed coffee rather than the eternal tea. Not that his parents hadn't wanted tea now and again. Coffee simply proved more common and easier to obtain.

He poured himself a cup of the strong, dark brew, eschewed the cream Chilcott offered him, and propped a shoulder against the mantel. "So tell me what was so important you had to follow me into the country."

Philo and Chilcott exchanged glances.

Meric gulped a mouthful of coffee to ease the tightness across his gut. "What's wrong?"

"The revenue men were by," Philo blurted out.

"They had some nodcock from the Somerset militia with them," Chilcott announced.

Meric's cup was half full. Still, coffee sloshed near the rim. He set it on the mantel and crossed his arms over his chest. "What did they want?"

"To know where you were last night," Chilcott said.

"To know where I—" Meric ground his teeth. "Why? Tell me what happened," he demanded.

"Prisoners disappeared from Dartmoor." Philo smiled as he reached for a sweet biscuit, but his hand shook, and he knocked two onto the table.

Meric closed his eyes and tried not to see the endless gray of prison walls, to smell the mildew and damp of the cell, to hear the clang of ironbound doors slamming in his face. Worse was an image of him repeating his father's actions of twenty-eight years earlier—fleeing in the night and sailing for America, his name forever blackened, unless . . .

"You assured them I had nothing to do with this disappearance, I presume?" Meric asked.

"I assured them you were not anywhere near the prison,"

Chilcott said in a too cheery tone. "You were entertaining the vicar until at least eleven of the clock, and that would not have given you enough time to get down to Dartmoor and sneak a bunch of Frenchmen—"

"Frenchmen?" Meric's eyes popped open and he stared at his steward. "Why would they think I would help Frenchmen?"

"Because the French helped Americans in the last war?" Philo suggested.

"We weren't anywhere near America in the last war." Meric snatched up his now cold coffee and downed it like a foul elixir necessary for life. "Our parents weren't anywhere near America in the last war."

"No, my lord," Chilcott pointed out, "but your father was, ahem, known all too well for, ahem, being rather lawless."

"And that's the rub of it, isn't it?" Meric scrubbed one hand over his face in a vain attempt to loosen the tension around his eyes. "Our father was never proven innocent of murder, and too many people believe the apple doesn't fall far from the tree."

"Precisely, my lord." Chilcott nodded. "From a murderer father to a traitor son is easy to accept."

"Then," Meric said, "that is all the more reason I need to prove Father's innocence."

If he could work out how to do so without the twenty-eight-year-old scandal rearing its head enough to cast a shadow over him.

Honore wore black for church on Sunday. Although the color—or lack thereof—enhanced the gold in her hair and the hint of roses in her cheeks, its dullness left her scowling at her reflection with displeasure. She must look fine, finer than other single ladies like Miss Carolina Devenish, if she was to persuade Lord Ashmoor to marry her.

If she should persuade Lord Ashmoor to marry her.

Still shaken from her brush with death and learning of her father's plans, Honore thought Miss Morrow's advice sound. If Honore wished to do anything to honor her father's memory, marrying the man he'd intended for her to wed seemed like an excellent start. Despite the reputation of his father and the fact he had been raised amongst those wild and rebellious Americans, Lord Ashmoor was a fine catch. Titled and wealthy, he possessed a handsome face and fine physique. He was young too, and kind, even if his refusal to take her to wife seemed less than good of him.

Honore did not blame him. No one wanted to marry her any longer. If her escapades with a handsome rake during her first Season had not been bad enough, getting caught kissing another gentleman in her brother-in-law's orangery—and then that man turning out to be a murderer—sent Miss Honore Bainbridge flying beyond the bounds of acceptability.

"It will all blow over in a year," her sister Lydia had assured her. "A new scandal will come along and your follies will be forgotten."

"But I'll be so old by then." Honore shuddered at the idea that by the next Season, she would be nearly one and twenty, practically on the shelf.

Lydia had been wed by twenty, and Cassandra betrothed. Honore had gone so far beyond the pale, her father had planned an alliance with a stranger, a foreigner.

"It is the same word in French," she murmured to her reflection. "*Étranger*."

"What is that foreign word?" Miss Morrow asked as she trotted into the room, a spill of pewter ribbon tumbling from her hands.

"Just musing about how *stranger* and *foreigner* are the same word in French." Honore lifted an end of the trailing ribbons. "What is this for?"

"I saw this in a shop yesterday and thought it might brighten up this gown without being too bold for church. See, a bit of it around your waist and a bow on your left shoulder." Miss Morrow demonstrated, slipping the jet grosgrain ribbon from the high waist of Honore's gown and replacing it with the satin. "Thank goodness you are out of crepe. That is so dull. And here's a bow I have made."

The loops of ribbon Miss Morrow pinned to Honore's shoulder more resembled a flower in the multiple loops of shining fabric than a mere bow. Honore stared in the mirror. Her boring black silk dress seemed to glow with a hidden light.

Her own eyes glowed. "You are a genius, Miss Morrow. Why

ever—" She stopped, not wanting to ask why her companion was so determined to make her look well enough to catch a husband.

Unless, perhaps, she wished for an excuse to leave Honore's employment, and getting her charge married off was the best way to do so.

A lump surely the size of the boulder broken from the cliff settled beneath Honore's rib cage. She started to turn from the mirror but caught another glimpse of herself from the corner of her eye.

"Amazing how you did that." She could not help but swing back to the mirror and stare.

With a few yards of ribbon, Miss Morrow had transformed a dull gown of social necessity for half-mourning into an interesting gown of fashion choice. On the other side of the room, she twisted more of the pewter ribbon around the brim of Honore's black straw hat.

"Why?" she could not help asking.

Miss Morrow smiled. "I like making things prettier. And you've been in black or white far too long. Meaning no disrespect to his lordship your father, but colors would suit you better."

"It has been nine months. That is more than long enough to be without colors for a parent. And Papa—" That lump under Honore's ribs pressed into her lungs, making breathing difficult. "He always spoiled me. Gave me whatever I wanted." She made a face. "Perhaps more than he should have."

Except he had not intended to give her the sort of husband she wanted—a man of refinement and polished good looks, sartorial excellence, and a sense of adventure. Papa had found a man who, if not the opposite of that, came far too close. At the same time, Ashmoor was titled and wealthy, and Miss Honore Bainbridge could no longer afford to be choosy. If Papa wanted her to wed Lord Ashmoor, then wed him she would. Even if he had changed his mind, she could change it back.

She accepted the refurbished hat from Miss Morrow and set it atop her curls at a coquettish angle, tied the ribbons into a bow beneath her left ear, caught up her reticule, and led the way downstairs.

Three carriages and a wagon awaited those of the Bainbridge household who wished to attend services at Clovelly All Saints. They could ride only part of the way due to the steepness of the Clovelly streets, but the two miles into town were too far to walk in one's good clothes, especially in inclement weather. No rain clouds dimmed the blue of the sky that morning, but most of the servants appeared to be crowding into the vehicles.

Instead of a footman holding the honors, Mr. Joseph Tuckfield, the Bainbridge steward, stood holding the family carriage door. "Ladies, may I join you?"

"Of course." Honore bit her tongue before she asked him what had changed his mind about going to services. She should simply be happy he was attending.

A glance at him looking at Miss Morrow, and Honore received her answer anyway—he seemed to fancy the pretty companion, though surely he was far too old for her.

For her part, Miss Morrow merely nodded her thanks as he handed her up the steps to the vehicle, but she said nothing to him then or on the short drive to the village. Instead, she kept her head bowed over her *Book of Common Prayer*.

Honore took the opportunity to ask him another question. "Have you been out to the cliff to see what happened there?"

"I have." Tuckfield's lips turned down at the corners. "I feel so responsible for what happened to you, Miss Bainbridge. If I had told you the cliff looked unstable, you never would have gone walking there."

"You did not know I would go for a walk on the cliffs straightaway."

"No, but I should have thought you might on such a fine day as we had most of Friday." Tuckfield's frown grew deeper. "I should have put up some sort of barrier to warn people. I had just noticed the problem that morning. Perhaps rain from the day before acted like the proverbial straw."

"Only that straw turned out to be me breaking the cliff's back." Honore shuddered and flexed her still aching shoulders, then made herself smile. "Can we do anything about it? I mean, can the cliff be shored up somehow?"

Tuckfield tapped his fingertips against his cleft chin, his most attractive feature. "It might be best to blast off all the loose bits."

"Could we get a mining engineer in to look at doing that?"

Miss Morrow raised her head from her prayer book long enough to give Honore a surprised look at that comment.

Tuckfield's dark eyebrows shot up to nearly join his hairline. "That is an excellent idea, Miss Bainbridge. I shall see who I can find."

"Whom," Miss Morrow murmured.

Honore snapped a glance in her direction, but the carriage stopped at that moment. They had arrived at the edge of the square, and they needed to walk downhill to the church. On a fine day, the walk invigorated Honore, giving her an alert mind for the service. On rainy days, dragging herself out of the carriage to descend the hill proved nigh on impossible. This bright, crisp morning sent her feet skimming over the stones, past gardens falling dormant with the first frost in the near future, up to the church, and—

She skidded to a halt like a runaway wagon whose brake had just engaged. Lord Ashmoor stood in the church porch, talking to the vicar. Beside them stood a young man who looked so much like his lordship that he must be a brother, and Mr. Chilcott, the Ashmoor steward.

"Come along, Miss Bainbridge." Miss Morrow tugged Honore's arm. "We will be late if we dally."

"We will not be late. The vicar is not even inside yet."

"And you want to greet his lordship, do you not?" Miss Morrow whispered in Honore's ear.

No, in truth, she did not. That lump beneath her ribs had increased, and an image of herself cradled in his arms as he'd carried her blurred her vision. His arms did not appear so brawny inside his fashionable coat, but she had seen the muscles through his shirt and felt their strength. Her cheeks heated despite the sharp wind off the sea.

"What was I thinking?" she murmured back to her companion. "I cannot persuade him to wed me if he does not wish to. Look at him. I doubt anyone makes him do what he does not wish to."

Miss Morrow tucked her arm through Honore's and propelled her forward by sheer force of will. "You are to persuade him, not make him."

They reached the steps to the porch. Ashmoor and the rest of his party left their post near the church door and swept forward to bow in greeting and receive introductions.

Honore held out her gloved hand to Mr. Philemon Poole. "Welcome to Devonshire. I hope you find it comfortable."

"Yes, it's . . . um . . . yes, ma'am, it's fine." The young man turned the color of a beetroot.

Beside him, Mr. Chilcott had also colored up to the line of his silvering hair, and Miss Morrow, forthright lady that she was, had fallen silent, her gaze cast somewhere between the first and third steps.

Honore narrowed her eyes in speculation, then snapped her attention around to the vicar, avoiding dialogue with his lordship. "Mr. Stanbury, we have a lovely day for a service, do we not?"

"Quite. Quite." He touched her outstretched fingers, his pale blue eyes gazing at her with adoration from a pleasantly plain face. "Must take advantage of these fine days before the autumn doldrums set in."

"I like autumn in the country."

From the corner of her eye, Honore regarded Mrs. Devenish and her gaggle of daughters swarming around Ashmoor like hens after a pile of grain.

"My sister," Mr. Stanbury was saying, "requested me to invite you and your companion to join us for a cold collation after service. Forgive the lack of notice, do, but we would so love to have you come."

The adoring look, not in the least faded since before she rode off to her first disastrous Season, warned her to say no. Honore understood what Miss Stanbury was up to—matchmaking Miss Bainbridge, with her dowry and connections, to her brother. Apparently those traits outweighed her unforgiven sins.

Not a yard away, the Devenish ladies tittered behind fans or gloved fingers. Miss Devenish actually simpered.

Honore felt ill. "I will have to ask Miss Morrow." She raised her own fan so she could observe the others without appearing to do so.

"Lord Ashmoor and his party are coming," Stanbury added as though that were an enticement.

Miss Morrow elbowed Honore in the ribs.

"We would be delighted to come," Honore said.

Who was she to stand in the way of a flirtation between her companion and the Ashmoor steward? At least it answered the question as to why Miss Morrow encouraged Honore to set her cap for the earl despite his declaration not to wed her. The more time Honore spent in his lordship's company, the more time Miss Morrow could spend in Nigel Chilcott's presence—theoretically. Mr. Tuckfield had better make hay while the sun shone if he did not wish to lose out.

The thought made Honore smile, and she bowed her head in acquiescence. "Please thank Miss Stanbury for me."

Miss Stanbury was inside the church, managing the barrel organ with the same three hymns the machine played every Sunday morning, signaling the congregation to move from the fresh, clear air on the porch to the dank stuffiness of the five-hundred-year-old stone building. That crowd on the porch had grown oddly silent. Instead of gazing at Lord Ashmoor, the Devenish girls now glared at Honore.

She shrank back a few inches at the power of those scowls. Her foot slipped off the step, and Lord Ashmoor grasped her elbow. "Chilcott told me that I have to escort you in because we are the two highest-ranked personages present."

"You needn't," Honore replied, her lips barely moving. "It is not a formal dinner party."

"But I do everything Chilcott says I must." Ashmoor released her elbow and held out his forearm.

Honore took it and understood why he had managed to lift her up that cliff and then carry her through the orchard. Beneath the smooth wool of his coat, his arm muscle was as solid as the stone beneath her feet, but far warmer.

Such an unholy thought to have before service. If she had not indulged in so many unholy thoughts and too many actions against her conscience's prompting, she would not be walking up the stone floor worn smooth after half a millennium's worth of churchgoers' soles had trod over them. Instead, she would be yawning her way through a service at St George's, Hanover Square, after a night of balls and routs.

Well, perhaps not balls and routs. More like a musicale or soirée, as she was still in half-mourning. Regardless, she would have been socializing in London instead of having had a quiet night in her brother's countryseat working on her Gothic novel.

She would not be enduring the stares of the local gentry on her way to the Bainbridge pew. Like the Devenish ladies, every female Honore passed began to whisper and giggle behind a fan or gloved hand. A few words rang off the cold rock around them. "Little more than she deserves" was followed by "Worst misalliance yet."

Not all glances were unfriendly. The local folk—the tradesmen from whom she purchased supplies, a few farmers' wives and daughters, even one or two of their sons—caught Honore's eye and smiled or nodded. They recalled the untamed, undisciplined, unfettered child she had been not so long ago, eluding her governess to fish or explore the caves. Now her status demanded that she do no more than nod in return, nearly shunning the only persons showing her kindness.

Not until Ashmoor opened the door to the Bainbridge pew for Honore and someone said far too loudly, "I cannot believe

Prudence Devenish is considering a match for her daughter there," did Honore realize the nasty remarks were directed as much at her escort as her.

She glanced up at him, trying to form an apology for her fellow Englishmen. She expected to see hurt or exaggerated indifference. Instead, he smiled broadly enough for it to reach his eyes, bowed to her with the stiffness of someone unused to the action, and crossed the aisle to the Poole pew.

Light-headed, she stepped up into the pew and slid across to make room for Miss Morrow. Mr. Tuckfield never joined the family in their pew, unlike the steward from Ashmoor. But then, Mr. Chilcott was the sixth son of a good if relatively poor family, and was more a secretary than was Tuckfield—a better match for Miss Morrow than was the Bainbridge steward. Honore must promote the union. Perhaps if she lost her companion to matrimony, her sisters would feel obligated to invite her back despite their confinements, and she could forget about her scheme to ensnare Lord Ashmoor.

That notion had seemed like a good one with rain lashing at the windows and her cliff ordeal mere hours behind her. She did not wish to die a spinster and wanted to marry immediately. She wanted to do something of which Papa would have approved. Marrying Ashmoor would indeed solve both of those goals. But a good night's sleep had compelled her to reconsider. Two good nights' sleep and his presence confirmed that she should not for a moment consider him as husband material. He was good-looking enough. To be honest, he was better than that. He seemed polite and had been considerate enough to give her the marriage contract—unsigned by him. And yet . . .

Nothing changed his foreignness.

Throughout the service, she watched him from the corner of

her eye. He sang the psalm responses with too much heartfelt pleasure in the music glowing on his face. He leaned forward, his face intent during the sermon, as though he actually listened to the vicar's words. He even nodded a few times, as though agreeing with a point Honore did not even remember half a minute after Mr. Stanbury made it.

What was the new Lord Ashmoor, some sort of dissenter? Or did he simply take his faith deeply to heart like her sisters and their husbands did?

Honore squirmed on the hard wood of the pew. She had done that not so long ago—believed she need only trust God to guide her life, to cleanse her heart, to love her. She had even attempted to make her relationship with the Lord personal. Then her second beau proved to be a murderer, and Papa died. Abandoned despite the proximity of her loving sisters, Honore gave up on believing God cared much about her.

"Be strong and of a good courage," Mr. Stanbury read from his Bible again, then he glanced at the congregation, at Honore specifically. "You are not alone. God promised to never forsake us, and His promises are true."

Honore bowed her head as though she acknowledged his words. In truth, she avoided his gaze in the event he read the doubt of her heart reflected in her face.

Not at all desirous of a cold collation at the vicarage, Honore rose for the benediction and then moved into the aisle. Perhaps she could plead a headache. It was not untrue. Her shoulders ached enough to set up a pounding at the back of her head.

"I think I escort you out too, Miss Bainbridge." Lord Ashmoor held out his arm to her.

Unable to refuse without embarrassing both of them, Honore took it and pasted a smile on her face as they retraced their steps down the aisle between the rows of the congregation. Outside, a blast of cold, damp wind buffeted their faces and brought a layer of cloud to haze over the earlier sunshine.

"Rain's coming," Ashmoor said quite unnecessarily, "which means we are to proceed to the vicarage, according to Miss Stanbury."

"That seems a bit odd if they won't be there." Honore stared at the street too narrow and steep for a carriage. "Perhaps I should simply go on home. Walking these streets in the rain is unpleasant at best."

"Please don't." His voice held genuine appeal.

Honore glanced up at him. "My lord?"

"Miss Stanbury scares me."

The organ music swelled out the doors of the church. Miss Stanbury, fifteen years older than and half again the size of her brother, was strong enough to crank the old organ into a volume high enough to drown out conversation within a hundred feet. She also played the pianoforte extremely well, cooked wonderfully, and knit mittens and caps for every child in the village each winter. She talked as loudly as she played and talked about whatever she liked.

"Are you her latest project?" Honore asked.

"I'm afraid I am." With Miss Morrow and the other two men in the Ashmoor party behind them, Ashmoor headed down a side street to the vicarage. "She insists she will prove to the parish that I am above speculation as to my loyalty to the Crown, that I deserve the title, and that I am an asset to the entire county, despite three months in an English prison upon my setting foot on these shores, and several visits from various branches of the military."

Honore halted in the middle of the lane. "What visits from the military?"

"Big brother is a suspicious character, Miss Bainbridge," Mr. Poole called out. "You're best off letting me escort you about."

"Stubble it," Ashmoor shot over his shoulder.

"What military?" Honore demanded. "Why?" She removed her hand from his arm and crossed it over her waist.

"The excise men, the horse guards, a gentleman who didn't say where he served." Ashmoor's face sobered. "Mind you, I use the term *gentleman* loosely. I've lived here long enough to learn that his accent was not up to snuff, even if his clothes met my valet's approval."

"Of course a man's accent matters more than dress."

His, for example, named him as a foreigner, regardless of his aristocratic English parentage.

"But that does not answer the why," Honore concluded.

Ashmoor shrugged and continued to walk.

She needed to either catch up with him or fall back and take Mr. Poole's arm instead.

She matched her pace with his but kept her hands at her waist. "They do not go visiting peers of the realm without good reason, my lord."

"They accused me of helping some Frenchmen escape from Dartmoor."

Honore gave him a blank look. "Why would you help Frenchmen?"

"An excellent question, madam." Ashmoor slipped his hand beneath her elbow to assist her over the ditch at the side of the lane and into the vicarage garden. "A pity I don't have an excellent answer."

"Now, if they accused you of helping Americans escape, I would understand that." Honore twirled her reticule strings between her fingers. "But then, perhaps you would not risk all for the sake of a few men who will likely be recaptured anyway."

"Besides trying to feed this insatiable whelp here," Ashmoor said with a glance back at his brother, "I have three more brothers at home, all of whom need to get a trade so they can survive in this world, and three sisters, two of whom would also like to marry one day and take something more than their pretty faces to the union. So, Miss Bainbridge, yes, I would not risk all of this for the sake of a handful of Americans who know the risk of going to sea against Great Britain."

"Bravo." Mr. Poole applauded.

"You have seven brothers and sisters?" Honore stared at him.

Mr. Poole laughed. "You make a fine speech, and she is in awe over the abundance of our family."

The front door of the vicarage opened to reveal a middle-aged maid with a decided mustache on her upper lip. "Do come in, Miss Bainbridge, my lord. The vicar and Miss Stanbury will be along shortly."

She led the way into the house. The rest of them followed the bobbing bow of her apron into a parlor smelling of beeswax and the coal of the fire on the hearth. Though she was not cold, Honore headed for that fire as an excuse not to sit. Experience warned her not to repose on one of the sofas or chairs in the chamber. She preferred sitting on rocks. They were more comfortable than whatever filled the cushions of the vicarage furniture.

"The chairs," she warned Ashmoor, "are character building."

"More like callous building." Mr. Poole hopped up from the edge of a sofa.

Miss Morrow and Mr. Chilcott said nothing, though they

had talked all the way from the church. They took seats across from one another.

"I will bring tea momentarily." Her upper lip stiff enough to make the fine hairs of her mustache quiver, the maid stalked from the parlor.

"Curb your tongue before servants," Ashmoor admonished his brother.

"I forget they're there." Mr. Poole placed his hands over his reddened ears. "Just not used to them, you know."

"I'd rather they weren't." Ashmoor leaned his elbow on the mantel and smiled down at Honore. "Thank you for believing me incapable of being a traitor. That makes one family in the county."

"Two," Mr. Poole said. "The Devenishes wouldn't believe it if they saw you personally leading escaped prisoners through the village."

"Now that they married off their eldest girl, they have another daughter of marriageable age." Honore grinned as she began to tug off her gloves. "Nearly two if you want to wait a year, Mr. Poole."

He shuddered. "No thank you. I mean, they're pretty enough, but those noises they make instead of laughing are enough to put me off my feed."

"Which is saying something," Ashmoor murmured. Aloud he asked, "How will we endure them for an evening tomorrow, Miss Bainbridge?"

Honore paused with one glove halfway off her hand. "Did they invite you to supper? Not a good sign."

"Not supper." Ashmoor glanced at his brother, then Miss Morrow, before his gaze settled on Honore. "It's some sort of evening gathering. A soirée, I think the invitation said. But surely you're coming too."

"No. No, I am not. I was not invited to the Devenishes' soirée," Honore said. The lump that had been pressing on her rib cage all morning suddenly rose into her throat. She swung toward the door. "I must be going. I have—I have a great deal of writing to accomplish this afternoon."

She would not weep in front of Ashmoor again, not over the lack of an invitation to a party she would not enjoy anyway. Miss Devenish was lovely, sweet, and kind, but her sisters were insipid and her friends too often mean. Still . . .

"Forgive me." She dropped a curtsy then exited the parlor.

Miss Morrow caught up with her before the front door. "You cannot leave, Miss Bainbridge. It would be the height of rudeness to the vicar and his sister, and you cannot afford to offend anyone else in the county."

"I believe I offend them with my very presence." Honore spoke through teeth clenched to keep her chin from quivering.

"Not the vicar." Miss Morrow tucked a curl back into Honore's chignon, a motherly gesture. "Come back and sit. The gentlemen—the Poole gentlemen—are comme il faut."

Honore sighed. "And the Stanburys are coming."

Miss Stanbury's voice rang from out front. By the time she and her brother entered the house, Honore had returned to sit in a torturously uncomfortable chair, Ashmoor was examining a Bible that appeared old enough to have been printed by Tyndale himself, and the others sat in stiff silence.

"What? No tea yet?" Miss Stanbury greeted them all. "I will see what that woman is doing to take so long." She stomped off through the house.

The vicar entered and told them the story of the Bible coming into his family two hundred years earlier. "It was one of the first ones printed under King James."

The others smiled politely.

Tea arrived along with the promised cold collation. Talk focused on nothing more important than the Christmas fete, three months off but needing a great deal of planning, and apparently the true reason for the invitation.

"We need a place to hold it that will accommodate a number of people," Miss Stanbury pronounced. "I was thinking that cottage of yours would work well, Lord Ashmoor, it being here in the village but having a fine garden."

"If you call a single tree a fine garden." Ashmoor spoke only loud enough for Honore's ears.

"She means your yard," Honore murmured back. "The yard of that house is a goodly size and walled to protect from the elements."

Ashmoor nodded. "I expect that will be all right."

"But we need a female's involvement." The vicar took up the planning. "And Miss Bainbridge is—"

"Not acceptable," Honore broke in. "If—if I am not being invited to parties . . ." That lump had arisen in her throat again. She swallowed. It stuck. She could not finish saying that she could not help with the fete if no one would invite her to their entertainments.

"But you are the highest-ranked lady in the parish." The vicar sounded as distraught as he looked.

Honore shook her head. She still could not speak. More afraid of making a fool of herself by weeping in front of everyone than offending them, she muttered an incoherent excuse and fled from the parlor, fled from the house.

She had not noticed the rain beginning. It poured from the sky like someone emptying a barrel of day-old wash water all dingy-gray and cold. Muddy water sluiced in twin rivers down the gutters of the street on their way to the sea. Not only had she forgotten to carry an umbrella, but her dainty slippers would be ruined in moments.

"Allow me, Miss Bainbridge." Ashmoor stepped out of the vicarage and opened an umbrella large enough to house a small family. "If you hold the umbrella, I'll lift you over the gutter."

"Really, my lord, you cannot continue to pick me up."

"I can as long as necessary." He thrust the handle of the umbrella into her hand. "Up you go." He scooped her into his arms as he had on Friday, as though she weighed nothing.

As she had done on Friday, she held herself stiffly, though she wanted to rest her head on his shoulder. She wanted to cling to him because he was so solid, so strong, so . . . warm.

Perhaps that was wrong thinking despite its truth. She would write Lydia and ask. Lydia always knew what was right and wrong, unlike the two younger Bainbridge sisters. Honore especially. She had behaved so badly she could not get an invitation to a local soirée arranged by people only a generation out of the shop.

"I'll take you to your carriage," Ashmoor offered. "It's too wet for you to walk."

"But Miss Morrow." It was the best protest she could manage.

Ashmoor grinned. "Mr. Chilcott will get her there."

"Ah, yes, Mr. Chilcott." Honore's desire to weep left with the appearance of his smile. "It would be a good match for her."

"Do, please, explain this social intricacy. I thought a companion would outrank a steward. And she's related to an earl."

"Chilcott is related to a duke. His great-uncle, I think. And Miss Morrow's connection to my brother-in-law is quite distant. A cousin several times removed."

"I suppose I have distant cousins like that." Ashmoor puffed a little on the uphill climb. "Am I expected to find them positions if they need them? Chilcott says not, but you might know better. Isn't there something like noblesse oblige?"

"Noble obligation? Yes. The Royal College of Arms can help you find your cousins if you like, but if they have not contacted you by now, I doubt they want favors from you."

"Offended that I inherited?"

Honore shifted her gaze to the rain pouring off the umbrella like a waterfall circling around them. "You are not quite English."

"Nor am I quite American." They reached the mews at the top of the main street, and Ashmoor set her down in the shelter of the carriage house. "Will you be all right here while I see that your horses are put to?"

"Yes, thank you." She shook off the umbrella and handed it to him. "You will need this."

He took it but hesitated in the doorway, raindrops bouncing off the lintel to land on his hair. It curled in the damp, giving him a boyish look for all his size. Nothing about his expression was boyish. The corners of his lips tightened, and lines showed at the corners of his eyes. "Miss Bainbridge, I am sorry you weren't invited to the Devenish soirée. It doesn't seem right to me."

"Carolina Devenish is a nice country girl."

Let him work out that Honore meant Miss Devenish was innocent and naive and must not be corrupted by the scandalous Miss Honore Bainbridge.

She smiled. "I shall have far more pleasure working at home, you will see."

"Working?" He raised one brow, a trick Honore had never been able to master. "On what are you working?"

"I am writing a Gothic novel full of adventure." Her smile broadened. "I am considering having my heroine nearly fall off a breaking cliff, only have the murderous villain rescue her instead of—" Realizing what she was about to say, she stepped farther into the carriage house. "You are getting wet standing there. Perhaps you should go."

"Maybe I should." His mouth flattened into a thin line as he turned on his heel and stalked through the rain to the stable without putting up the umbrella.

Not until she'd spoken those words did Honore remember that many considered his father a villain, a man wanted for the murder of an excise officer twenty-eight years earlier.

Meric seated himself as far from the pianoforte and other instruments as he could manage. Music played by skilled musicians thrilled his soul. Music played by rank amateurs grated on his ears like two pieces of tin rubbing together. With the three Devenish daughters and two of their friends swarming around the instruments, smoothing music upon stands, and rearranging chairs—all action accompanied by those delicate titters and little squeals—the fate of his ears for the evening seemed assured.

"If I'd known this was a musical evening," he muttered to Philo, "I would have brought some wax to stuff my ears."

"I can pinch a candle," Philo said.

"The offer is tempting."

Someone catching the earl of Ashmoor stealing candles from one of the wall sconces in order to stuff wax into his ears just might give this dull evening the spark it needed to make it interesting. So far, since he didn't play cards, he had enjoyed nothing more entertaining than a glass of fresh lemonade and no conversation livelier than a discussion of hunting deer. Lemonade was still a novelty to him, as his family had never possessed the resources to afford such luxuries. Hunting in England, however, was downright ridiculous, closer to shooting cattle in a pasture than stalking a wild animal through the woods. And although the English seemed to enjoy their venison, they didn't depend on it dried and cured to get through the winter without starving.

Mrs. Devenish apparently thought they should get through the evening by starving. Her refreshments had consisted of cakes no bigger than his thumb and as substantial as a handful of sea foam, and a rather good but sparsely supplied apple pie. Apple tart, she called it, complete with an edging of cream.

Beside him in the drawing room, cleared to accommodate the guests who didn't play cards, Philo's stomach growled like the roll of a bass drum. "Why do we have to eat supper after this gathering?"

"Because Wooland says so." Meric raised his gaze to the ceiling, knowing what was coming.

"He works for you. Why don't you tell him when you want the meals served?"

Meric held up a finger for silence. The young ladies had gathered around the pianoforte, a violin, and a cello. Two stood in the center.

"The singers," Meric said.

Philo paled. "There's a candle right above us."

"Take heart. They might be good."

They weren't good. Neither were they terrible. They simply sang and played with every note right and yet no heart. And Meric's heart ached for the music his family had produced. None of them played an instrument. They didn't have any instruments to play anyway. But all of them sang. They harmonized together. They felt the music of the old ballads Mother and Father remembered from their youth. The Devenish ladies sounded like an automaton playing a flute, which Meric had witnessed at some lord's house in London—pitch-perfect and soulless.

"I wonder if Mother and the children are singing tonight," he whispered to Philo.

Philo blinked hard, turned his face away, and shrugged. "They won't have anyone to do the low parts with us gone. And Kate might—"

"Shh," an old woman in a purple turban hissed at them from the row ahead.

Mr. Devenish's mother.

Meric cleared a thickness in his throat and stood. "Must go outside to cough."

He slipped along the row of chairs to the far wall and a French window that led onto the terrace. Cold, damp wind blew into his face, clearing his head and throat of candle smoke and too much perfume. The sharp tang of the sea greeted his nose, and he inhaled, missing the freshness of the lake at home, the tang of the forest in autumn. His heart ached.

"This wasn't what I meant when I prayed for the means to support my family, Lord." The ache grew into a clenched fist inside his chest. He pounded his own fist on the stone balustrade.

He wanted to leave, find a smuggler's vessel to carry him to France, where he could find an American ship to sail him back to New York. The most enjoyment he had experienced since deciding to take up residence in Devonshire was rescuing Miss Bainbridge from the cliff. He'd been useful there. No one else he'd met so far could perform such a feat. But the opportunity to pull maidens off crumbling cliffs didn't arise every day. The rest of the time he gave a nod to Chilcott's reports of the lands and other holdings, approved of the cook's food, and tolerated Huntley dragging him to a tailor or boot maker or some other sort of clothier.

"No wonder these people gamble away fortunes and drink to excess. They're bored to distraction."

Violin music swelled loudly enough to pierce the heavy glass in the doors.

"And suffer through bad musicianship."

Duty called, however. Duty always called him back. He opened the door at the end of the song. Apparently he did so at the end of the set of songs, for Miss Devenish rushed over to him, her cheeks as rosy as apples, her pale blue eyes shining, her golden curls bobbing. "My lord, thank you for enduring our performance. We know we aren't very good, but we so enjoy playing."

"You have a very pretty voice, Miss Devenish."

Which was the truth. She was a very pretty young lady, especially her sweet smile.

She blushed. "Why, thank you, my lord. Shall we get more refreshments? I know they were sparse earlier. We rather had a disaster in the kitchen this afternoon, but replacements should have arrived by now."

"What sort of disaster?" Meric offered her his arm—as he had no choice—and nodded to his brother, cornered by the elder Mrs. Devenish.

"Cook tripped over the cat and dropped the ham into the fire." Miss Devenish tittered. "That caused such an uproar, the bread burned and one of the maids dropped the trifle and . . . it was quite a mess. Mama was shrieking and threatening to dismiss them all, and Cook said she would give her notice if that was how thirty years of service was rewarded. It was like a farce at the theater."

"It sounds like it." Meric ran calculations through his mind as to whether or not he should take on more servants. "Did the servants get dismissed?"

"Of course not. Mama would not dare." Miss Devenish grasped his elbow like a tiller and steered him through the crush heading toward the dining room.

Too many persons greeted them, waylaid them along the way for further conversation. Not until he and Miss Devenish sat at a table set against the windows, plates of simple but abundant fare before them, did Meric gain the opportunity to ask, "So why does your mother dare not dismiss the servants?" He smiled to disarm any rude intent that might be read into his question. "I am learning the ways of the country gentry, you understand."

"Of course you are." Miss Devenish bestowed an understanding look upon him. "And we are a close company, you understand. Our servants talk to one another. And some of them talk to their employers. If one is unfair or unkind, it gets around and then hiring good workers becomes difficult."

Ah, so the servants were not entirely helpless.

"Did you not have this problem in America?" she asked.

"I have no idea. I didn't have servants."

She stared at him. "But who cooked your meals and did the shopping and the cleaning and—" She broke off this litany of chores as Philo and the violinist, a tall, slender girl with big, dark eyes, joined them at the table. "Penelope, Mr. Poole, how kind of you to seek our company." The chill of her voice and the tightening of her lips suggested feelings in opposition to her words.

"I heard about the kitchen disaster," Penelope Babbage said. "How did you get replacements so quickly?"

"Our cook is the sister of the cook at Bainbridge." Miss Devenish smiled at Meric. "As I was saying, everyone knows everyone else."

Meric set down his fork with careful deliberation and curled his hand around the edge of the table. "You took food from the Bainbridge household but didn't invite Miss Bainbridge to your party?"

He spoke a trifle too loudly. He spoke during a momentary lull in the hubbub around the food. He spoke at a moment when everyone in the room heard him.

"Um, Meric," Philo began, "maybe—"

Meric raised his hand. "I'll say no more on it. It is your concern."

Miss Devenish had paled right down to the apples in her cheeks, opened her mouth, but said nothing.

"Do, please, forgive me," Meric said.

Conversations resumed with a vengeance. Philo and Meric continued eating. Miss Babbage smiled as she nibbled at a hothouse strawberry.

Poor Miss Devenish stared down at her plate and didn't touch her food.

Meric touched her arm. "I'm sorry. I shouldn't have said anything. It's really none of my concern."

"Oh no, my lord." Miss Devenish gazed up at him with shining eyes. "It shows what a good and kind person you are that you could care about the feelings even of a female like her."

Across the table, Philo covered his mouth with his serviette and spluttered. His eyes danced.

Meric pushed back his chair. "I need some more air. Is it too cold or improper for you to join me, Miss Devenish?"

"No, my lord, not on the terrace."

Where the well-lighted rooms spilled their glow onto the flagstones and on anyone promenading back and forth. Besides, several others preceded them into the crisp night, but not so many that every word would be overheard.

"It was Mama's decision, you know," Miss Devenish said, "not to invite Miss Bainbridge. I wanted her here."

"Because of her reputation?" Meric asked.

Miss Devenish hesitated then answered, "Mama says so, but I think it is because she is so very pretty that girls like me have no chance of attracting the right sort of husband."

Meric's heart softened, warmed. He paused at the end of the terrace and smiled down at her, covering her little hand where it rested on his forearm. "I don't think that's true at all, Miss Devenish. You have an excellent chance of making a good match."

Her fingers trembled, and her smile was radiant even in the near darkness. "I do hope so. I wish to avoid going to London."

"Why? I thought all females wished a Season in London."

"I don't like the city. I don't even like going into Exeter or Plymouth."

"But what about the theater, the opera, the bookshops?" He named the activities he had found most enjoyable in the biggest city he had ever visited, then added one he thought all females would prefer. "And the shopping, of course?"

"I would like those things, I suppose, but for the crush of people." She shook her head. "I am too used to the open moors and sea here."

"They are fine." He resumed their stroll. "Do you like walks in the country, Miss Devenish?"

"I prefer to ride."

Meric tensed. Gorge rose in his throat at the mere thought of bouncing up and down on a horse. But Chilcott's voice rang more loudly in his ears than had the music, reminding him how he needed a proper wife to boost his own reputation, and what a fine choice Miss Devenish would make.

After taking a long breath as though planning to dive into cold, deep water, he said, "Then ride we shall. Tomorrow? No, Wednesday."

He mustn't seem too eager when all he wanted to do was learn more about her, to see if, indeed, he could spend the rest of his life in her company.

"I think . . ." She hesitated by one of the French windows. "I think perhaps Friday would do better. Father has some sort of business with the bishop, so we are traveling down to Exeter, and then Mama wishes to look at carpets in Axminster. So we may not return until Thursday or even Friday. I will send a note around when we return."

"You do that, Miss Devenish." Meric bowed, truly admiring whatever personage in the Devenish household who had made such traveling plans right after the soirée. Don't make the daughter too available to his attentions.

Laughing to himself, he followed Miss Devenish into the drawing room but kept going rather than stay and listen to the next set of music, this time performed by two middle-aged spinsters he had met at church the previous week. They glared at him as he exited the room. He smiled and bowed and continued on his way. Unable to locate Philo, he left a message with a footman and headed home. Two could play at the not-too-eager-to-court game.

The night was dark save for the brightness of stars, and the walk back to Clovelly was outside of five miles, but he needed the exercise. He got too little in England. Coal and wood came cut and delivered to his door. Servants carried buckets of water from the well. His suggestions that he go fishing had been met with expressions of horror and shock. If he wanted to row into a lake or river and fish, Chilcott could arrange a journey to

Scotland. The earl of Ashmoor could never go out in a smack like a common fisherman.

"And don't we need to worry about the French?" Philo had asked.

"They leave the fishermen alone, especially since they dare not come this close to our coast," Chilcott explained.

"Then I will be perfectly safe."

Chilcott seemed to have set out to dampen any opportunity for him to go out with the fishermen, for none would agree to take the earl aboard, Meric discovered when he tried to make arrangements for himself. He could easily purchase his own boat and go, but he didn't know how to sail. He had rowed on a lake. No one in England outside of the universities and Lake District seemed to row anywhere.

So he eschewed his carriage as often as possible and walked. Daytime, nighttime, rain, or shine, he took to the cliff path or the road.

The road passed by a stone wall and massive iron gates. Meric paused, realizing they belonged to Bainbridge. Somewhere up the lime tree–lined drive visible through the wrought iron, Miss Bainbridge spent the evening alone save for her paid companion and her Gothic novel. Next time they met, he would have to ask her if she had indeed endangered her heroine's life by having her nearly fall off a cliff.

And be rescued by the villain.

He resumed his walk. Not until he reached his cottage perched high above the village of Clovelly did he realize his trot had turned into a canter and then a near run, as though he were being chased, with each footfall accompanied by the same refrain. *A villain like your father. A villain like your father.*

If these people had known his father, they never would think him capable of murder. Yet they had known him twenty-eight years earlier—the older people—and amongst those, only the late Lord Bainbridge had believed him innocent of the crime. Apparently Lord Bainbridge hadn't passed his belief down to his daughters or his son, considering the latter hadn't contacted Meric in any way. Yet one more reason to court Miss Devenish. She and her family seemed unconcerned about his parentage. But then, a title and quantity of money covered up a number of family skeletons, especially when those barely removed from the shop wanted to elevate their social standing.

"Lord, I don't just want to cover them up, I want to erase them."

Restless despite the vigorous walk, Meric entered the library, shed his coat, and tossed it onto a sofa in a way sure to give Huntley apoplexy. He pulled the box of correspondences he had unearthed at Ashmoor off a shelf and set it on the desk. They were from his father. If any had been written *to* his father, Meric had never seen them. Father, however, had written to his brother faithfully for the twenty years he had been gone before he died.

Not one missive indicated where Broderick Poole had taken his family. The letters had been mailed from various ports—Philadelphia, New York, and Boston, even as far away as Charleston and Savannah. Father didn't write about the lakes or the woods, the hard winters or the brilliant autumn colors. In the early letters, he explained in clear, considered prose what had happened that fateful night. He gave an address in Trenton, New Jersey, where he could be contacted if the truth finally came out. Later, when that precious correspondence never arrived, he wrote about his growing family, his peace of mind and heart, his forgiveness of those who had lied about him.

"So where is everyone else's forgiveness?" Meric rested his chin in his hand and stared at the windows open to the cold wind off the sea. "And how do I start clearing his name?"

No answer came to him. None had come to him the other ten times he had read the letters. He didn't know the county, the coastline, or the people well enough to have a clue where to begin. The late Lord Bainbridge would have aided him. They had discussed it. But that option had been taken from him in a heartbeat. He needed an ally . . . an ally . . .

He didn't realize he had fallen asleep, his head on his folded arms atop the desk, until Philo wandered into the house mere moments before dawn.

Cold and stiff, Meric rose to greet—or confront—his younger brother and heir. "Where have you been all night?" He sniffed to detect the odor of spirits. He smelled salt spray and fish instead.

"I haven't been drinking, big brother." Philo grinned. "I've been fishing."

"You?" Meric frowned. "Why will they take you and not me?"

"I'm not the earl." Philo wandered to the steps, yawning. "By the look of things tonight, I won't even be the heir in a year or so." Chuckling, he stumbled up the steps.

Meric started to follow. "Maybe I should buy a boat and learn to sai—"

The front door knocker sounded with a thunderous *boom, boom, boom*.

"Wait for me to get that, my lord," Wooland called from the back of the house.

Something harder than a human fist and louder than a door knocker pounded on the door.

Guts twisted into a knot strong enough to hold up a ship's spar, Meric ignored Wooland and opened the door himself. Two red-coated soldiers poised on the stoop, one with the butt of his musket poised to slam against the door again.

"How may I help you . . ." He scanned the two men, one a sergeant, the other a lieutenant, judging from their insignia. "Gentlemen?" He allowed the question in the last word to convey his opinion of their early morning visit, and them for making it.

"We are here for Lord Ashmoor," the lieutenant said, hand on the hilt of his sword.

"Indeed?" With Wooland hovering behind him, Meric tried to imitate the lugubrious and stiff butler. "Do you intend to arrest him?"

"That is between us and his lordship." The lieutenant stood on tiptoe to peer past Meric's shoulder. "He must be home at this hour."

"That, fellow, is none of your business."

"It's the king's business, it is," the sergeant declared. "You'd best let us in if you knows what's good for you."

"And you," Meric drawled, "better know to whom you are speaking before you talk in such a manner. Now, if you will excuse me, his lordship does not receive callers of any sort before eight of the clock." He stepped back and slammed the door, shooting home the bolt.

The pounding resumed.

"That was well done, my lord." Wooland cast Meric the first approving glance since their acquaintance. "But you had best take yourself off so I can honestly say you are not at home."

"I shall." Meric exited through the library, snatched up his coat, and climbed over the windowsill into the strip of lawn the English apparently called a garden. From there, losing himself amidst the shops and early marketing servants was no trouble. He found himself a chophouse and purchased a meat pie for breakfast. In about an hour, he returned home the way he had come.

"They may as well open the gates of the prison and let all the Frenchies walk out," Chilcott informed him. "Another half dozen escaped last night. I assured the men you were at a party late enough you couldn't have been anywhere near the prison."

"But I wasn't," Meric said. "I left early and walked home, then was here by myself all night."

"Never you mind about that. It will not matter." Chilcott didn't sound quite sincere, and his lips turned down at the corners. "They are grasping at straws to find whoever is helping these men, and you are easy because you are new. But in the end, they cannot do much to a peer without awfully good proof."

But what about a peer's brother, who said he had been out fishing all night?

Honore tossed aside the sheaf of papers before her and stalked to the library window. If she did not find something more exciting in her life, her heroine's adventures would end up as boring as her creator's life.

"Did the cliff scene not come out right?" Miss Morrow asked from the depths of a wingback chair before the fire, where she curled up with a book.

"Worse than not all right." Honore glared at her reflection in the glass.

Every time she tried to write the villain pulling the heroine off the cliff so he could persuade her he was indeed a gentleman, she saw Lord Ashmoor's face. He was certainly not a villain. He had been kindness itself to her, and she repaid him by suggesting she might pattern her villain after his father.

She had not seen him since. He had avoided her on Sunday and, after service, walked off with the Devenish party.

"The soirée must have gone well," she murmured. "I suppose I am missing other gatherings here in the county?"

Miss Morrow said nothing.

"You know, do you not?" Honore pressed.

Miss Morrow sighed, and her book closed with a dull thud.

"You were not invited to the Babbages' dinner Friday evening either. There was dancing afterward, and some unkind talk about Lord Ashmoor—behind fans, of course—because he claims he cannot dance."

Honore could teach him. She was an excellent dancer.

"It did not advance his suit with Miss Devenish, as that Coleman boy monopolized her time."

"They looked close enough on Sunday."

The day had been cloudy but not yet raining, so no heroics of carrying maidens over puddles had been necessary.

Honore shivered at the memory of his arms cradling her the previous Sunday—their closeness, the easy dialogue—until she forgot entirely that he was the son of an accused murderer.

"Why," she demanded, beginning to pace around the room, "is he accepted in this county despite his father's reputation, but I am shunned like a leper?"

"I need not answer that, Miss Bainbridge. You already know."

"Yes, of course." Honore rested her hand on the latch of one of the long French windows that opened like a door for easy access onto the terrace. "I ruined my reputation all on my own."

"And do not have a title and twenty thousand a year." A cynical note in her companion's voice snapped Honore's head around.

"Miss Morrow?"

She shrugged and bent her head over her book. "Men fare better in this world, Miss Bainbridge. Were I a male relative of Lord Whittaker's, I could have asked him for work in one of his mills. I could learn the spinning and weaving trade and perhaps gain my own mills eventually. As it is, I have nothing. No trade, not a great deal of education—not enough to get me work as a governess or teacher—and fewer hopes of marrying with each passing year."

"But I thought you and—well, you and Mr. Chilcott appeared rather friendly even this past Sunday." Honore smiled. "And Mr. Tuckfield finds excuse after excuse to seek us out. Do you think that is for my sake? He needs none of my advice or approval for work on the estate."

Miss Morrow blushed. "Perhaps I am too particular, but Mr. Tuckfield is at least twenty years older than I. If I survive what few childbearing years I have left, I could end up a widow with no means of support."

"And here I am concerned about not being invited to parties that would have bored me anyway." Honore flung herself onto a chair across from Miss Morrow. "At least if I never overcome the scandals I have caused, my brother or one of my sisters will always take care of me. I will always have a home."

Miss Morrow said nothing, just stared down at her book.

"And you will always have a home with me," Honore added. "But a home of your own is far better, is it not?"

"One can always be relocated even amongst relatives," Miss Morrow said.

Despite the fire only a half dozen feet away, gooseflesh rose on Honore's arms. Her companion was precisely correct. Already in the past nine months, she had been shuffled from Lydia's to Cassandra's to Bath, back to Lydia's, and now to Bainbridge with someone paid to be her companion, her friend—her watchdog, in truth.

"I never thought of the consequences of what I was doing when I insisted I could go where I pleased, even to those gaming establishments in London . . ." She covered her face with her hands. "No wonder cousin Barbara is so fierce about staying with Mama and no one else. She is getting quite old and has no other prospects or home."

She had made Honore's life in Bath so miserable, Honore had written Lydia and begged her for hospitality. Lydia would never turn Honore down, had not last spring, and her husband was charming and kind. They did not intend to cut Honore out of their lives; they simply did not need her presence. Glances, smiles, a touch on one another's hands—all conveyed the impression they wished everyone else would go away. And Cassandra and Whittaker! Honore's ears grew hot at the memory of the way those two looked at one another.

More than embarrassing, though, the love, the adoration, and—dare she say it—the passion they so obviously felt for one another left Honore feeling hollow inside. Twice she had thought herself in love. Twice she had been wrong—wrong about her future plans, wrong about love, wrong about the man she chose. Next time she would wed for practical reasons—home, children, security. And feel none of the excitement around her spouse that her sisters so obviously experienced around theirs.

She leaped to her feet again. "Oh, why is it gone so dark already? I want a walk."

"Please, do not. With these prisoners escaping, it is surely unsafe outside at night."

"It is unsafe outside. It is dull as ditch water inside. I am a pariah in my own neighborhood with persons I have known all my life. If Papa were here . . ."

"You would be wed to Lord Ashmoor, I am thinking." Miss Morrow smiled.

"No, I think not. He would have learned by now that I am a scandalous miss and withdrawn from the agreement."

The thought of which served to increase the lump of lead settling around her middle.

Miss Morrow shook her head. "I think not. He would never

dare to defy your father. Nor would he go back on the contract and risk suit for breach of promise."

"Married by coercion. Not a good way to start a life together." Honore took two turns around the library, drew the curtains against the drab evening sky, rearranged books on the shelves so they lined up more precisely, and stared at her own writing on the top sheet of foolscap upon the desk.

> "Help! Help! Help! Someone, please help me! I am going to die!"

"What twaddle. I did not cry such nonsense." She snatched up the page and tossed it into the fire. "I think I could barely speak, let alone shout such banal words. I was too occupied trying to figure out if I dared bargain with God to save me."

"Yes, bargaining with God . . ." Miss Morrow thumbed the pages of her book. "I do not think that works. I am no longer convinced praying works, if it is not too disgraceful of me to say so."

"Not to me it is not." Honore pushed aside the curtains so she could open one of the windows to a blast of cold but dry air. "Grab your shawl. We can surely walk in the garden. That way we can discuss this topic without one of the servants overhearing us."

Miss Morrow went upstairs to do so, returning in a few moments with cloaks instead of shawls. "It is rather windy out there," she explained.

Bundled in the heavy cloaks, hoods drawn up to protect their hair, they crossed the terrace to the garden. Most of the plants slept for the winter months. The herbs had gone to seed and lost the pungency of their freshness—thyme and lavender, rosemary and mint.

Honore plucked a sprig of the latter, still pale green in the shelter of the wall, and rubbed it between her fingers to release its sweet, sharp fragrance. "I thought I was the only one who felt that way. My sisters are so strong in their faith, and I have tried, but I make so many mistakes I think God no longer listens to me."

"I think He has grown tired of me." Miss Morrow curved her shoulders inward. "I have prayed for a husband since I was fourteen." She hesitated. "I turned thirty last week."

"And you did not tell me? Miss Morrow, why ever not? I would have bought you a gift and had a little celebration."

Miss Morrow snorted. "It is nothing to celebrate. When I knew I was old enough to be your companion, I knew myself beyond the pale for matrimony or any hope of a home of my own. But do not mistake me"—she touched Honore's arm—"I am grateful—no, better than grateful. I am quite happy to be with you here. The house is comfortable, the countryside beautiful. And you do not at all need looking after, as I was warned you would."

"Looking after? Like I am a child?"

"More like you are reckless and headstrong and apt to create scandal."

"Bah." Honore dropped her sprig of mint onto the path and ground it into the crushed stone with the toe of her slipper. "There is my sister Cassandra, happily a countess when she and Whittaker . . . The least said about their behavior, the better. And Lydia a wife and soon a mother and gotten up to all sorts of things she will not talk about. Whereas all I did was fall for the wrong men."

"A traitor and a murderer, my dear."

Two stings of truth all the worse for being spoken in Miss Morrow's soft voice.

Weep or run shouting through the orchard to the cliffs—anything would do to release the knot twisting up her insides like a clockwork doll's spring. Another turn of the key and she might explode into a thousand pieces.

"That is why his lordship will not wed me, is it not?" she said in an admirably calm voice. At least she admired her own calm. "He could happily do so when I had my father's support behind me, but my brother will not do the same, so Ashmoor needs someone sweet and insipid and honorable like Miss Devenish."

"That is what your maid reports to me."

"My maid reports to you, not to me? Does no loyalty remain?" Honore increased her pace, welcoming the power of the wind trying to push her backward. "Then it will serve him right if I persuade him he cannot live without me. And you can then have Mr. Chilcott, as I will take you with me, of course."

"You are too kind. But when I made the suggestion, I did not realize his lordship was set on Miss Devenish."

"They are not engaged yet." Honore stopped in the center of the path and held out her arms so her cloak sailed around her like the wings of an enormous bat. "If God is going to ignore our prayers for husbands and homes of our own, I will take matters into my own hands and find them myself—for both of us."

"As much as I like your notion and encourage it . . ." Miss Morrow hugged her arms across her middle. "Is that not tempting fate?"

"Do you want to live in genteel poverty the rest of your life?"

"No, but—" She turned with Honore at the sound of a shout from the house.

Soames, the butler, stood on the terrace waving a letter. "Special messenger."

"One of the babies has come!" Honore broke into a run.

"Miss Bainbridge, dignity," Miss Morrow admonished.

Honore bounded up the steps and snatched the letter from Soames. "I shall read it here. No, not enough light." She retraced her steps to the library, slitting the wax seal with a thumbnail before she stepped through the French window.

But it was not from one of her sisters announcing the safe delivery of a baby.

"It is from Lord Bainbridge." Her throat tightened so badly she could scarcely tell the two people who entered the house behind her. "He is engaged and bringing his fiancée here to the house with her mother for a few weeks."

"That is wonderful," Miss Morrow said with a little too much enthusiasm. "We can give our own parties, and no one will dare refuse despite your presence."

"No, they will not need to concern themselves with my scandalous presence." Honore raised her head to look at her companion but could not see her face for a blur of tears. "He has asked me to vacate the house during their visit."

8

Considering what had happened less than a fortnight earlier, standing on the edge of the cliff was not the wisest action Honore had taken of late. Considering she did so near midnight was even more foolish. Considering the contents of her brother's letter, first sleeping had proven impossible, then remaining inside the house, then pacing around the grounds where any servant glancing out a window could see her. They could see her from the upper floors, but none would guess a lone figure perched on the north edge of Devonshire was Miss Bainbridge. She could be foolish—she had been foolish—but going to the cliff in the middle of the night exceeded many of her other exploits.

Her brother had told her to vacate the house.

Just for Deborah's visit. Once we are gone, you may return and stay as long as you like. Deborah has no interest in living in the country. She simply wishes to see my principal seat and meet the local people.

Namely Lord Ashmoor?

"What sort of baroness doesn't want to live in the country at least part of the year?" Honore had demanded. "A cit?"

Miss Morrow had hunted up *Debrett's Peerage* and found the lady's ancestry. Her father was Lord John Dunbar, second son of the marquess of Gilderoy. It was impeccable lineage. It was financially lucrative. She was the only child of a man who had done well for himself despite being a younger son.

"The impeccable heiress," Honore dubbed the young lady.

She doubted she would like her. She definitely did not like her brother, though they had always gotten on well. He was more Cassandra's peer with them only a year apart, but he was only two years Honore's senior, and they had seemed to have a comfortable relationship. He had been happy for her to take over Bainbridge, relieving him of the duties of the estate so he could pursue other matters in town.

"You said you were concerned about the wars!" Honore shouted the words into the wind trying to push her back from the edge of the cliff. "You lied. You were wife hunting."

He was young, but he needed a wife and heir. Marrying now was a wise choice. But he did not have to abandon his sister, send her out of the house as though she carried a terrible disease.

Tears stung her eyes. She wished she could blame the wind. She had already wept far too much since receiving Beau's letter. Abandoned, pushed aside, just like she and Miss Morrow discussed.

More proof that God was not listening to her prayers for . . . well, whatever she was praying for—a husband, a family, a home of her own. She did not want to live in a cottage on the land, a house small enough even Lord Ashmoor would consider it a hovel, writing her Gothic novels, raising cats, and waiting for the next quarter's allowance to restock her larder if she miscalculated and ran short.

"Miss Morrow is right—I need a husband."

She began to pace along the cliff, watching her feet as far as she could see them by starlight. Lord Ashmoor would never come along to rescue her from dangling off a cliff in the middle of the night. No one in his right mind was around in the middle of the night. Even fishermen were either tucked up in harbor or well out to sea. On a night with this kind of a gale, they would tuck themselves up in harbor.

Except a boat did struggle out to sea.

Honore caught a flash of light from the corner of her eye. She paused and looked toward the sea. The light flashed again, a lantern winking on and off, on and off, like a blinking yellow eye.

She paused, one hand raised to shield her eyes from the wind. If she squinted, she could see the craft, no more than a silhouette against the phosphorescent glow of the waves. It appeared to be what was typical locally—a single-mast fishing smack. Either it was taking on water or the vessel was in such poor trim the whole rigging listed to one side.

It would be taking on water in the kind of seas rolling down the Bristol Channel.

Honore was running toward the only path to the shore before she realized her intentions. Slipping, sliding, clinging to the striated rock wall beside the path, she did not stop until she was halfway to the water, close enough for spray to reach her, to brush her face like icy, ghostly fingers. Where the path turned, she hesitated. She could do little to help. Though Bainbridge possessed a boat, she was not capable of taking it out herself in such weather to effect a rescue. The closest thing she could do there on the beach was pull any survivors out of the water. She was better off running back to the house for help. By the time she reached Bainbridge, though, the smack would have already sunk and the sailors drowned.

A tiny cove sheltered the boat no Bainbridge had taken out for over a year, probably not since Honore's last foray onto the sea for a clandestine early morning fishing excursion with the daughter and son of the Bainbridge head groom. One of the gamekeepers sailed it to keep it in trim and for some fishing, so it bobbed and swayed at its mooring behind an arm of rock sheltering it from the worst of the wind-tossed waves. Figuring it would carry ropes at the least, Honore grasped the mooring line and tried to draw the craft close enough to the land for her to climb aboard. She did not possess enough strength. The water tugged the craft in one direction, and she tugged it in another. Her feet slipped on the wet planks of the dock, one foot going far enough for the toe of her slipper to peek over the edge. With a cry, she released the line, stepped back, and ran into something not solid enough to be the cliff side, surely too solid for a human.

An arm closed around her waist, steadying her. Definitely a human, warm and strong and . . . Her nostrils flared. She recognized the scent of something like a sun-drenched forest now mixed with the tang of salt spray.

"What are you doing down here?" she demanded.

"I could ask you the same thing," Lord Ashmoor responded. "Doesn't seem the kind of place for a lady at any hour, let alone this one."

"This is Bainbridge land." She tried to inject a note of haughtiness into her voice.

He laughed and released her. "Dare I hope you know how to sail this?"

"I do, but we cannot sail it. The sea is too rough. We will only drown."

"Then how can we help?"

"A rope. This boat should have a rope on it. I am afraid that is all we can do."

"It's better than nothing." Ashmoor leaped aboard the fishing smack and returned to land a few moments later with a coil of rope tucked under one arm. "Hang on to me. I'll not even ask if you have on anything but those silly slipper things you ladies think you can wear anywhere."

"I never intended to come out here." Honore shut her mouth.

"But it isn't beyond one of the feats of Miss Honore Bainbridge."

"We are all known in the family to misbehave. I just got caught." She spun on her slipper's flat sole and started for the narrow band of shore between incoming tide and jagged rocks.

Ashmoor caught hold of her arm. "Hang on to me, Miss Bainbridge. I don't want to have to fish you out of the sea."

"How will you fish them out of the sea?"

"I can brace myself on the rocks at the mouth of the cove. If they abandon that boat, they'll have a chance to find purchase on the rocks themselves."

"It is too dangerous for you." She hung on to him. She should have run back up the path to home, but she could not while that lantern continued to flash distress and the silhouette of the boat grew lower and lower. With the tide coming in, the boat would wreck against the rocks. She was not convinced the passengers would escape being battered too.

"Why would they go out on a night like this?" she cried above the roar of wind and surf.

"Smugglers, I expect."

"Smug—" For the first time, the cold of the night penetrated her cloak and her gown. Her feet went numb. "We cannot stay here and come face-to-face with smugglers. They—they will kill us."

"They will die if we don't stay."

And there they were as a wave as high as a farmer's cottage lifted the craft up and up, where it hovered as though suspended from the sky on string, then the wave hurtled it against the shore like the hand of an angry child discarding a toy.

"Wait here." Ashmoor ran forward, charged into the water near the smashed craft, and hurled the rope. Legs braced wide apart, he hauled like a fisherman with a struggling catch. A fisher of men.

Two men plunged over the side of the boat. They clung to its gunwale for a moment, staggering like drunken souls, then released the craft before the next wave struck. Ashmoor tossed the rope again and again as the men half swam, half stumbled toward solid and dry land. One of them went down and did not get up. Ashmoor stepped farther into the surf, and Honore covered her mouth to stifle a scream. But the other man caught the rope with one hand and dragged his companion to his feet with the other. Ashmoor lunged back, slipped, lunged back again. At last, the two sailors struggled ashore. Cursing and thanking Ashmoor in the same breath, they stumbled onto the rocks, then fell to their hands and knees.

"Are there more of you?" Ashmoor asked.

"No, sir. Just . . . two of us," one of the men gasped out between coughing up water.

"That was a fool thing to do, going out there in this weather, but don't say anything more to me. I won't ask what you were doing out there," Ashmoor said. "I'll just suggest you get yourselves home before I happen to see your faces."

Honore shrank back against the rocks and drew her hood over her own face. Like as not, judging from the man's accent, these were local men who just might recognize her even in the darkness.

Obediently, the men scrambled to their feet and, hands on one another's shoulders for support, staggered a few feet up the path, then one of them turned back. "We won't forget your help, my lord." Then they were gone.

"My not quite English speech, I suppose." Ashmoor spoke from beside Honore.

She jumped. "What?"

"They know who I am."

"Ah, yes, you do not quite talk English." She grasped his arm. "We need to get out of here or we will be trapped by the tide."

"Then let us go, by all means." He started up the path. "Where are you going?"

"Home, I think. That is—" Her throat closed.

Ashmoor stopped on the path and looked down at her, his face a pale blur. "What is it?"

She shrugged. "Nothing."

"I doubt that. You are brave enough that you intended to save those men all by yourself, even though they could have been the bloodthirsty kind of smuggler, but you choke on the word *home*. So don't tell me nothing is wrong."

"Nothing is wrong that need concern you."

"A lady in distress concerns me. A lady wandering on the shore in the middle of the night concerns me."

"Do you not know I am no lady? At least not fit for the company of ladies?"

"I know you made some mistakes . . ."

Of course he would not finish speaking his thoughts aloud. Even he rejected her for not being a perfect miss, the epitome of womanly graces worthy of being a countess. Oh, he deserved to fall in love with her.

She filled in the silence between them. "I needed some air to think over something, and I saw the boat in distress."

"You couldn't think in the garden?"

"Under the eyes of all the servants and Mr. Tuckfield in his cottage and whoever was sneaking about for a little clandestine behavior?"

He jolted as though attached to one of those electricity machines where someone wound the crank.

She smiled. "I shocked you with that remark. But you are forgetting my reputation."

"Probably greatly exaggerated in its . . . miscreant status?"

She caught the question of his remark but merely shrugged. Let him stew. He had chosen to believe the worst or he would have honored that marriage contract. Papa had done a great deal to help his lordship. The least Ashmoor could do for Papa in return—or his memory anyway—was marry the disreputable daughter and make an honest woman of her. She had not made herself socially unacceptable all that far. She had not contributed to her beaux' lawless activities but had merely been an innocent dupe.

All right, by her own willfulness she had associated with them too freely. Still, she had behaved far better than had her sister Cassandra and Lord Whittaker. Of course, they were now wed and all was forgiven.

If Honore were Lady Ashmoor, her brother would not dare remove her from the house. He would be begging her to welcome his fiancée into the family and the neighborhood, give her parties for the county. The county would not reject her.

"Those men did not even see who I was," she said too abruptly for the change of topic not to go unnoticed.

Ashmoor tensed. "Did you recognize them?"

"I should not say if I did. That is how people get themselves killed in these parts."

"What if—" He paused. "I suppose I should deliver you to the apple orchard gate again?"

"No, I came out a different gate. It's farther away, but it was the only key I could find in a hurry."

"Ah, you came out in a hurry." He resumed walking. "Did that light attract you or signal you?"

"What are you suggesting, my lord?"

He shrugged.

"And I can ask you the same. What are you doing here?"

He did not answer for the space of a hundred yards. Then he sighed. "I'm looking for my brother."

"Is he missing?"

"He's always missing at odd hours."

"And you're concerned he is as in league with criminals as I am."

"He's young and impulsive at times."

"Ah." Wind whipped her skirt and cloak around her legs and against his lordship's, nearly tripping them both. Gusts howled, masking the crunch of their footfalls, and clouds began to blot out the stars and quarter moon. An entire regiment of smugglers could fall upon them without them noticing until it was too late to run.

Then they slipped around the end of the orchard wall, and the wind dropped to a mere breeze. Their footfalls sounded loud enough to be a regiment of smugglers. With each yard passing beneath their feet, the new stillness emphasized the silence between them.

"Where is this gate you have—for which you have the key?" Ashmoor asked.

Honore smiled. "Ah, Mr. Chilcott even dares correct your grammar."

"My mother tried, but failed in much of her efforts."

"Your mother knew—but of course. Your mother was a Ludlow from Cornwall or something, was she not?"

"Not that that branch of my family wants anything to do with me." He sounded sad, not bitter, as he might have rightfully been. "I understand her parents are still alive, living in Bath, and I have an uncle who is unwed and childless."

"Which means you are likely the heir there too, or your mother perhaps, but probably you. No title would come to you, but they are well off."

"You know them?" He stopped and faced her.

She shook her head. "But I had to memorize the peerage before my come-out."

"They have not, apparently, forgiven my mother for running off with my father."

"She did the right thing, going with her husband."

"I know." He resumed walking until a dark patch in the wall suggested the switch from stone to iron. "Here?"

"Yes." She placed the key in his hand.

He slipped it into the lock and turned. The gate swung open on well-oiled hinges. "Don't come out in the night again, Miss Bainbridge. Besides being bad for your reputation, it isn't safe."

"I know. I was feeling . . . desperate."

She still was. The tears she had managed to hold at bay earlier now choked up her throat and burned her eyes.

"Good night," she managed in a whisper.

She snatched the key from him and fled through the gateway. She did not manage to hold back the first sob as she locked the gate and tried to flee out of earshot. She tripped over a hem she had not realized had come down just far enough to catch the toe of her slipper, and landed on her knees. She stayed there, her face buried in her arms, sobs shaking her harder with each effort at keeping them silent.

But not silent enough. Lord Ashmoor began to pound on the gate.

His pounding stopped her weeping. She flew at the gate, hissing, "Stop, stop, stop." With her arms flapping out of her cloak and her hair glinting pale in the sliver of moonlight, she looked like some sort of night bird, perhaps a particularly pretty goose with all that hissing, or a female peacock whose feathers were not dull.

"Got you to stop crying, didn't I?" He grinned at her.

She planted her hands on her hips. "A gentleman would have left me alone in my distress."

"Not where I come from. We see to females in distress. For all I knew, you'd injured yourself."

"I didn't." She turned her face away. "Please leave me."

Leaving her was the last thing that made sense at that moment. Perhaps she wept after moments of fright, but this time seemed far different from her near catastrophe on the cliff. She had never been in any danger tonight. The men who had come off that wrecked boat hadn't noticed her, let alone recognized her cowering back in the shadow of an overhang. So the deep, wrenching sobs made no sense if she was not in pain.

Meric reached through the gate and caught one of her hands in his. It was a tiny hand, narrow with long, slim fingers. A smooth hand. A lady's hand unlike the hands of his sisters, who, though possessing rather slender fingers and narrow wrists themselves, constantly battled red and roughened skin from the harsh soap and labors they engaged in to survive.

No more. They had better not be scrubbing and even chopping wood any longer. Yet he hoped they never lost the sturdiness of their hands.

Miss Bainbridge's hand felt anything but sturdy. Her fingers fluttered inside the curve of his palm like a small bird about to take flight, and he tightened his hold, smoothing his thumb across her knuckles. "Don't run off, Miss Bainbridge. Something's not right when you're out on the cliffs in the middle of the night and now crying like your favorite dog died."

"I do not have a dog. Papa did not like them much, but my sister had cats."

"And everyone in your family is well? You didn't get bad news about your sisters?"

"They all are well as far as I know." She tugged on her hand. "Please let me go."

"Of course." He released her.

She tucked her hands inside the sleeves of her cloak but didn't leave.

Meric leaned on the gate as though ready to stay for hours. "You know I have three sisters."

"I know that, but little more about you, my lord. People never talked about your family. That is, your father's branch of the family."

"No, I expect they didn't." He curled his upper lip. "I expect that was Christian of them."

"I think it was more a desire not to offend your uncle than not to gossip." She turned her face away, and her hair slid over her shoulder like a silk shawl.

He reached his hand through the gate bars again, then jerked it back. He had no business touching her hair, however curious about its softness he might be.

“The least said about why people didn’t talk about your branch of the family, the better,” she said a little too harshly.

“I was talking about my three sisters. They’re still young. The eldest is about your age. After five boys, my mother presented my father with three daughters. They’re tall and thin, but strong. Every one of them can shoot a musket or a rifle and wield an axe. Sarah is sixteen and a better tracker than any of us boys.”

“Why do you not bring them here so they can learn to be ladies as is their birthright?” She leaned just a little forward as she posed the question.

Meric tightened his lips to stop his smile. “It wasn’t safe for them to cross the Atlantic. For all I knew, I was going to get impressed onto a British man-of-war on the way and they’d be left to fend for themselves. So I had to leave them behind. Maybe when this war is over, if the second eldest hasn’t wed by then. The youngest better not be of marriageable age by the end of the war, that’s for sure.”

“How old is she?”

“Twelve.”

“I hope it is all over long before then.” She definitely took a half step forward. “But why are you telling me all this?”

“Because I want you to understand that my sisters are strong and courageous. The tales I could tell you about them hunting with us would curl your hair.” He glanced at the ripples of gold over her shoulders and allowed himself a smile. “Well, maybe for you they’d straighten it.”

Her teeth flashed in the dim light fading fast from the growing cloud cover. “I think they might find this country too tame.”

“Pamela, the eldest one, would like it. She’s gentle that way.

But it doesn't stop her from snaring a rabbit or five if that's what we need to eat."

Miss Bainbridge shuddered.

"But in spite of all that strength, they break down and cry too. Sometimes it's over the stupidest things, like a baby bird fallen out of its nest. Sometimes it's important, like when Pamela's first sweetheart got pressed into the British Navy despite his family living in New York for a hundred years. Sometimes they just want to be left alone to cry, and sometimes they need a brother's shoulder and a good ear."

"You are not my brother, my lord. I could not—I could never—" She ducked her head.

"I suppose not. People would get the wrong idea. But I have two good ears."

Which heard nothing but the surf pounding against the rocky cliffs, the wind howling and whistling around the garden and orchard walls, and the papery rustle of the tree leaves overhead. Miss Bainbridge said nothing, and dampness in the air warned of coming rain.

"I'll call on you tomorrow. No, that won't do. We are taking an early dinner with the vicar. Wednesday then. I'll call on you Wednesday afternoon."

Her head shot up. "Miss Devenish will not like that, my lord."

"Miss Devenish does not yet dictate with whom I associate." He touched her arm in lieu of her hand to shake and found himself with a handful of hair that was indeed as silky as it looked.

Too slowly for good manners, he drew his hand through the gate and stepped away. "If you're sure you can get to the house safely, I'll be on my way then."

"I am quite certain. Th-thank you." A hitch caught at her voice.

"I'm happy to help a lady in distress."

Perhaps a little too happy to do so.

"Good night." He strode off, wishing she had told him what distressed her so fully that she had left the safety of the grounds and fled onto the cliffs where she had nearly died just over a week earlier. And that bout of weeping, driving her to her knees, held a tale of its own, that was for certain. He recognized a female's heartbreak when he heard it in a sob. No man who loved his family and had sisters didn't know it.

"Who has broken your heart, Miss Bainbridge?"

Weeping for one of her beaux? Both had gone to their eternal reward—one shot while resisting capture, the other with the assistance of the Crown, he understood—so she wasn't likely meeting one of them. Possibly she had met someone else and he had failed to meet her rendezvous. That seemed highly likely with her past behavior.

The idea made him sick. No lady as brave and pretty and, yes, kind as Miss Honore Bainbridge should toss herself away on a rake or worse. Of course, his own grandparents thought his mother had done so. Despite her having to flee Devonshire in the middle of the night to keep his father from being arrested, despite her living hand to mouth more years than not in an attempt to feed their growing brood, the only part of life over the past twenty-eight years that Mother had not liked were the eight since Father's death. In word, deed, and simple glance, she proclaimed her love for her miscreant spouse.

A stab of pain struck Meric so profoundly he staggered under its impact. Whether it stemmed from missing his family or missing that kind of love in his life, he didn't know at that moment. He wasn't certain he wanted to find out. He had prayed for the right helpmeet in life for at least the past ten years, and all the

Lord was providing was Miss Devenish—acceptable, but not a partner in one's life.

That wasn't fashionable, of course. "No couple should live in one another's pockets," Chilcott had explained. "It is vulgar."

Meric didn't understand a society that tolerated a husband's unfaithfulness sooner than a husband who fawned on his wife. Not the society or the life he wanted. But for the sake of his family's future, it was the one he accepted as God's provision. He viewed Miss Devenish the same. She possessed all the qualifications he needed, just not a few he wanted.

"But God says He will supply all our needs, not all our wants," he reminded himself as the few still burning lights of Clovelly came into view around a curve in the road. "My needs are being met. I won't ask for more."

But he would call on Miss Bainbridge on Wednesday.

Meanwhile, an early country dinner at the vicarage and duty called to him. He dragged Philo along with him. Chilcott had insisted that he must ride down to Ashmoor to inspect the storage house for the apples. It couldn't wait another day.

"Actually, I will be gone for several days," Chilcott had explained. "This is a busy time of year on the estate."

"Then I should come," Meric offered.

"Do you know about farming, my lord?" Chilcott asked.

Meric just stared at the man.

"There is a difference between twenty acres and twenty thousand acres," Philo pointed out.

"We own more than twenty acres in New York," Meric said. Then he laughed. "Half of it is still stumps."

"Half of it here is sheep." Chilcott relented. "But your uncle hired me to oversee the farms, and that is what I will do. You will increase your social standing in the county."

And do everything he could to discover who might have wanted his father to take the blame for a crime he had not committed.

So Meric and Philo strode down the hill to the vicarage. Even before they reached the front door, savory aromas of roasting chickens and potatoes wafted into the yard.

"If it tastes half as good as it smells," Philo whispered, "I'll endure a lot of boredom."

"If we can get Mr. Stanbury to talk about Father, it won't be boring."

But Mr. Stanbury wanted to talk about Miss Bainbridge.

Halfway through the meal, with the soup and fish courses removed and two glistening and crisp fowl perched upon their platters in the center of the table, Stanbury set his fork across his plate and leaned toward Meric. "Since you are the highest-ranked gentleman in my parish, though the late Lord Bainbridge gave me my living, I do wish to ask for your advice."

"I doubt I'm qualified to give you advice on anything, sir." Meric set his own fork across his plate.

Miss Stanbury and Philo continued eating with the doggedness of two people not expecting another fine meal for weeks.

"You are a man of the world." Stanbury sat back, his hands folded on his lap.

Meric suppressed a sigh. He had been enjoying his roasted hen. Until the vicar resumed eating, however, he could scarcely continue himself.

Stanbury took a deep breath. "What do you think of my courting Miss Bainbridge?"

Philo stopped eating too. Miss Stanbury forked another bite of peas into her mouth.

It's a terrible idea, Meric considered shouting.

"Mr. Stanbury, that is your decision to make." He tried to smile. "Miss Bainbridge comes from a good family, and her brother holds the living, I understand."

"And she's beautiful," Philo murmured.

"She is pretty," Meric agreed.

The image of hair turning pale gold by a quarter moon rippled through his mind. Hair that felt as soft as the silk stockings Huntley insisted he wear when calling.

"I am concerned about the state of her soul," Stanbury said. "All that outer beauty should not cover an unrepentant heart."

The man talked as though he were sixty-five, not thirty-five.

Since Miss Stanbury continued to eat with mechanical regularity, Meric quite deliberately carved himself a chunk of fowl so he need not speak for several moments.

"I wanted to court her before she went off for her Season," Stanbury continued. "But his lordship, her father then, told me to wait until she saw a little bit of the world. Alas, she seems to have seen too much of the world. Still, my feelings for her have not changed."

Miss Stanbury paused eating long enough to remark, "And she has a fine dowry."

Meric tried to swallow too quickly and grabbed up his glass of water to stop himself from choking to death.

Lord Bainbridge had nearly allied himself to the vicar? Not Miss Bainbridge. She would make a terrible vicar's wife. She was too . . . alive for a vicarage existence.

Meric managed to swallow and face the vicar, a gentler approach to the truth on his lips. "Mr. Stanbury, Miss Bainbridge is still mourning her father. I think waiting is your best course of action."

"Wise counsel, I am sure. I do so think it is time to wed,

though." Stanbury scooped up a mouthful of pickled onion but did not carry them to his mouth. "Jane, you will be forced to remain here awhile longer."

"And who would manage the organ if I did not remain?" Miss Stanbury demanded. She rose. "I will fetch coffee for you gentlemen."

When the door swung shut behind his sister, Stanbury said, "She has been betrothed to a widower with five children for five years, but she will not leave me until I wed, no matter how many times I tell her I can hire a housekeeper and anyone can learn to play the barrel organ. So you see why I wish for a wife quickly."

"And Miss Bainbridge is available." Philo flashed a grin at Meric. "My brother needs a wife quickly too. I refuse to be his heir much longer."

"You do not have any choice until he has heirs in sons," Stanbury began, and then launched into a lecture on the duties of those who held titles and vast land holdings. Miss Bainbridge slipped into the background.

At least she slipped into the vicar's background of conversation. No one mentioned her name again until Stanbury suggested he should call on her the following day.

"I happen to know she's occupied tomorrow," Meric said.

He wanted no interruptions from the vicar. He didn't want to compete with the vicar for her attention.

The realization robbed him of appetite. He was courting an appropriate miss. Sweet, dull, and proper Miss Devenish, who, fortunately, liked riding a mare as docile as she was. He should not wish for time alone with Miss Bainbridge. The truth was, however, that he did want time alone with her.

He wrestled with that wanting for most of the evening and too much of the night. In the end, he decided not to call on

Wednesday. His conscience prompted him to send a note to the vicar to inform him that Miss Bainbridge would not be occupied after all, but he did not obey.

She did not want to share any secrets or distresses in front of Lord Ashmoor. Nearly two days' time and the cold light of day gave her more sense than to think she should confide in his lordship. If he did not wish to wed her because of her reputation, then telling him about her brother's rejection of her because of her reputation would not aid in her efforts to persuade him that he would regret rejecting her and repaying her father for all he had done for the new Lord Ashmoor. At the same time, he probably needed some explanation for her wandering about the cliff at midnight and her subsequent, not to mention revolting, imitation of a watering pot. No, worse, more like a demonstration of a fountain with hiccups.

Wednesday dawned cold and gray but dry, and Miss Morrow suggested they needed to clean out the dower house. "I understand it has not been used for years, so it will be beyond dirty."

"Grandmama died ten years ago. She was the last person to live there." Honore pushed open her bedroom window and leaned out far enough to catch a glimpse of the peaked roof beyond a row of conifers separating the house from the gardens. "My grandfather built it for his mother fifty years ago, but she died before it was finished. Then his sister lived there after she was disappointed in love and vowed to never marry. Grandmama lived there the longest." Her chest went tight. "It is a house where people go to die."

"Honore—Miss Bainbridge." Miss Morrow slipped her arm

around Honore's shoulders. "You are just turned twenty. I scarcely think you are going there to die."

"No, just be forgotten like a—like a—oh, I cannot believe Bainbridge is doing this to me." Honore slammed the window hard enough to rattle the panes of glass in their frame. "Is there no forgiveness?"

"Miss Morrow, we have a dozen maids in this house eating their heads off with little work to keep them occupied. Why do we not send them over to do the cleaning?"

"Because they are doing the cleaning here in preparation for the royal visit. I mean—" Miss Morrow's eyes widened, and she clapped her hand to her lips.

Honore giggled. "You read that tone into the letter too? And did a separate one arrive for the butler and housekeeper?"

"Instructions that everything should be polished to within an inch of its existence, which means every crystal on every chandelier and every globe on every wall sconce, every carpet taken out and beaten, every—"

"In short, they will get to us when they have time, which they likely will not."

"Or may not." Miss Morrow pulled a faded blue frock from the clothespress. "Your estimable housekeeper assures me that the dower house should be in fine repair. Someone inspects it every quarter to ensure the roof is not leaking and mice have not taken over the furniture."

"And no birds nested in the chimneys, I hope?"

"She did not mention that. But we shall look before laying any fires."

"Laying fires?" Honore stared at her companion. "Surely we get at least one maid? And what about food? We are not expected to cook for ourselves, are we?"

"We get two maids, and the scullion will bring over food from the Bainbridge kitchen."

"Cold." Honore sat on a trunk filled with shawls and fans and gloves. "If you wish to resign your position, Miss Morrow, I will understand. You were promised comfort, not servants' work and cold meals."

Miss Morrow clutched Honore's dress in her arms and stared into space for several moments before focusing on her employer again. "Do you know that verse in Proverbs?"

"'As a jewel of gold in a swine's snout, so is a fair woman which is without discretion'?" Honore asked.

Miss Morrow laughed. "No, no. 'It is better to dwell in a corner of the housetop, than with a brawling woman and in a wide house.'"

"We do not know if Miss Dunbar is brawling."

"Of course we do not, but I was thinking, were the dower house half the size and not so fine, I would prefer it to returning to living with my cousins. Oh, I could live with Geoffrey—Whittaker, that is. He and your sister would welcome me in an instant, and I could likely be a help with the baby when it comes. But they would feel obligated to have me to table for dinner, and I would feel like such an intruder."

"Do I not know that?" Honore's cheeks warmed. "They are rather embarrassing to be around sometimes." She picked at a loose thread on the front seam of her skirt. "Though I suppose they are fortunate in one another."

If she tugged on that thread, her seam would unravel and the skirt of her gown would fall into two pieces in front, exposing her petticoat. That was how looking at Cassandra and Whittaker made her feel—as though one tug at her heart would divide it into two pieces, revealing her longing to be loved like that.

She sprang to her feet. "I cannot clean today. Lord Ashmoor is coming to call. And that means I must change into another gown. This one needs repairs."

Feeling like dancing with the prospect of the call, she bounded to her wardrobe and began to riffle through it for something demure and complimentary to her looks.

10

By four of the clock Honore decided Ashmoor was not coming to call. There in the country, a visitor that late would expect an invitation to the early dinner served outside town so he could return home before the night grew too dark. Ashmoor might not know all the ways of English life, but he had been in the country long enough to learn the niceties of when calling was appropriate.

Heart heavy yet a surge of restlessness racing through her limbs, Honore ran upstairs and changed into the faded muslin gown she had owned for at least two and perhaps more years. The last time she had donned it, she had gone sailing with her brother before her Season.

"It is tight." Honore gestured to her front. "Am I getting fat?"

Miss Morrow laughed. "No, child, you have a charming figure, but perhaps we should tuck in a scarf." She pulled one from a chest and draped it around Honore's shoulders.

She tucked it into the straining neckline. "I would give this to one of the maids, but it is scarcely fit for more than rags."

"I doubt one of the maids would see it that way. It can be dyed."

Honore looked at Miss Morrow's faded gray dress, not one donned merely for cleaning but worn more than once, and then glanced at her overflowing clothespress. "You are smaller than I am. Taller, but smaller. Would I insult you by offering you things that are too tight for me?"

"I would appreciate some variety." Miss Morrow turned a pretty shade of peony.

"And nothing like a new gown to attract a handsome gentleman." Honore grinned.

Miss Morrow stuck her nose in the air. "It seems, Miss Bainbridge, that we have been abandoned by our beaux."

"Not that they were beaux. Well then, let us get to cleaning our new abode while we have light."

Armed with brushes and piles of rags, buckets, and strong soap, Honore, Miss Morrow, and two housemaids crossed the garden to the row of pine trees trimmed to symmetrical perfection inside a white painted fence. Beyond them, a tiny garden fanned out on either side of a flagstone path. That path led to the front door set in the exact center with four windows on either side—two upstairs and two on the ground floor. Even in the gray light, the rosy brick and white trim glowed. Uninhabited or not, the house was well taken care of.

Honore fitted the key in the lock and the door swung inward with a gentle creak. "Mavis, tell one of the outdoor men to come oil all the hinges and ensure the windows all open."

"Yes, miss." Mavis set down her load of cleaning materials and took a strike-a-light from her apron pocket. "I'll just be lighting some candles, if you please."

"I please. Thank you." Honore stepped into the room to the left of the front door. Her nose twitched from the quantity of dust layered over tables, mirrors, and holland covers for the furniture. She sniffed, seeking a hint of mice or dampness, but other than the dust, the house seemed all right. It did not even smell as musty as she might have thought a building that had been shut up for all but a few days out of the past ten years would have smelled.

"Where do we begin?" Miss Morrow asked.

"Take off the covers first and remove the carpets." Honore glanced outside. "No, those will have to wait until morning. Remove the covers and dust all the surfaces. No sense in working on the floor until the rest is cleaned. Bets," she addressed the other maid, "take a broom and knock down all the cobwebs you can find, then inspect the chimneys for nests and the like. When Mavis returns, have her—ah, there you are. Come to the cellar with me. I wish to inspect our coal supply."

Three more rooms opened off the entry hall. Beneath the steps, a fifth inside door opened into the kitchen and servants' area, the passage far too dark.

"I'll fetch another candle, miss." Mavis darted into the entryway and returned with a candle from one of the wall sconces. "We'll need to be supplying this house, I expect. No one would have left them for fear the mice would get to them."

"I would think mice would want only the tallow ones, not wax, but they seem to eat anything." Honore held out her hand. "I will lead the way. This will likely be unpleasant."

She held the flickering light at arm's length in front of her as though it were a shield against the darkness and cobwebs. Her heart sank lower and her stomach twisted into nausea with each step.

All two steps she took into the narrow passageway. Two was all she needed to have the light illuminate a ceiling free of spider housing and a floor clear of dust in regular patterns.

"Mavis?" Honore faced the maid. "You did not come back here yet?"

"No, miss." Mavis shook her head, her cap ribbons fluttering. Her face was white. "Those be too big for my feet anyhow." She stuck one foot out from beneath her black dress. In its sturdy clog of wood and leather, her foot appeared small enough for two of them, perhaps three, to fit into one of the prints before them.

"Did you—" Honore took a deep breath to steady her voice. "Did you notice any footprints when you were lighting candles in the other rooms?"

"No, miss. I weren't looking at me feet. I were looking at the sconces and the dust over all and the spiderwebs and . . ." She began to back toward the door. "There's been a body in here, Miss Bainbridge."

"Yes, I am afraid there has been. But it might have been one of the outdoor men. I was told they came to inspect things a month ago."

In a month, dust would have accumulated in the footprints. Cobwebs would have grown, especially as the days grew colder and even insects chose to live indoors rather than out. In short, no footprints would have stood out that clearly.

"Go ask anyway," Honore commanded more sharply than she intended.

"Yes, miss." Mavis spun on her heel and fled, the wooden soles of her clogs ringing on the wooden floorboards of the entryway.

Honore slammed the door to the back passage and wished for a key to lock it. She would have preferred to vacate the house altogether in the event someone was still inside, hiding in the pantry or cellar.

But that was nonsense. No one would have stayed once he heard the women arrive. No one would stay there anyway. The dower house was empty and sheltered from the rest of the property by walls and trees, but it was not isolated. To fear an intruder was foolishness, and she had work to do. If the coal supply was low, she needed to ensure it was filled immediately. Her brother could arrive as soon as Saturday and no later than Monday, according to his letter. That gave her precious little time to clean and get the dower house set up for her and Miss Morrow to reside in. She must move her clothes and books, her writing materials and foodstuff. She could not afford delays by imaginary interlopers.

Gripping a cleaning brush in one hand and the candle tightly enough in the other hand to soften the wax beneath her fingers, she marched forward along the line of footprints. Halfway down the passage, she paused to see where they led. If they did indeed lead to the cellar, she would not venture below stairs on her own. Someone could hide there regardless of how many people invaded the house. The cellar possessed numerous nooks and crannies of storage rooms from the days when the house had been inhabited for years on end, not temporarily, as was Honore's expectation.

The footprints did not lead to the cellar. They led from the back entrance to the door through which she had stepped into the passageway. From there, she would never work out where they led, as too many of them had trampled over the floorboards.

But no one had been upstairs yet.

No one from their cleaning party.

Candle flame flickering and creating weird shadows on the walls, Honore left the passageway and moved to the foot of the steps. No carpet ran down the center of the oak treads. Polished, they would be slippery and dangerous. But the same thick layer of dust lying over the wood assured Honore no one had climbed the steps in months, or even years. The outdoor man would have used the back steps to inspect the upper floor for roof leaks. And those footprints had definitely led toward the front.

"Miss Bainbridge?" Miss Morrow exited the parlor, a pile of holland covers over one arm, a cobweb trailing over one shoulder. "Is something amiss? I saw Mavis running across the garden."

"I sent her for one of the men." Honore gripped the newel post. "Someone—" No, she must not alarm her companion. "Someone else can inspect the coal room," she concluded in speech and decision.

"Of course. And I think we need more maids to help us. This house has been sorely neglected. If I may be bold enough to say so, perhaps it should have been rented out to someone, a gentlewoman in straightened circumstances."

"Mama always wanted it kept free for a relative, or if one of her children needed it. But it should have been cleaned more regularly so when one of us . . . does . . . need . . ." Honore's chest heaved with a sudden desire to repeat her mortifying display of weeping from the other night. She spun away. "I wish to see what sorts of reading materials are in the library and what I should bring over here."

She bolted around the steps and into the book room, her candle extinguished, trailing smoke and the stench of burned wax behind her. Mavis had lighted several candles in that room too, and Honore leaned her back against the door, blinking against surprising brightness and the halo of tears around each light. She should not need this place to live either. Should not. Bainbridge was her home, not the dower house. She had made mistakes, but not something too terrible other than falling under the influence of unscrupulous—all right, criminal—men. She had not helped them, not like that Miss Irving, who had let herself be a pawn out of family loyalty. She had not given up her virtue to them. She had even asked for God's forgiveness for her folly. Yet everyone still blamed her, from Papa increasing her dowry nearly half again as much in order to catch her a husband, to that man rejecting her because of her reputation, to her own brother banishing her from the presence of his fiancée. For all she knew, Cassandra and Lydia wanted her gone for fear she would taint their precious offspring.

"Hypocrites, all of them!" Honore cried.

She flung the scrubbing brush across the room. It struck a pile of books stacked upon a table. They crashed to the floor with a resounding and satisfying bang and a ring of metal striking wood.

Metal striking wood?

Honore ran across the room and dropped to her knees beside the books. Their jackets appeared surprisingly clear of grime for tomes that should have been sitting on that table for years. Their gilt titles flashed up at her, nothing she would have expected her grandmother to have read, though perhaps that great-aunt had left them behind. They were books printed the previous century—Fielding, Smollett, and Walpole. None of them should have chimed like a coin.

Careful to ensure none of their pages or spines were bent, she returned the books to the table also rather clear of dust and inspected the floor around the table. Seeing nothing, she rose and started for the candle lighted atop the mantel.

And her toe struck something wedged between wooden floorboards and stone hearth. It chinked against the rock. She bent, retrieved it, and held it up to the light.

It was half of a button. Half of an ornate silver button, a large silver button, such as a gentleman would wear on a fine coat. Embossed upon the silver, along with the feet of three figures, was part of a word—*égalit*.

Égalité? As in *Liberté, égalité, fraternité*?

She could not begin to comprehend why half of a French

button lay in the book room of the Bainbridge dower house. Yet something about the button looked familiar, as though she had seen it or something like it recently, which was highly unlikely. Men rarely wore ornate buttons anymore, and they certainly did not wear them in the country. Even more, Englishmen did not wear buttons with French revolutionary words upon them. Besides that, no man other than a servant should have been inside the dower house.

Feeling as though several spiders crawled over her skin, Honore dropped the piece of button into her apron pocket, rose, and retrieved her brush. Voices in the entry hall told her Mavis had returned with one of the gardeners, and Honore must resume her role as mistress of the house.

She opened the library door. "Ah, Riggs, will you inspect the cellar? I fear we may have had an intruder."

In the doorway to the dining room across the hall, Miss Morrow gasped.

"Nothing were disturbed when I come here a month ago, Miss Bainbridge," Riggs said. "But if anybody still be here, I'll send him packing."

He was of less than average height, but burly. Honore recalled something about him winning wrestling competitions at the county fair. He probably could send anyone packing. Yet sending him down alone was not quite right of her.

"I will go with you," she announced.

"Miss Bainbridge, you should not," Miss Morrow protested.

"I can go with him, miss," Mavis offered.

"I would rather you begin work on the book room, Mavis." Honore smiled at her companion. "I will be quite all right. I cannot imagine anyone would have remained here with us banging about. Where is Bets?"

"Here, miss." The girl's cap appeared in the morning room doorway. "'Tis frightfully dusty in he—*hechoo!*" She apologized and sneezed again.

"I'll help her first," Mavis said. "The dusting makes her sneeze something worse than usual."

"No one should have sent her here to clean then, if she cannot be around a great deal of dust." Grinding her teeth against the senseless action of the housekeeper, Honore started after Riggs.

"Miss Bainbridge." Miss Morrow stretched out a hand as though she intended to stop Honore.

Honore slipped past her. "I need to see for myself if anyone has been here. And there is still the matter of the coal. Riggs, take a candle and light mine."

The outdoor man did as she bade and led the way down the back passageway. He too paused and studied the footprints for a moment, shook his head without saying anything, and continued to the narrow doorway leading to the cellar steps.

If possible, they were narrower and steeper than the passage above, leading down and down into a blackness worse than a cloudy night, darkness that seemed to swallow the light from the candles. Somehow she must get her heroine into a cellar like this, perhaps without so much as a candle.

"This is like a cave," Honore said.

"Aye, miss, mebbe it were a cave. Lots of them about."

"Not deep enough in the cliff." She knew all too well how high the cliffs were here. "Do you know which way the coal room is?"

"Aye, miss, 'tis across here so's the coal can be loaded from outside the garden wall." He crossed the rough stone floor of the cellar and opened a door set a yard or so above the ground. Light from his candle vanished, then reappeared as a winking yellow eye in the darkness. "You'll be needing a load, miss. Not much left."

"Will you—do you see to that?" Her cheeks burned over the notion she even needed to ask such a question.

"No, miss, but I'll see it gets done."

"Thank you, I—"

Need not explain her ignorance to him. She had already demonstrated it enough, the neglect of a lesson her mother should have taught her had she not been so sickly these past four years.

She swallowed. "Should we look into the other rooms?"

"Aye, miss. I'll be looking. You stay here by the steps."

Good. She could run for help if anything untoward occurred.

She positioned herself at the bottom of the flight, listening to Riggs open doors, watching his candle disappear and reappear. From upstairs, more doors opened and closed. Footfalls clattered over floorboards. Voices rang out, the high, clear voices of the three other females at work, and—

"Riggs, I am going up. Someone is here."

She gathered her skirts in one hand and raced up the steps, down the passageway, and through the door into the front hall. Not until she saw Lord Ashmoor standing just over the threshold did she think how foolish her mad dash had been. But the thought came too late for her to back through the doorway and vanish into what now seemed the welcoming cellar. He had already seen her.

11

If not for the golden hair peeking from beneath her frilled cap and the startlingly blue eyes growing wide with horror from a smudged face, Meric might not have recognized Miss Honore Bainbridge. Her gown was a fright of dust, grime, and faded cloth stretched too tight where he had no business looking. A cobweb adorned her cap like a trailing ribbon. And she wielded a long-handled brush as though it were a sword. In short, she was possibly the most adorable lady he had ever seen.

And in that moment, a corner of his heart belonged to the dishonorable Miss Honore Bainbridge. He knew it. He couldn't stop it, not even with the notion he was supposed to court Miss Devenish. He could not be so rude as to spin on his heel and flee. He was already hours later than he should have been, pacing around his cottage arguing with himself, trying to convince himself he had no business calling on her.

He'd failed at the conviction. He'd failed at staying away. He'd failed partially at not succumbing to the feelings he'd suspected might descend upon him when he was at the vicarage.

He bowed to her as though she wore a fine ball gown and pearls. "Miss Bainbridge, I fear I have called at an inconvenient moment."

"Most inconvenient." She started to drop him a curtsy, glanced at her scrubbing brush, and merely bobbed her head. "We expected you hours ago."

A not-so-subtle rebuke.

A glance at her companion, the other part of "we" and not something spoken imperiously, presumably. "It is nigh on five of the clock."

Her poise in the face of her dishevelment left him speechless. At the social events he had attended, females shrieked and vanished like smoke against a gray sky if they so much as pulled a button from a glove. Then again, he had seen Miss Bainbridge slightly more than disheveled after her disaster on the cliff.

"Now that you are here," the companion said, "you may as well come into the parlor. I have finished with all but the floors, but the men will have to do that in the morning if the weather is fine."

"I am not fit to sit on the cushions." Miss Bainbridge swiped at her skirt with the cleaning brush. A cloud of dust wafted into the air around her. "I expect I am not fit to be receiving a gentleman." She glanced from the companion—Miss Morrow, that was it—to the two gawping maids. "Mavis, Bets, carry on here until it is time for your supper. Make certain you extinguish all the candles and lock the door. Tomorrow we will begin again bright and early, except for you, Bets. You will be assigned to the kitchen at Bainbridge and another housemaid sent over."

"But miss, I cannot." The girl wrung her hands. "I'll be dismissed for not being able to carry out my duties."

"Nonsense. His lordship has placed me in charge of the household staff, and that means I can make the assignments."

"Thank you, miss." Tears trickled down the maid's cheeks. "I do like working in the kitchen."

Meric stared, that softened corner of his heart stretching a little bit further. Thus far, he had yet to see a lady treat a housemaid with such consideration.

Then Miss Bainbridge turned back to him, and her eyes held no warmth, displayed none of the warmth for him he was experiencing toward her. "We delayed our cleaning for hours because you said you would call."

"Miss Bainbridge," Miss Morrow protested in an undertone.

"Now we shall have to invite you for dinner, and I am not at all certain that is proper."

"Perhaps if we serve it as mere refreshments before the parlor fire," Miss Morrow suggested, "no one would object to that."

"I hadn't thought about dinner." Meric's ears heated. "I can call tomorrow instead."

Miss Bainbridge marched toward the front door. "No, you cannot come tomorrow. We will be occupied cleaning here, as you can see. This house has been neglected for years and must be habitable by Saturday."

"You're having guests you banish to this—this—cottage?" He posed the question before realizing asking was impolite and the answer none of his concern.

"Not a guest." Miss Bainbridge dropped her brush beside the door and faced him. For a heartbeat, lightning flashed through her sky-blue eyes. "Me." Ungrammatical answer delivered, she spun on her heel and stalked down the three fan-shaped steps and onto the flagstone path.

Meric caught up with her before she reached the gate, Miss Morrow discreetly in his wake. "Are you closing up Bainbridge House?"

"Only to me, my lord." Her voice held no emotion. The tautness of her delicate jaw shouted volumes.

"And asking what that means is rude, I suppose." He smiled at her.

She turned her face away. "You already asked Monday night."

More like Tuesday morning, but this was not the time to quibble over dates. He understood the message. Somehow the cleaning of the little house in the garden and her bout of weeping as though her heart were broken were connected to one another. Something the size of a broadsword pricked his conscience.

"I am sorry I didn't come to call sooner today." His mouth felt dry all of a sudden. "And after I told the vicar you would be occupied today."

"The vicar?" She stopped beneath the branches of a conifer trimmed and trained to arch over the path like a gate head. "Why would you tell the vicar that?"

"Because he wanted to call."

"To discuss the plight of my immortal soul over my miscreant behavior?"

"No, Miss Bainbridge, to court you."

"The vicar wants to court me? Mr. Stanbury, Mr. Holiness himself, wants me with my tarnished reputation? Oh my." She threw back her head and laughed. "I am not good enough for the earl of Ashmoor, but a dear country vicar does not find me beyond the pale of acceptability. Oh my." She laughed again. Her cap fell to the ground, and twin tracks of tears showed the extent of grime on her face.

He handed her a handkerchief, then retrieved her cap. As he straightened, Miss Morrow hastened forward to take it from him.

"I will get her upstairs, my lord. Do go into the parlor and Soames will bring you something to drink while you wait."

"Perhaps I should leave?" He made the offer as a question because he didn't want to go.

The companion shook her head. "I think your company will do her good. But you should not have come alone this late, my lord. The road home might be unsafe after dark."

"Indeed." He remembered this pretty spinster and his steward casting longing glances at one another across the church, and added, "Next time I will bring my steward along."

Miss Morrow blushed. Even in her dirt and rumpled clothes, she looked rather pretty with color in her cheeks.

He smiled at her. "You should blush around Mr. Chilcott, Miss Morrow."

She blushed an even deeper shade of pink and hastened to fall into step beside Miss Bainbridge.

A wife for Chilcott would do him good. He spent too much time poring over estate accounts or writing letters. And Miss Morrow seemed like an admirable female. Then again, if she wed, Miss Bainbridge would be left alone.

In that separate house.

"Do you have a name for it?" he asked, coming up behind the ladies.

"For what?" they asked in unison.

"That little house. It is even smaller than the one you call a cottage in Clovelly."

"That is a dower house," Miss Bainbridge explained. "It is intended for the wife of the deceased baron. My grandmother lived there, as well as my great-aunt, whose sweetheart died in one of these endless wars with . . . Fra-ance . . ." She trailed off.

Meric waited for an explanation, but they reached the side of the house, and the ladies stopped.

"Go around to the front door," Miss Bainbridge directed. "Tell Soames to serve you whatever you would like to drink. We will be with you shortly."

He expected to wait at least an hour. They both needed a good scrubbing, like the dower house did. He spent the time sipping the cream-laced coffee a footman had brought him and flipping through the pages of a two-year-old copy of *The Gentleman's Magazine*. Then, just as the clock struck three quarters of an hour, the ladies appeared looking neat and fresh and, in the case of Miss Bainbridge, too pretty for a man's comfort. She wore a white dress with an overlay of some kind of gold stuff that had as many holes in it as a fishing net but suited her nicely, matching her hair as it did.

He rose and bowed, and this time she curtsied before extending her hand to him. He took it in his. She wore no gloves there in her own parlor with a meal expected. Her fingers were smooth and warm, and he didn't want to let them go.

She drew her hand free without looking at him. "I have ordered rather substantial refreshments to be served in here. I hope that suits you."

"Whatever is right. I didn't mean to come so late."

He hadn't meant to come at all, but he had walked and walked along the beach until the rising tide drove him up a path to Bainbridge.

"You are always welcome, my lord." Miss Bainbridge seated herself on a sofa before the fire, her companion beside her. Meric seated himself adjacent to the ladies, and the three of them sat staring at the coffee service for one. They were supposed to talk with one another, he and Miss Bainbridge, but he doubted she wanted her companion to know of the midnight excursion. No doubt Miss Morrow reported back to one of the sisters or the brother, and Miss Bainbridge would suffer worse than banishment to the dower house if any of her family learned of her exploit.

But they could talk about her brother—maybe.

"Is Lord Bainbridge coming to stay here at the house?" Meric asked at last.

"He is bringing his fiancée." Miss Bainbridge's upper lip curled. "We know nothing of her, as she was not out when I had my Season, but she must be a high stickler, for I am not good enough for her presence." She fixed him with eyes like a winter sky. "Then, my lord, you understand how that is."

Miss Morrow gasped. "Honore Bainbridge."

Meric waved the companion to silence and met the challenge head-on. "As I think you know, when I arrived in England last year, it was mere days after the country learned that the United States had declared war on Great Britain, probably an act of national suicide, but England has behaved badly to American sailors and shipping, and—but the merits of the war are not on point here. What matters is that I was immediately tossed into prison along with my brother under suspicion of spying. For months no one would believe we were heirs assumptive and presumptive to the Ashmoor title. Your father finally got a message and helped with the matter, and all was well until after his death. Once he died, the trouble began."

A scratch at the door was followed by the entrance of the butler and footmen to clear away the coffee service and set up a table with the supper buffet Miss Bainbridge had ordered, so they could call the meal refreshments and not be accused of having a single gentleman to dinner.

"Do let me serve you, my lord." She rose and made her way to the table, where she picked up a plate and fork. "Roast chicken? Some of this lovely fish?"

He removed the plate from her hands. "I believe the gentleman serves the lady."

"Well, um, yes, usually at a buffet . . ." She toyed with the golden netting stuff draping her skirt and avoided his eyes. "I just did not think . . . This is highly unusual, though proper enough with Miss Morrow here, and, um . . ." She fled back to the sofa.

Meric raised his eyebrows at the companion, who stood quietly on the other side of the table, waiting with her own plate.

She smiled at him. "Miss Bainbridge has a hearty appetite."

And something about his action had flustered her. Was she that unused to male kindness? Surely during her Season she had never lacked for gentlemen to serve her, not a lady with her looks and, when she chose, charm.

He rather liked her best when she wasn't being charming. When one was a nobleman with a substantial income, the world filled with charming females rather than honest ones.

Like Miss Devenish? Had he just considered that Miss Devenish was dishonest? Surely not. She was sweet-natured. He must remember that.

He carried a filled plate to Miss Bainbridge, then returned for his own. Once they were all seated again and the ladies eating, he asked, "Shall I continue?"

"If you think it is important information for us to have." Miss Bainbridge did not look at him.

"Of course I think it is important. I intended to tell you that day I brought you the marriage contract, only we got distracted by a little tumble off a cliff."

Her head shot up. "You told me quite enough that day, enough I insisted on walking home across the field and—" Her eyes widened. "That is where I—"

"Where you what?" Meric leaned toward her.

"Never you mind right now. Do, please, continue. Life has been difficult for you since my father died? I do understand. It has been difficult for me too. My family decided my mourning was a good reason for me to be hidden away as though they were ashamed of me." Her lower lip quivered. "As though they *are* ashamed of me."

Miss Morrow laid her hand on Miss Bainbridge's arm. "That will pass, you know. By next Season, something more interesting will have come along and everyone will forget about your unfortunate alliances."

"I keep hoping for the same." Meric smiled at the ladies. "But my alliances are blood ties I can't break."

"You mean your father?" Miss Bainbridge gave him her full attention. "You are being blamed for your father's . . . misfortune?"

"And for being raised in America with the two countries now at war." Meric speared a mouthful of some succulent-looking fish with enough vigor to flake it into bits. "Since my father was accused of murder and something akin to treason, I am potentially the apple that didn't fall far from the tree. In short, whenever something bad occurs locally—namely a smuggler landing or prisoners escaping from Dartmoor, some form of military men pound on my door and ask intrusive questions about my whereabouts."

The ladies stared at him, eyes wide, mouths agape, forks poised above barely touched plates.

"They still think you are helping prisoners escape?" Miss Bainbridge finally asked.

Meric inclined his head. "Yes, ma'am."

"But why would you take such a risk? Your life? Your liberty? Your family?"

"I wouldn't be the first man to do so for a cause he believed in."

"But you have given them no cause," Miss Bainbridge protested with gratifying vehemence.

Meric gave her a tight-lipped smile. "Other than being the son of an accused murderer."

"So you need to clear your father's name," Miss Morrow said in her quiet voice. "If you can."

"If I can. Until then . . ." He looked at Miss Bainbridge, every particle of his being suddenly aching as though he suffered from a fever.

Her hand shaking enough to rattle her cutlery against her plate, she set her service aside, rose, and crossed the room to the window. Not a good decision. With darkness having fallen outside and the candles and fire bright inside, her face was reflected in the glass, pale and working with emotion she was trying to control. Each pinching of her nostrils, every compression of her lips tugged at his heart, at his conscience.

He stood and joined her at the window. "I am sorry, Miss Bainbridge. Under other circumstances, I think we would have gotten along well together."

"But you cannot take a wife who has a reputation sullied by her association with a murderer and a traitor. Unless, of course, we learn who truly did kill that revenue officer and exonerate your father."

"If it's possible, it can't be a safe thing to do."

"I expect not. And more, we need to keep you safe from being accused outright of helping prisoners escape from Dartmoor."

"Another dangerous prospect."

She smiled at him in the glass. "I am willing to risk it, my lord."

"You cannot." Without thinking of the impropriety of it, he curved his hand around her shoulder. "This is work for my brother and me and has nothing to do with you other than . . . ahem . . ."

"Other than the reason why you cannot accede to the wishes of my father, the only true friend you had here in England—his desire for you to wed me." She faced him, and they stood far too close, close enough for him to see his reflection in her big blue eyes, close enough for him to smell her scent, light and sweet like wildflowers. "You need a wife above reproach. I already worked that out. But my father wanted to help you for the sake of your father, his friend. It is the least I can do."

Realizing his hand still rested on her shoulder, holding her with her bodice nearly touching his waistcoat buttons, he released her and took half a step away. "Your father would not want you risking anything."

"My father would not wish for a number of events that have occurred, like my brother banishing me to the dower house, or me living here alone with a companion, but that is the state of matters. I have nothing to lose."

"Except maybe your life."

She shrugged. "No one would dare harm the sister of a peer."

Meric gave his head an emphatic shake. "No, Miss Bainbridge, I will not allow it. I simply wished to give you a full explanation—"

"What if I may have information you can use in your hunt?"

"What? How?" He gripped his hands behind his back so he didn't seize her, as he might do with one of his younger siblings withholding vital information from him.

She smiled. "Will you let me help you?"

"No."

"Then I will hunt down the source of this myself." From the folds of her skirt, she drew half of a flat silver disc embossed in a way already familiar to him.

The other half of the button he had picked up on the pasture path the day the cliff nearly dropped Miss Bainbridge into the sea.

12

Stillness hovered over the library like an impending storm. In front of the fire, Miss Morrow bowed her head as though she were praying. In front of Honore, Lord Ashmoor hardened his jaw and glared down at her from eyes that held no hint of gold lights, only green and brown like the depths of a forest.

"Where," he asked in a rasping voice, "did you find that?"

She shoved the button back through the slit in her skirt to the pocket tied around her waist beneath her gown. "Our dinner is growing cold, and I know Cook has made gingerbread with a lemon custard for the sweet."

"Tempting, Miss Bainbridge, but not good enough to distract me." Despite his words, one corner of his mouth twitched as though he tried not to smile.

She shrugged. "The decision is yours, my lord. After all, would you not like a look at the footprints or any other things that might exist in the—" She clamped her lips shut as she realized she had nearly given away the location in which she found the button half.

"You know I would. I expect the authorities would too."

"But they are not interested in proving your father innocent—or you, for that matter."

He scowled at her for another moment, then laughed, a rich, rolling chuckle that seemed to vibrate through her even though he was not touching her. "I think you have me there, Miss Bainbridge. Against my better judgment, I will agree to let you help me so long as you do nothing rash." He lowered his voice. "Like the other night."

"That, I agree, was stupid. I was overwrought about my brother's letter . . ." She pasted a too-bright smile on her face. "Shall we return to our dinners—er, refreshments?"

Miss Morrow had placed their plates upon the hearth to keep them warm. Roast chicken and cod in aspic were a bit dry, but still flavorful. Although Miss Morrow must have heard every word—or most words—spoken by the window, more conversation regarding broken French buttons and nearly thirty-year-old murders directly beside her seemed inappropriate. The stiffness of her posture spoke disapproval.

After several mouthfuls and minutes of silence save for the crackle and shift of the coals on the hearth and the chink of silver against china, Honore set aside her plate, rose, and rang for coffee and the sweet. Instead of returning to the sofa, she began to pace around the room. Miss Morrow's eyes upon her told her that her action was rude. Her own upbringing told her that her action was rude. But she could not bring herself to stop. As though propelling themselves without her will, her feet kept placing themselves one in front of the other, from door to window to shelves of books, then back to the window. If a cold, damp wind did not rattle the panes of glass and seep around the edges, she might have flung open that window.

This was like the other night, when thoughts of her brother's letter had driven her out of the house and through the garden to the cliffs. She knew not what compelled her action other than a restlessness of body and spirit, the same kind of restlessness that had driven her to take foolish risks with her reputation while Mr. Frobisher and then Major Crawford courted her. Foolish, thoughtless risks that hurt not only her but also her family. Yet there she was, about to delve into another foolish risk with her reputation simply because . . .

Her family did not care what she did now. They shunted her off to Devonshire alone save for someone they paid to stay with her. Now her brother had gone one step further and banished her to the dower house. Perhaps she should count her blessings that he had not decided she was fit for life nowhere except a Channel Island, where no one they knew would encounter her.

She did not feel particularly blessed. Restlessness, hollowness that did not wish for food gnawed at her, driving her around the room one more time until she simply must fling open the window and dash across the terrace to the garden, to the cliffs—

The door opened and servants entered with more trays, some empty, some full of cake and coffee. The chafing dishes of dinner disappeared. Slices of cake with warm, yellow custard spooned atop it replaced them. Coffee steamed from a silver pot, fresh cream frothed from another. By the time the servants withdrew, Honore had regained her composure and acted as footman to Miss Morrow and Lord Ashmoor, laughing as though her doing so were a great jest.

Miss Morrow took her plate and cup while gazing at Honore with concern in her fine eyes. "Are you well, my dear?"

"Of course." Honore avoided her gaze.

His lordship took his service and allowed his gaze to move to hers, the gold lights sparkling in his eyes again. "I think you would like the frontier, Miss Bainbridge."

"Why would you say such a thing, my lord?" Honore seized

on the diversion as she had seized that half-dead sapling on the edge of the cliff. "Do tell us more."

"The western side of New York isn't much frontier any longer," he admitted. "It is still not all that populated, and the land is . . . untamed."

Honore glanced at Miss Morrow, a laugh bubbling inside her. "Have I just been insulted?"

"I do not think so—quite." Something sparked in the depths of Miss Morrow's eyes, making them more blue than gray, and a little smile touched her lips. "But do, please, continue, my lord. What is so untamed about the land?"

"The forest. I'm afraid clearing it to farm is an arduous task. And it's cold there more than half of the year, so the growing season is short. We lived a great deal on fish from the lakes and game from the woods."

"Why ever would a body choose to live there?" Honore held her coffee untasted.

Ashmoor cradled his cup between his hands, his long fingers and broad palms engulfing the fragile china. "My parents had little choice. Father wanted to hide. He wasn't sure if the Americans would send him back here for trial if they caught him, so he wanted to be away from civilization. And then they found they liked the land, the freedom."

"The hardship?" Honore spoke without thought.

Ashmoor flashed her a smile. "Yes, ma'am, the hardship too. They were both country born and bred, but to good families with lots of money and servants. Neither of them had to work before, but they discovered they liked it. Father said he had never been so satisfied as he was at the end of the day, knowing he was eating something for which he had worked. He said—" A muscle jumped in his jaw, and he looked away, sipped at his coffee.

"How long ago did he pass, my lord?" Miss Morrow asked into the silence.

"Eight years ago. I was twenty, the youngest a mere baby of four. She scarcely remembers him." Infinite sadness softened his chiseled features. "I hated leaving them."

"But you can make their lives so much easier now," Honore said. "Once this war is over, they can all come here to live. You can find good husbands for your sisters and wives for your brothers and—why are you shaking your head?"

"My mother won't come back here, and that means neither will the girls." His face brightened. "But they live in Albany now. I've . . . er . . . managed to get some money to them."

"Have you now." Honore gazed at him through lowered lashes.

Was the man quite as innocent of connections to the lawless as he claimed? She must be careful of that. She must not make another mistake like she had with Frobisher and Crawford, or she would find herself shipped off to Jamaica or even those western woods of New York.

She shivered. "Did you get a great deal of snow in those woods?"

"Feet of it sometimes." His expression grew dreamy, as though he remembered happy times. "I built us a sled when I was twelve years, and we spent many hours sledding down the hills. Then there are the lakes. They freeze so solid a body could drive a coach and four onto them. We ice-skated on them and chopped holes in the ice to fish."

"You fished through the ice?" Honore and Miss Morrow exclaimed together.

Ashmoor laughed. "Yes, it is very fresh fish. But the ice is dangerous. Sometimes one makes a mistake and goes through. The water is so cold a body can't survive long enough to get out."

That sorrow touched him again, and he set his cup and plate on the table. "I should be going, if you ladies will be so kind as to excuse me from this delightful interlude. I hear rain starting."

Honore had been too intent on the timbre of his voice to notice the raindrops pinging against the windows.

"I will order the carriage to take you home." She jumped up and dashed for the bellpull.

"No need. I walked here. I can walk home."

"Of course you cannot. Do not be a widg—that is—" She had barely stopped herself from calling the lord of Ashmoor a widgeon.

She opened the door and told the footman waiting in the hall to have the carriage brought around to the front door to convey his lordship back to Clovelly.

He had risen with her and now crossed the room to where she stood near the door. "Is it wise for the Bainbridge coach to be seen pulling up to my door?"

"Probably not, but I will not have you walking in this. Besides . . ." She lowered her voice. "If you are having difficulties with the authorities, they cannot accuse you of anything if you are first in our coach and then at home. I presume others are in your house tonight?"

"Chilcott hasn't yet left for the country, and my brother has chosen to stay at home tonight."

Miss Morrow's head snapped up at the mention of the Ashmoor steward.

Honore smiled. "Perhaps you wish to bring them with you tomorrow?"

"No, I think—" Ashmoor glanced at Miss Morrow and nodded. "I just may. Chilcott is an intelligent man who knows this area well. He might be of help. Is nine of the clock too early?

I know it would be in London, but perhaps you are well used to country hours?"

"Indeed I am. I like to ride by eight of the clock this time of year, weather permitting. Perhaps you would like to join me sometime."

He stiffened. "No, thank you."

"You do not ride, my lord?" She tilted her head and let her eyes laugh up at him.

"Not well. I've had little opportunity, other than once with a Devenish party." Shuddering, he added, "But I can drive a team hitched to a wagon."

"An admirable skill for a gentleman."

The footman scratched on the door, then opened it. "The coach is here, Miss Bainbridge."

"Thank you." Honore faced his lordship and held out her hand. "Thank you for coming."

"Thank you for your hospitality." He took her hand.

She was so used to herself and the gentleman wearing gloves when they shook hands, the touch of his warm fingers on her skin sent a jolt through her. She snatched her hand away and tucked both her hands behind her back as though he would grip them and not let go—surely a foolish notion, as he had already turned away from her and strode from the room. A moment later, the front door opened and closed. Carriage wheels crunched on the drive, then dwindled into the increasing flurry of rain against the windows. And still Honore remained by the door, her hands clasped behind her back, not to hide them from him but to preserve the sensation of warmth that had radiated from his fingers to hers.

"Oh, dear," Miss Morrow said from where she now stood in front of the sofa, "should we not have invited him to stay tonight?"

"Of course we should have. I—I am supposed to persuade him to marry me because I need a husband to make me respectable again and Papa wanted it, and—and—"

No, she would not say such a foolish thing aloud. She would not believe such a foolish thing. She scarcely knew him. She had made this mistake twice before. She would not make it again. Husband catching was a serious business, a business of the mind, not the heart. She was not even a little bit in love with Lord Ashmoor. No, not a little.

A great deal.

13

"I think," Meric said to his companions, "I am making a terrible mistake." He leaned his head against the high back of his chair and closed his eyes. An image of Miss Honore Bainbridge painted itself on the inside of his lids, all golden hair and creamy skin, pink cheeks and pinker lips. She was a minx, dangerous to his reputation in the neighborhood, dangerous to his peace of mind, dangerous to his courtship of Miss Devenish, who was the proper sort of bride.

"By staying here, I hope?" Philo's comment came as a welcome interruption to the direction of Meric's thoughts.

But he shook his head. "We have to be here. For one thing, returning to America is out of the question right now with the state of the war. For another . . ." He opened his eyes and fixed his brother and then his steward and secretary with a stern glare. "I have to find out who is getting prisoners out of Dartmoor and bringing them north to escape, or I and the rest of us may find ourselves hanged for treason, or whatever they do to punish peers for that crime. I do know that they take away their lands. And too many are depending on me having this land. If I don't clear Father's name of those old charges, I will be thought again and again to be the one guilty anytime something goes wrong. I need help."

"It seems to be an impossible task, my lord," Chilcott said. "That is to say, this is a long coastline to find one place where smugglers, or whoever they may be, are carrying men out of the country."

"I'd think they'd go south," Philo added.

"Which is why they are coming north." Meric rose and paced to the window, then the wall of bookshelves, before he realized he mirrored Miss Bainbridge's actions earlier that night.

How pretty she had looked with her skirt flowing around her, her hair catching the light of the fire and candles to shine like honey in sunshine. In repose, her face was exceptionally pretty with its fine bones and wide blue eyes, flawless skin and mouth—

He must stop thinking of her mouth. He was starting to court Miss Devenish. Thoughts of Miss Bainbridge—those kinds of thoughts—were disloyal, senseless, frustrating.

He stalked back to his chair and flung himself upon it. "I have a clue."

Philo and Chilcott leaned toward him, faces eager.

"To Father's innocence or the traitors?" Philo asked.

"The latter. Father's innocence will be far harder to prove, but maybe if I can do this favor for the Crown, they will help with the rest."

Philo sat back, mouth grim. "I doubt as much. They didn't try in '85. Why should they try now in '13 when he is gone?"

"Because I've proven my loyalty and asked it of them?" Meric's query held more hope than certainty.

Chilcott smiled. "It may be so, my lord. But what is this clue?"

"It's on Bainbridge land." His companions looking at him with blank faces, Meric added, "The clue is on Bainbridge land. A possible link to . . . something. Too little to go on, but something. Someplace to start."

"On Bainbridge land?" Chilcott shook his head. "Never."

"Why never?" Philo asked.

"They are too old a family. Bainbridge may only be a barony, but they are one of the oldest baronies in the land. They can trace their ancestors—" Chilcott broke off and grinned. "My apologies. I had to memorize all this as a lad."

"And it's helpful when I'm attending a party full of old names," Meric said. "But what does it have to do with treason?"

"The Bainbridges have always been known to be amongst the loyalists to the Crown through civil wars and revolts." Chilcott's pleasant face grew long. "Unless Miss Bainbridge's . . . er . . . propensity for getting herself into ill company has come here—my lord, are you all right?"

He wasn't—quite. His head had gone light as though all the blood had drained to his middle and turned to frozen mud.

Not for a moment, as she had gazed up at him with those summer-sky blue eyes framed by long, gold-tipped lashes, her lips parted as though she were about to speak or be kissed, had he considered that she might be leading him opposite of the direction in which he wished to go. He never considered that her association with less than savory men might have corrupted her loyalty to her family, her kingdom, her faith. Yes, her faith too. Her father had told him she was a good Christian girl, that all his daughters carried a deep faith in the Lord that had influenced him to take his own faith more seriously instead of just at church on Sundays. Yet even the best people fell away from their relationship with God. His own conscience pricked over how he had been less than devoted of late, scrambled in his prayer life like eggs beneath a whisk.

He bowed his face into his hands in hopes of bringing back sense, or at least the blood back to his brainbox. "I don't think she is disloyal."

Yet she had been on the beach the other night when those men had been foundering offshore in the high winds. Signaling them, or there because she was distressed over her brother's edict, as she claimed she was?

"Maybe I should avoid her completely," he continued.

"I should think," Chilcott said, "that this is all the more reason why you should stay near her, my lord. If she is guilty of helping, befriending her makes it all that much easier to discover."

"You're rather coldhearted, aren't you?" Philo gave Chilcott an admiring glance. "Wish I could be so sanguine about pretty females."

"I, um, have an interest." Chilcott's face turned the color of a particularly bright sunset.

Meric laughed. "An interest named Miss Morrow?"

Chilcott's face darkened to the color of a ripe plum.

Philo joined in the friendly mirth. "She is a nice lady," he said. "And so pretty when she smiles."

"She has a quiet spirit, a gentle strength . . ." Chilcott shot to his feet and stalked across the room.

"And you want to ensure she does not get swept into something dangerous," Meric offered.

"Yes, my lord." Chilcott leaned his brow against windowpanes that must be cooling to his fiery face. "She is fiercely loyal to her lady. I-I made the suggestion after church the other week that she find employment other than with a lady not acceptable to county society, and I thought she would bite my head off."

"Then maybe her judgment is sound." As he spoke the words, Meric wanted them to be true.

"We can only hope."

"And stay close," Philo added, his face eager.

"And pray," Meric murmured.

No one responded for several moments, then Philo asked, "What about Miss Devenish? Will you still be able to court her and keep a watch over Miss Bainbridge?"

"Of course." Meric spoke a little too sharply. "The situations are completely different." He rose. "And if I am to be at Bainbridge at nine o'clock, I had best get to my bed."

"Likewise all of us," Philo said.

"We are taking the carriage or riding." Chilcott made it a pronouncement, not a suggestion, as he faced Meric. "You must cease walking about the countryside like a vagabond, my lord. And this rain tonight is only one reason why."

"I came home in the Bainbridge carriage, and since I arrived dry, not soaked to the skin, I am inclined to believe you. We will take the carriage. Though I suppose I need to learn to ride better, as that seems expected of a gentleman."

"You would be better off learning that at Ashmoor," Chilcott suggested. "Better horses and terrain. Indeed, my lord, you should spend more time there."

"Once I am wed. For now, it is too remote from everything."

Especially Miss Bainbridge.

Discussing the merits of riding on a horse over riding in a carriage, of living in Clovelly over living at Ashmoor, they climbed the narrow staircase to their rooms. Once he was in his chamber, fatigue washed over Meric. Sleep would be easy.

Except it eluded him. He lay staring at the underside of the canopy, going over every word, every action of Miss Bainbridge's that night, in an attempt to work out whether she had been telling the truth or playing him for a fool. If she was guilty and knew what he intended, then she would want to keep him close as much as he intended to keep her close.

He didn't like the suspicion, the hint of deception. At the same time, with his sights set on marrying a quiet, respectable lady like Miss Devenish, his suspicions against Miss Bainbridge would keep him from having thoughts of her enticing mouth.

He hoped.

Honore stood in the opening of her clothespress, dithering over how to dress sensibly enough for going through the dust-layered dower house, yet not look as shabby and unkempt as she had the day before when Lord Ashmoor arrived. A good thing he had stayed for refreshments. He had an image of her in her cream and gold gown to take home with him rather than the ragamuffin in kerchief and faded muslin.

"Wear the lavender muslin," Miss Morrow suggested from behind her.

Honore jumped. "It does not fit me at all well any longer. Parts of me seem to have grown, and the more I tighten my stays here"—she indicated her waist—"the larger things seem to grow here." She waved her hands in front of her chest. "It is quite, quite mortifying."

Miss Morrow laughed. "I expect most young ladies envy you, and gentlemen . . . well, gentlemen should at least pretend they do not notice. If they do not pretend as such, they are not gentlemen, whatever their station."

"I have learned that, to my regret."

Frobisher and Crawford had looked where they should not have. She had been flattered at the time. What a pickle her vanity had gotten her into. She wanted none of it now.

"I will wear that black muslin with the grosgrain ribbon trim." She reached for the gown. "It is more than modest."

"And will sadly show every speck of dust. Let us see." Miss Morrow mused over the selection before them. "This gray with a pretty fichu?"

"That will need to be washed. No, I will wear the black. If he cannot find me appealing in black, then . . . then . . . well, I'd just as soon err on the side of modesty."

She eschewed the apron. If she ruined her gown, so much the better.

Once dressed, she descended the steps to the morning room, whose cheerful wallpaper, covered with the bright yellow of primroses and yellow and cream striped cushions, reflected sunshine on clear days and tried to substitute for it on cloudy ones. The dower house boasted nothing so welcoming in the morning. In the name of symmetry so popular fifty years earlier, every room on the ground floor was the same size.

Counting how many mornings she could still enjoy her breakfast in the manor house, she seated herself at the gateleg table before the hearth and lifted her cup to her lips just as Soames entered to inform her Mr. Tuckfield wished to speak to her.

"I believe the engineer from the mines is here, miss."

"In that event, send them in." She hesitated, wondering for a moment if she should order more cups and coffee, then decided against it. "Take them into the library."

Lord Ashmoor could go about with his steward, for the man came from a noble family and acted more as a secretary than an agent to the land. Tuckfield was of common stock and never invited to social events. Who knew from where a man who worked with mines originated.

She waited until she heard voices pass the morning room, then a few more moments to let them settle in the book room, before she made her way down the hall to the more formal setting. The man took his cue from Mr. Tuckfield, stood, and bowed upon Honore's arrival.

"Mr. Polhenny from Truro," Tuckfield presented the engineer.

He was a young and handsome man in a simple but well-cut coat. "My pleasure, Miss Bainbridge." His smile was broad, his Cornish accent broader. "I understand you wish to know how to stop your cliff from falling to bits."

"Yes, that is precisely what I would like." She folded her arms across the high waist of her gown. "Can it be done?"

"I suspect the ground beneath is riddled with caves, and caves are not so different from the mines. So aye, it can be done in most situations." He glanced from her to Tuckfield. "But I'll need to be looking all up and down the cliffs. Is there access to the base?"

"There is. Mr. Tuckfield can either show you or provide you with someone who will." She hesitated then said, "Of course, any serious work needing done will have to be approved by my brother, but he will be here in a few days."

"He will?" Tuckfield exclaimed. His face reddened. "That is, I am happy to hear this, Miss Bainbridge. I need to hire more men for the harvest, and the cliff problem and all will need his attention. I was just surprised, as I've heard nothing."

"Saturday or Monday." Honore nodded to Mr. Polhenny. "Do, please, carry on as you need, and come to me if you have any difficulties you need sorted out before my brother arrives."

She left the library and returned to the morning room to find

Miss Morrow replacing the neglected coffee with fresh. "We will need to hurry. It is nearly nine of the clock."

Indeed, Honore had barely finished the coffee and taken a bite or two of a bread roll before carriage wheels crunched in the drive, heralding new arrivals. She wiped her fingers on a serviette and entered the hall to greet the visitor.

Visitors. Mr. Chilcott and Mr. Poole accompanied his lordship. They strode into the house, bringing with them the scent of cold autumn air, wood smoke, dried leaves, and the sea. Their gaits were easy, confident, their smiles warm, Lord Ashmoor's handshake warmer.

Once again, neither of them wore gloves.

She tucked her hands beneath her elbows. "Shall we get ourselves started? I am not certain what we can learn, but we can look at where I found that button half and what's left of the footprints."

Miss Morrow brought her a shawl, a paisley one prettier in its blues and greens than was wise for the dirty house. Together, the five of them left through the library's French windows and across the terrace and gardens. Mr. Poole commented that the greensward beyond the flowerbeds would be perfect for some sort of game. Mr. Chilcott walked beside Miss Morrow with neither of them speaking or looking at one another.

Lord Ashmoor fell into step beside Honore. "Chilcott tells me that you brought in a mine engineer from Truro to look at the cliff."

"Does not news travel swiftly? I just met him this morning."

"He arrived last night, apparently. Does he think the cliffs can be shored up?"

"He is inspecting them today to see. He said the caves here can be trouble." She smiled. "I know the revenue service thinks so."

"I imagine they are a boon to the smugglers."

"Indeed. Many a house along the coasts has routes directly from caves into their cellars. But not us," she hastened to add. "Papa made certain of that. He was too politically savvy to allow even a hint of those sorts of goings-on here to cloud his reputation."

But not enough to ensure his spoiled youngest daughter did not.

She suppressed a sigh, and her chest hurt at not redeeming herself before he died. Marrying the man he'd wanted for her would help.

"The dower house cellars are not deep enough to reach the caves," she continued. "They are little more than a series of storage rooms and the coal room that abuts the wall so coal can be delivered easily."

"And that wall faces which way?" Ashmoor paused at the gate beneath the arching tree branches. "A side lane, I think?"

"Yes. There's a lane that leads off the road, but it ends in a pasture before it reaches the sea. We grow very little here in Devonshire other than sheep for wool and a little fruit. We have some farmland in Somerset, but the house there is very old and small and we never go there."

Except her brother could banish her there if she was not careful. Perhaps her association with Lord Ashmoor would help her consequence in her brother's eyes. Of course, if he was amongst those who believed Ashmoor's blood was tainted from his father's alleged crimes, then the association would harm her further.

She shook off that worry and led the way up the flagstone path to the front door. Mavis peeked around the corner of the building, then crept forward as Honore unlocked the door.

"We'd've gone in the back way, miss," Mavis said, "but 'tis locked."

"I should hope that it is." Honore twisted the key in the lock. The latch clicked, and she pushed the door open, then started to step over the threshold.

Lord Ashmoor rested a hand on her shoulder to stop her. "If there was someone in here before, there may have been again, so I think we should go with caution."

"I brought a strike-a-light again," Mavis offered. From her pocket, she produced the implement that resembled a small gun. "Should I be lighting the candles first?"

"Just one or two will do," Ashmoor said.

"One for each of us," Mr. Poole spoke from behind them.

"Three for us gentlemen," Ashmoor added. "Miss Bainbridge and Miss Morrow and you girls can wait—"

"No, we cannot." Honore snatched the strike-a-light from Mavis, stepped over the threshold, and lifted the globe off a wall sconce. She pulled back the trigger. Steel rasped against flint, igniting a spark that created a flame of oiled waste at the end of the barrel. The candle flared, dull against the glow from the fanlight above the door.

His face a mask of resignation, Ashmoor lighted another candle from hers. "At least let me go first."

"Do you know which way to go?" Honore gave him a sweet smile.

He sighed.

She laughed and led the way across the hall to the book room. She flung open the door at the same time the clouds outside parted and sunlight streamed through the windows. As though someone had suddenly lighted ten score candles at once, the golden beams washed over the gleaming wood of the furniture and floor, sparkled off the brass inkstand on the desk and the handles of the fire tools, and shimmered in the glass of candle globes and doors covering part of the bookshelves.

The room was spotlessly clean.

14

If not for the rumble of wind around the corner of the house, a pin could have fallen on the upper floor and been heard. Not so much as a sniff or a gasp of breath, the scuff of a shoe sole on the floor, or a whisper of clothing from an arm moving a fraction of an inch disturbed the next several moments.

Then Miss Bainbridge cried, "How?" She spun on her heel and glared around at the assembled company. "How could this room have gotten clean overnight? No one was here. I would declare it in church."

"Obviously someone was here." Meric stepped away from her and made a circuit of the chamber. He ran his fingertips across the mantel, a bookshelf, the desk. His hand came away clean. He turned back to Miss Bainbridge. "And this is the room in which you found that piece of silver?"

"It was on the table where those—" She broke off and scowled, her lips pursed so tightly they puckered as though . . .

He forced his gaze back to her eyes, seeking truth. "What, Miss Bainbridge? What are you claiming now?"

"I am claiming nothing. I am telling you there was a pile of books lying on that table. They are not here now. They are—"

She ran to the wall of shelves and began to hunt. "Here." She pulled off a thick tome bound in red Moroccan leather. "And here." She drew out another one. "And—oh, this is too, too strange."

Afraid she was about to burst into tears, Meric focused his attention on the others still crowded around the doorway. "Let's go inspect the other rooms and see if they have been visited by the cleaning spirits too." He didn't try to mask his sarcasm.

None of them moved.

"What I want to know," Miss Morrow said, "is why someone would do this. It would have taken several people all night to accomplish this."

"I expect," Meric said, "they worked out that Miss Bainbridge already knew someone had been in the house, so they wished to remove any possible traces of who they are."

"Which means," Miss Bainbridge said from close behind him, "that someone is near at hand. I mean, who else would know I am being . . . banished to live here but someone on this estate?"

"Or in our household." Philo looked and sounded far too cheerful for someone announcing a traitor in their midst. "We were talking about it last night, and with the way servants pad around spying . . ." He shrugged. "Anyone in Devonshire could have known by midnight."

The two maids backed away with those silent steps they seemed trained to use, their faces red.

"I'm going to take a look around outside if I may, Miss Bainbridge?" Meric turned to her. "The rest of you—"

"I do not care what the others do, but I am coming with you." Miss Bainbridge seized his arm like a limpet, and only force would dislodge her. “Mavis, Gracie, finish cleaning upstairs so we can have the men come in and do the carpets.”

“Are we sure no one’s been upstairs?” Meric asked.

“They had not been yesterday.” Miss Bainbridge nudged his elbow like a collie nudging a sheep.

Left with no choice without being rude, Meric started out of the room. The others scattered away from the doorway and reassembled around the steps. Dust still lay thick upon them and the banister. Unless the person flew, no one could have gotten to the upper floor.

“Easier to see those windows from the house,” Miss Bainbridge said. “Go ahead up and get started, girls. And since this is a fine day, open as many windows as you can to give the place a good airing.”

“Yes, miss.” The maids bobbed curtsies, gathered up cleaning materials, and headed up the steps.

The rest of them looked from room to room, ending in the kitchen. Like the library, every surface had been cleansed of its accumulation of dust. Not so much as the smudge of a finger or boot heel marred the furniture and floors. It was the work of someone good at cleaning, and in what must have been only candlelight. He couldn’t imagine Miss Bainbridge doing the work on her own, but Miss Morrow was loyal to her, and the maids obeyed her commands without hesitation. Yet suspecting her was absurd. Still, who else had access to the house? Who else could move about the grounds without interference?

His innards uneasy, he allowed Miss Bainbridge to steer him into the garden. Now falling dormant save for a few hardier herbs, it appeared to be a miniature version of the lawns around the main house. Walls surrounded the property on three sides, more to shelter from the sea winds than to provide protection from intruders, as the front gate was open. The main house and grounds boasted a wall, however, making access difficult, though not impossible.

"Where is this coal chute?" he asked Miss Bainbridge.

"Outside the wall." She released his arm at last, leaving a cold place through his coat, and led the way through the same gate she had entered the other night, the one she said she could obtain a key for without difficulty.

That thought rattling around in his head, he followed her along a lane just wide enough for a wagon, and she showed him a door cut into the wall and covered with a wooden hatch. It wasn't large enough for a grown man to squeeze through unless he was quite small, but a boy or average to small female could fit just fine.

Miss Bainbridge was an average to small female.

He gave her a head-to-toe assessing glance to see if he was right. She flinched away from him as though he had touched her, and turned her back on him.

"As you see, it would not be easy to enter the house," she said.

"But not impossible." Philo stooped by the coal hatch. "This hasn't been opened in an age. Look how warped it is. It'll take a sledgehammer to get this unstuck."

"I had best notify Mr. Tuckfield before I get my coal delivery." Miss Bainbridge tucked her hands beneath her upper arms as though her fingers had grown cold.

They probably had. The day, though bright and clear, held the hint of winter coming just around the corner.

"If you would like to do so now," Meric said, "feel free to go about your business. We should be on our way."

"I should go to the cliffs and see what the mining engineer has to say." Miss Bainbridge shivered. "I want them to be safe again."

"If you are going to the cliffs, you need more than that shawl," Miss Morrow said. "It has gotten colder out here."

Meric removed his coat and draped it about Miss Bainbridge's shoulders. "Will that do for the time being?"

"You must not. You will get cold yourself." Even as she protested, she grabbed the sleeves of his coat and tied them in front of her like cape strings.

She looked so adorable with the wide collar framing her creamy skin and her golden hair beneath a ruffled cap, he doubted he could get cold while she was near.

"I'm all right. Remember, I'm used to a harsher climate than this." He turned his face into the wind off the sea and met his brother's eyes.

Philo said nothing, just raised his eyebrows.

Feeling even warmer, Meric offered his arm to Miss Bainbridge and led the way down the lane toward the sea. Behind him, Chilcott walked beside Miss Morrow. Meric had seen his secretary offer the lady his arm, but she had refused, tucking her hands inside her shawl instead.

"Isn't there a poem that says, 'The course of true love never did run smooth'?" Philo asked.

"Shakespeare," Miss Bainbridge said. "But what are you—"

Meric pressed her fingers against his forearm and glanced over his shoulder.

"Ohhh." The drawn-out sound puckered up her lips.

Meric welcomed the low wall where the lane ended. It distracted him with the necessity of climbing over it, then offering his hand to the ladies. Miss Morrow seized his hand as though it were a lifeline. Philo aided Miss Bainbridge, then offered her his arm, the jackanapes.

"My big brother is a bore, always worrying about everything,"

Philo was saying. "I shall entertain you with all the random quotations my mother managed to stick in my head."

Miss Bainbridge laughing, Philo carrying on with those random quotations, they trotted across the pasture, scattering sheep to the four winds.

"Your brother is charming," Miss Morrow said to Meric. "Do you hope to marry him off while he is here in England?"

"The thought hadn't occurred to me, especially not with—" Miss Morrow's fingers dug into his arm, and he cleared his throat. "That is to say, I suppose he's old enough, but I think he has interests back in New York."

"He should find a nice English girl, perhaps even an heiress," Miss Morrow said, "as long as he is your heir. Even afterward. You know more than most how the line of inheritance can shift."

"True. But I don't think he likes England much."

"He looks happy enough right now." Chilcott spoke in a dull tone, as though he were anything but happy.

"I won't make him wed or not." Meric tried to use the same kind of decisive accents he had noted in his butler and valet.

It must have worked, for none of them spoke again until they reached the far barrier of the pasture and the cliffs beyond. That close to the sea, even with the elevation above the foaming waters, the roar of wind and surf made talking to anyone not right at one's shoulder difficult. It wasn't an easy path to traverse, with rocks and vegetation clinging to the ground with the expectation of being swept away at the next storm. Meric didn't even try to be companionable as he examined the path, sometimes stooping to get a closer look at the shrubbery or a scar where a rock had been moved aside. The path told a tale of recent activity—but from a smuggler's pack, a phalanx of

French prisoners marching to escape vessels in the dark of the night, or just ordinary persons using the shortest route between two points?

A dower house sitting empty for years but being used, only to have someone clean it in an instant—clearly giving its usage away yet eliminating any hope of a clue to an identity. A broken button embossed with the symbols of the French Revolution and still cried by the followers of that greedy man Napoleon. Too, too little to clear his name once and for all. Certainly too little to come close to clearing his father's name.

"How does the saying go?" Miss Bainbridge spoke from behind him. "Finding a needle in a haystack?"

"Something of the kind." Meric peered up the path and caught a glimpse of two men standing near where the cliff had broken away and nearly taken Miss Bainbridge down with it to smash upon the rocks. "I believe we have found your steward and the mine engineer."

Tuckfield stood with his arms crossed over his broad chest and his face taut and grim. If possible, his mouth grew even tighter at their approach, until Miss Morrow stepped up beside Miss Bainbridge. He smiled then, lighting his whole face. "Ladies, what brings you out here on such a windy day?"

"I need to remind you of the need for coal in the dower house," Miss Bainbridge said. "And—" She drew Meric's coat more closely around her, as though feeling a suddenly deeper chill.

Meric felt the heat of the sunlight, for all its autumnal paleness, and strode to the edge of the cliff. "Is it safe now?" he asked the man he presumed to be the mine engineer.

"Aye, sound enough, but I'm wishing to go into the caves. Mr. Tuckfield seems to be a bit leery of me doing so."

"Is he a coward?" Chilcott spoke just a little too loudly.

Meric stared at his quiet and polite steward and secretary. "Why would you suggest—ah."

Tuckfield had his head bent low over Miss Morrow's, and she was smiling shyly without looking at him.

"What's that all about?" Meric asked softly.

"He is inviting her to accompany him to some assembly in Clovelly." Chilcott shuddered. "A public assembly for a gently bred lady like her."

"It seems to me," Meric observed, "that she likes the notion."

"Huh," Chilcott grunted.

Miss Morrow nodded and glided forward to join Miss Bainbridge with the mining engineer, while Tuckfield flashed Chilcott a triumphant smile and followed the ladies.

"I wouldn't like to say as yet why I think the cliff gave way," the man was saying. "The ground seems sound enough here, but you never know what can go wrong. Water runoff, maybe. Vegetation digging its roots into the rock. I must study further and go below."

"I'll go with you if Tuckfield is . . . concerned about it," Chilcott offered.

"What would you know about caves?" Tuckfield demanded. "Ashmoor does not have caves."

Meric's lips twitched. Beside him, Miss Bainbridge covered her mouth with her hand, but her eyes twinkled.

"No, Ashmoor has no caves." Chilcott smiled. "But my family home does. When would you like to go, Mister . . ."

"Polhenny." The mine engineer inclined his head. The men shook hands.

"When would you like to go?" Chilcott asked again.

"Should you not ask your master first?" Tuckfield glanced to Meric.

He shrugged, enjoying the tug-of-war between the two men. "He can take the rest of the day if he likes. I'm for home after I see the ladies safely to the house."

"I will come with you." Tuckfield offered Miss Morrow his arm.

"Please come report to me when you are finished, Mr. Polhenny," Miss Bainbridge said before she slipped her hand into the crook of Meric's elbow. "We can discuss effecting repairs."

"That is not necessary, Miss Bainbridge," Tuckfield said. "With his lordship coming home soon and—"

"To me, Mr. Polhenny," Miss Bainbridge reiterated.

Chilcott smirked at Tuckfield being overridden, but the smirk faded into a scowl as he realized his lady was walking off with the other man.

Meric smiled at his employee, then turned his attention to Miss Bainbridge. Her fingers were cold through his shirtsleeve. She wore no gloves, having believed she would be cleaning or, at the least, inspecting a dirty house. His own hands felt warm enough, so he covered her fingers with his other hand and avoided his brother's questioning gaze.

"Don't say anything," Meric murmured to her. "They might hear you."

"May I laugh?" Her eyes danced. Her fingers warmed beneath his.

"No." But they both chuckled.

"What is so amusing?" Philo asked.

"Dogs tussling over a bone," Meric said.

They all laughed, and a soft warmth radiated through Meric, a lessening of a tension he hadn't been aware plagued him until it melted away beneath the silvery peal of Miss Bainbridge's laugh, the shimmer of her gaze, the warmth of her fingers.

Instinct warned him to run. Now, more than ever, he could not. The key to whatever misdeeds had been going on in the county, regarding prisoners at Dartmoor, centered on Bainbridge, Miss Honore Bainbridge's home.

15

The inner warmth of peace—he would even go so far as to say the first happiness he had felt since leaving America and his family—began to dissipate as soon as he bade Miss Bainbridge goodbye and started for home with Philo. Now that he was away from her charming determination and forthright manner, not to mention her fair face and form, thoughts of treachery—thoughts treacherous all in themselves—stole into his mind and overwhelmed his spirit.

"That they'd use Bainbridge makes a great deal of sense," he told Philo. "The family has been away from the house for over a year."

Philo propped his feet on the opposite seat of the carriage and leaned into a corner. "The steward has been there."

"He lives in a house outside the walls and rarely goes to the house."

"How would you know a thing like that?" Philo yawned. "Not that it matters."

"Chilcott told me. I think it was to show his superiority to Tuckfield, since he lives in the house and dines with the family."

Philo laughed. "Those two growling and snapping over Miss

Morrow. She's pretty enough, but must be even older than you are."

"And they are older than that. She is a pretty and kind lady. And her birth is impeccable, you know."

The brothers laughed at Meric's imitation of Chilcott's prim pronouncement regarding people's family connections.

"Ours aren't." Philo rubbed his eyes. "You were born aboard a derelict merchantman, and I was born in a log cabin in the woods. Hardly noble birthplaces."

"It's what's in the blood that matters here." Meric scowled at the passing scenery beyond the window. The cliff ran close to the road there, and a vista of sea and sky opened like the vast plains of grass beyond the great Mississippi River that Meric had read about and sometimes thought might be worth seeing. "And ours may be tainted from Father's."

Since Philo seemed to doze in his corner, neither of them spoke until they slowed to enter the mews where the carriage and horses were stabled at the top of the cliff-set town. Then Philo dropped his feet to the floor with an impact that rattled the vehicle and sat forward. "It's hopeless, isn't it? We'll never clear his name."

"Or keep me from getting arrested for doing something treasonous? Sometimes I am afraid not."

"Mother would say to pray about it."

"Mother says to pray about everything."

But her prayers hadn't kept Father alive nor put enough food on the table those first years after his death. On the other hand, God was providing now—abundantly.

If only You will show me the right way to go.

For that day, the right way to go—socially, if not spiritually—was a picnic with the Devenish family and others. Expecting poor fare as he had received on his other visits to the Devenishes, he dined on bread and cheese before he left. Philo joined him, then declined to go along.

"I thought I'd go down to Ashmoor and do some riding." Philo's gaze shifted around the room and color touched his high cheekbones. "I find I like the odorous beasts."

"One of us should. You can learn to ride well, and then you can teach me instead of one of these uppity English grooms." Meric grinned. "But Miss Babbage will miss you."

"Miss *Baggage* had best keep missing me with every handkerchief she drops my way."

"Miss Baggage?" Meric raised a brow.

Philo grimaced. "She is not as virtuous as these ladies all pretend to be. The other night . . . But I'm not a gentleman if I tell."

"She got a bit bold, did she?" Meric's lips twitched. "You looked a bit red when you came into the drawing room."

"And I'll say she looked pleased with herself. Is she trying to get me in a compromising position or something?"

"Maybe she is, but tell her you're going back to America as soon as I set up my nursery, and she'll run as fast as she can."

"No, she won't." Philo shook his head. "She says she will persuade me to stay."

"A pair of willing lips on a pretty girl has persuaded many a man from more important courses."

"Perish the thought." Philo shuddered, then rose and went to the door, where he hesitated a moment before saying, "Unlike you, I don't have torn loyalties. I am an American, born and bred."

Long after his younger brother left the dining room, Meric stared at the blank panels of the door, the bread turning to the consistency of unleavened dough in his middle. Philemon Poole felt no loyalty to England. To him, it was the land that had made a false accusation against his father, condemning him and his family to a life of back-breaking labor that ultimately killed Father, then imprisoned the heirs for no crime other than not leaving for Britain early enough to arrive before the war began. With that attitude, Philo just might have fallen in with a bad crowd there in Devonshire, a crowd bad enough to get him to help French prisoners escape from Dartmoor with the purpose of freeing American prisoners eventually.

Meric gave himself a hard shake like a dog coming in from the rain. This was ridiculous. If he kept up with his string of suspicions, he would be blaming the vicar and his sister for conspiring against the Crown.

With images of Philo's fatigue, though they had all been in their rooms by midnight the night before, Meric climbed the steps to his room to consult with Huntley as to proper attire for a picnic. "Something I can move in freely."

"I am afraid, my lord, that you will not look fashionable in such attire." Huntley looked like he held half of a lemon's juice in his mouth. "The best I can do is a pair of buckskins and that dark brown coat."

"And a kerchief instead of a cravat?" Meric asked hopefully.

An invisible hand inserted the rest of the lemon's juice. "My lord, I would never be able to hold my head up with the other gentlemen's gentlemen if you did such a thing. For shooting, perhaps. For riding alone about your estate, perhaps. But to a social event? Never so long as I draw breath."

"Heaven forfend I should shorten those breaths." Laughing despite the notion of getting trussed up like a chicken going to market, Meric allowed his valet to choose his garb and guide him through the intricacies of tying a cravat.

"You are learning well, my lord." A sugarplum's sweetness replaced the lemon juice.

Meric departed, hands in his coat pockets to stop himself from running a finger between the collar and his throat. He took the carriage again. He would have to find some way to exercise if he didn't walk around the countryside. Otherwise, he feared resembling Mr. Devenish, Carolina Devenish's brother, more Philo's age than Meric's and already sporting a paunch barely concealed beneath his fine coats. For now, he settled himself back against the cushions—called *squabs* for some reason no one could explain to him—and tried to think of appropriate avenues of conversation for the afternoon.

The weather—fine.

The harvest—acceptable.

The viands—not at all appropriate considering Mrs. Devenish couldn't set a fine table. The only time she had provided decent refreshments was that night of the musical soirée, when a disaster got them begging from people they wouldn't invite to their house.

When he arrived in the garden, where the picnic consisted of tables moved outdoors instead of set inside the house, Meric discovered his efforts at conversational gambits were unnecessary. Everyone was speaking of Lord Bainbridge's imminent arrival in the county.

"Such a pity he is bringing his fiancée," Miss Babbage was saying as Meric approached the small company. "I thought one of us would surely have the opportunity to make a—ah, Lord Ashmoor, welcome. We are discussing Lord Bainbridge's arrival. Have you met him, the new one, that is?"

"I haven't had the privilege."

And hoped he didn't. He might be tempted to plant him a facer for how he was treating his sister.

"We have known him all our lives." Miss Devenish's cheeks were pink. "I thought him well deserving of the name Beau."

"Beau?" Meric stared at her. "Bainbridge's name is Beau?"

"Not really," Miss Babbage said. "It is something dull like Richard or John, but his family called him Beau from the time he was an infant."

"And he is." Miss Catherine Devenish sighed.

"So I think we shall have to have a ball in their honor," Miss Devenish said with haste.

"And speaking of Lord Bainbridge," Miss Babbage said in her languid way, "will you have to invite the sister?"

"When even he will not have her in the house?" Miss Devenish tossed her head, sending a cloud of rose scent wafting around the now flowerless garden.

Half expecting a swarm of confused bees to arrive, Meric took an involuntary step back. He hadn't noticed her giving the perfume too lavish a hand in the past, nor being spiteful to another female. But the look on her face at the mention of Miss Bainbridge was downright hostile.

Defense of Miss Bainbridge burned on the end of his tongue. The way the young women and a couple of men, whose names eluded Meric, leaned toward Miss Devenish said no defense would be accepted. So he excused himself to procure a cup of tea, since no coffee was apparent, and fall into a conversation about hunting with the fathers of the young ladies.

Hunting, he had long since learned, had nothing to do with stalking deer to put food on the table. It meant riding to hounds somewhere in the northern counties in pursuit of a fox that had likely done no one harm. Men broke their limbs and even their necks in galloping across fields full of rabbit holes and leaping over hedges, but it stopped none of those who were hunting mad.

"You are welcome to join us at our hunting box in Lancashire," Devenish said to Meric. "Can set you up with a fine gelding up to your weight."

"Not this year, thank you." Or the next, or the next . . . "I have other matters I should be seeing to," he concluded.

"Like setting up your nursery, eh?" Devenish nudged him in the ribs hard enough to slosh the tea in his cup.

Meric gave him a noncommittal smile, made his excuses, and wandered to another group of men discussing the American war.

"They are fools if they think they can defeat us."

"We will get our colonies back and then some, mark my word. They cannot win a land battle to save their lives."

"Or their country."

The men laughed.

Meric bit back the urge to remind these men how many British merchantmen had lost their ships and cargoes to American privateers. The United States might lose everything to Great Britain's superior strength, but they would see that the island empire suffered in the meantime.

But he dared not voice his opinion on that either.

He glanced around for another group of people to join, one with whom perhaps he could express his viewpoint on even a minor issue. None materialized from the score or so of people present, so he turned toward his hostess, forming some excuse to leave.

Miss Devenish latched on his arm. "Oh, do come back and join us, my lord. We are considering getting up a party to attend the harvest moon assembly in Clovelly tomorrow night. It will be full of yokels, but ever so much fun for that. We will dress up like peasants like Marie Antoinette did."

"Have a hankering for being guillotined?" He smiled to make a jest of his words.

Miss Devenish and the others who had joined her laughed.

He refrained from pointing out that a true harvest moon was the full moon within two weeks of the autumnal equinox, which October eighth was not. No sense in spoiling their pleasure. No sense in staying home alone with a gloomy Chilcott either.

"All right," he agreed, "I'll come."

"And do bring your brother." Miss Babbage's smile held something in it that Meric called less than ladylike.

He shook his head. "He's off to Ashmoor for a few days. And now I should be off home too. I have ledgers calling my name."

A bevy of protests rained upon him. He bowed over several hands, nearly carried Miss Devenish's to his lips, remembered how dull the afternoon had been with him having to keep his mouth shut at literally every turn, and refrained.

Did he truly want to commit himself to a lifetime of this? It surely could not be what God wanted for him.

Inside the house, he waited in the entry hall between two stone-faced footmen while his carriage was brought around. If he were walking, he could have simply departed and been a mile toward home by the time the vehicle rumbled up to the door. Climbing up for the solitary journey to travel inside a wooden box like a piece of jewelry, he considered learning to drive a showy team and purchasing a curricle. That way he could drive himself. His coachman could teach him. The man never spoke a word, but he drove well.

The idea of taking up sporting driving was such a fine notion, he began to envision the sporting vehicles he had seen in London—the colors that would suit him, the sort of team, if he would hire a boy to stand behind—

A giant's fist seemed to slam into the side of the carriage, knocking Meric into the corner of the seat. His head struck the side of the vehicle. Ears ringing from the impact, he tried to right himself. His head spun. He was still off balance. Sunlight blazed too brightly through one window, the sea shimmered and sparkled far below the other.

Sea in one, sky in the other.

He wasn't off balance. The carriage was tilting, teetering on the edge of the cliff.

He flung himself at the window. Too small for him. The door was on the downward side. If he exited that way, he would tumble two hundred feet to his death. But if he didn't get out, he would tumble two hundred feet to his death.

He shoved at the hatch in the roof. The carriage rocked, swayed, slid farther over the edge.

And the hatch didn't move.

Shouting he knew not what, he kicked at the window, smashing glass, splintering the frame. Each blow rocked the carriage further. Wood and steel creaked and groaned. No coachman shouted. No horses whinnied. Only the vehicle protesting and his boot heels slamming, slamming—

A panel sprang free of the carriage's side. Meric threw himself through it, ripping his coat, his shirt, his arm on the splinters.

He landed on scrubby vegetation and rocks at the top of the cliff. Clung to all, clambering to the road. Behind him, the carriage gave a final groan and rolled down, down, down, then the drop grew precipitous and the coach took flight until it smashed on the rocks at the edge of the sea.

The horses and coachman did not go with it. They were nowhere in sight.

16

"You will go to the assembly with me tomorrow night, will you not?" Miss Morrow's eyes pleaded with Honore from across the dinner table.

Honore widened her eyes back. "And not allow Mr. Tuckfield to have you all to himself for once? I doubt he will appreciate that."

"I need a chaperone, and who better than you?"

Honore laughed. "Almost anyone, I expect the rest of the county will say."

"But the rest of the county will not be there. At least not those who . . . would disapprove of you. It will mostly be freehold farmers and tradesmen and the like. They will be honored at your presence."

"Possibly."

None of them shunned her in church as did her peers. On the contrary, they treated her with the same affectionate respect they always had.

"But I doubt my brother will approve."

"Your brother, if you will forgive me for speaking so bluntly, has not placed himself in a place to approve or not." Frost dripped from Miss Morrow's tone. "And he is not your guardian, is he?"

"No, Christien—that is, Monsieur de Meuse, my sister Lydia's husband—is my guardian. Still . . ."

The idea of music and dancing and spinning around the floor to a reel, even with some ham-handed farmer as her partner, sounded better than sitting in her bedchamber half emptied of her belongings as the maids and footmen carried them to the dower house.

"You know you love to dance," Miss Morrow pressed as though reading Honore's mind. "And it has been long enough since your father's death for a local party like this."

"Yes, nine months for a father is quite long enough, and yes, I love to dance. But it will be odd to arrive with my steward." She tilted her head and observed Miss Morrow through her lashes. "I am surprised you are not going with Mr. Chilcott."

"Mr. Chilcott did not invite me." The frost turned to icicles. "And I would not have gone with him had he done so."

"Indeed? Why is that?"

Miss Morrow bowed her head as though concentrating on making a cross with her knife and fork, then an *X*, and then a cross again. "He is not even officially courting me and thinks he can tell me what is good for me."

"Indeed? Such as?"

Miss Morrow pushed back her chair. "Just do, please, come with me. The likes of the Devenishes and Babbages will not be there to criticize you."

Nor, in that event, would Lord Ashmoor. But a night filled with music and Cornish pasties would keep her from moping over the fact that his lordship had gone off to a picnic at the Devenishes' house that afternoon. She hoped he choked on chicken as dry as Devonshire rock. She hoped he recalled the fine repast she had served him though she had not expected a guest. She hoped he had an absolutely terrible time and left early.

"All right," she said, "I will go."

"Wonderful." Miss Morrow went to the door. "Shall we go see what we can wear?"

Nothing too fancy for the expected assembly. Honore pulled out a gown from her Season the previous year, one of the few in a color other than white—a pale rose muslin with a pattern of silver leaves embroidered around the neck and hem and a broad band down the front of the skirt. She gave Miss Morrow a similar dress in pale primrose with gold embroidery, and they settled themselves in a small parlor to add a flounce to the bottom to accommodate for Miss Morrow's greater height. As with most of their evenings, this one ran its course in quiet talk of books, of the novel Honore was trying to write when she found the time, of things they must remember to take to the dower house the next day in the event Lord Bainbridge arrived on Saturday.

Honore had just risen to order some light refreshment when someone hammered on the front door as though using a battering ram rather than the knocker. She jumped, yanking the bellpull so hard half of it broke off in her hand. Miss Morrow stabbed a needle into her finger and gasped with a little squeak.

"Bad news!" Honore cried. "No one knocks like that except with bad news."

One of her sisters had died in childbed. It happened all the time. Nothing else mattered so much to make such a cacophony.

She darted for the door, eyes burning.

"Miss Bainbridge, wait," Miss Morrow called.

"I cannot. If it is Lydia or Cassandra, I promise I will—" She flung open the parlor door.

Lord Ashmoor stumbled over the threshold, fairly knocking Soames off his feet. "Where is that mine engineer?"

"My lord, I—"

"My lord!" Honore's cry rang above the butler's protest.

Ashmoor's coat and shirt were torn. Blood stained the ragged edges. Dirt streaked his face, and his hair looked as though someone had shoved their hands into it and tried to lift him by the roots.

"Miss Bainbridge, I beg your pardon for this intrusion." He was breathing hard as though he had been running, was in pain, or both. "If you please, I must speak to Polhenny."

"Then fetch him, Soames," she commanded the butler.

"Miss Bainbridge—"

She glared at him. "And fetch tea—no, coffee—into the parlor immediately." Softening her voice, she turned back to Ashmoor. "My lord, do come sit by the fire."

"There's no need. I can wait here."

"And fall down on this marble floor? I think not." She clasped his hand and led him into the parlor.

"I'll get your chairs dirty."

Honore rested her hand on his shoulder and pushed him onto a plain wooden seat. "This will wipe clean. Now tell us what happened. An accident? Were you set upon by highwaymen?"

"I honestly don't know. I was returning from the Devenish picnic, and my carriage—" He stopped. "I shouldn't trouble you ladies with this."

"If you stop—" Honore did not need to come up with an appropriate threat, as a footman arrived with the news that Mr. Polhenny had been sent for and would arrive momentarily.

Calmer after the servant's departure, Honore turned back to Ashmoor. "My lord, you know I am no milk-and-water miss, and neither is Miss Morrow."

"I know, but this—" He covered the jagged hole in his sleeve with his hand.

Miss Morrow stood. "I shall have one of the footmen see you to a room where you can make yourself a bit more presentable. The housekeeper has a fair hand at doctoring. She can see to that gash on your arm."

In moments, servants whisked Ashmoor away. They would attempt to find him something to wear, but none of the Bainbridge men had ever been quite so large as Ashmoor.

Honore looked to her companion, shaking and lacking the will to hide it. "What could have happened?"

"He has been attacked in some way, that is obvious."

"But why the insistence on seeing Mr. Polhenny? That is, I suppose he could have been foolish enough to walk home from the Devenish party and had difficulties with the cliffs too. But that seems highly unlikely. I haven't heard of the cliffs falling away twice in one year."

"And only at all after hard rains, which we have not had," Miss Morrow murmured.

Honore started to ask what her companion meant, but a footman arrived with the requested coffee plus several platters of simple viands—apple slices and cheese from the Cheddar Gorge in nearby Somerset, a plate of macaroons, and another of tiny cakes.

"Cook is so good to me." Honore's eyes stung. She was turning into a regular watering pot of late. "We shall wait for his lordship." She tried to sit but managed to for only a handful of minutes, then sprang up and paced the room, tried to sit again, leaped up and paced some more.

What felt like an eternity later but was only a quarter hour by the hands of the ormolu clock on the mantel, Ashmoor returned wearing a clean but many times mended shirt that must have belonged to a groom or gardener, for it fit him well in shoulders and arms. Whose ever it was, Honore would give him two new ones for being so generous. As for Ashmoor, his face, though free of dirt, still looked pale, his eyes the dark swirl of forest hues, absent of the flecks of gold.

He returned to the wooden chair despite his breeches having been brushed clean, accepting a cup of coffee from Honore with a smile that did not quite reach his eyes. "You are hospitable as always." He cradled the cup as though his hands were cold. "I should have gone on to Clovelly, but my brother isn't home, and I would like Polhenny to look at something on the cliffs, if you will be so kind as to lend him to me."

"Of course, and you are welcome here." Honore called on her training to remain a gracious lady rather than a silly chit who too easily tumbled head over heels for the wrong man. "But please, tell us what has happened to you."

"Of course." He downed half of his coffee, and some color returned to his face. "I think I must tell you." He set his cup on a side table and clasped his hands on his knees. "My carriage went over the cliff."

"The horses, your coachman!" Honore cried.

"How?" Miss Morrow demanded.

"How indeed?" Ashmoor nodded at Miss Morrow. "That is why I wish to see Polhenny for his opinion. As to the horses and coachman?" He turned his gaze on Honore, and the gold lights returned with a softness that set her belly quivering. "You are kind to think of them, but all I can tell you is that they did not go over the cliff with the carriage—or me, as I believe I was expected to go."

"Believe you were expected to go?" Honore slid off her chair to her knees. "But, my lord, that would mean someone—are you saying someone tried to kill you?"

"That's exactly what I mean. The coachman freed himself and the team while I was teetering on the edge of the cliff."

"But how? Why?" Honore persisted.

"The coachman would simply have had to jump off the box and cut the traces for the horses." He breathed hard as though running. "Disappearing is easy, especially if he was paid to do me in and he sells the horses."

"How did you free yourself, my lord?" Miss Morrow asked. "I presume the door was on the downward side if you were returning home."

"Yes, indeed it was. And the hatch appeared to be jammed shut." He stared at the mangled toes of his boots. "I kicked out the side of the carriage, and not a moment too soon."

Honore's head spun. She pressed her hands to her temples to steady herself. "This is awful. This is beyond awful. We should send for a constable. We must find your coachman. Where is your brother? Shall I send a groom to fetch him? No one goes about trying to send peers off the cliffs. It is barbaric, unconscionable. It is—"

"Shh." Ashmoor crouched before her. He cupped her chin in his hand and brushed the pad of his thumb across her lips. "I'm alive. That's all that matters for the time being. It might have simply been a terrible accident and my coachman ran off to fetch help. Right now he might be frantic, thinking I am at the bottom of the cliff with the carriage."

"Yes. Yes." Honore's heart raced. Breathing proved difficult, and the affirmative words emerged in a breathy whisper.

"May I send a groom to Clovelly and down to Ashmoor to assure them I'm well?"

"Yes, of course, straightaway. I will give the order." Honore started to rise.

"I will go." Miss Morrow sprang up and left the room.

Ashmoor caught Honore beneath the elbows and lifted her to her feet, then stood holding her arms and gazing down at her. "You are kind to a man who all but jilted you outright, Miss Bainbridge."

"You saved my life. This is the least I can do."

"Indeed." He released her and stepped back hard enough to send his chair skittering across the floor. "I believe Mr. Polhenny has arrived."

"Has he?" Honore heard nothing through the roaring in her ears, the racing and pounding of her heart.

She did not care about mine engineers or carriage accidents. She wanted to cup her fingers over her lips and preserve the tender caress of his thumb, somehow more intimate, more appealing than the naughty kisses she had received from the two men who had lured her into their nets, then ruined her reputation.

She dropped onto her chair before her knees gave way.

Mr. Polhenny, with Tuckfield and Miss Morrow close behind, entered the parlor. No one invited the men to sit. Miss Morrow moved to stand beside Honore's chair, her hand on her shoulder, and the three men stood in the center of the carpet while Ashmoor told his story again.

"What is it you wish to know, my lord?" Polhenny asked at the end of exclamations over the incident.

"If the cliff gave way on purpose or by accident." Ashmoor's tone was calm, matter-of-fact.

Honore shivered. Miss Morrow's hand tightened on her shoulder.

"I see. Aye, that makes sense to wonder under the circumstances." Polhenny clasped his hands behind his back and glanced around the room. "'Tis strange circumstances to me. And I can do naught now. Even with the moon nigh full, 'tis still too dark for a good inspection."

"I doubt anything will change by morning," Ashmoor said. "Can you meet me there at, say, eight o'clock in the morning?"

"Aye, but I can tell you one thing now, my lord."

"Not in front of the ladies," Tuckfield admonished him.

Honore made herself rise. "What, Mr. Polhenny? Have you learned something about our cliff?"

"Aye, and I think you've a right to know." Polhenny glared at Tuckfield.

"I am trying to spare your sensibilities, Miss Bainbridge. His lordship—Lord Bainbridge, that is—can hear—"

"Tell me." Honore barely stopped herself from stomping her foot. "I was the one who nearly fell off that cliff when it broke. I have a right to know why it happened."

"Aye, that is my thinking." Mr. Polhenny gave her a slight bow, then looked to Ashmoor. "You see, that cliff didn't break apart from natural causes."

17

Miss Bainbridge turned as white as the kerchief around her neck, and Meric closed the distance between them to clasp her hand between both of his. Beside him, Tuckfield slipped his arm around Miss Morrow, also the color of new-fallen snow.

"Why?" Miss Bainbridge whispered. "Why would someone be so—so cruel as to risk someone's life?"

"I suspect that's the idea." Meric's jaw hardened. "To take a life."

"But why?" Miss Bainbridge repeated.

"Who is usually in the way of walking those cliffs?" Polhenny asked.

Everyone looked at Miss Bainbridge.

Her fingers moved convulsively in Meric's, and he laced his fingers through hers, holding them fast. Improper or not, she needed something solid to cling to, and he was the most appropriate person present.

"Don't be too hasty," he told her. "You had just gotten home, hadn't you?"

"The day before, but it was raining, so I did not go for my usual walk. Oh my, oh my." She pressed her free hand to her brow.

"'Tis sorry I am to overset you so, Miss Bainbridge," Polhenny began.

"I told you not to tell her," Tuckfield lashed out. "See how you have distressed the ladies?"

"No, no, I am glad he told us." Miss Bainbridge didn't release Meric's hand. "I am all right, truly, just a bit shaken. No one would wish to be rid of me, I am quite, quite certain. It makes no sense. Killing me off solves nothing."

"And killing me off only benefits my brother," Meric said. "And I wouldn't suspect Philo for a moment."

He wouldn't say why. No one needed to know that Philo's loyalties lay with America and the last thing he would want was an English peerage. These Englishmen and women wouldn't understand caring about anyplace but Great Britain, especially not an upstart nation like the United States with its joke of a Navy and poorly led Army.

"We do not know for certain anyone wanted you dead on purpose, my lord," Tuckfield pointed out. "But I understand why you presume so." The steward turned to Miss Morrow, who wasn't objecting to the man's arm around her. "Do you still wish to attend the assembly tomorrow?"

She smiled. "Of course. We shall all attend. It is just the thing to distract us. But right now, I think I would like to go to my room. Miss Bainbridge?"

She slid her fingers from Meric's with gratifying slowness. "I must go too, then. Mr. Tuckfield, will you see that Lord Ashmoor has everything he needs? A way home? And all of you, feel free to eat what is here. No sense in letting it go to waste." Dropping him the most graceful curtsy he had seen a female give anyone, Miss Bainbridge followed her companion from the room.

"I think I'd prefer to walk home," Meric said.

"My lord, it is all of five miles," Tuckfield protested.

"Then I shall fortify myself first. But right now, I feel safer on my own feet than in any vehicle. I only wish I had a horse pistol along."

"I can help you with that if you feel more comfortable." Tuckfield glanced at the plates of food from Miss Bainbridge, such a kind and generous lady.

Kind, generous, and poised. The news had overset her all right, but she had regained her composure in moments and intended to go to a party the following night—a party he was committed to attending with the neighbors who had decided to ostracize her.

Foreseeing a different sort of trouble brewing beyond damaged cliffs, Meric asked the two men to join him, then proceeded to quiz Polhenny about how he knew the cliff had been tampered with.

"Even after these two weeks or more, my lord, a body can see the marks of hammer and chisel. There are natural cracks in the rock, and someone drove in wedges to make them worse. If a body could look, I'd wager we'd find those spikes in the sea."

"Along with Miss Bainbridge's shoe," Meric murmured.

The two men stared at him.

He shook his head. "Never mind me. Thinking aloud. Do continue, Polhenny."

Polhenny continued with descriptions of erosion marks from rain and wind and roots digging into the rock versus those fissures created by the hand of man. Meric knew which they would find in the place where his carriage had gone off the road and struck the edge of the cliff.

That he'd gone off the road in the first place suggested something quite, quite amiss. The coachman had participated all the way. If he hadn't done the planning, he had at least carried out specific orders for someone else. If they ever found him . . .

But the coachman and horses were gone. A few minutes later, Chilcott arrived with the information that neither servant nor team had returned to the mews stables.

"I have informed the constable," Chilcott said, "but I doubt we will ever see man or beasts again."

Chilcott had ridden out to Bainbridge and brought an extra mount for Meric, a beast he agreed to ride back simply because it boasted a brace of pistols with the saddle. On the way back to town, they dismounted long enough to study the area where the carriage had left the road for its final journey over the cliff. Scarred rock gleamed white in the moon's glow.

"Why?" Meric asked aloud.

"Someone doesn't want you finding answers," Chilcott suggested. "Either whoever is smuggling prisoners out of the country, or whoever killed that revenue man twenty-eight years ago."

"They wasted their efforts. I have no knowledge to even hint at whom it might be."

"You must know something and not realize it," Chilcott said.

The thought plagued Meric in sleep that night and upon waking the next morning. The thought plagued him as he met Polhenny at the site of the mishap, heard him say the carriage's iron wheels had created too much damage of their own for any other marks to come through with clarity. "I do not know why this has eroded so, though, milord," the mine engineer admitted. "Seems odd."

"And should be repaired at once?" Meric suggested.

"Aye, that it should." Polhenny stroked his chin and stared into space. "It cannot be done until spring, I'm thinking, like the Bainbridge cliffs. The weather is too uncertain."

"Then we must put up warning signs," Meric said.

Polhenny shrugged. He was the engineer. Warning signs were not his duty.

"Are the Bainbridges having their cliffs repaired in the spring?" Meric asked.

Polhenny sighed. "Tuckfield tells me nothing can be done without his lordship's permission, and that I may not receive before I must return to Cornwall."

"I will talk to his lordship," Meric said.

He would try to get the work done before spring, he decided, then nearly forgot the cliffs as he made plans with Chilcott to purchase new carriage horses and order a new coach. He would get his curricle at the same time. Now, more than ever, he was determined to drive himself about rather than sit back and be delivered like a sheep to the slaughter.

Not in the best of humors, he would have begged off from meeting the Devenish party at the harvest moon assembly ball that night, but Miss Bainbridge would be there. He couldn't leave her to her own devices like a canary amongst a colony of cats. He should have warned her ahead of time. Yet if he had, she wouldn't attend, and the dear girl needed some entertainment in her life. From the way they had talked the day before, the Devenish crowd merely intended to make an appearance then leave. They would expect him to leave with them. If Miss Bainbridge was there, he had no intention of doing so.

Fortunately, everyone walked to the public assembly rooms, as they stood halfway down the steep hillside upon which the village perched. No vehicle except perhaps a handcart could maneuver the steep incline of the main street.

At Huntley's advice, Meric didn't arrive too early. Music and dancing was well under way by the time he and Chilcott strode into the main room. At least two score farmers, tradesmen, and their ladies cavorted around the floor to country dances bearing little resemblance to their more sedate counterparts performed in the ballrooms of the haut ton. The thunder of roughshod feet on wooden floorboards nearly drowned out the two violins and a flute. A pity too. From what Meric caught, the musicians possessed more than a modicum of talent.

"They are not here yet," Chilcott called above the tumult. "I wonder if they have changed—" He broke off, for Miss Morrow sailed past at that moment, her hands firmly in the grip of a red-faced farmer.

The farmer was grinning from ear to ear. Miss Morrow's whole face glowed from the brilliance of her smile and bright eyes. She wore a pale yellow dress with a lacy frill at the bottom that swung out with each turn, displaying just the hint of a dainty ankle.

Meric felt rather than heard Chilcott's sigh.

He grinned at his steward. "You'll have to cut in, I believe it's called."

"Terribly rude. I shall wait until the music ends."

But the music didn't end. Each set spun directly into the next. By some form of signals, partners changed, the lines of dancers shifted into the right formation, and the skipping, spinning, and dipping commenced again.

Without a sign of Miss Honore Bainbridge.

If Miss Morrow was present, surely Miss Bainbridge was too. Meric stepped over the threshold of the door left open to allow the brisk night wind off the sea to keep the chambers cool. Even so, the odors of burning candle wax, perspiration, and a quantity of perfume created a cloud in the room nearly thick enough to see. Through another doorway, Meric caught a glimpse of tables and older women laying out a veritable feast for what would surely be famished dancers. He skirted the crowd to peer inside the dining room for a glimpse of Miss Bainbridge. She wasn't there either. Unless she had gone outside, which she would surely never do alone in town, she must be in the room with the dancing.

With care, he began to skirt the chamber. A few chairs had been set against the walls. All were occupied by older persons—fathers and mothers chaperoning their daughters, or maybe men accompanying younger wives to the festivities. Two chairs were occupied by young women whose plain appearances had probably condemned them to going without partners. So unfair. They deserved to enjoy themselves too.

Vowing to invite both of them to join him for a set, Meric turned another corner and found Miss Bainbridge. She sat behind the two men with violins, whose size had blocked her from view and whose instruments had drowned out the tinkling of the ancient harpsichord she played.

For several moments, he could only gaze upon her. She perched on the edge of a three-legged stool, her back straight, her head tilted so her eyes rested on the other three musicians. And her fingers flew over the keys as swiftly as the bows swooped across the violin strings. A smile played about her lips, a secretive smile, as though she knew something no one else had yet worked out.

There was something Meric was working out—the state of his heart whenever he found himself in her company. It began when he saw her so bravely clinging to that sapling on the edge of a crumbling cliff—the prick of Cupid's arrow. Watching her in her gown the color of a rosebud with silver sparkling at each movement of her arms, her joy in the music . . .

The arrow nearly struck all the way home.

Logic, the same sense that told him she was exactly the wrong wife for him, warned him he should run. He should go home and avoid all contact with her in the future. Yet he could not. He needed her help. Whatever was amiss on the north shore of Devonshire, Bainbridge was somehow involved. She was possibly involved. He needed an excuse to call at Bainbridge, and she was the best one.

She was indeed the best one.

She understood they could have no future together, that he needed a wife above scandal and rumor to lend his own sullied name consequence. She had offered him friendship, nothing more. She had, without realizing it, shown him that in no way could he wed Miss Carolina Devenish.

As though the very thought brought her near, a flurry of movement in the doorway drew his attention—drew everyone's attention. The music ground to a halt. The dancing slowed and stopped like an automaton whose clockwork mechanism had run down. Across the chamber, half a dozen ladies and gentlemen spilled into the room wearing what was apparently their notion of country dress. The ladies wore bodices that laced up the front, but not quite far enough for modesty, and wide dark skirts a little too short. On their feet they wore their satin dancing slippers, in absurd contrast to the plain cotton of their other garb. Likewise the young gentlemen wore rough woolen breeches, waistcoats, and full-sleeved shirts with no coats. They, at least, wore boots instead of evening pumps.

"Do not stop on our account!" Miss Babbage cried. "We have come for the dancing also."

"But we need partners," Miss Jane Devenish said, then burst into a peal of giggles.

A young farmer with bold, dark eyes strode forward and

grasped her hand. "I'll partner with you then, milady. Music, lads. Get up the mu—"

"Wait!" Miss Babbage's cry froze everyone in place. "Is that not Miss Bainbridge at that wreck of a harpsichord? How droll that she has stooped so low. Do play something for us, dear Miss Bainbridge. I see the gentleman I wish to invite me to dance." Her gaze fell on Meric.

He bowed. "I beg your pardon, Miss Babbage. I am spoken for this dance, and so is Miss Bainbridge."

Before she could give him a by-your-leave, he clasped Miss Bainbridge's hand and drew her from the stool. With his other hand, he dropped a crown into the open violin case on the floor. "Play a good long set."

"My lord, you cannot," Miss Bainbridge said through clenched teeth. "They will never forgive you."

"And for what Miss Babbage just did, I will never forgive her."

Not a Christian thought to have. At that moment, he felt none of the spirit of love and grace he knew he should. No forgiveness reigned where a young woman could make mistakes in her youth—where she had been left too much to her own devices, neglected by the standards his parents had employed with the eight of their surviving children—and be not merely ostracized but publicly ridiculed by her peers.

He pulled her into the nearest set as the music began with a few hesitant notes warbled on the flute, then a long string of notes drawn out from a bow, and then the full swing of the music launching into the atmosphere.

"People here like you if they asked you to play." He managed to get the comment out before the dance separated them.

Feet stomped, skirts flowed out like draperies billowing in a high wind, the lines of dancers moved. Meric spun Miss

Bainbridge into the hands of a green grocer and found himself partnered with a pretty matron no taller than his middle waistcoat button, then he was with Miss Morrow. She took the time to mouth, "Thank you," and then he held Miss Bainbridge's hands again.

"They did not ask me. I invited myself," she told him.

"Hiding out?"

From the corner of his eye, he spied Misses Devenish and Babbage pressed against the wall near the door as though afraid someone would trample on their satin slippers. Their male companions had entered the dance, and Miss Jane hopped and skipped with the best of the country folk, but the two who had initiated this mockery of the harvest ball and then tried to humiliate Miss Bainbridge had joined the wallflowers.

As he had instructed, the music played longer than a usual set of three dances at a time, adding three more. By the time they drew the last reel to a conclusion, everyone was mopping brows and calling for refreshments.

"I'll fetch you some cider," Meric told Miss Bainbridge.

She took a step back from him. "No, do not. I-I shall fetch my own. You must make repairs with the Devenish crowd." Spinning on her flat-heeled slipper, she ducked beneath the upraised arms of two stonemasons and vanished toward the refreshment room.

Meric could not follow without pushing aside two men larger even than he. Only one path lay open to him, a path directly past Misses Devenish and Babbage.

"Time for my medicine," he grumbled, then he headed straight for them.

They stuck their pretty noses in the air, nostrils pinched as though he smelled bad, which he just might after all that vigorous exercise. The notion made him smile.

"You may smile now," Miss Devenish snapped, "but you won't be smiling when we neglect to invite you to our next social engagement."

"Mama was just about to send out the invitations to our harvest ball," Miss Babbage added. "After she hears about tonight, I expect yours will be removed from the list."

"A pity," Meric said. "I'll have to seek a wife farther afield."

"As if anyone of note will have a man who consorts with the likes of that Bainbridge baggage." Miss Devenish's cheeks burned with hectic color, and tears shone in her eyes. Rage or frustration?

Both. She knew her words held no teeth. A number of eligible females would be more than happy to accept his suit. He had hoped not to have to leave Devonshire but would if he must.

"She demeaned herself by playing music with these . . . ruffians," Miss Babbage persisted. "It is almost worse than dangling after a traitor and a murderer. Once Mama tells her brother, I expect he will send her into isolation."

"I believe," Meric drawled, "that the rest of you already have. Now I am off for some refreshment, so I shall bid you good night." He bowed to them, then slipped through the crowd to the refreshment room.

He couldn't find Miss Bainbridge in there. He procured a tankard of freshly pressed cider, drained it, then kept searching. After a quarter hour or so, he found Miss Morrow hemmed between Tuckfield and Chilcott as though they were about to grab her arms and begin a game of tug-of-war. He considered offering to rescue her. She, however, was laughing, so he simply asked if she had seen Miss Bainbridge.

"I thought she was with you, my lord." Miss Morrow's face sobered. "Perhaps I should go—"

"No, no, I'll go find her."

He continued his hunt through a withdrawing room for those wishing quieter entertainment, and once again into the ballroom. The Devenish party had departed, and Miss Bainbridge was nowhere to be seen.

He started asking people in the crowd. They all knew who she was and offered to hunt for her, but none had seen her for several minutes.

"Why'd that lady have to be so unkind to her?" one little maid asked. "She never does naught but be kind to folk."

"Some ladies are jealous," Meric said.

The girl nodded. "She is pretty."

She was better than pretty. She was strong and kind and intelligent and—

"Milord." An apprentice tapped Meric on the shoulder. "The young miss you're looking for is outside." He leered. "It's a fair night."

It was a fair night, but she had no business being out in it alone.

Meric thanked the boy, handed him a sixpence, and slipped outside. Many people milled about the lane, all couples with arms or hands entwined and faces turned up to the brilliant yellow glow of the full moon sailing right overhead. Meric passed them without so much as a nod and entered the main street running up and down the hill. No diminutive feminine figure descended the hill to the harbor, but a hundred feet up the incline to his left, a torch burning outside a shop lit a flash of pink and silver.

Meric closed the distance in seconds and dropped a hand onto her shoulder. She jumped and gasped, but didn't scream. She went perfectly still.

"You're lucky tonight, Miss Bainbridge, it's only me and not whoever wanted you to fall to your death on the rocks." His tone was deliberately harsh, and her shoulder rippled beneath his hand.

"I did not think about that," she whispered. "I just wanted to get away, to breathe air not befouled by those—those cats."

"Do not, please, malign the feline species. I happen to like cats."

"You happen to like Carolina Devenish too." She shrugged off his hand then and recommenced walking.

He joined her, tucking her hand beneath his elbow. "I don't care for the Devenishes much now."

"You will when you receive no more invitations."

"I doubt it."

"Ha! You will wish to make up to them and shun me like the social leper I have become. I understand how it is."

"I don't think you do understand."

A throng of inebriated-sounding young men charged up the hill, singing a song not fit for anyone's ears, let alone a lady's. Meric drew Miss Bainbridge into a side lane and stood in front of her, blocking her from the men's view, his hands over her ears.

They passed, and he slipped his hands from her ears but found his fingers entangled in her hair, masses of her hair rippling around his hands like skeins of silk glowing golden in the moonlight.

"I don't think you do understand," he repeated.

And then he kissed her. Her lips parted beneath his in an instant, perhaps in surprise, perhaps in a protest she didn't express in word, sound, or movement, or perhaps in welcome. The welcome of his caress was what mattered, the full softening of her mouth beneath his, her person leaning against him, her arms sliding around his neck. She tasted of cider, sweet and sharp just like her. She smelled of perfume, sweet and soft just like her. She felt like a lady he wanted the right to kiss every moonlit, dark, cold, wet, or balmy night—and again in the mornings.

The late Lord Bainbridge had been right. His third daughter was the perfect choice to be the next Lady Ashmoor. In those moments, as he gloried in the contact of their lips, he forgot why he had thought otherwise.

Then she drew away slowly, as though reluctant to do so, and murmured, "My reputation, my lord."

And he remembered she had associated with a traitor, and the taint could destroy his fragile hold on respectability. He remembered that she was practiced at kissing, by all reports. He had fallen into a trap of moonlight, a sweetly curved mouth, and a womanly figure, and she wasn't as innocent as she should be. Too close an association with Miss Honore Bainbridge could damage his reputation beyond repair until his own innocence was established.

With even more reluctance than she had shown, he let her go and ordered his heart not to demand he draw her back to him.

18

He had known what she meant by her reputation. He understood in an instant she had not meant that her consequence in the county would suffer if someone caught her kissing a man in a dark lane off the main street of the village. No, she meant *his* consequence would suffer for kissing *her* in a dark lane off the main street of the village. And the impact of him releasing his hold on her could not have hurt more had he shoved her tumbling down the hill and into the icy waters of the harbor.

She reached up to assess the damage to her coiffeur, found her hair a tangled mass of curls around her shoulders, and took a step back. "You had best return to the assembly rooms. You still may have a chance to repair the damage you created dancing with me in public."

"I can't leave you here alone." He reached out his hand to her. "I'll take you back to Miss Morrow."

"Looking like this?" Her hair was not merely a disaster, her lips felt . . . kissed, softer and fuller, still tingling.

All of her still tingled, except where her heart ached like a bruised limb.

"The church is along here. I will tuck myself upon the porch while you fetch Miss Morrow for me," she said.

"I wouldn't feel right leaving you alone with these drunken yokels cavorting about."

"Do you want to escort me home all the way to Bainbridge?"

"I, um . . ." He shoved his hands into his coat pockets and turned his face up to a moon that looked close enough to touch. "I'll be happy to escort you with Miss Morrow."

"And call on me tomorrow for a walk along the cliffs?" Honore swallowed a sudden lump in her throat. "Perhaps you will call on my brother when he arrives and ask permission to court me, though I do believe the kissing comes after the courtship has progressed, not before it s-s-starts."

"It takes two to kiss, Miss Honore Bainbridge, and I didn't feel you resisting, with or without a courtship."

"And that makes me a lady beyond the pale of acceptability, while you are merely a-a dashing rake and all the more desirable to the ladies of the haut ton." She crossed her arms over her waist and gripped her arms hard enough to hurt. "Well, that is quite all right then. Just do your dashing—right off to your acceptable ladies. I am going to the church."

She spun on her heel and tried to march along the lane. She stumbled instead, her toes catching in the rough cobblestones, her chest expanding to bursting with the wail of pain demanding release.

There just was no forgiveness. Her transgressions had occurred sixteen and eleven months ago. She had repented. She had spent hours on her knees begging God to set aside her follies with the male gender, make her a truly new creature, and give her a purpose in life, especially the kind of love her sisters enjoyed. Instead, this attractive rogue of a foreigner pulled her away from certain death, was kind to her, and won her heart. Another man who would do nothing for her reputation. He needed a respectable wife to ensure his reputation did not tarnish any more than having spent three months in prison—through no fault of his own—a father accused of murder, and suspicious military men dogging his heels at every lawless action in the county.

He dogged her heels. He said nothing, but he followed her down the lane to the church. She let herself through the gate and quite deliberately shut it between them, held the latch down so he could not release it from the other side, and scowled at him from over top of the bars.

"I am safe here," she assured him in a voice as cold as she could manage around the burning pain inside her. "Go back to the respectable ladies who do not kiss you back and will not tarnish your name . . . further."

The last was a jab, a mean and nasty one she regretted in an instant, yet did not admit she regretted.

"Miss Bainbridge." He released his breath in a drawn-out sigh and smoothed a lock of hair away from her brow with such tenderness, tears pooled in her eyes and clung to her lashes. "Honore, I shouldn't have done that. I can make excuses about the moon and the dancing and probably a dozen more things. The truth is simpler than that. I've wanted to kiss you since I pulled you up that cliff. You are beautiful and brave and—"

"Everything a wife should be except respectable. I know. If you ally yourself with me, as you saw tonight, you lose the rest of the county." That was the simple truth, making her throat so tight she could not speak above a whisper. "You need those people to find out who could have hated your father enough to want him hanged for a murder he did not commit."

"And I need you as my friend." The mere timbre of his voice was a caress.

Her knees wobbled. She leaned against the gate for support and laid the truth at his feet, made his choice for him, to salve the conscience a man like him would have. "You have a mother and seven brothers and sisters dependent on your largess to keep them from starving, probably to provide dowries for your sisters too. If you are shunned by the haut ton, you might find yourself in prison, even hanged for being a traitor. That means staying out of the company of a lady known for an association with a traitor who met a traitor's death. We both know duty calls you away from me, even if you do care for me." She made herself laugh, a high, tinkling trill. "But I doubt you do. It was the moonlight."

"No, Honore Bainbridge, it's you." He leaned forward and kissed her lightly, a little too long for a mere fare-thee-well. "It's you. You are everything your father said you are and more."

"And were he still alive, he would sweep aside anyone who dared ostracize me. He had that kind of power. But my brother has neither the power nor the will to do so. On the contrary, he is making matters worse for me. But I will not make matters worse for you. I could not live with myself if I ruined you and brought worse suspicions down on your head." She screwed up her face. "I can hear the cats now. 'Miss Bainbridge has set her cap for him, so he must be guilty of something wrong. A murderous father, and he was not born here, therefore—'"

"Shh." He brushed his finger across her lips.

She shook her head. "You know it is the truth, the way people think. All that the vicar and my sisters preach is wrong. There is no forgiveness. Now go fetch Miss Morrow for me. I need to go home."

"I can't . . . I wish . . ." He pressed the back of his hand to her cheek as though checking to see if she had a fever. "I want to argue with you, but I can't. It seems everything I pray for grants me the exact opposite. I feel like everything I've been accused of—the worst of traitors—even thinking of leaving you here."

"But I will always have a home and food. It may not be the best nor what I want, but I will have it. Eventually, Society will accept me again, or my family will buy me a husband. Your family cannot afford for you to end up on the block. So go." She turned and walked away from him.

"This is why I love you," he said behind her in a tone so low she might have only imagined the words. A moment later, boot heels scraped on the cobbles and the sense of his presence left the gate.

She swung back. Stark moonlight shone where he had stood. He had made the right decision. He could not ally himself with her. He and his family need not suffer because she had made poor choices.

"But where is forgiveness, God?" She leaned against one of the porch's support pillars. "Why do You keep punishing me when I have been the model of respectability since last year?"

First Papa had gone. Next her sisters were given excellent excuses to send her away from their homes where she had taken refuge. On the heels of that, her brother banished her to the dower house. And now, worst of all, she had found a man she believed truly worthy of her love, and he was not free to return her affections.

Unless he was not what she thought and God was protecting her from making a third mistake.

For the first time since she had fled from the assembly rooms without her shawl, Honore felt the cold of the October night engulfing her like an icy bath. Gooseflesh rose on her arms. She began to shiver, teeth chattering. She pulled the rest of the pins from her hair and drew the tresses around her like a cloak, but it helped only in a minimal way. The chill reached clear through her, forming a ball of ice in her middle.

She was mad to think so. He was so gentle, so kind, so concerned for his family, he endured a life he did not want in order to provide for them. Her father thought him worthy of marrying Honore, admittedly the late Lord Bainbridge's favorite child. He had saved her life.

From a cliff someone had made to break apart when walked upon.

"What if—" She could not say it, could not even think it.

She pressed her hand to her mouth, the mouth so recently, so thoroughly, so tenderly kissed by the man she was about to accuse of heinous crimes. Surely he could not talk of caring for her and yet be betraying her and the Crown in the same hour.

But of course he could. It would not be the first time for her. Two other men had kissed her. Both had turned out to be scoundrels. She would not—she should not—be surprised if a third man paying court to her ended up the same.

So she had not truly repented. She had fallen into the same trap as before, allowed flattery—more subtle from Ashmoor, but flattery just the same—to sway her right into the arms of a rogue. Yes, he had admitted that he loved her. But Gerald Frobisher had done the same. Major Crawford had wooed her with tales of his difficult rise through the ranks of the military without a proper sponsor. He, at least, had been telling the truth. Ashmoor was likely telling the truth—at least about the needs of his family. She only wanted to believe the rest in her anguish over her brother's treatment, her loneliness, her aching desire to be settled like her sisters.

He'd said everything he prayed for got the opposite response. How well she understood in that moment. She prayed for a husband and got . . . nothing but another kiss to make her restless and anxious, empty and hungering for more.

She pressed her fingers against her lips. Kissing Ashmoor had been different from the other two. With them, she felt possessed. With Ashmoor, she felt cherished. They had been forceful, something she thought made them manly and exciting. Ashmoor's gentleness melted something she had not known was frozen inside her. The memory now melted the knot of cold fear inside her.

"I cannot think the worst of him just because of the others."

But what about because of him?

She did not have the opportunity to pursue that line of thinking. The sound of voices in the lane sent her scrambling onto the porch to hide behind a pillar. The gate swung open on hinges she now noticed needed to be oiled, and Miss Morrow called, "Miss Bainbridge?" in a voice pitched to carry only the few feet to the front of the church.

Honore descended the steps to the front path and greeted her companion along with Mr. Tuckfield and Mr. Chilcott. She could not stop herself from scanning the street behind the group for a tall, broad figure. He was nowhere to be seen.

"Thank you for coming for me," she said. "I am sorry to interrupt your enjoyment."

"It was getting too boisterous," Tuckfield said.

"And I could not enjoy myself while worrying about you." Miss Morrow tucked her arm through Honore's. "Are you all right?"

"Yes, quite. I simply needed to get away from the cats."

If Ashmoor liked cats, she needed to find another term for hissing, spiteful females.

"The four-footed variety is well enough," Tuckfield said. "I have four of the beasts, I admit. As well as a pup."

"Why, Mr. Tuckfield," Miss Morrow exclaimed, "I would never have guessed you could be so sentimental."

"Or ridiculous," Chilcott muttered. He then turned to Honore. "If you are well, Miss Bainbridge, I shall let your companion and steward see you home. I feel the need to go to Ashmoor and repair the damage—ahem."

"Do what you like, Mr. Chilcott." Honore did not allow the merest hint of warmth into her tone. "But you know as well as I that the Devenish crowd will take him back for the price of a bouquet of flowers for Miss Carolina Devenish."

"I . . . they . . ." Chilcott spluttered to silence.

Honore turned her back on the Ashmoor steward. "I want to go home."

They left the church and climbed the hill to the mews at the top where the carriage awaited. Even with the full moon, driving at night necessitated driving slowly, and over an hour passed in near silence. At last the torches left burning at the gates to Bainbridge loomed out of the night. The carriage turned between them and stopped for Tuckfield to descend. He lived across the road in a little cottage on the estate. He bade them good night, holding Miss Morrow's hand a little longer than proper, and strode off into the darkness, whistling one of the tunes played at the assembly. The coachman shut and latched the gates behind him, and they continued up the drive to find the house, which should have lain in near blackness at that hour, ablaze with light.

"Oh no!" Honore cried. "Oh no, oh no, oh no, oh no! Coachman." She rose enough to rap on the hatch. "Stop here."

"Miss Bainbridge, what—"

The front door flew open. Light from the opening spilled over the blond hair and lithe figure of Lord Beau Bainbridge.

Honore's brother had arrived a day early.

19

"Beau!" Honore leaped from the carriage without waiting for the steps and dashed toward her brother.

He held up his right hand, palm toward her, as though warding her off. "Get back into the carriage and continue on to the dower house."

"I cannot tonight," Honore protested. "My things are still in the house."

"I will have your maid pack them up and bring them over." He turned his back on her. "I will meet you there within the quarter hour, so do not think you can sneak off elsewhere."

"Where . . . else would I go?" Honore asked of empty air.

Beau had already disappeared into the house.

Her insides cringing from the pain of being hollowed out with a sharp knife while still alive, she stumbled back to the carriage. A footman had let down the steps, and she half climbed, half crawled inside, as her legs were refusing to fully cooperate in holding her upright. Her back tended to bow, and only a lifetime of training stopped her from curling in on herself like an overcooked prawn.

"Carry on," she told the coachman.

He could not have heard her, but he had heard her brother.

Anyone within fifty feet had heard her brother. Presumably that did not include her future sister-in-law.

"I am going to be ill," she whispered.

"No, you are not." Miss Morrow's tone held an extra bracing note. "You will face him down for the unnatural brother that he is."

Honore shook her head. "He is not unnatural. Many brothers with a sister like me would have sent her to the remotest estate they own or someplace where she would never mix with polite company."

"It was not your father's wishes for you to be treated thus. The more Lord Bainbridge treats you this way, the worse it makes the scandal."

"Scandals," Honore corrected her. "Two of them. I barely escaped a gaming . . . establishment with my life after going there with a traitor—not that I knew him as one—and then I was caught kissing a man who turned out to be a murderer. Everyone tried, but no one can keep these things secret. Servants know. Servants talk."

"But your father wanted you to wed."

"Yes, a man who doesn't wish to wed me." Honore pressed her hand to her mouth. "I am good enough to kiss, but not good enough to—"

Miss Morrow gasped. "He did not."

"He did, and I quite happily kissed him back. I thought, after he made such a show of support, perhaps he had changed his mind."

She closed her mouth. She closed her eyes. She would not cry. Beau must not find her weeping. He should not find her with her gown rumpled and her hair disheveled, but she had no time to make repairs without so much as a comb moved over to the dower house yet, let alone more hairpins. He had seen her dress, so changing it would raise his suspicions further.

She wrapped her shawl more tightly around her against the chill in a house without fires, and set about lighting candles in the front parlor. Light would at least give her the illusion of warmth.

"I can light a fire." Miss Morrow knelt before the hearth and began to do so.

It was just taking hold when Beau strode in without benefit of knocking to announce his presence. From now on, that door would be locked.

"Where have you been that you come home at midnight looking like a wanton?" he demanded of Honore without preamble.

She did not answer his question. She swept him a mocking curtsy. "So good to see you too, brother. And how was your journey?"

"Fatiguing, now answer me."

She stared at him. He was only two years her senior, and they had always gotten along well. They were not as close as he and Cassandra had been while growing up, but he had always been a kind and thoughtful brother. Somewhere between being a carefree young heir to an ancient title and comfortable fortune and becoming the baron, he had changed. She must write Cassandra and Lydia and tell them. If they were not too preoccupied with their babies, surely born by now, perhaps they could give her advice on how to manage this new, officious brother.

He strode up to her now and loomed over her. "I asked you a question."

"And I did not answer."

"That is obvious. Now answer me this time. Where have you been and why is your hair down?"

"Because a man buried his fingers in it and pulled it down while kissing me. Is that what you want to hear?"

"It is not." He raised his hand.

For a heartbeat, Honore feared he intended to strike her. Nonetheless she held her ground, meeting his gaze full on.

Instead, he cupped her chin and turned her face to the light of the nearest candle. "But you are telling the truth, are you not?"

Honore sighed. "I am, I regret to say."

"Is he another criminal?"

Honore winced. "I do not know."

Miss Morrow caught her breath. "Miss Bainbridge, surely not."

"I think perhaps I have fallen in love with him, so that does not bode well for his veracity." Her lower lip, still feeling the tenderness of Ashmoor's kiss, protruded, quivering. "Though Father approved of him."

"Father?" Beau jerked back. "Ashmoor? Are you telling me you have been . . . carrying on with Ashmoor?"

"Not carrying on. There was an assembly in Clovelly and a full moon. I thought . . . Never you mind. I am too scandalous for his lordship. He wants to remain above reproach, and association with me will not help him do so."

Because he needed to ensure his position of innocence, a position he did not deserve?

Honore pressed her hands to her temples. "Do not think you can make Ashmoor wed me over a mere kiss, Beau. He will not."

"Someone will have to, or I fear you will continue this behavior until you lose your looks. Once Miss Dunbar and I are safely wed, we will arrange a marriage for you."

"Is it not Christien's role to find me a husband?" Honore could not resist the taunt. "After all, he is my guardian, not you."

Beau stalked to the door. "De Meuse is too preoccupied with his new family."

"Did Lydia—that is, has she—" Honore stumbled on a delicate way to ask the question.

"No, the *petit paquet* has not yet arrived that I know of. I expect word any day now." Beau scowled at Honore. "Do not leave the grounds of the dower house for any reason while Miss Dunbar and her mother are here. Your maid shall arrive with your things shortly, and I will see that you have adequate foodstuffs sent over."

"How magnanimous of you." Honore sneered at him. "Bread and water for the prisoner."

"Do not be pert. Your latest escapade carries you quite to the edge with me."

"And only a little push will send me over?"

"I expect you know what you mean by that," Beau said. Then he was gone, closing the door behind him with too hard a slam.

Honore did not know what she meant by that. She could not suspect that her brother had arranged for the cliff to give way beneath her. He had not known when she would arrive at Bainbridge. Still, her fall would have benefited him well, apparently. The dower house was not far enough away from this fiancée, who must be quite a termagant or high stickler at the least to refuse to be in the same house with Honore. Her brother was seeking an excuse to send her off to Somerset, to a house that might not even be habitable.

She should declare that she would never give him a reason to send her packing, but she knew she could not. If she wanted Ashmoor, she must clear his name, and that would entail taking action about which her loyal companion would probably tattle, if she found it necessary to stop her. Yet now that she was immured in the dower house, she could seek clues. Surely whoever had been using the miniature manor for a hiding place had missed another clue when cleaning the place. She could hope.

She could pray.

No, not that. She had moved beyond reconciliation with the Lord. He did not want her. Well, no, that was not true. The Bible told her He did, and she believed in her head that was right. In her heart, however, she merely felt punished and unworthy, battered with her sins, with too many events in her life like Ashmoor's rejection because of her past mistakes, and her brother exiling her to the dower house and wanting to exile her further. In truth, all of her family wanted to exile her further away from them.

In that moment, with the chill still on the dower house and the creaks and snaps of a settling building in the chill of the night, she wished for the conflict with America to end. Perhaps on the other side of the ocean she could make a new start.

But the war was not over. She must manage her life right there in Devonshire. She would begin with finding out who had been using the dower house while it stood empty, and why. It would help her family, especially since the purpose was surely lawless, considering the half a French button having been in the book room.

So someone on the estate had to have been a part of the wrongdoings in the building. Only someone with access to the grounds had access to the dower house. That left no more than three or four dozen people to consider. And they might even be gone, having given a key to the gate to someone else.

"Every lawless element in Devonshire," she grumbled. "Not difficult at all to sort out."

"Sarcasm is unbecoming of a lady, Miss Bainbridge." Miss Morrow sounded prim, but her lips twitched.

Honore laughed. "Not at all becoming, but far too true."

"Let us go to our beds. I believe I hear someone coming. Perhaps they are bringing our personal effects." Miss Morrow rose and went to the door.

Mavis entered with a box containing nightclothes and other personal items. "I'm to stay here and do up the fires and the like in the morning."

"What about tea or coffee in the morning?" Honore asked.

"I can do that too, miss, so long as there's coal enough for the stove."

"I hope so. I ordered it." She headed for the cellar steps. "If not, we shall go to the main house and get enough for fires in the morning. I do not intend any of us to freeze and have to wash with cold water."

She yanked open the narrow door. The blackness below seemed to swallow her candle flame while breathing forth the stench of mildew and the sour reek of a long-ago spilled cask of wine. For a moment, she hesitated, one foot on the first tread, the other still in the back passageway. Descending into that cellar looked too much like her future if she did not make something change, if she did not accomplish a feat that would wipe clean her slate of sins.

Shivering, she stepped back onto the ground floor of the house and closed and locked the cellar door. She had descended into a place named for the netherworld once and nearly lost her life. In no way did she intend to descend into a cellar alone at night when someone had been using the house for illicit purposes.

She turned, sending smoke and candle flame streaming in

an arc around her. "I will look in on the coal in the morning. Tonight we shall ascend to our beds."

Miss Honore Bainbridge wasn't in church Sunday morning. Three strangers occupied the Bainbridge pew—strangers to Meric. He studied them from beneath half-lowered lids. A young man whose fine features, honey-colored hair, and sky-blue eyes marked him as Miss Bainbridge's brother perched between a plain-faced girl with hair the color of spring wheat and eyes an uncertain shade, and an older, prettier version of the young lady. The fiancée and her mother, most likely.

"What's the protocol here?" he murmured to Chilcott after the service. "Do I approach him or does he approach me?"

"Neither," Chilcott explained. "You are called peers for a reason."

"So not approaching him is snubbing him?"

"It could be construed as such; however, if you do not wish to speak to him, I think his current preoccupation can excuse you without causing too much difficulty." Chilcott inclined his head. "The earl of Ashmoor, being the newcomer to the neighborhood, can be expected to think he must wait for the older peerage to approach him first."

"Older? Oh, because the barony has been around for several hundred years, and my title is relatively recent."

"Exactly. A hundred and fifty-two years, to be exact." Chilcott nodded like a tutor to a particularly bright student. "You can wait for him here. He will see you and come over quite quickly unless he wishes to cut you."

"I do wish to speak with him, but not here."

"Then do not look at him without catching his eye, or it

may be construed as the cut direct. You may nod to him and move on."

Meric did so, then headed down the aisle. Rather hoping he could escape the churchyard altogether before Bainbridge finished talking with the vicar and a handful of parishioners surrounding him and his guests, Meric exited the church to rather watery sunshine, a biting wind off the harbor, and two young ladies who tried to make up for the cold day with the warmth of their smiles and greeting.

"Good day, Lord Ashmoor," Carolina Devenish and Penelope Babbage chorused.

He bowed but said nothing. After the way they had behaved Friday night, they could make the first step toward apology.

And what about the way you behaved? his conscience prompted him.

He winced, as he had been for a day and a half of restlessness, guilt, and the sense that someone was using a dull spoon to hollow out his chest.

What had possessed him to kiss Miss Honore Bainbridge and then compound the error by saying he loved her? He didn't. He couldn't. He had been raised with better manners than to treat a lady like that.

Those manners Mother had drilled into him prompted him to speak. "I trust you ladies are well."

"Well enough." Miss Devenish's lower lip quivered. "I will do much better if I know you will forgive me for my disgraceful behavior the other night."

"It's quite forgotten."

Which is a lie, his conscience jabbed at him.

Miss Babbage sighed. "If only we could believe that. Such a scold we got when we returned home." She tapped his arm with her fan. "But you can show us all is forgotten if you come to my house for dinner. Just a small affair with the Devenishes, of course, this being Sunday in the country, but we would so appreciate your presence."

"I don't know right off, ma'am. May I send around a message?"

Both young ladies' faces fell. Miss Devenish positively pouted, not nearly as prettily as did Miss Bainbridge. But then, few females could look as pretty as Miss Bainbridge.

"Yes, of course," Miss Babbage said. "But not in too long a time. We keep country hours."

"And must be on our way." Miss Devenish dropped a curtsy and spun away, her lips pursed.

Miss Babbage did the same, her lips curved into a satisfied smile.

Lord Beau Bainbridge replaced the ladies before him with a slight bow and no female companions. "Good day, Ashmoor. Welcome to the neighborhood."

"Thank you." Meric looked down on the younger man from more than a head's advantage. "I trust you had an uneventful journey here. And where is your sister this morning?" The question burst from him unbidden, the most important thing he had said all day.

Bainbridge started. "Honore? I cannot have my sister coming to church with my fiancée and her mother. She is not . . ."

"Fit for the Lord's house?"

Chilcott's touch on the back of his shoulder alerted Meric to how he had fisted his hands against his thighs. He uncurled his fingers and sought for a more congenial tone. "I would like to call on you later, Bainbridge, at your convenience."

"Anytime in the afternoon is acceptable." Bainbridge also grew more affable. "Unless you wish to join me on my morning rides?"

"No, thank you. I shall call in the afternoon."

"So long as it is me on whom you call and not my sister. She has enough trouble without . . ." Bainbridge trailed off, perhaps realizing that what he had been about to say could get him slapped across the face and invited to meet Meric, were he so inclined.

If ever a practice was stupid, it was dueling, but Bainbridge didn't know that about him.

Meric pretended he hadn't noticed the near insult and bowed. "I will be calling at some time. Your father was a great friend to me." He strode out of the churchyard and along the lane to the main street, Chilcott trailing in his wake.

"Do you plan on going to the Babbages' today?" the steward asked.

"No. I'm not."

"Bainbridge, then?"

Oh yes, he intended to go to Bainbridge, but not to call on the baron, who hadn't allowed his sister to come to church with him. Isolating her from worship with the congregation was beyond acceptable behavior, and he would not himself continue to join the likes of the baron in hypocrisy.

20

Honore stared at the pages of her Bible. She had just turned all the pages in the book of James, but she doubted she had actually read anything. She certainly recalled nothing of the words, at least not from this reading, though her eyes ached as though she had read the entire New Testament in one sitting.

Beau had not allowed her to go to church. No, that was not quite right. He had informed her that the carriages would not be available. She could have walked the five miles into Clovelly. But then she could not have joined them in the family pew.

"Why is he being so awful?" Honore covered her face with her hands. Her Bible slid off her lap and onto the floor with a thud. "He did not seem to mind my escapades with Frobisher last year."

But that was before Major Crawford came on the scene and nearly killed Cassandra. Not that Honore had helped Crawford's murderous attempts. All she had known of the man was that he was a guest in the same home as she and was devastatingly handsome.

As Frobisher had been.

Not like Ashmoor. Oh, he was beautiful in his inelegant

brawn, but his hair was dark, and his eyes . . . too compelling to be anything but disturbing.

But none of this had anything to do with how Beau had begun to treat her as though she had taken to the streets to earn her pin money.

"Why, Miss Morrow?" she demanded of her companion.

Miss Morrow looked up from the little book she was writing in. "I wish I knew, Miss Bainbridge. It seems a bit too much. If Miss Dunbar were of the middle class and bore a large dowry your brother needed, I might understand. The middle classes are terribly high in the instep and concerned about their reputations, especially when buying their way into the nobility." She sounded bitter.

"You seem to disapprove of the practice."

"It is acceptable if the parties are amenable." Despite her words, her lips had formed a thin line.

Curiosity aroused, Honore leaned forward. "Miss Morrow, did this come out badly for someone you know?"

"You might say that." She bent her head over her book but did not dip the pen in the ink to resume writing.

Honore waited in the silence broken by a gust of wind battering the side of the house and rattling loose windowpanes. A cold draft defied the heat of the fire and swirled around her ankles. She shivered.

A dozen feet away, Miss Morrow tucked her gray skirts more tightly around her legs and sighed. "I was betrothed when I was nineteen. I had a bit of a dowry then. Not much at all, but it was acceptable. And the gentleman had a title. I thought he loved me. But apparently he had a bit of a gaming habit." She delivered the story without expression on her face or in her voice. "And when he lost nearly everything at the tables, he found a rich city merchant's daughter to wed him in exchange for his title."

"I would say you came out the fortunate one," Honore said.

"I would tend to agree, except life with a gamester is preferable to life as a spinster."

"Reduced to earning your bread being companion to the likes of me."

"Oh no, Miss Bainbridge, you are the kindest of employers. I count myself blessed for being able to stay with you in your exile."

"Like all those people who were imprisoned with Mary, Queen of Scots?"

Miss Morrow laughed. "Something of the kind." She sobered. "But you are delightful company and not at all demanding and—well, I have two suitors here, where before I haven't had one since I was jilted for a cit ten years ago."

"Perhaps I should look for a city merchant for a suitor," Honore mused. "Except they are probably as much high sticklers as is Ashmoor." She could not stop the break in her voice when saying his name.

"Is he a stickler or simply protecting his family?" Miss Morrow's soft eyes held speculation. "I would think a high stickler would not kiss you in the moonlight."

"Yes, he is protecting his family and himself. I cannot fault him for that."

Nor for kissing her. She had done nothing to stop him.

She picked up her Bible and carried it to a shelf in the book room. "But I can blame my brother for his treatment. Surely my sisters would not approve of him marrying a female who would treat me so."

Yet had her sisters not treated her so? Were their imminent

confinements mere excuses to be rid of their troublesome younger sister?

"But if I want Ashmoor to be free to court me," she said with haste, "I will have to clear his name for him."

"How will you do that?" Miss Morrow was gripping her pen so hard the quill bowed between her fingers.

"Begin with this room and search the rest of the house. Someone was using it secretly, which means for no good pur—"

The door knocker sounded.

Honore headed toward the door. "Who could that be?"

"Sit down and let Mavis get it." Miss Morrow stretched out a hand as though she could draw Honore to a seat.

"But perhaps it is news from my sisters or my brother or—"

"A courier would not arrive on Sunday, and neither would the mail. As for your brother . . ." Miss Morrow grimaced.

"No, no, I suppose it would not be him." Unable to force her legs to carry her to sit primly in a chair, Honore fairly bounded across the room to the window. It looked out on one of the walls that surrounded three sides of the dower house and its garden. The faded sun of the morning was rapidly disappearing behind cloud banks that promised rain within the hour. She would get no walk today. Once their caller departed, she would begin her search of the house, Sabbath or not. It was not work if she was helping a fellow man. She could no longer sit still with her future growing as bleak as the day.

Behind her, Mavis scratched on the door. Honore braced herself for her brother's arrival, for more condemnations and restrictions on her movements.

"Come in." Weariness with the whole matter lent an edge of annoyance to her tone.

The door opened. "His lordship, miss," Mavis fairly squeaked.

"What do you want?" Honore snapped.

The door closed with a gentle but decisive click. "I suppose I deserve that," Lord Ashmoor said.

"My lord." Honore spun on the flat heel of her slipper, sending the flounce on the bottom of her gown swirling out in a cloud of creamy muslin. "What—what are you doing here?"

"I've come to call." He closed the distance in two long strides and bowed. As he straightened, he met and held her gaze. "I . . . owe you an apology."

"Oh no. No, no, no, not that." She would break down in tears if he went on about what a mistake the kiss had been. "I was as complicit as you."

"I took advantage of you, of the situation, and said and did things—"

"Stop." She clapped her hands to her ears.

His lips kept moving, those lips that had moved on hers and nearly driven her to her knees with a longing that shredded her heart.

Gently he drew her hands away from her ears and held them in his. His hands so broad and strong and tough, with calluses along the base of his fingers even after a year as a gentleman. Perhaps he still chopped wood.

Or rowed a boat?

She should pull away, command him to leave if he did not intend to pay court to her. If he stayed, she was uncertain of her power to resist his nearness. If she did not resist him, if he had changed his mind and said he did intend to court her in spite of everything, she knew he was not innocent of crimes against the Crown. That was simply how the men in her life fell, the ones she cared about and those who pretended to care about her.

She yanked her hands free and tucked them beneath her

elbows. "You have spoken your apology." She made her voice drip with icicles. "You may go now."

"Miss Bainbridge," Miss Morrow admonished.

Ashmoor grinned. "I think your eyes are even bluer when you're angry."

Her palm itched. If she could have stepped back, she would have. Never in her life had she wanted to slap anyone—except perhaps her brother Friday night. It was not an impulse she was proud of.

She made herself speak with exaggerated calm. "My lord, I have been a fool for pretty compliments in the past, but no more. My behavior has been above reproach for nearly a year except . . . except . . . Perhaps I am at fault. If so, I am sorry. Now leave."

"I cannot."

"I beg your pardon?"

"I need your help."

Why did he have to say that with his voice soft and his eyes softer?

Honore's arms dropped to her sides. "How?"

"This house. This room." He stepped back at last and swept an arm out. "There's something key here."

"Of course there is. I will look and keep you informed if I find it." She managed to step around him and place half a room's worth of distance between them. "Now you may go court your respectable young lady."

"I realized I can't court any lady until I have a completely clear name, and that means my father's name too."

"No one?" She staggered against a table, sending a precarious pile of books sliding to the floor with a series of thuds like heavy footfalls. She stooped to pick up the books.

Ashmoor stooped to pick up the books.

Their heads collided. They rocked back on their heels, hands to the tops of their skulls. Their eyes met and they started to laugh.

"You two." Laughing too, Miss Morrow rose from the desk and crossed the room. "Do you need help up, or perhaps a physician?"

"Or the nearest passage to a madhouse." Gold lights danced in Ashmoor's eyes.

"These books are going to be ruined." Miss Morrow stooped, managing to do so without clashing heads with anyone, and picked up the nearest tome. "I have never read Mr. Latham's work." She flipped the cover back and stared at the front page so hard, Honore leaned over to see what was so fascinating.

And so did Ashmoor. Their heads clunked together again.

The three of them sat on the floor laughing hard enough to press their hands to their middles. Tears dripped down Honore's cheeks. Wiping them away, she started at the sight of Mavis standing in the doorway, mouth agape.

"If-if I didn't know better," she stammered, "I'd say you all have been at the wine."

"Considering there is none in the house," Honore managed to respond in a somewhat sober tone, "that is not possible."

"But there is, miss, begging your pardon for contradicting you. There's a half dozen casks—"

The three of them were on their feet in unison like marionettes shot up by their strings.

"Where?" Honore reached the door first, the swiftness of her movement sending Mavis scurrying backward into the corridor.

"The-the cellar. I were looking for more candles and maybe more coal. We're frightfully low and—"

Honore led the group down the narrow passageway to the cellar steps. She paused only long enough to snatch a candle from a stand on the entryway table. Slowly, hand gripping the rope serving as a railing, she descended the steep steps to the packed dirt floor of the cellar. Her nose wrinkled and twitched. The sourness of old, spilled wine permeated the air, tickled her nose.

She paused, turning her head in search of the scent's source. "I know my grandmother did not drink spirits of any kind."

"It isn't wine." Ashmoor paused beside her. "It's brandy."

"But how?" Honore stared up at him too, too close to her.

"Someone's been using the dower house for storing contraband, apparently." His face was taut.

Mavis gasped. "But that means smugglers been in this house." She began to back toward the steps. "I don't want nothing to do with smugglers. They-they kill people who interferes with them."

"Yes, they do." The chill of the cellar penetrated to Honore's bones. "But I thought when they cleaned to remove any traces of who they might be, they would have taken away everything leading back to them. So why would they leave casks of brandy that is so obviously contraband?"

"And how did they get it here?" Ashmoor, who had also procured a candle, strode forward. "Where are these casks, Mavis?"

"In-in that room." Mavis's teeth chattered.

"Go upstairs," Honore told her. "You're freezing."

"No, miss, I'm scared. I don't want to go alone."

"Miss Morrow, will you go with her?" Honore tossed the suggestion over her shoulder as she followed Ashmoor.

"And leave you down here alone with his lordship?" Miss Morrow laughed. "I would be remiss in my chaperoning duties."

"There is nothing to chaperone." Honore's tone was sharp.

Miss Morrow just laughed again and stood her ground.

With a sigh of exasperation, Honore entered the side room after Ashmoor. Not until she stood in the opening surveying the half dozen casks, one of which was obviously leaking onto the floor, did she realize that she had been there once before and hadn't realized what the sour stench had been.

"Lord Ashmoor." She swallowed, for her teeth had begun to chatter as well. "These are new here. I mean, I smelled this on Thursday, but not on Wednesday."

He faced her. "Are you saying someone brought these in Wednesday night?"

"They must have, the same night they cleaned. But that's absurd." She pressed her hand to her lips.

Ashmoor drew it away and curled his fingers around it. "Don't look so scared . . . or so sweet. The temptation to kiss you is powerful."

Honore gulped. "Then do not touch me."

"Or look at you."

"Or be in the same room as I am."

"Not possible if I'm to get any answers."

"My lord." She stepped back, though he still held her hand. "I want to prove your innocence for my own sake. For if you are guilty, I am afraid—afraid—"

"I'd never hurt you under any circumstances."

"No, I do not mean afraid like that." She tugged, and he released her fingers. She wished he had not. "I am afraid I will never trust anyone again. I had already asked Papa to find me a husband because of Frobisher and Crawford. But now you . . ."

Ashmoor stared at her, his eyes dark in the flickering candlelight. "Are you saying you think I might be guilty of treason against England because of your other suitors turning out to be scoundrels?"

Honore jutted out her chin. "Yes."

"Or because of my father?" His voice could have cut the iron bands on the contraband casks.

"I have little knowledge of your father's crime." The instant she spoke, she sucked in her breath as though she could draw the words back.

He turned away from her. "So, like father, like son?"

"I know not. No one talks about your father much anymore. It was a lifetime ago. It was—"

"Yes, his lifetime." He glared over his shoulder. "If he hadn't been hounded out of England like a mad dog, he would never have drowned beneath the ice while trying to feed his family. He was the best of men, yet here he's been tried and convicted without a trial, and by association of my blood, so have I." He turned away. "If it wasn't for the money I can smuggle back to America for my family, this wouldn't be worth the trouble." He strode from the room. A moment later, the steps creaked beneath the thuds of his boot heels.

Honore ran after him, ignoring Miss Morrow's and Mavis's cries to know what was happening.

"My lord." Honore's candle extinguished and she tripped over her hem, tearing loose the stitching and falling to her knees on the top step with an "ooph" as the air was driven from her lungs.

"Honore Bainbridge." The hardness had gone, the tenderness had returned as he retraced his steps and held his hand down to her. "Am I forever going to have to pick you up?"

She smiled. "My father thought you good enough to elevate me."

"Yet I seem to be your downfall."

They laughed, and the strain between them broke. She felt it slip away like a knotted sash finally coming loose. She took his hand, scrambled to her feet, and let him lead her back to the book room. He set her in a chair and removed the candle from her fingers, then built up the waning fire.

"Let me tell you the story about my father that he told me." He seated himself across from her. "My mother verifies it, for what that's worth. They were wed. Had been for about a year. And they were living in the Clovelly house."

"Is that why you are living there?" Honore asked.

"Because it was theirs? No. It's nicer than the hall on Ashmoor. Not as drafty."

"Wish I could say the same of this place." Honore shivered. The clouds of earlier had begun to fulfill their promise of colder temperatures and rain. "I will have Mavis make us some tea."

"I expect they are already at it. Shall I wait?"

"Please." She leaned forward, holding her hands out to the blaze. "Why do you think the brandy casks are down in my cellar?"

"For the same reason the smugglers ensured you'd know they had been here by cleaning the house." He grinned. "I have no idea."

"It makes me angry. Someone is invading my property to do this. I know not how they are managing it. To get here, they would have to cross the lawn and the garden in plain sight of the house."

"No secret passages into the caves?"

"We're two hundred feet above the sea here. It seems unlikely."

Ashmoor started to speak, then stopped and rose at the entrance of Miss Morrow with a tray.

"Tea," she said. "And I hope you did not walk, my lord."

"I did." He took the tray from her and set it on a low table. "After nearly going off the cliff the other day, I am disinclined to get in a carriage again."

"You can ride." Honore gave him a sidelong glance through her lashes.

He grimaced. "Eventually. My brother is the one taking to riding like a centaur. I'm ordering a curricle so I can drive myself."

Honore's insides softened like a stale cake dropped into a cup of tea. Liking, sympathy . . . love for the man across from her? Dangerous, whatever the emotion. She must simply prove his innocence so she would know she had not gone and kissed another villain. That was all. She must not forget that. She could not care and get hurt again.

Yet his admission of apprehension regarding being inside a carriage, of not riding well—in short, of feeling helpless if he was not good at something—plucked at her heartstrings until they sang. All too well she recognized the tune.

She would love him even if he were a villain.

Such a fool for men. Three hundred years ago, her father could have done her a favor and locked her in a nunnery. Now she must face down life with the knowledge that she never chose right in heart matters.

Suddenly the isolated farmhouse in Somerset looked rather good. Right now, stranded in the Devonshire dower house, she set about pouring tea, then sat back with her cup cradled between her hands. "You were going to tell us about your father, my lord?"

"Yes, my father." He too cradled the delicate teacup. It disappeared inside the curve of his palms. "He was a bit on the lawless side. If he hadn't been, no one would have believed what happened that night. He told me he'd been going on runs with the smugglers for years. He wanted to get enough money together so he and my mother could marry and purchase a small estate. I believe your father was considering selling them some property he owned in Somerset."

"It's a dairy farm," Honore confirmed. "The house is a hovel, but the land is excellent."

Ashmoor nodded. "It wasn't so much of a ruin thirty years ago. Apparently my uncle was more than happy to have them go. They were living in the Clovelly house and my uncle wanted the rent from it. Father said he intended only one more year of runs to France, but then Mother became . . . that is . . ." His ears turned pink and he lifted his cup to his lips.

Honore smiled. "Your father changed his mind with a family to consider?"

Ashmoor nodded. "So Father decided to just work on this side of the channel instead of crossing. He would take his boat out and collect goods the smugglers had dropped into the sea."

Miss Morrow looked blank. "I'm from the Midlands. I do not understand what you are saying."

"The smugglers carry the cargoes over here from France on bigger vessels like sloops, then they drop it into the sea with weights when they get close to the coast, so the revenue cutters cannot catch them with goods aboard. Then men pretending to be fishermen lift them out and bring them ashore in smaller batches that are harder to detect."

"Smaller boats." Honore's eyes widened with the recollection of a craft tossing and turning and swamping on too high a sea for anyone to be out upon. "That's what those men—"

She stopped, realizing she could not say anything in front of Miss Morrow. The other two stared at her.

"Never you mind. Go ahead, my lord."

He flinched. "Do you really have to keep calling me that? It seems . . . wrong."

Honore shook her head. "I can scarcely call you by your Christian name, and calling you by just your title is too . . . friendly."

"I'd . . . rather we were friendly," he said with touching uncertainty.

"Ashmoor." She tasted the name on her tongue. It slid off the tip like anything but something burned and dry, more a touch, a whisper caressing and gentle. "All right."

Their gazes clung.

Miss Morrow cleared her throat. "So your father was pretending to be a fisherman?"

"Yes, a fisherman." Ashmoor swallowed more tea and set his cup aside. "It was all well until the riding officers got wind of a run one night and were there on the top of the cliff to meet the men. There was a pitched battle, with the smugglers only armed with knives and the revenue men with pistols and muskets."

"Hardly fair." Honore's hands had turned her tea cold, and she set her cup on the table. "But if it was a battle, how could your father have been accused of murder?"

"There was a witness . . ." Ashmoor rubbed his hands over his face. "It was no battle. More like a massacre. The men looked to my father as their leader, so he got behind the riding officer's captain and held a knife to his throat, threatening to slit it if the others didn't lay down their arms."

Miss Morrow breathed a quiet prayer.

Honore sat so still a breath seemed like too much activity.

"It worked." Ashmoor closed his eyes as though he saw the fight for himself. "The revenue men laid down their weapons and the surviving smugglers ran."

Honore opened her mouth, but the inevitable question did not emerge.

Ashmoor smiled at her. "I know. Everyone says my father tossed the officer off the cliff and everyone heard his screams for a mile around."

"A gross exaggeration," Miss Morrow murmured.

"A flat-out lie." Ashmoor picked up his cup, set it down again without tasting the dregs of tea in the bottom. "That is, the man went off the cliff, but Father didn't do it. He pushed the man in the other direction so he could run before he was caught too."

"Could he—?" Honore gulped. "Could he have been mistaken in the direction in which he threw the officer?"

Ashmoor gave his head an emphatic shake. "He said one of the other revenue men did it. I know that's just his word, but he was not the murderous sort. And your father believed him. They had been friends all their lives."

"But the riding officers would never betray one of their own, even over the life of a captain." Honore felt sick, partly with the notion that men sworn to uphold the king's laws would break it and let another take the blame, and partly because she was uncertain as to the truth of it. And if Ashmoor's father had committed murder—

She jerked herself upright and away from that line of thought. "So they arrested your father?"

"Yes. They arrested him to wait for the assizes. He would have been hanged. Few people believed he spoke the truth except my uncle and your father."

"Two people one would think would know him best." Honore nodded.

"Except they were not witnesses." Miss Morrow's voice sounded as dry as newspaper.

"He would have been hanged," Ashmoor repeated. "But he escaped from prison, and he and Mother ended up on a ship bound for New York."

Honore arched her brows. "Somehow they escaped?"

"I expect my uncle, maybe even your father helped."

"I suppose none of your father's old smuggling gang would testify for him for fear of prosecution." Honore leaned her head against the curved back of the chair and closed her eyes.

She saw the white-capped waves, the fishing smack tossed about like a cork, the two men Ashmoor drew to safety. Two men with a mission important enough to go out in such weather. A mission like rescuing kegs of contraband from the bottom of the sea.

"Could we find any of these men?" She leaned forward, her tone excited. "It is too late for them to testify, but they may know something of that night they would tell his son."

"They might. But I can't do it on my own. I don't know the people here."

Which was why he was there. His presence had nothing to do with her, with regretting kissing her, with changing his mind about courting her despite her reputation and his need of a wife above reproach. No, he was there for help from the only person he knew who would be willing to give it.

She would weep about that later in private. For now, she offered him a smile that might have been a little too bright. "Of course I will help you. I already planned to start finding out who has been invading my property, especially now that we have a half dozen kegs of contraband in the cellar and no way of knowing how it got there."

"Thank you. If we can clear this up, my entire family will be better off for it. They can—"

The door knocker sounded for the second time that day.

Honore jumped to her feet. "Who would come calling in this weather?"

"And at this hour?" Miss Morrow glanced at the clock.

Ashmoor rose and glanced about as though seeking a bolt-hole. "I shouldn't be seen here."

"Oh no, of course not." Honore made no attempt to disguise her sarcasm.

In the entryway, Mavis was greeting and exclaiming over the wetness of someone's garments. The responding voice was unfamiliar but female.

"I am afraid, my lord," Honore said with a chill to her tone, "you are caught."

"By whom?" Miss Morrow asked.

Mavis scratched on the door, then popped her head around the edge of the panel. "Miss Bainbridge, Miss Dunbar is here to see you."

Ashmoor looked blank. "Who is Miss Dunbar, if that's not rude of me to ask?"

"Send her in and bring more tea." Honore addressed the maid, then turned to Ashmoor. "Miss Deborah Dunbar, my future sister-in-law."

21

Miss Deborah Dunbar entered the room like a will-o'-the-wisp gliding across a nighttime field—as pale and filmy as mist. Her hair, a silvery blonde, sprang from its pins in fluttery curls. Her eyes were a silvery gray, her complexion pale. Even her gown, a smoky silver gauze, drifted around her delicate frame as though it were created of vapor, not fabric.

"I apologize for the intrusion, Miss Bainbridge." She spoke in a thin little voice. "I have been anxious to make your acquaintance for simply ages, and Mama will never allow it."

"Apparently not." Honore's tone was dry. "So how did you manage this?"

"Manners," Miss Morrow murmured.

Honore held her ground. "I should think now is the least of appropriate times for you to call."

"Not at all." Miss Dunbar halted halfway between door and chairs. "Mama is resting after dinner, and Bainbridge is in his study and thinks I am resting also."

"And would not approve of you calling on me any more than does your mama." Honore clasped her hands behind her back to stop herself from reaching out and drawing this fragile creature to the heat of the fire. She could not be kind to the reason for her exile, for the final humiliation of being denied a ride to church.

"What Mama does not know keeps her from killing all of us." Miss Dunbar giggled.

And Honore melted. The giggle, the absurd remark, the flash of light in those silvery eyes announced that Miss Deborah Dunbar only appeared frail. That flash was likely the bar of steel running through her.

"Then come here and get warm." Honore stepped aside so Deborah could have her chair, the one closest to the warmth. "Lord Ashmoor, let me present Miss Deborah Dunbar, my brother's fiancée."

She curtsied. He bowed. He gave Honore a look of concern.

"I will tell no one you are here, my lord," Deborah said. "I do hate to hear Mama acting like the cit she is and haranguing Bainbridge about his disreputable family. If she goes on too long, he just might change his mind about marrying me, since he scarce needs my dowry."

"And that would break your heart." Honore was about to turn into a puddle at this young lady's feet. As apparently her brother had already become. And no wonder. She was not exactly pretty, but her ethereal looks and sweet yet direct manner held a body captive.

"Of course it would break my heart. I've adored Bainbridge since he came home from school with my brother for the first time five years ago."

Ah, the connection.

"Then why have I never met you?" Honore asked.

"I never made my come-out. First Grandpapa died, and then my younger sister, and then Papa. But my brother is sitting in the Commons now, so we finally went to London last year."

Deborah grimaced. "But I am far too old for all the trappings of a first Season."

She looked about sixteen.

"I am three and twenty." She seized Honore's hand in a surprisingly strong grip. "So please be patient. As soon as we are wed, your brother will be able to stop fearing Mama will withhold her consent and make me wed horrible Mr. Chumley back in Worcestershire."

Honore shook her head and caught Ashmoor's eyes. They were dancing with amusement, the rogue.

"I think," he said, "I should be on my way. Pleased to make your acquaintance, Miss Dunbar. I'm certain we will meet again."

"I am certain we will." She curtsied again. "Mama told Bainbridge he must invite you to dinner soon."

"I'm not surprised." Ashmoor's tone was sardonic. His lips twitched. "Titles cover a multitude of sins."

"Then I should find one for myself," Honore snapped. "Do you think I can be knighted for a service to the Crown and then be respectable in spite of my misdeeds?" The words sounded bitter. They tasted bitter.

The other three in the room stared at her.

"Do sit down, Miss Dunbar." Honore suppressed a weary sigh. "I will see his lordship out, since Mavis is occupied making more tea." She marched to the door and yanked it open.

Ashmoor preceded her into the hall, then stopped and faced her. "I think you've just heard a promise of restoration from your brother, so why are you crying?"

"I am not."

"No?" With a fingertip, he traced the track of a tear down her cheek.

"One tear is of no consequence."

"And your lip is quivering." He brushed her lower lip with the pad of his thumb.

All of her quivered right down to her toes.

"We'll get this all sorted out, Honore." His voice rumbled over her ears like velvet against her skin. "And you'll get your respectable life and a title if you want it."

"Of course. I am simply unworthy before I do something important." Turning her back on him, she flung herself at the front door and yanked it open. A gust of wind and icy rain swept into the entryway. "Try not to catch a chill, my lord. You have not yet set up your nursery."

"Honore . . . um, Miss Bainbridge—"

"Do not fret, my lord. I will still assist you in locating your father's men, if any are left alive. But right now, I have a guest awaiting me."

Mouth grim, he stepped over the threshold, then turned back, rain streaming off his hair and face. "If I were the only one who mattered in this—"

"I have a guest waiting for me." She slammed the door and shot the bolt. For several moments, she remained by the portal, half expecting him to knock. When he did not, she retraced her steps to the book room just as Mavis emerged from the kitchen passage.

"I will take the tea in. And Mavis, do not tell a soul of Miss Dunbar's or Lord Ashmoor's visits."

"No, miss." Mavis's green eyes sparkled. "This is exciting doings here. But I'll keep mum."

Honore took the tray from the maid and entered the book room. Miss Morrow and Deborah glanced up but did not cease their dialogue about some people they both knew. Both ladies sat back in their chairs, relaxed and calm, their lips curved up, companionable and comfortable.

"Do either of you want tea?" Honore managed to ask during a lull in their dialogue, her tone a little too bland.

"I am sorry, Miss Bainbridge." Miss Morrow sprang to her feet and took the tray. "It seems that Miss Dunbar's eldest sister is married to my sister's husband's brother."

"I think I followed that." Honore sat, a fresh cup of tea in her hands, her gaze on her soon-to-be sister-in-law. "So to what honor do I owe this secret call, Miss Dunbar?"

Deborah looked surprised. "Why, who better than you to introduce me to the tenant farmers' wives?"

"My brother?"

"Bainbridge has scarcely spent any time here between school and university," Deborah pointed out. "I doubt he knows the tenants, let alone their wives, as you must."

How many of the tenant farmers' wives did Honore know? She had spent too little of her time visiting those who labored on Bainbridge land since her return to Bainbridge, but she had known them all before she left for London. She should have been spending more of her hours calling on the sick or old and infirm, and ensuring those with children had all they needed. Many of those wives and mothers had been her childhood playmates, exploring the caves, stealing apples from the orchard, and playing games of tag upon the cliffs. She should not neglect them simply because she was now Miss Bainbridge. From their shy, friendly smiles at church, they had not forgotten those youthful bonds, and neither should she. They were proving kinder than her peers.

"I will do my best to introduce you," Honore said. "I have met all of them at one time or another, except perhaps some wives brought here since I left for London last year. But how will you keep that from your mother?"

"She spends two hours resting every afternoon." Deborah smiled. "She is really reading novels but does not wish me to know she indulges in them, so we pretend she needs the rest. And as for Bainbridge . . . " She shrugged. "I will be in my room resting too."

Not certain this act of deception was a good way for her brother's fiancée to begin a relationship, Honore still hesitated.

Then Miss Morrow caught her eye across the teacups. "What a fine way for you to reacquaint yourself with the people who live here, especially those who have been here for nearly thirty years or more."

Honore stared. Miss Morrow was speaking nonsense. Most of the families of the tenants had been there for more than three hundred years, let alone nearly thirty.

Nearly thirty . . . As in twenty-eight.

Honore nodded. "All right. We will go Tuesday, I think. Tomorrow will be washing day, so that is not good. But Tuesday is ironing, so we can visit without disrupting their work."

"Lovely. Do we walk?" Deborah looked a bit dubious.

Honore smiled. "I see no other choice."

They discussed how they might get out a pair of horses or even a dogcart. But Bainbridge's carriage house did not contain the little two-wheeled vehicles any lady could drive on her own, and a groom would insist on accompanying them with horses. In the end, Deborah conceded that Honore was right, and they arranged to rendezvous there at the dower house.

"Trouble there." That was Miss Morrow's observation after Deborah's departure. "She has a will like yours."

"Then perhaps my brother likes me after all, if he likes females with strong wills."

"Stronger than his own, if I may say so." Miss Morrow's

chilled tone suggested she did not care in the least if Honore minded her criticism of Beau Bainbridge.

Honore did not. Deborah might claim her mother would loosen her hold once they were wed, but Honore doubted it. Lady John would get her way in all things unless Deborah chose to disagree.

It did not bode well for Honore's future.

All the more reason to accomplish something that would either create a scandal powerful enough to obliterate her escapades or set Ashmoor free to marry her.

"Except he is always free to marry me." Honore came to the conclusion Monday night as she brushed out her hair before her dressing table mirror. "He is simply choosing not to."

She flung the silver, enamel-backed brush onto the table and propped her chin in her hands. He claimed he had to keep himself above reproach for the sake of his family, but in truth, the revenue officers would have to find a great deal of proof against a peer of the realm—as in catching him in the act of treason—to do anything about him. Of course, someone could lay information against him and he might be carried off to London for questioning by the House of Lords, but surely his assets would not be seized until he was decided guilty. That could take months, even years. In the meantime, he could have smuggled enough money and other valuables out of England to set up his family for life.

So of course he had just been toying with her, dallying with her. She was a passably pretty girl with a reputation for being flirtatious, so why not kiss her in the moonlight? He even told her he loved her so she would not feel bad about acting so recklessly.

"A test. It was a test, God, and I failed."

She dropped her face onto her folded arms, suddenly too

weary to braid her hair or even get up and go to bed. For the third time, she was making a fool of herself over a man who was unworthy of her regard.

Or at least she said he was. Perhaps she was the one unworthy—unworthy to be loved, to be respected, to be a part of the lives of good and decent people.

Self-pity is unbecoming. Miss Morrow may as well have been in the room speaking the words in Honore's ear, so clear did her brisk tones come across.

"I am going to indulge for a while anyway." Honore spoke aloud. No one was near enough to hear her.

Yet she heard another voice, Cassandra's quiet tones, reminding her that God loved her, that He accepted her with all her flaws. If anyone understood being loved despite flaws, that person was Cassandra. Honore's head knew the truth of God's acceptance. She could recite many Scriptures referring to God's love. She had even accepted it in her heart once. Now, however, after a year of her being rejected by Society, her own family, and a man she wanted to be worthy of her love, her certainty of being loved had vaporized and left behind a hollow in her heart that seemed to grow larger that night.

She did not cry. She fell asleep sitting on the dressing table stool. Sometime in the night, the barking of a dog woke her. She stumbled to the window and stared over the wall to the orchard and sea beyond. Nothing stirred. Even the tree branches hovered motionless in the night, so she crawled into bed despite cold and damp-feeling sheets.

Not until morning did she wonder how she had heard a dog barking. As far as she knew, no one close enough for the animal to be heard owned a dog. So someone had walked by in the night. It meant nothing. She was seeing shadows and suspicious movements everywhere. Now she would meet her future sister-in-law with her eyes puffy from lack of sleep.

"And I will learn nothing." She grumbled over her state to Miss Morrow across the breakfast table. "This is a hopeless wild goose chase for a man who does not love me."

Miss Morrow gave her a sympathetic smile. "I wish I could assure you that he does, but I would think he could perhaps be a bit more forthcoming."

"Like caring about me more than his reputation? Perhaps he has no reputation to protect."

There. She had spoken her fears aloud.

But Miss Morrow showed no surprise. "The notion has occurred to me."

"That he is as much a roué as the others I've lost my reason to?" Honore set down her coffee cup before she smashed it against the farthest wall. "We say that someone had to know this and know that, and of course it could easily be him. Which means I am once again a dupe being used for someone else's gain."

"Or a scapegoat."

"You are so comforting." Honore made no attempt to hide the sarcasm in her tone.

Miss Morrow rose, pressed Honore's shoulder, then left the room without another word. She did not reappear until moments before Deborah knocked on the dower house door and Mavis let her in. Then Miss Morrow descended to the entryway with cloaks over her arm.

"It is clear but cold out. You will need this, Miss Honore."

"Miss Honore?" Honore stared at her. "When—? Well, I suppose it is better than 'dishonor.'" She snorted at her own jest.

Deborah giggled.

Miss Morrow flushed. "I should not be so presumptive. You are my employer. I forgot myself."

"Do not be absurd, Miss Morrow. I am weary of this 'Miss this' and 'Miss that.' You are like one of my elder sisters now." Honore frowned. "Better than they. You have stayed in contact with me."

"But your sisters have written!" Deborah exclaimed. "Did no one bring over the letters?"

Honore stiffened. "No. When?"

"They were on the hall table Saturday morning. Your sisters are both delivered of healthy baby boys just two days apart."

"Saturday." Honore's head felt about to explode. "I did not know." And no one had thought to tell her. "I will write them, if Bainbridge will frank the letters," Honore murmured.

"Whittaker will frank them at his end if you send them there first." Miss Morrow squeezed Honore's hand. "Do not see malice in all actions, my dear. Sometimes people are simply forgetful."

"Of course." Honore compressed her lips and started for the door.

If they walked around the dower house and exited the garden through a side gate, they could leave the walled grounds and emerge onto the lane without anyone from the house seeing them. They moved quietly, as though someone might hear them if they did not creep. Her own words stuck in her throat, but she must let that go, swallow down the hurt and frustration for the sake of meeting the tenants again, gaining their trust, garnering information. Perhaps she could not gain a title or knighthood for her efforts, but she could possibly gain the approval of society.

Society, not Lord Ashmoor. If he could not love her tarnished and all, then he was not worthy of her love in return. She was weary of being good enough for clandestine alliances, a secret companion and friend, or a lady to be kissed in the shadows. She would be courted in public or nothing.

Marching along the lane to the road and cottages beyond, she practiced her smile, the phrases of introduction she would utter. She would make note of any repairs needed to cottages or any sickness in the houses. Tuckfield had always been good about repairing houses and other buildings on the estate. Honore had received no complaints from anyone since her arrival, and the dwellings she had seen appeared sound. If she found want anywhere, she would find a way to fulfill it. For all his ill treatment of her, her brother would surely follow in their father's footsteps and authorize repairs and other assistance to the tenants. And if she took care of the tenants, if she found out who was smuggling French prisoners out of England, if she even discovered who had really murdered the revenue officer, then perhaps she would be acceptable, her past sins forgotten, if not forgiven. Apparently they would never be forgiven.

By the time they reached the first cottage, Honore had schooled her features into a warm smile. Once they were inside the spotlessly clean house smelling of hot irons and some kind of simmering stew, her smile became natural. The wife, a newcomer from Cornwall who had married one of Honore's childhood cohorts, appeared genuinely happy to see them, and a child of perhaps three or four peeked out from beneath the kitchen table with brown eyes wide and a thumb in his mouth. While Deborah spoke with the wife, Honore crouched down and tried to persuade the toddler out. She vowed to send—no, bring—some boiled sweets in the near future.

The next house belonged to a couple whose children had married and moved elsewhere. The wife moved with a stiffness suggesting arthritis, and Honore made a note to dig up liniment from the Bainbridge apothecary stores. The stillroom had been neglected since Cassandra abandoned chemistry for Plato a few years earlier, and Mama never made medicaments, preferring to purchase hers, but Honore expected the housekeeper made a few things for the servants' needs.

They returned to Bainbridge, not wanting to be too long, but promised more visits on Thursday.

"Bainbridge will be off to Exeter for some business," Deborah explained. "We can stay out a bit longer then."

"And tomorrow?" Honore asked.

Deborah turned away, muttering something about other occupations. They were occupations that brought a dozen carriages to the house in the afternoon, an at-home to introduce Deborah in a more informal setting than a ball or dinner party.

"I am tempted to walk in on them," Honore told Miss Morrow. "But I like Deborah, so I will refrain." She wondered if Ashmoor came to call, then kicked herself for caring. "Saturday we shall go into Clovelly to the market so I can buy sweets for the children and perhaps bulbs for the wives to plant flowers around their front doors."

"An excellent notion. Daffodils will look fine in the spring."

On Thursday, they visited two more cottages. Both appeared fine inside, with comfortable chairs in the parlor and some rather nice china dishes set on the dresser in the kitchen. The wife in the first cottage proved to be the eldest sister of one of Honore's playmates, and the second housewife the youngest. Honore's friend had married and moved to Dorset.

The table in the second house bore a row of loaves made from the coarse grain that was the usual in the country tenant homes—bread that Honore had preferred to the fine white bread she received at home. When Honore, Deborah, and Miss

Morrow departed, the wife wrapped up a loaf in a fold of newspaper and pressed it into Honore's hands. "For helping me Tom." She whispered the words.

Honore stared at her. "Who?"

The woman glanced at the other ladies, then moved even closer. "Me Tom nearly drown t' other night, but you and your young man saved him."

"But I—" Honore caught her breath. Her heart began to race. With an effort of will, she managed not to crush the loaf against her chest in her excitement.

She must not be excited. This could mean nothing but that Tom had been out fishing on that windy night she and Ashmoor had gotten the rope. Then again, it could mean this woman's husband worked with the smugglers and trusted Honore enough to thank her for her help, little as it had been.

It also meant he and his companion knew she had been out in the middle of the night.

She must not concern herself with that. She must concentrate on the gift of knowing the identity of one man who might be able to help her obtain the information she needed for her mission.

"If we can ever do aught to help, miss," the woman said, "never you hesitate to ask."

"Thank you. I will remember that."

Honore fairly bounded to catch up with Deborah and Miss Morrow. "She gave me a loaf of bread." Her breathless explanation was unnecessary.

Deborah's brow furrowed. "Odd she would not give me one, as I will be mistress of this land soon."

"She likely thinks you too grand to want such humble fare." Honore smiled.

Deborah did not. Her lips turned down at the corners, and

she said nothing all the way back to the gate behind the dower house. Instead of coming into the dower house as she had on Tuesday for a cup of tea, Deborah declined Honore's invitation to taste the bread.

"That woman is right. I only like the finest of white flours." She drifted off toward the house, gown, cloak, and hat ribbons floating behind her.

"If I had not seen them," Miss Morrow mused, "I would think that child had no feet."

"Child?" Honore snorted. "She is a year older than Beau."

Miss Morrow gave Honore a sharp glance. "Why have you taken against her?"

"Her remark about the bread. It was truly arrogant."

"You cannot imagine she would go untouched by her mother's attitude, can you?"

"I had hoped." Honore sighed. "Or maybe she was just hurt that farm wife gave it to me and not her."

"Yes, quite possibly." Miss Morrow gave Honore a sidelong glance. "So perhaps you should tell me why she singled you out."

Honore started across the garden to the dower house. "I would rather not."

"I was afraid you might say that, which means you have been indiscreet again."

"Yes, I have. I mean I was. I mean—oh no." She stumbled to a halt at the sight of her brother glaring at her from the book room window.

Too late to go in another direction. She must simply brazen out whatever had brought him to the dower house in the middle of the afternoon.

She mounted the fan-shaped steps and flung open the front door. "What do you want, Beau?"

"To know where you have been." He stalked out of the book room and stood in the middle of the tiny entryway with his arms crossed over his chest. "Where you have been with my fiancée."

"Ask her. I do not answer to you."

"You are under my roof."

"No, I am under the roof of the dower house. When you exiled me here, you washed your hands of controlling my movements."

"I am responsible for you." For a moment, his expression softened. "And Deborah. I do not care so much that she has called on you. It is in her nature to be kind, but if you have led her astray—"

"I have not. We called on some tenants is all." Suddenly Honore wanted to go to her bed and sleep for about a week. "Now will you leave me?"

"As long as you assure me you were not meeting some man," Beau said.

Honore snorted quite indelicately. "No, I was not meeting some man. I have decided not to marry until someone sensible finds me an acceptable husband I can trust to be upright and honest."

Beau's eyes narrowed. "Not Ashmoor?"

Too weary in body and spirit to dissemble, Honore said, "There is no hope there, Beau, if nothing else because I care for him."

Miss Morrow gasped.

Beau's eyebrows nearly reached his hairline. "You cannot think he is . . . like his father."

"Or my last beau?" Honore curled her upper lip then shook her head. "No, not that. If his father was a murderer, it did not pass down to the son. But you can trust me not to be tossing my hat over the windmill for Lord Americus Ashmoor." The very words hurt her heart.

Unable to speak any longer, she brushed past her brother and started up the steps, still carrying the loaf of bread.

"Miss Bainbridge." Miss Morrow hastened to follow. "Honore." She caught up with her at the top of the steps and laid her hand on her arm. "Surely you do not think Lord Ashmoor is guilty of the smuggling."

"I love him, which makes me fear something is wrong with him." There, she had admitted it aloud. And in front of her brother, who stood at the bottom of the steps scowling up at her.

"If he is up to chicanery," he declared, his face fierce, "I will find out no matter what it takes to protect you."

"Never fear, Beau, I am already making plans to do the same." Or she would be as soon as she reached her bedchamber.

But she did not need to go as far as her bedchamber to know the time had come to ask favors of the childhood friends and their relatives with whom she had become reacquainted.

With Philo and Chilcott on either side of him like some sort of bodyguards, Meric strode down the hill to the market. They followed a crowd of mostly housewives, maids, and a handful of men in common garb with baskets and market wallets tucked beneath their arms. Every man, woman, and child amongst them checked at the sight of the men from Poole House. Most glanced quickly away. Others tried to pretend they weren't staring from beneath bonnet and hat brims. A few stared openly.

"A curiosity to have us here, apparently." Meric didn't attempt to make his voice inaudible to anyone close.

Philo glanced askance at his brother. "It's not as though we're buying fish and fowl for the dinner table."

"Or buying anything at all." Chilcott's sigh gusted enough to flutter the ribbons streaming from the back of a maid's hat brim too close in front of him. Or maybe that was simply the breeze off the harbor lifting the black streamers.

"Why are we here?" Philo asked the question while focusing his attention on the young woman with the ribbons. "Pretty little thing, isn't she?"

"Quite beneath you, Mr. Poole." Chilcott's breath should have shone with frost, so cold was his tone. "You might have wed a farmer's daughter in New York, but here you need to think higher in the event you are the heir."

"And any more accidents, he just might be." Meric shuddered.

Two days earlier, he had received word that his horses were boarded in an inn stable on the Portsmouth to London road, and would he collect them or pay up. Philo had wanted to go after them, but Meric refused his request in the event the message was a trap. He sent two grooms from Ashmoor instead. If all went well with that, Meric intended to go to Hampshire himself and make enquiries regarding who had left the horses there. His miscreant coachman, obviously, but the innkeeper or servants might know more.

"You are more cautious now, my lord." Chilcott laid a hand on his hip. Beneath his greatcoat he wore a pistol, as did Meric and Philo.

Not that a pistol would have saved him from going over the cliff if the carriage had slid down any faster.

Meric paused on the steep descent and peered over the heads of the crowd to the harbor still a long way down. Never before had heights frightened him. He hadn't flinched when rescuing Miss Bainbridge. But now he woke in the middle of the night with the sensation that he had been tumbling and tumbling and tumbling, and wakefulness had barely saved him from striking bottom.

As he stood there on the steep Clovelly street, the sensation returned. He would have gone back home to the flat land and secure walled garden of his house—or, better yet, the inlands of his estate away from cliffs—if he had been alone, if he didn't expect to find Miss Honore Bainbridge somewhere in this throng.

A note had arrived the day before telling him to do so, though not that directly. *I am considering attending the market day tomorrow*, had been her precise wording. *You should come. You never know what you might learn.*

The note had sent a surge of excitement racing through him that he quickly suppressed. Nothing he or Philo had tried had revealed information thus far. Indeed, people shut their mouths when either of the Pooles drew near.

They certainly did there in the market. A wave of silence rippled out as though they were stones tossed into a still pond. Once they reached a point too far away to hear the words of anyone, the conversations recommenced.

"I feel like a prisoner on the way to the gallows." Philo made no attempt to lower his voice. "Or do the crowds cheer when they pass?"

"Depends on the crime." Chilcott took the question seriously.

Meric continued to scan the crowd in search of a hat that appeared more expensive than the rest bobbing around the street. Or maybe a glimpse of honey-gold hair or a lovely face with eyes the color of the October sky and lips so pink they looked rouged or recently kissed.

He flinched at that. For shame. He never should have kissed her without being willing to offer for her. He wanted God to honor his prayers while he behaved in a way that did not at all honor the Lord. And she hadn't forgiven him, which made forgiving himself difficult.

Seeing her made repenting of his actions difficult. All Sunday afternoon, he wanted to hold her, tell her to forget about his duty, about the reputation he must keep clean to protect his inheritance for the sake of his family, about her reputation that might damage his. He wanted to kiss her until her tears sprang from joy, not anger and frustration with him and his inability to put her in front of family.

The intervening days hadn't stopped the longing.

If not for the promise of information he might like, Meric would have turned around and headed back up the hill and avoided seeing Miss Bainbridge again. As it was, he paused beside a woman shouting about the winkles she was selling and opened his mouth to tell Philo to find Miss Bainbridge and obtain her information.

But she appeared beside him in that instant. One minute a phalanx of schoolboys pushed noisily through the throng, and the next Miss Honore Bainbridge touched his arm, sending a lightning bolt through him. "Let's go examine that table of wooden toys." She slipped her arm through his so that he could not evade her without being unforgivably rude.

As if he hadn't already been unforgivably rude to her.

"They look more like ornaments than toys." He nodded to Miss Morrow.

She gave him a half smile and fixed her attention on a table piled with embroidered handkerchiefs. Chilcott joined her there and she started to move away, but he pressed a bit of muslin into her hand, so she had to stay or appear to steal it.

"Clever man, my steward." Meric bent his head toward Miss Bainbridge so she would be sure to hear him. "She seems to be refusing to speak with him as long as he thinks I should stay away from you."

"No, as long as he thinks *she* should stay away from me." She twisted up her face. "Like the rest of the county, except for my charming future sister-in-law."

"Ah, Miss Deborah Dunbar of the wispy voice."

Miss Bainbridge laughed. "She does seem wispy, but she's a strong girl in many ways. It gives me hope that she will send her mother packing as soon as she and Bainbridge are wed."

They reached the table of wooden carvings. None rose more than two or three inches, and the subject matter centered on animals—most real like cats and dogs, the rest fanciful creatures like griffins, dragons, and even a harpy.

Miss Bainbridge picked up the latter. "I can think of half a dozen ladies to whom I could send this, though I suppose that would not be nice of me."

"Not at all." Meric picked up one of the felines, a fat creature with a definite sneer. "Maybe this instead?"

"Oh, the cats." Miss Bainbridge laughed.

He smiled into her sparkling blue eyes. Their gazes locked. Then he remembered when they had discussed whether or not to call Misses Devenish and Babbage cats, and his gaze dropped to her mouth.

She released his arm and stumbled as though he'd shoved her. "Do not." Her voice was hoarse. "I need to tell you something. We can discuss from there whether or not we can or should do anything else, if this means anything, if—" She covered her own mouth with gloved fingers.

Meric turned to the wizened old man behind the counter of carvings. "I'll take all three of your cat carvings."

"One and six," came the laconic response.

Meric handed the man a guinea.

"He means one shilling and sixpence," Miss Bainbridge said.

Meric's ears heated despite the cold of the day. "I still get the money confused."

"One of them there rebels, are you?" The old man frowned. "Not sure I can be selling to no traitor to the Crown."

"Do not be absurd, Mr. Ricks," Miss Bainbridge snapped. "This is Lord Ashmoor. It is not his fault he was raised in foreign parts."

"Humph." Ricks took the two shillings Meric gave him and made no move to give him the sixpence he owed him in return.

"Mr. Ricks," Miss Bainbridge said in severe tones, "you owe him sixpence."

"Let him have it." Meric turned away without picking up the carvings.

Not since he had gone down to Albany with Father for the first time as a lad of twelve had he made such a stupid error with money. By dark, the story would range the entire breadth and length of Devonshire of how much of a dolt was the new Lord Ashmoor with his coin. And they would remark on his companion, a lady he should not be near in public.

He crossed the street to where Chilcott and Miss Morrow still stood beside the handkerchiefs. They gazed at one another as though no one else were around. Neither even blinked when Meric strode up to the table.

Philo had vanished from sight.

But Miss Bainbridge did not. She bustled up to him with a parcel beneath her arm and sixpence shining on her palm. "Take this." She thrust the package at him. "But perhaps you need a real cat from someone who will not try to steal from you."

He took the package and dropped it into one of his capacious coat pockets. "I hardly notice less sixpence, Miss Bainbridge."

"You will if you give them away to everyone. Goodness, my lord, do you need a keeper?"

He did around her, someone to drag him in the opposite direction.

"Just more lessons on the money cant. Now what is it you need to tell me? We've already made enough of a spectacle today, not to mention those two." He glanced at Chilcott and Morrow.

Miss Bainbridge giggled. "She cannot decide which man

she prefers. They are both eligible and they both adore her, but Chilcott thinks he can tell her what to do and with whom to associate." Her face suddenly sobering, she bent over the handkerchiefs, sorting through a pile with various initials embroidered on one corner. "How much, Mrs. Lee?"

Did she know everyone?

"Sixpence. They be only muslin." The middle-aged lady in widow's black gave Miss Bainbridge a gentle and kind smile. "For you, Miss Bainbridge, I'd be selling them for three for a shilling. And they're as soft as you please now, as I washed the cloth many times before doing the stitching."

They all knew her and liked her, apparently not caring about her past misdeeds.

Or maybe having forgiven her for them as a Christian should?

Meric shifted from foot to foot, suddenly uncomfortable in the crowd and with the smells of raw fish and overcooked sausages. He needed a walk in the open. Better yet, a walk through a forest where he could smell the drying leaves crunching beneath his feet this time of year and sniff for a hint of snow on the wind.

Beside him, Miss Bainbridge handed over two shillings. "It's exquisite stitching. I'll take six." She selected one with an H and then others with flowers along one edge.

The woman offered to wrap them for her. Miss Bainbridge declined and tucked five of the squares into the little bag hanging from her wrist, making its sides bulge. Then she started to walk away from him, dropping the sixth handkerchief at his feet.

He stooped to pick it up, and when he rose, she had vanished into the crowd. But she had left him a message tucked into the folds of the kerchief.

"Dropping her handkerchief for you, is she, my lord?" The widow behind the table winked at him. "You won't be finding a nicer lady in all the county and likely further. No matter what t' others say of her, she be a good girl. Spoiled, allowed to run wild, but good for all that."

"Yes, ma'am, I believe you're right." He smiled at the woman and turned back to again look for Miss Bainbridge.

No, not "Miss Bainbridge" anymore. Whatever propriety insisted, he and the youngest Bainbridge had passed from formality of address to . . . something else that still confused him.

Chilcott and Miss Morrow had vanished too. With Philo nowhere around, Meric headed up the hill to his house. Not until he reached his front steps did he open the message and read it. Then he read it again, scarcely able to believe that she suggested he meet her ten miles away. No matter that she assured him she would be well chaperoned, it all seemed shockingly improper. On the other hand, it would be private, away from prying eyes and the possibility of him encountering those who would know him in an instant. Possibly those who would know either of them in an instant. They would be all right if properly chaperoned.

At that moment Chilcott arrived in the street leading one horse, a groom behind him leading two more. "Ready, my lord?"

"You know." Meric's words held no question. Of course Chilcott knew.

But he nodded as if Meric had asked a question. "*Mon amie* will be there to make us respectable."

Ah, his friend. His lady friend. Miss Morrow.

But ten miles on a horse . . .

Meric suppressed a groan and descended the steps to mount. "Philo coming along then?"

"Yes, my lord. He said he will not allow you out of his sight, as you seem to get into trouble when he is gone and he does not wish to inherit."

"How benevolent of him."

Philo was certainly not responsible for his accident with the carriage, but the missing French prisoners might be another matter. Philo wasn't much fond of England and might decide to earn a little of his own money helping England's enemies. If it were so, Meric would find out immediately if he had to lock his younger brother up for days until he confessed. Yet even if he did, it didn't answer the problem regarding who had tried to kill Meric and who had falsely accused his father of murder.

Maybe Honore had gained some useful information. She had better have found out something to make this journey worth the discomfort of riding on a horse for an hour and a half. She was probably in a cozy carriage.

But she was not. Wearing a veil over her face, she arrived behind the Ashmoor party with Miss Morrow in the back of a dray wagon along with its barrels of provisions for the inn. The instant the drayman lowered the back of the wagon, she leaped to the ground and held up a hand against anyone speaking to her, then slipped inside the inn.

Meric followed. Bowing with perfunctory courtesy, the landlord showed Meric and his companions into a private parlor.

"I have ordered some refreshment," Honore said from across the room. "Do, please, be seated, gentlemen."

Meric remained standing and propped one shoulder against the mantel. He didn't speak until the landlord left. "Why this clandestine meeting if I was to meet you in the market?"

"To throw anyone watching us off the scent." Honore's smile flashed through the gauze of her veil. "We know we have a traitor in our midst, do we not?"

"I know no such thing." Meric glanced at the other three occupants.

Miss Morrow flushed but met his gaze.

"How does that help if it is one of us here?" Philo asked.

Honore toyed with the hat ribbons beneath her ear. "Elimination, Mr. Poole. If this news gets out, then we know it is one of you."

"Me?" Philo shot up from his chair.

"Down, boy," Meric drawled. "She is being general."

"I suspect she means me." Chilcott's mouth worked as though he struggled against either smiling or frowning.

Miss Morrow ducked her head so her hat brim hid her face more completely than did her filmy veil.

"It's all nonsense." Meric made his tone harsh. "Like schoolchildren playing games in the woods."

"This is no game." Honore took a step toward him, holding out her hands palms up. "You came too close to dying, and so did I. French prisoners are escaping from Dartmoor, going free to kill Englishmen, and only an Englishman can be helping them."

"Or an American," Philo said.

"Or an American," Honore agreed. "Though I—"

The door opened to admit two maids with trays of coffee and viands. No one spoke until the food trays stood on a table and the maids departed. Then they talked only of serving matters for several more moments.

"What news I have," Honore said at last, "is so miniscule it emphasizes to me that we have to do something drastic, something daring, or we will learn nothing until perhaps it is too late to prevent a disaster like a fatal fall off a cliff or a few drops of poison in someone's soup."

"Poison is a woman's weapon," Chilcott said.

Honore smiled. “Why do you think we are not considering a female here? Am I not suspect because of my past alliance with a traitor?”

How she managed to kick him in the middle from across the room, Meric didn’t know, but his gut sure felt like she had managed the feat. Or perhaps his conscience had kicked him in the middle.

“No one could suspect a lady like you.” Philo glared at Meric. “Can they?”

Meric sighed. “Not seriously.”

“Or Miss Morrow,” Chilcott added.

“Why not?” Miss Morrow’s tone held asperity. “I might wish to feather my nest for the day Miss Bainbridge no longer needs my services.”

“What is your information?” Meric let the question lash like a whip crack before an argument disrupted the meeting.

“It is very little.” Honore lifted her veil and raised a Shrewsbury biscuit to her lips, took a bite, and returned it to her plate, leaving a dusting of sugar behind.

Meric raised his hand as though he could reach her from a dozen feet away and brush the sugar away with his fingertips. Except he didn’t want to use his fingertips. He wanted to taste the sweetness . . .

He had no right to even think in that direction if he didn’t intend to offer for her.

He looked away. “You never know how the smallest seed will grow.”

“Quite true.” Honore licked away the sugary crumbs and avoided his gaze. “This made me think—but I am getting the cart before the horse. All I learned is the identity of one of the men you rescued that windy night. His wife thanked me with a loaf of bread, the kind I loved so well when I was a child and ran wild with the tenant farmers' children."

"I won't ask," Philo murmured, "how she knew Miss Bainbridge was involved, Meric, you dog."

"I think," Miss Morrow said, "some further explanations might be in order."

"Not now." Honore pulled her veil over her face again, then flung it and her hat aside and leaped to her feet. "It is unimportant, all that. Knowing the identity of one of two men who were out picking up contraband despite the weather is unimportant. They know nothing of French prisoners escaping."

"But might know something of the murder blamed on my father," Meric said.

"They might, but because of that murder accusation and escape, you, my lord, are going to get accused of these disappearances in a way your rank will not prevent, now that my brother knows you called on me last Sunday."

"Why did you tell him?" Meric asked.

She glared at him. "Why presume I told him? Miss Deborah, though good-intentioned, cannot keep secrets from her fiancé. So now Beau thinks you must be . . . if you have taken interest in me . . ." Her lower lip quivered and she turned away. "So I have decided we need to earn the trust of Dartmoor prisoners and see if we can learn anything from them."

"Why would they trust you?" Philo asked.

Honore smiled. "Do you all know that my brother-in-law was a prisoner in Dartmoor for a while?" She flicked a glance at Ashmoor. "Christien de Meuse, the man who is officially my guardian by my father's appointment should I not be wed at his death. He said the conditions in Dartmoor are such that they will do anything, trust anyone they think will get them out of there before the end of the war, especially the French. Some have been there since the prison was built four years ago, and who knows when the war will end? It's been going on for twenty years already."

"But Miss Bainbridge—" Chilcott stopped speaking and shook his head.

Meric stared at her. Chilcott and Philo stared at her. She gazed back at them with eyes as calm as an August sky.

"You want me to go make the acquaintance of Dartmoor prisoners, convince them I'll help them escape, when I'm under suspicion?" Meric finally managed to get the words of incredulity past his lips. "My dear Miss Bainbridge, you must be mad."

"Not at all." She smiled. "I do not expect you to go. That would be madness. But they have a market every Wednesday, and I can go."

23

Honore did not care that the others spent half of an hour trying to dissuade her from her chosen course of action. She intended to go to the prison. At present, she saw no other course.

"If we can stop whoever is taking French prisoners out of the country," she pointed out, "we can stop the military from trying to blame you, Ashmoor."

"Ashmoor, is it," Philo murmured. Then he grinned at Honore.

She turned her shoulder to him and fixed her gaze on Ashmoor. "If we clear your name of these suspicions, then the old murder will not matter."

"The old murder," Ashmoor responded, "will always matter so long as the majority of the county thinks my father committed it."

Honore shook her head. "Most of the county does not think that, though. You are the one invited everywhere. You have been invited everywhere since you landed here."

"Including a three-month visit to one of your cozy prisons." Ashmoor's mouth was set in a thin, grim line, and she wanted to smooth it with her thumb as he had touched her lips, soften it with a kiss . . .

Her insides quivered, and she rose to draw on her hooded cloak and veiled hat. "I am going to the prison if I have to go by myself. Miss Morrow?"

"Miss Morrow," Chilcott exclaimed, "you will not allow her to go, will you?"

Miss Morrow smiled sweetly. "How do you intend me to stop her?"

"Why, you can . . . her brother will not . . . that is to say . . ." Chilcott spluttered to a stop.

"Have me dismissed?" Miss Morrow also rose and began to draw on her cloak. "I am shocked one of you gentlemen will not rise and assist us."

Ashmoor shot to his feet. "I beg your pardon." His ears reddened. "We are forgetting our manners in our shock. Miss Morrow, allow me." She was closer to him, and he reached for her hat resting on a table.

Chilcott reached it first.

Philo reached Honore first. "We are a couple of colonial yokels, aren't we?" He took her cloak from her hands and swirled it around her shoulders, then handed her hat to her. "I think you're mad for this scheme of going to the prison market, even if ladies do go there, but you have such pluck, I wonder my brother can bear to so much as talk to Carolina Devenish."

Honore fastened her cloak and adjusted her hat before saying, "She is a remarkably pretty girl." She set her mouth tight so she did not curl her upper lip or gag on her prim way of speaking.

Philo laughed and turned to his brother. "Meric, you are a fool."

"Probably." Ashmoor's gaze touched Honore's face, met her

eyes, dropped to her lips, then snapped back to her eyes. "You cannot do this for me, Miss Bainbridge."

"I am not doing this for you, my lord. I am doing this for myself." She flipped her veil over her face so it appeared as though she viewed him through green fog. "I hope one day I can say that I did not love three rascals in a row."

Not waiting for a response, she spun on her heel and stalked from the room before anyone could leap forward and open the door for her.

As the portal slammed shut behind her, she heard Philo say, "She as good as accused you of committing some crime."

"Wrong," Honore murmured to herself. "I did not accuse him of a crime per se. I simply pointed out it was a possibility." After all, she loved him. She could as easily have chosen a scoundrel three times in a row as she could be hoping that three times was the charm for her. She already knew it was not. He had made up his mind she was not good enough for him, that he could not accept her with her sullied reputation.

She wanted to be gone before the Ashmoor party exited the room, but Miss Morrow would not remain inside alone with the three men, and Honore needed to wait for the drayman to return with his wagon. The journey home would be slow, bumpy, and fatiguing. She had not ridden this many miles in over a year. The carriages or horses, however, had been out of the question.

Now she must work out how she would reach the prison. She could not find a farmer or drayman who would take her there. Again, if she used a Bainbridge horse or carriage, doubtless the head groom would tell her brother, who would scold, even forbid her the use of the horses also. That might make reaching the prison difficult. And Chilcott might tell Beau of her planned expedition. Or perhaps she should draw Deborah into the wild goose chase of a scheme. It was the equivalent of going someplace like Bartholomew Fair or to some other raucous entertainment, populated by the great unwashed rather than the haut ton.

Deborah would never go without a large escort.

The Ashmoor men did not wish Honore and Miss Morrow to ride home without escort, even veiled as they were. They crowded out of the private parlor as though all tried to exit the door at the same time, and surrounded Honore.

"It's the least I can do for you after your help." Ashmoor rested his hand on her shoulder and spoke quietly into her ear.

Honore shrugged off his hand. "I am not doing this for you, remember? And your brother is right. I have just about accused you of a crime."

"You know it's not true."

"I know I would rather it were not true. Ah, here is my conveyance." She swept out the door.

Ashmoor followed. "I'll help you climb up."

Honore accepted his aid. Settled on the straw-stuffed bolster the drayman had produced for a seat, she leaned toward Ashmoor and rested her hand on his shoulder. "If you are lying to me, please tell me now."

His eyes flashed, and he walked away without saying a word.

Not a denial of guilt. Not an admission either. As good as saying she must reach her own conclusion.

She rode home, not saying a word, not listening to Miss Morrow, and wishing she still prayed. No, that was not quite right. She still prayed. She simply did not believe any answers would come if she did not take drastic actions.

Going to the prison was not precisely a drastic action. Many ladies did visit the prisons with blankets and soaps and coin to buy the trinkets the prisoners made to sell or exchange for such luxuries as the means to cleanliness and warmth. Her brother would likely send her to Somerset or lock her up if he found out, though, which meant not daring to let Deborah know of the excursion.

But Deborah seemed determined to spend as much time as possible with Honore. She arrived on Monday with a plate of macaroons and cakes. On Tuesday she drew up outside the gate in a little dogcart Beau had purchased for her for tooling about the countryside. Miss Morrow had to stay home, for which she expressed a great deal of pleasure.

"I was thinking of baking apple pies, if I may be so bold."

"I love apple pie. How many did you plan to bake?" Honore asked.

Miss Morrow blushed. "Three."

"We cannot possibly eat all three if we do not wish to be as fat as Christmas geese, but—oh." Honore laughed. "One for each of your suitors?"

Miss Morrow tossed her head.

"Then bake four and we will take one to the prison."

On Wednesday, Honore and Miss Morrow rose extra early to take out two horses before Deborah could plan their day for them. First they made some calls on more of Honore's childhood friends, cementing their loyalty to her. Then they started for the prison.

They were halfway to the prison, riding cross-country on their mounts, their faces heavily veiled, when Honore realized the guards might not allow the pie inside. "We might be smuggling something inside it."

"We are," Miss Morrow said in her calm fashion. "Coins for bribing guards if we must."

Dartmoor was bleak, with high, barren rock and scrub where the wind blew ceaselessly and always seemed colder than the rest of the county. Sheep and a few wild ponies wandered about the landscape, but few people ever ventured there except on business pertaining to the prison.

The Crown had built it four years earlier to house French prisoners. Now Americans joined the crowded facility, and the fortress appeared far older, bleaker, formidable.

"Odd to think my sister met her future husband here." Honore poised outside the gates. They stood open so men, women, and children could stream in and out with baskets and small carts full of goods. The scene resembled the entrance to a country fair more than a prison except for the Somerset militia in their red-coated uniforms and bayoneted muskets.

Suddenly trembling, Honore dismounted, paid a waiting boy a shilling to watch the horses, and led the way to the gates.

"Whatcha got there?" One of the guards grabbed for the pie.

Honore smiled and held it out. "Just an apple tart, sir."

"Dunno. Did you bake more into it than apples? Hee hee." He stuck a none-too-clean finger through the golden top crust. His eyes widened, and he stuck in his thumb with a well-bitten nail and drew out one of the crowns Miss Morrow had included in the ingredients. "I think you can take it in to your sweetheart, though why you'd be wanting a Frenchie for a sweetheart rather 'n a good Englishman, I dunno."

"Not a sweetheart, sir, just Christian charity." Honore dropped him a curtsy he did not deserve, then she led Miss Morrow into the teeming prison yard.

"This place is teeming with vermin," Miss Morrow muttered.

Indeed, the stench nearly knocked Honore back out the gate.

The appearance of the men brought tears to her eyes. Most wore little more than rags cobbled together with tied twine and rough stitching. Their hair and beards were long and unkempt. Worst of all, only a few men appeared to be eating enough.

"Even if this proves to be a useless journey," Honore declared, "we are returning with food and blankets."

Blankets that others had apparently brought to the prison now served as cloaks against the damp chill in the air inside the high stone walls.

Miss Morrow's apple tart, as large as she had made it, looked ridiculously inadequate. It served as a lure. The men ranging around the edges of the market square, carefully watched over by guards, stared at it with hungry, hollow eyes. One man close to the entrance dared to reach out toward the confection.

Honore danced away and spoke in her schoolgirl French. "I am buying information."

"I don't have none," he said in an accent similar to Ashmoor's.

"You are an American." Honore flinched back. "You cannot help."

"If you want a Frenchman, you have to go over there." He pointed across the yard. "But I'd pay a pretty penny for even a bite of that pie."

He even had hazel eyes like Ashmoor's, and the longing look chopped a hole in her heart.

Miss Morrow tugged on her arm. "We must be going."

"Wait." The man stepped forward and lowered his voice. "What sort of information?"

"Who is helping the Frenchmen escape?" No sense in dissembling. That would take too long.

The man sighed and looked away. "Nobody willing to help us Americans. To some, we're the greater enemy."

"But you are not—" Honore clenched her teeth from further words.

Of course he was the enemy. Ashmoor could be the enemy. Just because they both spoke English—sort of—did not make them friends and loyal to the Crown. Yet he was a man, and if nothing else, she could at least honor the Lord through helping her fellow man with something trifling. Next week she would do more.

"You—you may break off a chunk of the tart," Honore said.

Miss Morrow jabbed her elbow into Honore's ribs.

The man looked at her as though she had sprouted wings and a halo, then broke off a chunk. His contained no silver, yet his action brought such a swarm of prisoners sweeping toward Honore and Miss Morrow, two of the militia had to leap forward and raise their muskets as a barricade.

"Move along, ladies," a lieutenant commanded.

Miss Morrow walking close behind her, Honore spun on her heel and headed for the French side of the prison. Not wanting to make a spectacle again, she handed the tart to the first man they encountered, a sailor as short as Honore with twinkling blue eyes and a gap-toothed smile. He thanked her in a guttural French she did not comprehend and darted away, weaving and bobbing beneath the outstretched arms of his countrymen.

Trembling from the cold now, as well as from sadness and fatigue, Honore headed for the gate.

"This was as bad an idea as I feared it would be." She rubbed her temples through her veil. "Could we ever make enough pies for them all?"

"Not big ones, but perhaps small pies and cakes." Two tears dropped from beneath Miss Morrow's veil.

Neither of them spoke until they were nearly to Bainbridge, then Honore sighed and glanced at her companion. "It is rather useless. We could go for weeks and learn nothing. Going back seems like a waste of time unless it will possibly help my standing with the Lord."

"Your good works aren't necessary for that, child. He likes us to do good things, but we need not earn grace. It is freely given if we repent."

"Then why," Honore demanded, "am I not forgiven even though I have repented? I have even given up pursuing Ashmoor until I am certain he is innocent, in the event he is not. Yet nothing changes for the better in my life."

"That is not the Lord's doing, Miss Bainbridge. That is people. We are commanded to forgive as we have been forgiven. You know that."

"I do, but it has been difficult to accept as truth these past few months."

Yet was not all that the Bible said truth? She could not pick and choose what she believed like delicacies on a buffet table. Either she accepted the entire Word of God or she rejected it all.

She could not do the latter. Faith had been too ingrained in her heart. And yet, what good was faith if all believed she was beyond the pale of associating with others calling themselves Christians?

"What good is God's forgiveness if others still shun me?" Honore's voice emerged tight from a constricted throat. "I can do no good as an outcast."

"Miss Bainbridge—Honore, how can you say you can do no good? You have brought so much joy and comfort to those around you these past weeks, including me. All these people"—Miss

Morrow waved her arm to encompass the countryside—"they love you. And above any humans, God loves you."

"I do not feel loved."

At that moment, her heart felt as bleak as the moorland rising behind them, as useless as the scrub vegetation clinging to the rocks.

But of course she was loved. She knew it. Her sisters, Miss Morrow, and the local people around Bainbridge and Clovelly loved her. She knew God loved her too. She knew it. She must not doubt it just because the one person she wanted to love her refused to give in to his feelings for her.

I have a solution to this, my girl—do not love him, she told herself. *He might belong in that prison with those Americans.*

Except no one deserved to be in that prison.

Honore, as usual, shoved aside thoughts of her relationship with the Lord and, of lesser importance, her relationship with Ashmoor, and began to plan how they could get back to the prison with cakes and pies and other necessities. Perhaps Deborah could be of use. Honore resolved to tell her brother's fiancé about the prison and the poor conditions.

"But why should we help these men?" was Deborah's first response to Honore's suggestion. "They are enemies of England."

"They are human beings being treated worse than swine," Honore responded. "But ask Beau if we can do anything to help. I would not want to go against his wishes in this."

Deborah gave her a skeptical glance and agreed to do so.

Sunday after church, she arrived at the dower house with Beau in tow and announced they had decided to help.

"The sermon was on loving our enemies," Deborah explained, then she winked at Honore. "And the vicar asked where you have been. He said he misses your pretty smile in the pew."

Honore wrinkled her nose. "He needs to recover from his *tendre* for me. If I am not good enough for a wealthy earl, I am most certainly not good enough for a godly vicar."

"Saw Ashmoor today," Beau said. "He says he needs to talk to me about Father. Something about the night he died."

Honore's stomach clenched. "That was the night Ashmoor was supposed to—" She compressed her lips against allowing the rest of that information out. Ashmoor did not wish to talk about signing the marriage contract, after all. Likely he wanted to ensure that Beau would not hold him to its terms. "Father was a great help to him," Honore concluded instead. "Now then, shall we go to the prison this week? We have to ride. Getting a carriage over the moor is too difficult and probably dangerous."

They made plans for taking supplies to the prison. Miss Morrow expressed a wish for Bibles in French. These being impossible to obtain, they wrote out cards that said simply, *Le bon dieu vous aimez*. The good Lord loves you.

Unable to wholly accept the truth of God's unconditional love, Honore felt like a hypocrite with each sentence she penned. She comforted herself with her novel in between times. She had nearly finished writing the tale full of adventure and romance. If only she knew how to make the ending happy and not one of those terrible books where the heroine died of a broken heart because she had behaved badly, like Clarissa Harlow or Charlotte Temple. Her happy ending would come when she found someone to publish the story for her and make her independent, or at least possessed of some money beyond her quarterly allowance, much of which she had already spent helping a man who had not so much as sent her a note for a week and a half.

If she learned anything at the prison, she would contact him.

But of course she would not, not for weeks. Too many men swarmed through the marketplace and beyond the inner gates to where they lived in stark, ugly buildings. Meanwhile, she took comfort from having her brother treat her with more warmth than he had shown her in a year.

She watched his and Deborah's faces as they entered the prison. They too stared with pinched mouths and tight eyes. Deborah blinked her pale lashes several times but failed to always hold back her tears. With a guard following them, they gave food and clothing to as many men as they could before their supplies ran out. Most of the men thanked them, blessed them. One American insisted that he pray for them. A handful cursed them as filthy English, for which Honore did not blame them. She did not know how her countrymen could call themselves civilized and herd men into these pens. Nor did she approve of an Englishman helping them escape. They might deserve to be treated better, but they were still the enemy.

Her arms lighter but her heart heavier, Honore turned toward the gates. She had been right the week before. Learning anything inside the prison was as unlikely as learning anything on the coast without watching along the shoreline every night.

They reached home. With a firmness that said Honore was still not allowed in polite company, her brother bade her good night at the gate to the dower house garden.

"No wandering about," Beau concluded before following Deborah to the house.

"What could you possibly mean by that?" Honore posed her question to Beau's back.

He either did not hear her or chose to ignore her. Grinding her teeth, she began to stalk toward her own door and shoved her hands into the pockets of her cloak.

Where she found a folded scrap of paper that had not been there when she left for the prison.

24

The last person Meric expected to see standing in the entryway of Poole House was Miss Morrow. The sight of her shot his heart into his throat, thoughts racing through his head of Honore falling into another disaster.

Yet calm and dry-eyed, Miss Morrow balanced on the balls of her tiny slippers as though ready to rock forward onto her toes and bolt or throw a right hook at the least provocation. In front of her, Wooland appeared ready to present her with that provocation. His long face had been drawn down to abnormal proportions with a frown as deep as an upside-down smile, and he had narrowed his eyes.

Meric paused in the shadow of the staircase to watch the show unfold. That Miss Morrow didn't appear distressed left him more curious than concerned. If something had happened to Honore, Miss Morrow would surely be distraught.

"We do not receive females of your sort here. Milord is a Christian gentleman for all he is a foreigner."

"And what sort of female do you think I am, sirrah?" Miss Morrow, half a head taller than the butler, looked down her long, thin nose at him from her own narrowed eyes.

"It is night, and you are a lady at a gentleman's establishment." Wooland's nostrils pinched. "Does that answer your question?"

"I believe"—Meric stepped forward into the pool of light cast by two branches of candles—"it answers my question, Mr. Wooland, as to whether or not I should dismiss you."

"Milord." Wooland jumped back as though Miss Morrow had struck him. "I am merely protecting your interests."

"You have just insulted a fine lady. If she is here, there must be some emergency." Meric held out his hand to Miss Morrow. "Do come into the parlor, ma'am. My housekeeper will come to act as your chaperone."

"My lord, I would rather ruin my reputation than have another hear what I have to say."

"I see."

He saw more than he wished. More than likely Honore was in some sort of trouble from which he must extract her. He never should have agreed to let her help seek out the men smuggling prisoners from Dartmoor. He never should have let her go to the prison.

As if he could have stopped her.

Guts twisting, he turned to Wooland. "Bring some coffee and have the fire built up in the parlor."

"Milord, you do not seem to understand." Wooland wrung his hands.

"Even though I am a foreigner, man, I understand that you are required to take my orders and enact them."

"Yes, milord." Head high, shoulders stiff, Wooland stalked through the swinging door into the kitchen area.

Meric opened the door to the parlor. "I was just about to come in here with Mr. Chilcott, as my brother has taken over the library with a few young men of his acquaintance."

To emphasize this explanation, a burst of laughter rang from the library.

Miss Morrow started, then took a deep breath and preceded Meric into the parlor. "I do not wish anyone to hear, my lord."

"I gathered that. May we wait for Chilcott?"

"I, um—" Now she was wringing her hands.

He smiled at her. "We'll wait for him."

She turned the color of a boiled lobster.

Meric stepped out of the doorway so a maid could pass and build up the fire. He could have easily done so himself and probably more efficiently, but employing servants was so little money out of his pocket, he hired as many as he reasonably could and, according to Chilcott, a few more, considering he rarely stayed at Ashmoor.

Once the maid left, Meric strode to the hearth and stood with one booted foot on the fender, his elbow on the mantel. He didn't want her giving her news before Chilcott heard it, nor before the coffee arrived with Wooland's excuse to be outside the door and possibly overhearing something, but he could wait no longer to ask the question burning on his lips. "Is all well at Bainbridge?"

"All? Yes." She held his gaze. "Miss Bainbridge has completed her Gothic novel and sent it off in the hope that someone will publish it."

"Is—is that what's been occupying her time? That is—"

What was it? If he wasn't going to court her, he had no business asking for more details.

Miss Morrow's cold glance told him that was her thought too.

He ducked his head, felt his hair slide across his brow, and thought how he needed a haircut. He had also scuffed his boots, and the knees of his buckskin breeches bulged. An unkempt Yankee. He knew the epithets the Londoners had used against him before they knew who he was, and even the men afterward, his peers in the House of Lords. They held him in such low regard for his American upbringing and three months in prison, he doubted they would give him a fair trial if suspicion grew strong enough to see him brought up on charges of aiding and abetting the enemy. That someone had tried to kill him made no matter. He had survived. Some might make the claim he had engineered the entire incident.

Chilcott said he needed a wife with connections, that he was quite likely setting his sights too low with Miss Devenish, only a generation removed from the shop.

Higher than Miss Devenish meant higher than a disgraced lady. That meant going back to London before everyone retired to their country estates for the Christmas and winter seasons. That meant leaving soon and accomplishing nothing toward clearing his father's name or his own.

It meant giving up on Honore.

"If I need to flee the country," he said aloud, "I will have to leave her too."

"Are you attempting to convince yourself of that or me, my lord?"

Wooland's entrance with a tray of coffee and cups and cream cakes prevented Meric from the need to answer. Chilcott followed on the butler's heels. The former departed, still cowing. The latter leaned against the parlor door with his arms crossed.

"In the event someone tries to eavesdrop," he said by way of greeting, "I will be here to notice and prevent them. Now tell us, Miss Morrow, to what we owe this unprecedented visit. An unwise visit, I might add, though apparently employment with Miss Bainbridge has damaged your ability to adhere to propriety."

"As has employment to his lordship robbed you of a sense of human feeling." Miss Morrow looked straight at Chilcott as she spoke.

She may as well have shot a crossbow bolt through Meric's chest. Or maybe his throat, since he choked on a sharp inhalation of breath.

"Miss Bainbridge has risked her safety and health going to Dartmoor Prison on your behalf, my lord, and you have done naught so much as send her a missive of enquiry after her wellbeing in nearly two weeks." Miss Morrow rose and began to pace around the room, surely a habit she had learned from her employer. "I only came so she would not damage her circumstances further, nor suffer the humiliation of this sort of treatment. She is distraught at the moment, to say the least, and will do something terribly foolish if you do not assist her."

"She is likely to do something terribly foolish regardless of whether or not we assist her," Chilcott murmured.

Miss Morrow stopped her pacing long enough to glare at him.

Meric did much the same. "That is enough, Nigel."

Chilcott flinched at the use of his Christian name. "I only attempt to protect the two of you from destroying any hope either of you has of being fully respectable. Miss Bainbridge has such a reputation for choosing her gentlemen unwisely, you will appear guilty of a crime simply by associating with her, my lord."

"Precisely what she thinks." Miss Morrow returned to the table and began to pour cream and coffee into the thin china cups. "Which is the only reason why she is trying to help—she needs to know she has not chosen unwisely yet again."

"The only reason?" Chilcott curled his upper lip.

Meric seated himself adjacent to Miss Morrow and studied her calm, pretty face. "What has she learned, Miss Morrow?"

"Wait." Chilcott yanked open the parlor door. Philo's upraised fist barely missed punching him in the nose.

"Sorry, Chilly." Philo strolled into the room and took the third cup of coffee. "My friends have departed for more convivial company than I provide. They don't seem to understand that I like watching racing horses without gambling, playing chess rather than games of chance, and drinking coffee over distilled spirits. Drunkenness, to me, is not entertainment." He quaffed the coffee and poured himself more—black this time. "But the three of you look anything but entertaining. What gives you all such somber faces?"

Chilcott closed the parlor door. "Miss Morrow has brought us some sort of news she was about to impart."

"Forgive the intrusion. I shall depart then." Philo headed back to the door.

"Stay," Meric said. "You may be of assistance too."

Philo paused by a shelf containing a rather large and ugly Chinese vase and leaned against it. "If you like. Haven't been any help thus far."

"Go ahead, Miss Morrow." Meric gave Chilcott a stern look. "You keep your opinions to yourself."

Chilcott shrugged.

Miss Morrow began to stir her as yet untouched coffee round and round with the silver spoon tinkling against the china, in rhythm with her explanation about the visits to the prison, the success of her pies for getting attention, how Honore dared talk to the French prisoners in her halting, schoolgirl words.

"And when we got home," Miss Morrow concluded, "she had a folded piece of paper in her pocket. Someone slipped it in there without her knowing it."

"Rather a frightening notion," Chilcott murmured.

Meric gave him another warning glance, then returned his attention to Miss Morrow. “What did this piece of paper have on it?”

“A date and a time.” At last she stopped stirring and lifted what must be cold coffee to her lips.

Meric stared at her. Philo stared at her. Chilcott grimaced and opened his mouth.

“Stubble it, Nigel.” Meric interrupted even the intent to speak. “It’s quite obvious this is a trap.”

“The conclusion Miss Bainbridge also drew.” Miss Morrow wrung her hands. “There is one difficulty with it.” She fixed her gaze on Meric. “Miss Bainbridge intends to go regardless of whether or not she thinks it is a trap, in the event it is not.”

“Of course she does.” Meric sighed, yet he could not stop his smile. “Which means I have to go too.”

25

For once, Honore thanked the Lord her wardrobe consisted of so many black gowns and gloves, kerchiefs and cloaks. She donned all of these garments, tucking her bright hair into a kerchief like a countrywoman and leaving an end loose to veil her face. Afraid Miss Morrow would join her despite her insistence that the companion remain as far from these matters as possible, Honore locked her dressing room door. Miss Morrow owned nothing black but might be tempted to borrow something of Honore's.

She was going alone. No one else must be subjected to danger that night. If Ashmoor insisted on coming, as Miss Morrow said he would, that was on his head. He should know better. He held more at stake than did she. Her reputation was already in shambles. Adding being in the presence of smugglers to his stock just might land him in prison again.

Yet she would be glad of his presence. She would be glad to see him. The elements of love she included in her Gothic novel did not substitute for the companionship of the man she still loved, even if she told herself a dozen times a day he did not deserve her. The heart did not care about whether or not the loved one was deserving.

As God does not care whether or not you are deserving. Lydia's voice rang inside Honore's head. *None of us are, but He loves us anyway.*

He had an odd way of showing His love. Even her earthly father, for all his neglect in the name of his political ambitions, had made plans for her future, had ensured that she was safe and maintained her role in Society despite her errors in judgment.

And she was off to make one more error in judgment—helping a man who might as soon be in league with the men on whom she was about to spy, if they were there, as be the innocent one seeking answers. Not, of course, that she was doing this for him entirely. No, she needed to know for herself. And she was bored now that she had finished her novel.

So why did she blame God for not loving her when she so blatantly went her own way?

The question giving her pause, she stopped on her bedchamber threshold and pressed a gloved hand to her lips. The Bible said God loved her no matter what, and forgiveness was hers for the asking. Yet she rejected God's love and forgiveness, damaging her once close bond of faith with every willful act.

Your willfulness does not stop God from loving you. Though she had said no such thing precisely, Miss Morrow's voice still rang in Honore's ears.

Honore locked the truth away, as she was tempted to lock Miss Morrow into her bedchamber. She slipped downstairs and exited through one of the parlor windows, then pulled it closed behind her. Mavis would not look to see if it was locked. Honore had deliberately taken that chore upon herself for just this sort of occasion. Only a draft of the frosty night air would take the maid into the parlor to see if a window had been left open and then to wonder why. Worst of all, she would close and lock it, stranding Honore outside in the cold and darkness.

Nearly complete darkness. The dark of the moon had been only a few days earlier, and now thick clouds covered the starlight. She could not see her black-gloved hand before her face. Only her movements would draw attention, so she proceeded with stealth, slipping along the tree line and out the gate to the garden of Bainbridge. The outside of the dower house fence gave her fair shelter until she reached the gate in the wall. She slipped the key into the lock—and froze.

The lock was not engaged.

Always this gate was kept locked except when large deliveries of goods needed to be brought to the back door or a member of the family went riding. Never in her twenty years had Honore found this gate unlocked. That it was this night left her blood as cold as the iron beneath her hands. A traitor, someone in the household involved with the smugglers, or both?

Both, for certain.

Instinct warned her to race back to the dower house and climb into her bed, safe and warm. Better yet, she should go to her brother and tell him someone he employed was likely in league with traitors and should be discovered and stopped.

But he would wonder what she was doing out at night trying to unlock an already unlocked gate. No, he likely would not ask. More than likely, he would simply lock her into her bedchamber while preparing for her exile to Somerset. She could send her pleas for Christien and Lydia to rescue her from there and wait for weeks for a response—if her letters reached them. Until he was firmly leg-shackled to Deborah, Beau was not likely to allow her to mingle with polite company, if it was in his power to stop her.

And it was in his power to stop her.

She took the only choice that made sense, other than staying home. She left the gate open.

The instant she left the protection of the wall, the wind slammed into her in a staggering gust off the sea. No sailor in his right mind would go out in this. He could never go farther than the mouth of a cove without being dashed against the rocks, even if he received the great fortune of a strong ebb tide. No tide was strong enough to counter this kind of a gale.

She was uncertain as to whether *she* was strong enough to withstand this kind of a gale. She started to flatten herself against the wall for as much protection as she could manage, then realized how much her black garb showed in contrast to the pale limestone. Head down so her kerchief remained over her hair and face, she trudged along the edge of a field on the far side of the road. Her skirt tangled around her legs. She gathered it in one hand and held it up to her knees. No one was about to see her calves in their black lisle stockings.

One yard. Two. Twenty. Twenty times twenty yards from the gate, she reached the low wall for the pasture. She climbed over it. No sheep remarked at her intrusion into their terrain. Sensible if stupid animals, they were tucked up together in a sheltered corner. If she screamed, no one would hear her.

"I do not have a reason to scream," she said aloud.

The wind snatched her words and howled them away.

She increased her steps. She was not going to become involved in anything. If she was quick enough, no one would even know of her presence, perhaps not even Ashmoor.

She hoped he would not know. Nearly two weeks away from him was good. She must keep it that way until he was proven innocent.

If he was—

She brought her thoughts up short from going in that direction. The low wall on the other side of the field brought her up short with the next-to-the-top row of stones slamming into her knees. Gasping from the pain, she bent over, her hands on top of the wall, the smell of dried grass and salt spray thick in her nostrils, the taste of blood from a bitten lip in her mouth. She could not recall if she had cried out. She must not, not this close to the cliffs.

If she did not pay more attention to her whereabouts, she would walk right off that cliff. Coming close to falling off it—or, more accurately, having it fall out from beneath her—had been quite enough of a close call for her in that regard.

Grimacing with the ache in her knees, she climbed the wall and dropped the edge of her kerchief from her face so she could see. Though the water swelled and frothed two hundred feet below, it lent more light to the darkness. So did the white scar where the cliff had broken away.

Had been helped in breaking away.

She stopped halfway over the wall, knowledge blooming in her head like the nighttime fragrance of jasmine. The cliff's destruction was not targeted at her. She knew that. The timing of her fall would have been too uncertain. But to make someone fall. To make the cliff look unstable, too dangerous to approach from above or below. To keep people away.

So perhaps this was indeed a legitimate night for the smugglers.

For half a dozen heartbeats, she poised on the low wall, ready to drop back into the meadow and retreat to her bed and safety. A trap that she knew of, she could either elude, since she was prepared for it, or talk her way out of. But real smugglers—especially those facing the attainder of treason and not merely transportation to Australia or a few years in Newgate for smuggling—would be more difficult to convince she was not a danger to. They would not care whether or not she was a Bainbridge or a nameless traveler, a lady or a laborer. They would kill her.

Continuing down to the shore was simply stupidity. Running home was simply cowardice. She could not live her life knowing she might have had the opportunity to learn something of the truth and had run from it.

She dropped down on the seaward side of the wall.

A hundred yards along the top of the cliff, she began her descent to the shore. The tide had not quite begun its ebb. Salt spray, whipped into a froth by wind and rocks, spewed into the air, wetting her slippers, her skirt, and then her cloak the closer she drew to the water. She continued, shivering from the icy water. She must be in place before the tide began to recede. Otherwise, she would be too late, could walk straight into the smugglers, one of the escaping prisoners—anyone daring to use Bainbridge land for their unlawful activities, as though intending to implicate one of the family in their treacherous crime.

She ground her teeth, clenched her free hand into a fist, and walked into Lord Ashmoor.

With the kerchief pulled over her face, her vision was obscured. She had moved down the path with the aid of a hand against the wall and her feet sliding forward with care. She had kept her head down to avoid getting salt water in her eyes and saw no one until the top of her head collided with something solid—not as solid as the rock but solid enough to send her tumbling backward.

He caught her arm and hauled her up before she struck the ground. For a moment, she stood nestled in the curve of his arm against his side. His wool coat with its scents of the sea and some distant forest, and something she could not identify, tickled her nostrils, teased them to find that elusive something else, teased her with an ache deep inside.

She tilted her head back. Her kerchief fell away. "Is it you?"

"Be glad that it is." Pitched below the roar of the wind and sea, his voice was rough, close to harsh.

"You should not be here."

"Neither should you." He released her slowly enough she thought perhaps he did not wish to do so. "But since you are, we need to get into place. I was thinking beneath the overhang."

"I was seen last time I thought I was hidden there. I have a better place." Honore headed across the shingle, the pebbles bruising the soles of her feet in their thin slippers.

She should have worn half boots, but they tended to make more noise when she walked. Not that the crunch of footfalls over small stones would be audible at that moment. And with slippers, she could better keep her balance on the slippery rock fragments.

With the tide barely retreated from the base of the cliff, the shingle gleamed in the phosphorescence from the wave crests and sea foam. She could hold on to neither her kerchief nor her cloak. Her garments flapped about her, threatening to lift her off the ground like wings. Her considered hiding place would not be comfortable. If either of them was inclined to seasickness, they would surely experience it here and now.

She reached the tiny inlet and the fishing boat large enough for only two, which her father had used upon occasion when he wanted to talk to a political colleague and be certain of not being overheard. He had fished from it too, and sometimes Honore had gone with him. She had gone out with her brother once or twice, and more often with the local children. Cassandra used it when she spent one summer collecting marine life to dissect and study, a short-lived interest, fortunately, since the smell she carried with her was worse than her later chemical concoctions.

Honore caught hold of the salt-stiffened painter and drew the craft close to the miniscule dock. "Climb aboard, my lord."

"We're waiting in there?" His tone conveyed his horror.

"Nowhere else—" A swell of the sea yanked the rope from Honore's hands. "Nothing else will conceal us quite so well."

"I'm not so certain about that." He reached past her and grasped the painter.

Together, they dragged the boat against the tug of the undertow. Crouching, Ashmoor held the craft steady. Or as steady as he could with wind and water swirling around the gunwales.

"If only I could wear breeches." Honore started to lift her skirt, then dropped it again. She could not show him her legs all the way to the knee. Her stockings covered them, but still . . .

"I won't look." He turned his head away. "Just hurry."

Honore picked up her skirt, petticoat, and cloak and climbed onto the boat's deck. The vessel did not boast of anything as luxurious as a cabin, merely a covered area at the stern behind the single mast—currently not stepped—and the tiller. She scrambled for the shelter and seated herself on the hard wooden bench seat. A glass stern light protected occupants of the shelter from the worst of the spray, but some of it managed to spew over the deck and beneath the overhang. If only she possessed some of those oiled skins she had heard of. They were supposed to keep a body dry.

"Keeping hidden is safer," she reminded herself aloud.

A thud vibrated through the deck to her feet. Tall and dark against the night sky and cliffs, Ashmoor covered the distance of the deck in a handful of paces and ducked beneath the shelter.

"Now what do we do?" He settled on the bench beside her instead of the one opposite.

Though he must be as wet as she, warmth radiated from him. Sliding closer than the hand span of space between them would be highly improper, and yet she had to hold herself taut to stop herself from doing just that.

"We wait." She wrapped her arms across her middle.

"This is highly improper, of course. If we're caught, you will be hopelessly compromised."

"No one will force you to wed me, my lord." She made her tone as cold as her hands and feet.

"Maybe if they did—" He broke off and leaned forward. "What was that?"

Honore shook her head. "I did not hear anything."

"Hmm." He remained in that position, alert, listening, poised to spring up at any moment, but he tilted his face toward Honore. "So you think this is a trap?"

"The information came to me too easily, do you not think?"

"I think indeed. But a trap by whom, for what reason—" Again he stopped speaking in the middle of a sentence and held up a hand, dark in its leather glove.

Above the howling wind and lashing surf rose the rattle of falling stones, the scrape of boot heels on rock, voices the wind reduced to a mere murmur.

Honore's insides coiled like the insides of a clock with someone still twisting the key. She could not have moved if the Prince Regent himself ordered her to do so. She was not certain she breathed.

Beside her, Ashmoor stiffened as though his middle had also been wound to the snapping point. The only thing on him that moved was his hand. He reached out and clasped hers, his fingers strong and warm even with two layers of gloves between them. Strong and warm and as taut as a harpsichord string.

In moments, they would know who approached the shore—smugglers turned traitors in helping French prisoners escape, or riding officers ready to spring a trap with Honore and Ashmoor inside.

Another shower of stones preceded a sharp command. *"Arrêtez-vous!"*

A sharp command to stop—in French.

Bile rose in Honore's throat. This was no trap. This was the enemy coming to escape to once again fight against Englishmen.

She leaned to whisper in Ashmoor's ear. "How do they intend to get away? There is no boat here."

He turned his head, and his lips brushed across her cheek before touching her ear with words so soft they felt more like breaths than speech. "Except the one we're on."

Madness. No one could round the Lizard at the end of Cornwall, the end of England, then cross the channel—not even to a Channel Island—in this little fishing boat.

Except they need only reach Ireland.

Her heart seemed to stop beating. The blood left her head, and she dropped her face to her knees. One breath. Two. She would not be sick. She would not faint.

Ashmoor's hand settled on her back, strong, steadying. When she started to straighten, he held her down. He slid to the deck and tugged her down beside him. He did not speak. The Frenchmen and whoever directed them stood on the dock, shuffling, muttering, making far too much noise in a sudden lull of the wind.

Then the boat jerked forward, bumping into the dock with a thud that resounded off the cliff. Someone had pulled on the mooring line. They were going to board.

"Attendez." Again a command in French, but now that the owner of the voice stood so close, his English origin became obvious.

An Englishman, a traitor, stood not a dozen feet away.

They crouched in the corner of the boat shelter, Ashmoor's arm around Honore's shoulders. Her ears ached from trying to hear the slightest nuance of movement or voice. Her eyes ached from staring into the near total darkness. Her body ached from her awkward position, the cold, a longing to simply lay her head on Ashmoor's shoulder and forget about smugglers, traitors, and decades-old murders.

She remained motionless. So did Ashmoor beside her. Honore's heart thudded so loudly the men on the dock must surely think someone marched along the cliff to the rhythm of a drum. Her heart beat so hard she felt rather than heard the thump of a person landing on the deck. Her eyes widened, her breath caught in her throat. One man of average build, judging from all of him visible as a silhouette against the pale cliffs, strode toward the stern and straight to the shelter.

"Come out." His voice was a mere rasp. "I have a gun and can't miss at this range."

Tears stung Honore's eyes. A trap. It was a trap, and she had led Ashmoor straight into it.

"Don't move," he murmured to her. Then he rose, too tall to stand upright beneath the low overhang. "A gun will be heard for miles around and could cause rocks to fall. But I have a knife, and at this range I can't miss. You'll die without a sound."

26

Of course both of them were wrong. The man could miss in the dark, cause a ricochet, and injure himself. Meric could miss with the knife, receive the shot, and leave Honore vulnerable to this man and the others still ashore. If he did nothing, however, Honore and he would be in more trouble than either of them wanted or needed.

"You can only hit one of us," Meric pointed out in a calm tone.

"But the Frenchmen will take whoever is left to protect themselves." The man laughed with a low, mirthless chuckle. "In the event it's the young lady, they might just take her."

Meric was moving, diving low, knife in hand, before he realized the man had made his crude remark about Honore for just that reason. The chuckling laugh rolled across the deck again, and then the shot came, a blast of sound, a stab of light over Meric's head.

"Honore!" He cried out her name in the silence, then he struck the man at the knees, sent him tumbling onto the deck with a resounding thud.

The Frenchmen chittered like squirrels after acorns. One tried to come aboard.

"Non, non, non." The man on the deck issued the negative, and then the distinctive click of a cocking pistol sounded nearly as loud as had the shot. "Get off this boat. I can't miss her with this one."

The rasping growl of the man's voice grated across Meric's ears like a razor over dry skin. He rolled, his knife still in hand, and took in the scene of Honore poised not two feet from the barrel of the pistol. The little fool. She should have stayed in the dark beneath the canopy. She was safe, appearing unharmed, only for the moment.

The man was right. He wouldn't miss from that distance. Meric could stab him, and Honore would still be shot before the knife gained its end.

"We will go." Honore's voice held little more strength than a puff of summer breeze, but it was steady and clear.

"The Frenchmen?" Meric asked.

The man didn't answer. He gestured for Honore to go before him, prodded her with the barrel of the pistol when she passed closely enough to him. Meric's hand gripped his knife hard enough to bruise his palm through his gloves. He'd been bested. The man had known they would be there. Someone had betrayed them again.

Probably grinding his molars to pulp, Meric led the way to the bow and grabbed the painter with one hand. It wasn't enough to drag the craft against the dock and away from the tug of the ebbing tide. He needed to slide his knife back up his sleeve and grasp the line with both hands.

A yard away on the dock, the Frenchmen set up a murmuring chatter. Meric thought he knew some French from the Canadian trappers he had encountered upon occasion. The French of these prisoners sounded like gibberish to him, with the occasional comprehensible word poking through, enough of the latter to indicate they were confused, concerned, a little angry.

Meric understood how they felt. Instead of holding on to Honore, ensuring her well-being, he held on to a rope and drew a boat to shore with a gunman threatening the lady he had determined to protect at all costs.

Other hands joined him, hands from the men on the dock. They were coming aboard. They would escape. They would escape in the Bainbridge fishing boat, with Meric none the wiser of who was behind the smuggling of prisoners out of the country.

He released the line and glanced behind him. If he could distract the man away from Honore long enough, or maybe stab his gun hand—

"Hands on the rope, Yankee." The hoarse, growling voice ripped through the air like canvas shredding in a gale. "My gun is at the back of her neck."

"Is that true, my dear?" Meric posed the question without intending the endearment.

Of course it was true. Only something that deadly could silence his Honore.

No, not his Honore. He had rejected her in that way because she wasn't good enough for him. Yet she had risked her life for him.

"It is true, *mon chou*." Her voice was slow and steady and clear, as it had been on the cliff when a shredding shrub was all that was between her and death.

He didn't understand the last two words, but he read her tone—warm and affectionate. Her own endearment to him.

His chest tightened. "Let us go free then." He grasped the line, now to hold the craft against the dock rather than close the distance, as the Frenchmen had done their work. The best he could do now was get Honore away to safety—like her own house.

Another sharp command in French came from the ringleader. The Frenchmen moved aside, still holding the mooring line. "Get ashore, Yankee." This time the command came in English.

Meric climbed ashore, then turned to grasp Honore and lift her over the gunwale and onto the dock.

"Start running." The command lashed out. "And don't spy on us again." A shot emphasized his words, a blast close enough the pistol ball buzzed past Meric's ear.

He grabbed Honore's hand. As one, they began to run. Behind them, the Frenchmen cried out, words that sounded like curses and protests. He mustn't look back. No time. Not safe. Must get Honore away, home, locked behind a solid door.

They reached the path. He nudged her before him.

"What's afoot?" She was gasping for air or from fright.

"Never you mind now. Just go." She went. He followed.

So did others. Their footfalls crunched on the shingle. Their voices rattled off the cliff.

The Frenchmen hadn't gone on the boat.

Meric dared a glance back. A swarm of men poised at the edge of the sea, waving and shouting at the boat bobbing about on the surf like a bucket in a stormy pond.

The man with the growling voice had cut the mooring line and left the prisoners behind.

"He will never survive." Honore grasped his arm. "Those waves will swamp him. He doesn't have rigging."

"And who knows what the French will do to us if they come to their senses. If I had more than just a knife, I'd round them up and deliver them back to the prison. As is, they can overwhelm us by sheer numbers."

And they had turned, their faces pale in the glow from sea and stars breaking through the clouds. One man started forward, heading toward the cliff path. Another joined him. A third. A fourth.

"Honore, start running—now."

She ran. Her skirt and cloak gathered in her hands, she sprinted up the path. Meric paused long enough to gather handfuls of stones and fling them at the Frenchmen in pursuit. *Rattle, rattle. Thud, thud, thud.*

Nothing he had thrown should thud. No human footfalls made that much noise.

Horses' hooves made that much noise. Horses. Several of them cantering along the cliff top. Too fast for the location. Drunken horsemen or—

Grabbing Honore's hand again, Meric sprinted across the cliff top to the pasture wall. He lifted her over, then dropped to the grass, drawing her down beside him.

"Halt in the name of the king!" The voice trumpeted the command like the end of the world.

"That answers that question." Meric dropped his head against Honore's soft curls for a moment, inhaled the sweetness of jasmine, then jerked away. "It was a trap."

Just as his father had been trapped, lured to the cliffs with riding officers who were warned he would be there.

"I think," Honore murmured, "it still is a trap. We aren't exactly safe here."

Indeed not. Anyone who glanced over the wall could probably see them even in the darkness, especially if they carried torches.

They carried torches. Their light suddenly flared from above. Meric raised up enough to peer over the wall. The riding officers headed down the path to the shore and the bellowing Frenchmen.

"Time to go." He scrambled to his feet, drawing Honore up after him.

They began to run across the field. It seemed a short distance on a stroll during the light of day. At night, with a likely hangman's noose about to catch up with them, the pasture looked a dozen miles long. Miles of open territory with not a hint of shelter.

If only the clouds had remained. If only fog as thick as porridge covered the countryside. If only he had found a way to lock Honore in her room to stop her from coming out to the rendezvous.

"Halt or we shoot!" The shout soared across the field, too close for comfort. Meric changed their course. Changed it back. Honore stayed with him, following his lead. If shooting started, they would not make good targets, running and not in a straight line.

"Halt!" A gunshot accompanied the command.

"Not even close," Honore gasped out.

Meric smiled. That was his Honore.

Ha. If he had any honor he would marry her.

But wasn't that the difficulty? He wouldn't marry her so no one questioned his honor? He was a lout. A fool, a—

Another shot boomed through the night.

This one didn't miss.

Beside her, Ashmoor grunted and staggered. His fingers loosened from her hold.

"What is wrong?" She caught him around the waist with one arm.

"That one . . . got me." He leaned against her for a moment. "Go on. They won't want you once they have me."

"What? Are you mad? I will not leave you to hang. Come

on." She laid his arm over her shoulders and clasped his waist. "We are almost there."

"I don't think—"

But they had reached the far wall. Honore poked, prodded, and partly rolled him over. He landed on the ground with a thump. She crouched beside him below the level of the wall, listening to the revenue men bumbling about in the field, calling to one another about how they saw a man fall.

"Where?" she asked.

"Shoulder. Back. Hip. I can't rightly tell." He started to groan, swallowed it down. "All three?"

"There is a great deal of blood." It covered her arm, sticky and metallic, gagging her. "Let me help you up. If we can get to the gate . . ."

She could lock it. The men would have to go to the house to gain access to the land. Perhaps she could hide Ashmoor by then. No one would believe Miss Bainbridge had been out with Frenchmen. Not even Miss Bainbridge.

"You can't lift me." He lifted himself to his knees with the aid of the wall.

"I can get you up the rest of the way." She grasped him under the arms and tugged.

He sucked in a sharp breath but got one foot under him, then another.

"Good, good, good. Let us go now. I think they are coming."

Difficult to tell in the dark with men shouting, a horse neighing, another gun exploding. Sounded like chaos in the field and beyond to the cliff. Good. Darkness and chaos worked to their advantage.

She staggered under Ashmoor's weight. Likely half again her own eight stone. She would not fall and drag him down. He might not get up again. She would be responsible for his death.

God, if You love us . . . No, that was testing God, was it not? God loved them no matter what.

God, if You get us out of this . . . No, that was bargaining with God.

She stopped, not knowing how to talk to God. With Father, she wheedled, bargained, or tested his love to get her own way. She was not supposed to do any of those things with the Lord, but how else did she treat a loving but distant parent?

"Please, Lord, just help us." She said the words aloud. "You are not supposed to be a distant parent but here with us always."

"Does God help those who do stupid things?"

"We are still alive, are we not? After all the stupid things I have done, I should probably be dead. But this was not entirely stupid. I think—"

"Not now."

He was right. Now was no time to talk. The riding officers were still in the field, though sounding closer, and the gate loomed before them. Honore fished the keys from the inside pocket of her cloak.

And another shot accompanied a demand for them to stop.

The gate was not locked. She had found it unlocked and left it thus. She shoved the latch down and pushed Ashmoor through with the opening gate. She closed it with the merest click and turned the key in the lock. That would slow the officers.

The wound slowed Ashmoor. What felt like a quarter hour passed before she half supported, half dragged him into the shadows beyond the wall. It must have been only a few minutes, but long enough for at least two revenue men to reach the gate and begin to rattle it, then shout.

"Keep moving." Honore stood on tiptoe to whisper in Ashmoor's ear. "Almost there."

Almost to the dower house garden. The house was not far beyond. What then? The king's men might insist on searching the dower house, if they were allowed to search the property of a peer. She did not know. She could not take the risk. Ashmoor needed care, doctoring, at least bandages and perhaps even the lead ball removed. She could not do any of those things.

She might have to. She must keep him safe until then or until she could go for aid.

"Your cellar." Gasping, Ashmoor leaned against the gate to the dower house garden. "No, not your cellar. Leave me out here. I can say I got here on my own."

"I will not leave you alone. You stay here, I stay here."

"Why?" He stroked her cheek. "I'm a—a—"

She pressed the fingers of her clean hand to his lips. "No talking. Save your breath for staying alive."

She opened the gate, caught Ashmoor as he lurched forward. He grew heavier with each step toward the dower house—the dark dower house. Either Miss Morrow had not awakened, or she had decided she would remain quietly in her chamber until Honore returned home so as not to alert the two maids sleeping on the third floor. Whatever the reason, Honore breathed a prayer of thanks for the dark stillness of the house. Even the fire in the kitchen hearth glowed as mere banked coals, more testimony to no one being awake and needing fire to boil water for tea or light candles.

But where to put him in the event the revenue men could search the house?

She paused just over the threshold into the kitchen. "I wish we had a secret room of some sort, but this house is too modern for that kind of interesting place."

"You have—" Ashmoor sagged against the wall, gasping for breath. "You have a lot of rooms in your cellar . . . Will do."

"Our cellar. That brandy."

More trouble.

She had not known what to do with it, so she had cleaned up what had spilled and smelled so badly and left the rest. Now it screamed some sort of collusion with the smugglers, cried out that the house had been used in an illicit manner. No riding officers finding the brandy would stop until they found a man they suspected was a traitor, the man they had been suspecting of treachery since his arrival in the country.

"I can hide behind the brandy." Ashmoor's hand closed on her shoulder with reassuring strength. "They find that, they may stop looking."

"May." She said nothing of suspecting it would spur them on to search for more. "Can you get down the steps?" she asked instead.

"Of course. It's just a scratch."

From the quantity of blood soaking into his coat and her cloak, the wound or wounds were more than a scratch. He could be dying. But he took a step, then another and another on his own, before he stumbled and grabbed for the edge of the worktable. A wooden bowl tumbled to the floor with a bang like a sounding gong.

"So sorry." Ashmoor breathed with quick, shallow gasps like someone who'd been running. "Hide . . . trees . . . instead . . ."

"You'll catch your death and someone will find you in the morning."

Or find his body.

She hesitated only a moment. "Sit here." She pulled out a chair. "I will return."

She eased him into a chair, yanked off her cloak and wrapped it around him, then picked up her skirts and raced upstairs.

She needed help. That was all that mattered. She needed Miss Morrow's help.

The door opened the instant Honore turned the key in the lock.

"What happened?" Miss Morrow asked.

"I will tell you all later. Right now—" Honore's throat closed at the prospect of speaking her fears aloud. "Ashmoor has been shot and I am so afraid—" A sob broke into her words.

"Where is he?" Miss Morrow grasped Honore's arm and drew her into the hall.

"Kitchen." Honore swallowed hard. "We were thinking . . . the cellar."

"Of course."

Calm, decisive, sure of herself, Miss Morrow led the way down the back steps and into the kitchen. "My lord, how bad is it?"

He did not answer. He was slumped over the table, his head on one arm. The faint light from the hearth coals revealed none of the extent of his wounds, but the metallic stench of blood filled the kitchen.

"Let us get him downstairs. Where down there?" Miss Morrow asked.

"He suggested behind the brandy barrels, but we can't move those."

"The coal room then."

Honore stared at her companion, though her face was merely a blur in the dark. "That is a terrible idea. It's dirty. It will be uncomfortable."

"It is only half full, and its very dirtiness will keep anyone from looking further." Miss Morrow's shudder ran through Honore. "Besides, coal dust will absorb the blood."

If he were still bleeding. If he were not, then either the wound was indeed a mere scratch or he was dead. If he still bled, he could soon be dead if they did not stop it.

A whimper escaped Honore's lips.

"We have time." Miss Morrow's tone soothed. "No one is looking for him."

"Yet."

"Precisely. Let us get him downstairs."

Getting him to his feet proved nearly impossible. He had lost consciousness, a bad sign. Talking and tugging, patting his face, and attempting to lift him did nothing but come too close to toppling him from the chair.

"Get some cold water," Miss Morrow suggested. "I will see what I can find of this wound."

In the far corner of the kitchen, Honore located a cup and a barrel of cold water. She dipped the former into the latter and carried them back to Miss Morrow.

Her companion leaned over Ashmoor, muttering beneath her breath. "It is not good, but it could be worse," she said aloud. "Where is that water?"

Honore gave her the cup. "It is not much for cleaning a wound."

"I do not intend to clean a wound with it." Instead of explaining, she simply upended the cup over Ashmoor's head.

He gasped and spluttered, then jerked upright with a muffled groan. "What in the—ohhh."

"My apologies, my lord," Miss Morrow said, "but we had to get you awake. I have padded your wound with my shawl. It is not the doctoring you need but has slowed the bleeding."

And how did Miss Morrow know so much about wounds?

She would ask later. For now they needed to get Ashmoor on his feet and down a steep flight of steps.

"I'm all right." The thready consistency of his voice spoke volumes to the contrary.

Yet he pressed his right hand onto the table and levered himself to his feet. Honore slipped her arm around his waist on one side and Miss Morrow on the other. Between the two of them and his own flagging strength, they got him across the kitchen and into the passage from which led the cellar door. There they stopped to figure out how to get him down the steps.

"We will go first," Honore decided. "You can lean on us, and if we are together, we can stop you from falling."

She hoped. They were more likely to all three of them fall into a broken heap at the bottom of the flight.

But they did not. Each step seeming to take a full minute, they maneuvered the stairway from coal-lit gloom to stygian darkness. Not one of them had thought to bring a candle. Too late. Ashmoor could not wait any longer before settling in one place.

Honore still balked at the coal room door. "I do not think this place is good for him."

"Prison would be less good for him," Miss Morrow countered.

Briefly, Ashmoor's arm tightened on Honore's shoulders. "She's right, my dear."

His dear. The second time he had called her that this night. For the second time, her heart stopped, warming with a spark of hope.

All the more reason to keep him alive and out of prison until she found proof that her suspect was indeed the culprit. All the more reason to keep *herself* alive and out of prison.

Honore opened the door to the coal room. The oily stench stung her nostrils. Surely it was no place for a well man, let alone a wounded one. The smell would be overwhelming with the door closed. Except a draft rushed through the room, possibly from the wooden chute high up near the ceiling that Tuckfield had had unstuck for a coal delivery.

A meager coal delivery. As Miss Morrow had said, half the room lay empty. Their shuffling feet encountered mere clumps of obsidian. Honore kicked those aside to make a clear place on the floor in one corner. Then they eased Ashmoor to the ground, Honore and Miss Morrow breathing hard from balancing his weight, him dragging breaths through his teeth.

"We will return with blankets." Honore rested her hand on his head, the thick, soft hair. With all her will, she turned away without leaning down and kissing him.

They would return if they could.

She closed the door behind her and Miss Morrow. In silence, they groped their way to the steps and climbed back to the kitchen.

"I need to light some candles and wash up any blood," Miss Morrow said.

"I will help."

"No, you go change and wash. You are all over blood."

Honore gasped and looked down. She could not see the stains against the black gown, but she felt the drying substance. "What do I do with this dress? If someone looks here and finds it . . ."

"Hang it in the wardrobe under another gown. Always hide in plain sight."

Honore opened her mouth to ask Miss Morrow how she knew so much about subterfuge, but that, like wound care, needed to wait until later when they could talk over tea and crumpets.

Honore fled upstairs. Through the fanlight above the front door, she caught a flash of light. She ran into the front bedroom, the one facing the main house. Her heart dropped into her middle. Lights flared in window after window there, as though everyone had awakened or people moved from room to room without extinguishing lights in the previous chamber searched.

The riding officers had gained entrance and permission to search her brother's house for miscreants—for her and Ashmoor. Their arrival at the dower house loomed in mere moments.

She spun on her heel and reached her own chamber as thunderous knocking sounded on the front door.

27

Buttons flew as Honore tore off her gown. No matter. The king's officers were not searching for something as small as a button. They wanted Ashmoor and his companion—her. They would know she was with him, or suspect it, from the blood on her hands.

She tucked her gown into the wardrobe beneath another black dress. While the knocking continued, accompanied by some shouting, she poured water into her basin and scrubbed her hands and right arm. They came clean, but the water glistened pink. She must get rid of it. The knocking had ceased, and voices rose in a low rumble from the entryway.

Nothing for it. She opened her window and poured the contents onto the plants below. No one would notice in the dark—she hoped.

She reached for her nightgown with its dozen tiny buttons down the front. She would look as though disturbed from bed—

But her bed was undisturbed.

She dragged back the covers and once again started to don her nightgown.

"Honore? Honore Bainbridge, get out here," her brother roared from the hallway, then pounded on her door.

She shoved her nightgown beneath the bedclothes and dragged on her dressing gown. No gentleman would look too closely to see what she wore beneath the heavy brocade robe.

Not that riding officers were gentlemen. On the other hand, they would not want to offend her brother, a peer of the realm.

She yanked open her door, hoping her disheveled appearance would be taken for having been aroused from her bed. "What is wrong?"

"I have been rousted from my bed by these gentlemen"—he cast a sneer over his shoulder—"who claim a renegade has come this way."

"How could they with the gates locked?" She pretended to rub sleep from her eyes.

"The gate isn't locked," Beau said.

"Not locked?" Honore covered a yawn with her hand.

Beau knew as well as she did that few people had access to a key, and two of them stood in her doorway—but she had not unlocked it.

From the look of her brother, his hair standing on end, his eyes red-rimmed and puffy, his clothes haphazardly donned, he had been sound asleep indeed and had likely been with Deborah and her mother before that. The aging butler or housekeeper leaving the gate unlocked? Not likely. But one or two others . . .

"What do they want with us?" Honore thought to ask.

"They have already searched Bainbridge." Beau grimaced. "As if we would harbor a traitor, and a wounded one at that."

"A traitor? Wounded?" Honore covered her mouth to hide her trembling chin. "How could they think that of a peer?"

"Because the peer's sister has been known to consort with traitors," Beau snapped.

Honore staggered back a step as though he had struck her.

"I never consorted . . . I did not know . . ." Tears spilled down her cheeks.

"Now, my lord, we ain't that cruel to a young lady." The sergeant of the revenue troop moved into sight behind Beau. "We just want a bit of a look around so we can tell our commanding officer we made a thorough search. We'll never find anything here, I told him, but he insisted."

"Of course, sir." Honore smiled through her tears and widened her eyes. "Look all you like, though I can assure you there are no traitors or anyone else in my chamber."

But in her cellar . . .

She pressed one hand to her middle to calm her jumping stomach. She could not be sick in front of these men.

They treated her with more courtesy than had her own brother. Each man touched his hand to his hat as he passed her. They barely touched her possessions, mainly looking under the bed and giving the armoire a cursory glance. Taking up a candle, she followed the officers and her brother from room to room. Miss Morrow joined them downstairs in the kitchen, where she and Mavis were calmly brewing tea and slicing up a plum cake.

Dark plums. Dark like dried blood. Surely a trail of it led right down to the cellar. She looked but saw none. But the yawning opening to the cellar gaped in front of her like an abyss, the very pit about which the psalmists wrote.

God, if You protect us—

No bargaining with God. All she knew to do was ask purely and simply. *God, I have made amok of this, of everything. I do not deserve Your help, but I am asking for it anyway. This time I am simply going to believe You are here with me.*

The sergeant began the descent into the depths of the house. The stench of that spilled brandy invaded Honore's nostrils again, though she was certain she had cleaned thoroughly. They would be led right toward it. Accusations would fly. Surely she already felt iron shackles binding her feet, felt the noose tightening around her neck. Even her own brother would not try to gain her a pardon. He had reminded her of her folly with Frobisher right in front of the riding officers. He would be well rid of her.

If only Father had not died. He had never wanted to be rid of her despite her mistakes with men. He had loved her.

No one would love her in about two minutes when the revenue men found Ashmoor tucked into the coal room. She was not going to love herself when she was sick on the cellar floor. She shrank back against the wall at the foot of the steps and waited for the axe to fall.

Candles glowing in the blackness, the officers and her brother tramped from room to room. In five, four, three, two seconds they would open the one with the contraband brandy.

Miss Morrow tucked her hand beneath Honore's elbow and squeezed. She said nothing, simply stood there with her calm, quiet strength and unwavering loyalty.

The door opened. The officers stomped in. Honore pressed the back of her hand to her mouth.

"Nothin' 'ere, sir," one man called.

Nothing? Honore's knees buckled.

Miss Morrow held her upright. "How did ten barrels of brandy vanish?" She asked the question so softly it was a mere brush of air around Honore's ear.

She shook her head, light-headed and confused.

And still shaking with fright. The coal room came next. Perhaps if she fainted she would distract them. Or she might simply give away everything.

Blood roared more loudly in her ears with each passing

moment in which the revenue officers drew closer to the coal room door. It took forever but happened in the blink of an eye. They opened the door. A few chunks of coal dribbled from a pile inside the opening. A pile that had not been there earlier.

"Coal room," one of the men crowed. "Good way to get inside—through the chute and all."

The sergeant stepped over the threshold and raised his candle. "Too small for a man to get through that opening."

And Ashmoor was not a small man. Indeed, he was so big they should have seen him by now, or they would as soon as the sergeant lowered his candle.

He lowered the candle. Honore wondered how fast and far she could run before they captured her and hauled her off to Bridewell or some other place where they housed women prisoners. Perhaps they would be lenient because of her social rank and just send her to Australia. Or perhaps hanging was quick enough not to hurt too much.

Papa, if you were here this never would have happened.

No, she would be wed to Ashmoor by now, a respected lady, a countess like Cassandra. She would not be on the verge of expiring from sheer terror.

"Nothing here," the sergeant announced. He turned to a tight-lipped Beau. "Our apologies for disturbing you and your fair sister tonight, milord. You are right. No one came this way."

"You are simply doing your duty." Beau sounded more weary than annoyed. "Now will you leave us to get what sleep we can?"

They left, refusing Miss Morrow's offer of tea and cake before they continued their searching. The front door closed behind the men. Mavis shot the bolt home and burst into tears.

"I never been so afrighted in my life," the maid sobbed.

Honore held her. "It is all right. They would never have

harmed you anyway. Now you have a nice cup of tea and slice of cake and return to your bed. Sleep as late as you like in the morning."

"But the cake be for you, Miss Bainbridge."

"And I give it to you."

She would never be able to stomach plum cake again.

Her head would explode from the blood pounding into it if she did not get down to the cellar and look. She met Miss Morrow's gaze over the top of Mavis's head and read the same confusion, concern, and relief.

At last they got Mavis calmed down and tucked into her bed. Then Honore and Miss Morrow took candles and descended the steps to the coal room. They would look at the room where the barrels should be later. Ashmoor came first.

Honore opened the door. Nothing but coal lay in the room. Ashmoor had vanished. Unless he had vanished beneath a pile of the fuel. The configuration of the pile looked different than it had earlier.

Honore began to paw through the coal, sending lumps of obsidian flying and rolling and ricocheting off the walls. Not that much coal lay in the chamber. Surely not enough to crush him. But in his weakened condition, his wound . . .

She began to kick at the lumps, sending clouds of dust up to choke her.

"Miss Bainbridge, Honore, stop it." Miss Morrow grasped her arm. "You will set us all alight if that dust reaches your candle."

"Oh, oh, of course." Honore allowed Miss Morrow to remove the candle from her hands, then dropped to her knees and began to dig through the mess with her hands. "He will not die. He will not die instead of that treacherous, lying—"

Except surely the true traitor had already died. He could not possibly have survived those seas in that little fishing boat. But if he did not live, how would they ever prove it was him?

Haphazardly, she flung a large lump of coal against the wall. A shower of dust and bits of plaster rained upon her head.

"Come away, Honore." Miss Morrow spoke with gentle care. "He is not in there."

"Buried?"

"I do not see how. Now come. You need half a dozen buckets of water to wash away the coal dust."

"I will keep looking. Save the water."

"And what will the riding officers think if they come back?"

Honore stopped tossing coal about and hauled herself to her feet. "Of course, you are right." She glanced at Miss Morrow. "How do you know so much about intrigue and wounds?"

"I, um—" She looked away so her loosened hair hid her face. "I had a brief attachment with a man involved with the Luddites. He was wounded and fled the country to avoid hanging."

Honore stared at her quiet, sober companion in awe. "A renegade?"

"Yes, and I am not proud of it. I am only fortunate that no one but my cousin, your brother-in-law, knows."

"Which is why he thought we would suit."

Miss Morrow smiled. "He knew I had learned my lesson and thought I could bring pressure to bear on you, as well as urge you to wed. I never thought I would fall in love."

Miss Morrow's words yanked Honore's thoughts away from Ashmoor and her fears for him. "With whom have you fallen in love?" She posed the question with exaggerated care.

"Nigel Chilcott, of course. He is—"

Honore waved her hand. "I need not hear his virtues. He is an excellent man. I am so, so very happy for you."

"But I will not wed him." Miss Morrow turned away and headed for the steps. "Water."

"Why will you not?" Honore ran after her.

"I will not leave you, especially now that your brother has banished you here."

"And is likely to send me to Somerset tomorrow. Not that I will go. First I must find Ashmoor and find out where—where a certain person has gone."

If he had survived his bucketing about on the sea.

Miss Morrow spun around so fast her candle flame trailed a line of sparks through the darkness. "Who? Besides Lord Ashmoor, that is?"

"I believe—" Honore stopped and shook her head.

Miss Morrow had spent a great deal of time with Mr. Tuckfield. She might be telling Honore she had given her heart to Mr. Chilcott to throw her off the scent, send her down the wrong foxhole, or gather information on what Honore knew.

"I would rather not malign anyone without knowing for sure."

If they ever could know for sure. With Tuckfield dead and Ashmoor vanished, who would care about the truth? They would blame Ashmoor, not Tuckfield, a stolid Englishman from a solid English family. But Honore knew. Even before she was sure she recognized his voice, though he attempted to disguise it on the boat, she knew it must be him. Several persons in the household could have taken the gate key, but none of them were the sort to command a group of prisoners or have the riding officers listen to them enough to set the trap he had. No one else would have the audacity to damage the cliffs for the simple reason of scaring off anyone from going near them. No one else from Bainbridge—and the culprit had to have come from Bainbridge to use the dower house.

"I need to wash off this coal," Honore said on her way up the steps. "And we should send word to Mr. Poole and Mr. Chilcott. They can help us search for Ashmoor."

But they could not send for Mr. Poole and Mr. Chilcott in the middle of the night. Nor could they search for Ashmoor now and take the risk of running into riding officers. As much as she chafed under the practicality of their situation, Honore knew she must wait and pray. Yes, she would pray. And in the morning, the Lord willing, she would hunt for Ashmoor.

But in the morning, before Honore had wiped the sleep from her eyes, her brother pounded on the front door, demanding admittance.

28

Meric staggered to his feet and leaned against the orchard wall. Pain seared down his left side like a sword dipped in a forging fire and stabbed into him again and again. His breaths rasped through his lungs, each one an effort. But he was free—free of the coal cellar, free of the dower house, free of Bainbridge land.

He was not free from pursuit. The riding officers had departed from searching the Bainbridge houses and grounds, and they might come back again once they found no sign of him in the countryside. That would be his time to move—when the officers gave up on the immediate area. If he could get down to the shore, he just might manage to get home to Clovelly. If not, maybe he could hide in one of the caves honeycombing the cliffs. Either way, he took no one down with him, not even his family.

Except he would take them down. If he was found guilty of treason, his estates would be confiscated. He must survive. He must continue to provide for them. He must stay alive to find out what Honore thought she had learned and add it with what he thought he had learned. Together they might complete the answers they sought.

Together they were formidable. He had been such a fool to turn down marriage to her because of her reputation. Who was he to think he deserved better—a fugitive now, the son of a fugitive until his death? She was exactly the wife for him, headstrong and impulsive yet courageous and kind, generous of heart and passionate of spirit. Not good enough for him now that he was an earl? More like far above his touch were he a royal duke. If he came out of this, whatever the consequences, he would go down on his knees and beg her to have him. He wouldn't for a moment be shocked if she turned him down. He would deserve it. Pride did indeed go before a fall.

Yet a fall had gotten him free. Deciding he needed to leave the dower house or turn himself over to the revenue officers so as not to implicate Honore or Miss Morrow, he had started to get up but had fallen into the piled coal—and found the tunnel the obsidian concealed. It was too low for him to stand upright in and barely wide enough for his shoulders, but it was clear of detritus like spiderwebs and fallen dirt or rock, testimony to recent use. Gradually it sloped upward until it ended at a row of stones that gave way with a push, and he found himself near the path through the sheep pasture.

No wonder he had found half a Frenchman's button on this path. The true traitor must have been using the dower house for years to smuggle, to bring prisoners to hide out. They could have hidden in the dower house for days without anyone noticing—long enough for the hunt for them to die down or the dark of the moon to arrive.

He replaced the stones so no one would find the opening and be able to blame Honore for harboring a criminal. Crawling from there and across the pasture seemed like the wisest action. His head tended to spin when he stood upright. He could crawl with only one arm. His left arm seemed reluctant to work and started bleeding again through the shawl and lady's cloak bound around his shoulders and chest. He could crawl for miles if necessary. Surely he could. Surely . . . surely . . .

He reached the far wall and slumped against it. Climbing over the yard-high structure seemed impossible.

Then he heard voices and thought climbing over it seemed unwise at that moment. Maybe in that time between night and dawn, when the stars faded and the sun had not yet risen over the horizon, searchers would miss him in the lee of the wall.

Footfalls grew nearer. The voices grew louder, clearer, clear enough for the distinction of a clear English voice and—an American one?

Meric raised his head over the edge of the wall to listen. Yes, yes, it was them!

"Philo." He gasped out his brother's name.

Philo and Chilcott kept going. In a moment they would pass him. He tore up a clump of autumn-dead grass and threw it over the wall.

The voices ceased.

"Philo. Nigel." His voice was so weak he could scarcely hear it himself.

But they must have heard him, or the flying clump of grass caught their attention enough to draw them to the wall. Their footfalls drew nearer, rattling loose rock and crunching the pebbled dirt of the path. Then they loomed above him, dark silhouettes against the sky.

"Meric?" Philo sounded uncertain.

"Here." He leaned his right elbow on the wall.

"You are hurt, my lord." Chilcott vaulted over the wall and crouched beside Meric. "Where? How? Never you mind. We know. You are who the revenue men are searching for, are you not?"

"Yes. Afraid so."

"Then there's no time to waste." Philo leaned forward. "Can you walk, or must I carry you?"

"He looks to be in a bad way," Chilcott said. "Carry, I think."

"Walk." Meric tried to rise. His legs refused to cooperate.

"What did those English—" Philo growled in his throat. "It was a trap, was it not?"

"Yes, similar to what happened to Father."

"Then we will get you away before they can put you in prison. I have a boat ready."

"No," Meric began.

But Philo stepped over the wall and picked him up with Chilcott's assistance, and the world tilted, swirled, began to fade in and out.

He never quite lost awareness for long—at least not at first. They seemed to carry him forever, bouncing him up and down. At one point, someone said something about him bleeding again. He needed stitched up. Honore could have stitched him. Honore would keep him alive simply by being present.

When they reached the sea, roaring with the incoming tide, his brother and his steward set him on a shifting platform, and Chilcott examined the wound. "Bad," was all he said before his probing and pressing shot pain too intense through Meric, and the world went black for a few minutes.

Or a few hours. When he came to himself again, sunlight blazed around him and the sea swelled beneath him—or rather the boat on which he lay.

"Where are you taking me?" He tried to sit up, managed to prop himself on his right elbow and glare at Philo a yard away at the tiller. "What do you think you're doing?"

"Getting you to safety while Chilcott remains behind and

convinces the riding officers you have merely gone down to Ashmoor."

"And you take me—where?" Meric was too weak to feel a surge of anger. It was more like a trickle, but a trickle strong enough to help him lever into a sitting position against the rail. "Where?"

"Ireland and then a ship for France and then home."

"No."

"What?"

"I said no." Meric spoke through clenched teeth. "No, you will not take me to Ireland or anywhere else but back to Devon."

Philo sighed gustily enough to be heard over the sea and wind rumbling against the single sail of the fishing smack. "Go back to sleep. We patched you up as best we could, but you look like you lost a lot of your claret and need rest."

"I need to go back." Meric closed his eyes against the brilliance of sun and blue sky reflected in the sea. He breathed the clean air and his own metallic stench. "I can't run away, brother. I can't be a coward."

Philo said nothing for a few moments, then asked, "Are you saying Father was a coward when he ran away from England?"

Meric flinched but could not deny the truth. "Yes, I am afraid he was. He did not stay to prove his innocence. We grew up with far too little. Mother was born a lady and yet is now estranged from her family and looks older than she should. And all this time Father could have been proven innocent."

"Or have hanged."

"Maybe."

"Probably. It's not a risk I'm willing to take with you."

"Philo." Meric put all the strength he could muster into his next words. "It is not your choice to make. I would rather stand trial and lose than know all my life that I never tried to learn the truth."

"Other than us being poor, Father never suffered from not knowing the truth."

"Did he not?" Meric slid back down to lie on his good side. "I read his letters home. They were not the writings of a man content with his life. He loved Mother and us deeply and felt he had harmed us all by his actions. In the end, he did."

As Meric would have harmed Honore by his actions. As he had already harmed her by his actions.

His left shoulder throbbing, he felt unconsciousness grabbing at him again. He forced himself to stay awake until he could persuade Philo to turn the smack around. "I need to see her again. If I leave, I will never see Honore again." He breathed slowly and as deeply as the pain allowed. "I need to ask her to marry me."

Philo said nothing for so long Meric figured he was being ignored. Maybe when he reached Ireland or France, he could hire a boat back to Devon, back to Honore. Even if he was arrested, at least she would know that he no longer cared more about his status or even his safety than he cared for her.

"All right." Philo heaved another one of his gusty sighs. "We'll go back. At least as an earl you get judged by the House of Lords instead of a jury of commoners."

Meric laughed. Even though it hurt, he laughed aloud. "Philemon Poole happy about me being the earl at last."

And if it made him eligible to marry Honore, it made him happy too.

"What. Have. You. Done?" Beau bit out the words as though they were chunks of poisoned meat he needed to be rid of. "Never in my life have I been expected to find excise men pounding down my door in the middle of the night."

"Nor have I." Honore pretended to be annoyed and bored. Bored she was not. Annoyed she was—with her brother.

Beau glared at her from across the entryway, all the further she had allowed him to go. "Are you mocking me?"

"No, I am perfectly truthful at this." Honore yawned, not a pretense. "I was never so sc-shocked in my life."

"Scared." Beau's eyes narrowed. "You were about to faint. Those men might have thought it likely you were simply frightened by their presence, but I know you better than that. If you were not guilty of something, you would have found it a grand adventure."

"Yes, well, I am finished with grand adventures."

And right then, she was finished with Beau.

"Where is your steward, Beau?" she asked.

"My steward?" He looked blank.

"Yes, Tuckfield. Have you seen him today?"

"I have not, and do not change the subject. What were you expecting to find in that cellar?"

"Contraband brandy." Honore smiled at the shock on Beau's face and the way he spluttered rather than responded in words. "It was here when I moved into the house. Barrels of it, but it has been removed."

"What did you do with it?"

"I?" She sank onto the bottom step of the stairway, too weary to remain upright any longer. "I did nothing with it. If I had, I would not have been afraid the revenue men would find it."

"Humph. How could contraband brandy have gotten into the house?" Beau demanded.

"Precisely. I doubt it was Grandmama. But who has keys to this house besides you and me?"

"The steward."

"Twice a year when he came in to ensure the roof was not leaking, or the like."

"Are you accusing Tuckfield of smuggling?" Beau gave his head a hard shake. "Unlikely. Probably that beau of yours, considering your history."

Honore winced. "I knew no one would believe me. Never you mind then. I will have to confront him myself." She rose. "Now, if you will excuse me, I need to get to my bed."

"You do look haggard." Beau went to the door, opened it, then turned back. "If I go call on Lord Ashmoor today, will I find him at home?"

A yawn masked Honore's start. "I have no idea. I am not good enough for him, remember."

That pain would surely diminish in time.

"You had best hope he is, or you will find yourself living in Somerset until you are one and twenty."

"Ten months," Honore said as the door slammed behind her brother.

Somerset would be all right. She would not have the cliffs and the sea, but it was lovely country, and she could visit Mama in Bath. She would have more than enough time to focus on getting her heart in order.

So weary she could scarcely place one foot in front of the other, she climbed the steps to her room with the intention of sleeping. But sleep eluded her. She needed to know if, indeed, Ashmoor would be at home that morning, if he had somehow gotten out of the cellar when everyone was focused on the excise men, and if he had made his way to safety and care for his wound. Or would she receive a report that he had perished somewhere along the way? Or—worst of all for a man like him, who so appreciated fresh air and freedom—was in prison?

She climbed from bed and dressed in a round gown that did not require anyone to fasten hooks or buttons for her. She went walking outside, examining the garden, then the surrounding area outside the dower house fence, for signs of someone having passed through. She dared not look outside Bainbridge's walls.

Defeated in the grounds, she made her way down to the cellar, candle in hand. Once she managed to open the chute through which coal was delivered, she did not need the candle. With daylight streaming through the opening, she studied the room with the full blast of sunlight. Nothing. Not a whisper of evidence that anyone had lain bleeding in the chamber. Yet Ashmoor had gone, vanished into thin air, apparently.

Behind her, the steps creaked. She slammed the chute door and faced Miss Morrow. "I do not understand it. He is simply gone."

"I know. I fretted about him all night." Miss Morrow held up her candle and peered at Honore. "So did you."

"I did." Honore worried the fringe on her shawl. "I, um, went walking outside at dawn. No, do not scold. I know it was foolish, but I feared I would find him lying dead in the middle of the pasture or the orchard. But I found no sign of him."

"You will not, and neither will the excise men." Miss Morrow's face softened. "Mr. Chilcott is here to talk to you about last night."

"He has news?" Honore brushed past her companion and bolted up the steps like a hoyden in short petticoats.

"He did not say," Miss Morrow called after her, a laugh quivering her voice.

Honore sped down the passage to the entryway. She had not asked where she would find Mr. Chilcott. No matter. The choices were few—the parlor, the book room, the dining room, the sitting room.

She found him in the book room, the only one where a fire had been laid on that cold but clear morning. He stood with his back to the fire, his hands clasped behind him. Like Miss Morrow's, his eyes showed the redness of too little sleep. But he smiled at Honore's entrance and smiled wider when Miss Morrow followed at a more sedate pace.

"Will you ladies close the door, please?"

Miss Morrow did so and then turned the key in the lock. "You do not care for refreshment?"

"Not yet. I would rather not be disturbed while we talk." He gestured to the chairs grouped around the hearth. "Do sit down, ladies."

"Do talk, sir," Honore responded. But she sat. If she did not, neither could he, and he looked about to fall down. "What has happened to Ashmoor?" she demanded.

"He is on his way to Ireland and then France and then America." Chilcott delivered the news in a quiet and gentle tone.

Honore's heart stopped. Or at least it felt as though it had. She could feel no movement inside her chest, could hardly breathe for the pressure building up behind her ribs. She managed to squeeze out three words. "He is gone?"

Chilcott gave Honore a sympathetic glance. "His brother thought it the safest thing. The riding officers had been at the Clovelly house and were possibly heading down to Ashmoor. They are convinced he is guilty."

"And it will not help if I say he is not." Honore did not realize she was crying until tears dripped off her jaw. "They will be convinced he is guilty because of me. All along he was right to reject me. Even me helping him has made matters worse."

Ashamed of her tears, Honore rose and paced to the shelf of books. She had been such a wayward child, demanding adventure and action regardless of the consequences. Yet Papa had loved her all through it. He had strived to make matters better for her, while he surely knew the potential consequences of an alliance with her. He had still loved her . . . loved her . . .

Verses learned long ago from a sermon or a governess ran through her head, something Jesus said in one of the Gospels. *If a son shall ask bread of any of you that is a father, will he give him a stone? or if he ask a fish, will he for a fish give him a serpent?*

Papa had never given her anything but what she wanted, and she became wayward and rebellious. And when God tried to give her a chance to gain understanding and wisdom, she had rejected Him for not giving her what she wanted. And all the while, the Lord was giving her more bread and fish than she could need—a time to reflect, to be obedient, to make her heart right with the Lord.

And He had shown her the depths of true love.

A lifetime of sermons, Scripture readings, and, of late, Miss Morrow's wise reminders coalesced in Honore's heart. Peace filled her, warmed her. God had never been giving her stones; He had loved her all along. He had been more than generous with loving patience. He had been with her all along. She had simply not reached out and accepted the truth.

She reached out now. *Lord, I cannot take one more step without You beside me.*

Not certain what she was about to do was right, yet feeling perfect peace, she spun on her heel and looked at Chilcott. "I must follow him. Will you help me arrange passage? Directly to France, if possible, or through one of the Channel Islands would be safer, I expect."

The two of them stared back at her. "Have you lost your reason, my dear?" Miss Morrow asked.

"No, I have just found it. I will not allow Ashmoor to go into exile alone."

"But what you are giving up . . ." Chilcott gave Miss Morrow a helpless glance, then turned back to Honore. "If he forfeits the estates, he will be back where they started save for what he managed to smuggle out of England. And even people with money do not live as comfortably in America as they do here."

"I care not for that. I am learning to cook and I sew well." Honore fairly skipped to the door. "I will be ready inside an hour. If you will not assist me, then I will go away on my own."

Meric and Philo reached the dower house after dark. They had put into a small port in Cornwall so Meric could be tended by an apothecary, who declared Meric's injury as a mere flesh wound that wasn't likely to kill him, and took several guineas for his promise of silence about their presence. For good measure, he provided Meric with some worn but rather well-fitting garments not stiff with dried blood.

Philo did not set the smack in the harbor at Clovelly. "The Crown is still looking for you, I expect. We'll set in at an inlet and try to get horses or some other mode of transportation to Bainbridge."

"And hope the riding officers aren't there too?" Meric hoped the mode of transportation would be some means other than horses. As bumpy as carriages often were on the country roads, riding a horse would be worse. "Can't we simply put into a cove near Bainbridge and walk?" he asked.

Philo gave him a disgusted glance. "You couldn't walk above a mile right now."

He was probably right. Mention of his weakness tempted Meric to lie down and sleep. If he did, though, Philo just might turn around and again set sail for Ireland.

Philo found a cove below a village that was little more than a cluster of hovels around an inn. But one of the local farmers was willing to take them in his wagon as far as Bainbridge—for a consideration. The guinea Philo gave him was likely the most money he saw in a month or more.

"How much money did you come away with?" Meric asked his brother in the back of the jouncing wagon.

"Not nearly enough." Philo leaned against the side panels. "You are a fool, brother. I hope I never fall in love."

"I hope you do. It's a good place to fall."

If the lady loved in return. Meric had believed at one time that Honore loved him, but lately, since he had kissed her at the harvest moon ball, she had seemed less inclined to look at him with the adoration he had known before. She claimed she helped him for herself and not for him.

"But I can hope—"

"Hope?" Philo's tone held disgust. "I hope it's more than hope you have. If you've risked your life and freedom for the mere hope of a female's love, you are a fool."

"No, it's more than that." Meric clutched at the lump of bandage beneath his coat. "I need to prove my innocence for all your sakes. I've given up too much to get this far. I won't sacrifice it to the Crown over suspicions."

Philo spat over the side of the wagon. "We were all right without this wealth. We were all together and had enough."

"No dowries for the girls? No education or training for trades for all of us? Too little land to support us beyond the minimum, let alone with families added? No, Philo, it was not enough. We prayed for God to provide all these things, and this is what happened."

"And if you're found to be a traitor, we lose it all and you. Is that God providing?"

An excellent question.

"That's where faith comes in."

Listen to him talking about faith, something sorely lacking in his life of late. Faith, trust, believing God's promises were true—all those things his parents taught him had vanished little by little the more he lived in the world of the haut ton. He had believed what they said. He had believed that Honore Bainbridge was worse for him than no wife at all. Yet he had loved her and hurt her by denying that love in exchange for doing what others told him was best.

If you can find it in your heart to forgive me, my dear . . . He formed his speech to Honore.

But in truth, he needed to ask the Lord for forgiveness. He had allowed the pressure of society to steer him from a right and godly course. He had not trusted the Lord to provide; he had tried to provide for himself by shunning Honore, by courting a young lady with good family and little character, in order to protect his reputation, his self-interest.

If the inheritance was the Lord's way of providing, then the Lord could transcend any power of the Crown to take it away. He knew that. He had not lived it.

He closed his eyes and covered his face with his hands. "Lord, I've been wrong. Please forgive me for trusting in men and not You. Whatever happens, I know You are not surprised and will provide for us in our bodies and our souls." He could not stop himself from adding, "And our hearts. Please do not let my bowing to the world keep me from my love, from—"

The farmer drew the wagon to a halt outside the Bainbridge gates, jarring Meric from his prayer.

"Far as I go, gentlemen," the farmer said.

"Wait until we see if we gain entrance." Philo leaped to the ground and tugged at the bell rope.

A moment later, the porter stumbled from the gatehouse, grumbling about late callers being indecent, though the hour could not be later than seven of the clock.

"Who is it?" The old man sounded less than gracious.

"My lord Ashmoor," Philo snapped out.

The porter said nothing but swung the gate open.

Philo returned to the wagon, paid the farmer a few more shillings, then assisted Meric to the ground. "Can you walk all the way back to the dower house, or should we get the wagon in?"

"If the wagon carries us in, the main house will know of my presence." Meric gazed up the drive. It looked to be a score of miles long. "I'll manage."

"Crazy, milords," the porter muttered before slamming the gate closed and shoving home the bolt. "Suit yourself. Wagons and walking . . . Not sure you are Ashmoor."

Meric decided ignoring the man would go further in convincing him of the truth, and started up the drive leaning on Philo's sturdy arm. At halfway, Philo stopped to cut a stout walking stick from one of the overarching trees. It helped. Meric's knees threatened to buckle with every other step, but the drive was only a mile long, not twenty, and the dower house was merely a few hundred yards behind it. He could manage. He could, with the image of Honore's face before his mind's eye, so lovely, so sweet, so stubborn . . .

The main house appeared deserted. No light shone in any of the windows. Perhaps Bainbridge and his guests had departed for the city.

No light shone in the windows of the dower house either. The gate to the garden stood open, however, and Meric, knees buckling from more than simple fatigue, barely managed to reach the front door and pound the knocker. No one came. Surely Honore would not have gone with her brother. Yet she would not have gone to bed this early.

He applied the knocker to the door again. This time, the flicker of a candle through a side window flashed in the corner of his eye. A moment later, the door opened to reveal the little maid shaking hard enough to send her candle bobbing like a jig dancer.

"Who—milord? Oh no." She covered her mouth with her hand, and her eyes rounded.

"Is something wrong with Miss Bainbridge?" Meric asked.

"N-no, milord. But she ain't here."

"What?" Meric sagged against the door frame. "How can she be gone? That is . . ."

"I'll fetch Miss Morrow." The maid took the steps up two at a time.

Meric and Philo stepped into the entryway and closed the door behind them. If Miss Morrow was there, Honore should not be gone. If she was gone, his journey was in vain.

No, not in vain if he managed to stand firm and prove his innocence and, he hoped—no, he prayed—the innocence of his father.

Miss Morrow sped down the steps in a fashion more akin to Honore's manner than the staid companion's. "My lord, what are you doing here? Mr. Chilcott said you had sailed for Ireland and then on to—"

"Where is Honore?" Meric demanded.

"My lord, she has gone after you."

If ever a man needed proof of a lady's love, it was Honore's foolhardy journey to follow after him. The knowledge warmed Meric, lent his weakened body strength.

So he could somehow catch up with her and stop her.

Miss Morrow gave him as many details as she could manage. If they could somehow get to the Clovelly harbor . . .

That proved easier than not with Bainbridge and his fiancée gone. Miss Morrow ordered the grooms to saddle up two horses. She looked concerned over his ability to ride, but he managed to haul himself into the saddle and hold the reins in his right hand. Five miles to Clovelly felt like five hundred. More than once he found himself slipping to one side or the other, ready to collapse and land on the ground. But at last the lights of the village shone in the distance. The earthy scents of the stables rose in the fresh night air, and the harbor glistened below with several boats getting ready for the night's fishing.

Chilcott would get Honore on one of those. That would make the most sense. No one questioned a fishing boat that went out night after night. That was why smuggling was so very easy.

Getting down the hill to the harbor was not easy. At least a dozen times, Meric stopped to catch his breath. He, who had thought nothing of walking ten miles rather than riding a horse, could scarcely walk a few hundred yards down a hill—a steep hill, but a hill nonetheless.

At last he and Philo reached the water, black and oily beneath the lights of bobbing lanterns. "We're seeking a boat that might have a young woman on it," Meric began to ask . . . and ask . . . and ask . . .

Mostly, blank stares and shaken heads were the response. Then a grizzled old man who smelled like a barrel of three-day-old fish pointed toward the mouth of the harbor. "Gone."

"How long?" Meric tried not to sound too eager.

The man shrugged. "Quarter hour."

"I expect you can't catch him?" Meric suggested.

"I can catch anybody on t' water," the old man declared. "How much is 't worth t' you?"

Meric didn't bargain. He paid the fee the man demanded. Then they climbed aboard the fishing smack and clung to the rails while the old man and his crew—two loutish-looking youths—set the single sail and sent the small craft skimming over the bay . . .

To nothing but open sea. Yet open sea with distant lights bobbing on its surface like floating stars.

"They are probably going to dump us overboard after killing and robbing us," Philo muttered.

"He can't possibly know which boat is the right one," Meric said loudly enough for the fisherman to hear.

The old man shot a glare from the tiller. "'Course I can. We all have our places."

"But this boat won't be going to a place." Meric leaned forward as though his action could drive the smack faster.

"He'll go thatta way." The old man shoved down the tiller, sending the sail swooping over the deck. The fishing boat's starboard rail nearly dipped into the sea in the change of tack. Capsizing seemed imminent.

"Move back," Philo admonished.

"Chilcott?" Meric called.

The two boats came abreast, swooped dangerously close to locking a jibboom over the taffrail. Half climbing, half crawling, Meric mounted onto the bowsprit and dropped onto the deck of the other craft, where two men with darkly stubbled faces met him, their hands on their hips, likely ready to draw weapons.

"Do you have a lady aboard?" Meric asked.

"Maybe," one of the men said.

"Or maybe not." Philo started to leap aboard the squat craft. "Where?"

"She's below." The fisherman jutted his chin toward the cabin. "Let's go." He shoved off from the other craft with a boat hook.

"Wait!" Philo ran to the end of the jib.

"Wait for my brother," Meric added.

The fisherman, who smelled as clean as the old man on the other boat reeked of fish, and his mate ignored Philo's attempts to get on the larger smack. The latter turned the tiller over hard, and the lugger dipped, plunged into the trough of a wave. The sail flapped overhead, then caught the offshore breeze and bellied out, sending the craft skimming for more open sea.

Meric lifted a hand to his brother. "I'll be back."

"I would not count on that, my lord."

Meric spun toward the voice, lost his balance on a wave of dizziness, and grasped the railing. "Tuckfield?"

Indeed it was Tuckfield, with Honore in the crook of his arm—an arm that ended with a pistol pointed at her middle.

A gut shot rarely killed—immediately. It killed slowly from infection, causing days of agony. If Meric took one step toward the Bainbridge steward, that would too easily be Honore's fate.

"Why did you come back?" she asked in her soft but steady voice.

"Leaving was the coward's way out." Meric smiled at her. "And I couldn't leave without telling you I love you."

"Touching." Tuckfield curled his upper lip. "And stupid, just like your father."

Taunting him just like the man on the boat the previous night, a lifetime ago. This time he would not fall for the pressure to attack. He would not risk Honore's life.

"Why?" was all Meric said.

Tuckfield shrugged one shoulder. "Money. Power. I am tired of not having enough of the latter to get away from taking orders from females or nodcocks like Bainbridge."

"You don't have enough in—what, thirty years of smuggling?"

"Power comes from knowing I'm fooling all these people who think they're better than I am." Tuckfield pinched his nostrils as though smelling something foul. "Watching you all speculate and worry has been far more gratifying than taking the money and running."

"I see that now. It must be difficult having to take orders from a young female like Honore Bainbridge."

"One stupid enough to let me lure her onto my boat." Tuckfield looked smug.

Honore ground her teeth hard enough for Meric to see her jaw work. He looked away from her and concentrated on Tuckfield. "But my father . . ." Meric slid one foot a half step forward. "Why did you set him up to take the blame for murder?"

Tuckfield's face screwed up. "Your father." He spat over the rail. "He intended to leave the gang. He'd gotten so pious, I thought he was going to turn on all of us."

"But he didn't know who you were." Meric slid the other foot to join the first. "He never said a word in all those years."

"I am so sorry, Ashmoor." Honore met and held his gaze in the light of the bow lantern.

Beyond her, the crew of the lugger went about their work of handling the tiller and sail as though one of their passengers were not holding another at gunpoint. They had sailed beyond sight of the harbor and other boats. The open sea lay beyond, black save for crests of white glowing against the horizon.

Meric smiled at Honore as though they spoke in her parlor. "Why do you apologize, my dear? My love."

She bowed her head. "I thought for a bit that you might be involved with smuggling prisoners out of the country."

Meric flinched. "You still thought me a traitor?"

"Just like everyone else now." Tuckfield laughed, an eerie sound for the genuine amusement in its rumbling tones. "No one will think a thing when the two of you disappear. They'll presume you fled from England and your brother stayed behind to try to keep the estate from being seized by the Crown—or to inherit."

"I suppose we will never see America?" Meric tried to sound casual, though his heart pounded like waves in a hurricane.

"You won't see Ireland." Tuckfield waved his free arm. "There's all this water to take you."

"Sometimes the sea gives up its dead." Meric glanced back toward the invisible bulk of the land.

"Two lovers drown while eloping." Tuckfield snorted. "We all expected Honore Bainbridge to do something that dishonorable—run off with a traitor or a murderer. Why not another traitor, the son of a murderer?" He threw back his head and roared with laughter.

With the man's focus off of him for the moment, Meric loosened his knife from inside his right sleeve and tucked the hilt into the palm of his hand.

"Every other man I thought I loved ended up being something awful," Honore said. "And when you would not wed me because of my reputation, I thought perhaps you wanted to ensure respectability."

"I did, but that wasn't the way to go about it, denying that I loved you, making poor excuses like needing to feed my family. That's why I came back. If I am arrested, I will stand trial knowing I did not run away from the risk, nor from you." He held her gaze again. "I love you, Honore Bainbridge. Please trust me."

"You came back for me. That is all I need."

Except for him to get her free.

Despite the gun pointed at her middle, her eyes glowed like a sunlit sky. If only she understood the double meaning of his message regarding trusting him. If she panicked, all would be lost—such as her life.

"You got away last night, Tuckfield. So why did you come back?" Meric asked.

Tuckfield jabbed the pistol into Honore's middle. "To get rid of her. I thought she might have recognized me. She's known me all her life."

"Because my family kept you employed all my life and more." Honore stomped her booted foot onto Tuckfield's instep. He grunted and shoved the gun harder into her middle. "Do not do that again." He called her a vulgar name. "I should have killed her last night, but could not with all those Frenchmen about and the excise men expected. Had to get away so they could catch you with the French."

"But you failed." Meric let himself gloat. "I presume you failed at killing me with the carriage accident as well."

Tuckfield scowled. "That man was incompetent all around. I should have found a way to do it myself."

"But you didn't do it yourself and failed in your choice of assassins." Meric shook his head. "I didn't get caught. I even found your secret passageway into the dower house."

"Secret passageway?" Honore's eyes and mouth rounded. "Truly? And I did not get to see it?"

"Behind a pile of coal, my dear. I'll show it to you when we get home."

Tuckfield snorted. "Unless you are strong swimmers, you won't get home."

Strong swimmers indeed. The sea rolled in five-foot swells beneath the lugger's keel. No one was that strong a swimmer, especially not a small female and a wounded man.

But those swells could be used to their advantage aboard the vessel. Tuckfield had his back propped against the side rail, but he still needed to brace his legs to hold his balance and hold on to Honore at the same time.

Meric merely balanced with his legs—legs wobbly from the wound weakness, unstable from the pitch of the lugger. On the next swell, he addressed Tuckfield.

"How did you survive that sea last night with no sail?"

The lugger climbed the wave up, up, up to the crest, hovered for a moment as though reluctant for the drop.

"These fellows were—"

The boat plunged into the trough. Meric "lost" his balance and lunged forward. His right hand sent the knife flying past Tuckfield's eyes, the blade glinting in the lantern light. Tuckfield flinched back, free arm flailing at air.

"Honore, drop!" Meric shouted.

She dropped. At the same time, Meric's left shoulder struck up the pistol barrel. The gun fired into the air, then spun out of Tuckfield's hand and into the sea.

Tuckfield bellowed and lunged for Honore. Blood seeping through his bandages, Meric kicked Tuckfield. His boot heel caught the other man beneath the chin. He landed on the deck hard enough to shake the craft.

So did Meric. He sprawled unheroically at Honore's knees. "So—so sorry, my beloved."

Laughing, Honore grasped the rail and stood on Tuckfield's chest. "I will not let him go anywhere."

Tuckfield could have thrown her off with one heave, probably knocked her into the sea. But he lay still enough to be dead. Meric checked for a heartbeat. Without Tuckfield, he could not prove his innocence.

His heart beat strongly. He was simply unconscious, a bruise rising on his jaw.

"Nice kick." Honore grinned. "Now to get these men to turn their loyalty to us."

"Just a minor detail."

Meric levered himself upright and called to the man who had let him aboard. "Why did you work for this man?"

The skipper shuffled forward, eyes narrowed. "Loyal to him."

"Why?"

Tuckfield groaned. Honore stepped on his middle. "Do not move."

Tuckfield gasped for air. "Do . . . not help . . . them, Rogers."

"Why not?" the skipper asked. "Seems like they got you cornered."

"I . . . can still talk." Though the swelling of his jaw was slurring his speech. "You know . . . what I know . . ."

"Unless it's murder," Meric said, "I will see you get either a pardon for your past or enough money to start a new life, if you take us back to England."

"I will hunt you down, Rogers," Tuckfield declared.

"Not if you're swinging from a gibbet." Rogers nodded. "Got your word, milord?"

"My word." Meric held out his hand.

The men shook, and Rogers turned away to give orders.

Tuckfield began to curse. Honore pulled her sash from her gown. "I think we should tie him up."

"If you have a handkerchief," Meric said, "we should gag him too. You shouldn't hear that kind of language."

She smiled at him. "I keep repeating you calling me your beloved and do not hear a word he says."

"My dearest beloved." Heart melting inside him, Meric used the satin ribbon to tie Tuckfield's hands, then stuffed a handkerchief into his mouth. He didn't have a way to affix that, but it would take Tuckfield awhile to work it loose, with his inability to move his jaw properly.

"As long as he can talk enough to confess," Meric said.

"Do you think he will?" Honore knelt beside Meric.

"He might, for transportation over hanging. But it doesn't matter. With us bringing him back this way, the riding officers will look for evidence pointing to him and find more than enough. It's there, especially since you worked out who was guilty."

"I should have told you, but I thought he surely died at sea last night. And I thought I would see you again." She rested her head on his shoulder. "Why did you run away without me?"

"I didn't. That's why I came back." He wrapped his arm around her and tilted her face up to his. "Do you forgive me for not marrying you when I should have?"

"I do. I understand why, and I love you for it." She laid her hand against his cheek. "I was not ready to truly love someone anyway until now when you came back, and—mmm."

He kissed her. Two of the crew cheered.

Laughing, Meric lifted his head. "Let us go home so we can get married and I can do more of that in private, my Honore."

Epilogue

Honore had always expected an elopement for her nuptials. Instead, she stood in her bedchamber at Number Sixteen Cavendish Square on a shockingly cold February day three months after Ashmoor's proposal. Everyone wanted to see her married and braved the cold and snow that seemed ever present that winter to attend the affair.

"Everyone" included Lady John Dunbar, Beau's mother-in-law. Now that Honore was to become a countess, she thought her respectable enough to join the family.

"I shall be the picture of propriety from now on." Honore made the pronouncement to the room at large.

The company included Lydia and Cassandra, both with their sons in their arms more than with the nursemaids; Deborah, already looking matronly after a mere month of marriage; and Miss Morrow, whose own wedding would take place in Clovelly in a month, after she and Chilcott returned to Devon and the banns were read. All four ladies swarmed around Honore, tucking in a curl, adjusting her hat, plucking off one pair of earrings and exchanging them for another, as though she were a fashion doll. Not one of them commented on her claim for future respectability.

She frowned at them in the dressing table mirror. "You do not believe I can be respectable?"

"My dear," Cassandra declared, "now that you are a countess, nearly everything is considered respectable. No one is the least scandalized by me flying in a balloon except for Geoffrey himself."

"You should not have gone up when you were nearly at your confinement," Lydia scolded. "If you had crashed, you would have done in the heir as well as yourself."

"But I did not crash." Cassandra stroked the chubby cheek of her infant son. "I rather wanted to ensure that he would inherit my passion for flight instead of his father's fear of heights."

"And everyone thinks Lisette's penchant for cooking is merely because she is French and therefore a little mad." Lydia smiled when speaking of her sister-in-law. "Of course, we should know anyone who willingly separates herself from the ground to fly is a touch eccentric."

Miss Morrow heaved an exaggerated sigh. "I expect I will have to live a staid and sober life."

Everyone laughed, for no one expected anything else from Miss Morrow and Nigel Chilcott. Only a few of them knew that Miss Morrow had enjoyed enough adventure for her life.

Deborah said nothing. Her life was already sober and staid as Beau's wife. Her gentle smile and calm eyes suggested she liked things that way.

Honore glanced from her sisters to her companion to her sister-in-law and shook her head. "I think I will leave spies and traitors to themselves from now on. Ashmoor and I shall drive off to his house in Surrey and enjoy the quiet until spring. Then we shall return to Devon to see what we can do about making Ashmoor more habitable. It is terribly drafty and uncomfortable. And, of course, as soon as the war is over, he wants to bring his mother and siblings back here, if they will come."

"So sad you could not have waited to marry until they could be here," Deborah said.

Honore and her sisters stared at their brother's wife as though she had grown an extra head.

"Perish the thought of waiting," Cassandra murmured. She smiled down at her son.

Honore's cheeks grew warm.

Before she could say anything, though, the clock chimed the half hour. Eleven thirty. Marry on a rising clock hand to satisfy tradition. Marry before noon to satisfy the law. The drive down to Surrey could not come fast enough for her.

She started for the door. Cassandra and Lydia grasped her arms.

Cassandra squeezed her hand. "I know you are anxious, but you must not be unseemly about it." Her eyes twinkled.

Honore laughed. "You are telling me not to be unseemly when you and Whittaker . . ."

"Yes, well—" Cassandra blushed. "We are respectable now, except for my ballooning, that is."

"And Whittaker chasing Luddites," Honore added.

Cassandra shuddered. "The rebellion is over. At least Whittaker's role is done once and for all. I suppose some unrest will continue for a while yet. But that is too sober a thought for this day."

"Tuck in your lace." Lydia adjusted the white lace fichu set into the neckline of Honore's silk gown, the same blue as her eyes. "There now. We shall go seat ourselves and you will follow."

Someone knocked on the door. Lydia opened it. "Ah, Beau, here you are."

He looked past her to his bride. "Everyone ready?"

"Three months ago," Honore muttered.

Laughing, the Bainbridge daughters descended to the drawing room, where the chairs had been arranged to accommodate two score guests. Ashmoor had paid for a special license to enjoy the ceremony in the privacy of the house with only family and close friends present. Though Tuckfield's arrest and conviction of murder and treason had cleared any scandal from the Poole family, Society tended to ask rude questions and likely would until another sensation stole the public's attention.

Ashmoor stood at Honore's entrance. Their gazes met and locked across the width of the chamber. His sparkled with golden lights and held so much warmth and love that Honore's knees weakened and she stumbled.

In a few strides, he reached her side and gave her his arm. "Do I need to carry you?"

"You need not continue to pick me up, my lord."

"I intend to continue picking you up for the rest of our lives."

Laughing, Honore reached the vicar while clinging to Ashmoor's arm and, still glowing from within, made her wedding vows in a clear, strong voice.

The vicar closed *The Book of Common Prayer* to indicate the end of the ceremony. Honore gazed at Ashmoor in wonder that she was finally his wife.

"I think we are supposed to lead the guests into the dining room," Ashmoor said.

"I would rather set out on our journey."

Ashmoor kissed her lightly, much to the delight of the guests, and shook his head. "I, for one, am starving."

They led the guests into the dining room for the wedding breakfast. Honore sliced up the rich, fruity bride cake with its marzipan and sugar icings so each guest could have a piece and the single females could take theirs home to slip under their pillows.

"I never did anything so silly," she told Ashmoor. "It is good I did not. I never would have dreamed of someone like you."

He wiped a bit of marzipan off her lower lip with his fingertip and tasted it. "You mean an uncouth, American-raised rascal?"

"I mean honest and faithful and true to his faith."

"All those things were badly tested, but God showed me the right way in the end." He rose. "Madame de Meuse says we can go now."

Honore leaped from her chair and spun toward the door. "Blessings to all of you!" She blew a kiss to the room at large, then fairly skipped from the chamber, leaving ripples of mirth in her wake.

"I think," Ashmoor said, laughing, "your eagerness has amused half your guests and scandalized the other half."

"Is it wrong of me not to be a shy, shrinking bride?"

"Never." He started to draw her close, but suddenly all the Bainbridges and their spouses surrounded them with embraces and kisses and advice for Honore to act like a countess.

"I will. I will," she promised. She just wanted to be gone.

She and Ashmoor ran from the house and through the bitter cold to the carriage warmed with hot bricks. Once inside, Honore huddled in her fur-lined cloak. This was the first time she had been alone with Ashmoor since the night they caught the traitor, and her tongue suddenly wouldn't work. Ashmoor settled beside her, and he too said nothing. In silence, they watched Cavendish Square roll away while heading for London Bridge and the countryside beyond. Ashmoor's hand closed around hers, and still neither of them spoke. They glanced at one another, then quickly away.

Finally, Ashmoor turned to her and tilted up her chin. "What's wrong, my dear?"

"Nothing." Oh, the look in his eyes made her breathless. "That is, I am not certain I know how to be a countess."

"More than I know how to be an earl." He kissed her. "But I do know how to love you."

She closed her eyes and melted against him, expecting more caresses. But he was staring out of the window and all of a sudden reached up to knock on the roof. "Stop, coachman."

"Why? Whatever is wrong?"

"Nothing. There's a frost fair on the river."

"Is there?" Honore leaned toward the window and gazed with racing heart at the revelries spread out on the frozen Thames. She opened her mouth to ask if they could stop for just a moment, but closed it again.

"Have you ever danced on the ice?" Ashmoor asked close to her ear.

Honore shook her head. "I do not think countesses dance on the ice."

"Ha! Mine does." And he lifted her from the carriage.

Acknowledgments

These last three years have probably been the craziest years of my life. Thanks to the calls, emails, texts, and Facebook messages of a whole lot of supporters, I have come through them a stronger and, I hope, better person. The list is long, so I'll highlight a few especially special ones—Debbie Lynne with her little gifts, and Marylu, Louise, Ramona, and Patty with their prayers, advice, and willingness to set me straight with loving honesty. Deb K. and Pam M. for their warm welcome in Chicago; Pam B. at the Laredo Public Library; and all the staff of the Laredo Books-a-Million for their tremendous support of my books. Thank you, June and Billy, for your hospitality in Dallas.

I must not forget to mention my agent, Tamela Murray of the Steve Laube Agency, for calming my hysterics, and the patience and tact of my editors at Revell. Last but definitely not least, my husband, for getting me new cats when the others had to be left behind (in a good home) and putting up with frozen dinners way too often while I traveled and met deadlines.

Laurie Alice Eakes used to lie in bed as a child telling herself stories so she didn't wake anyone else up. Sometimes she shared her stories with others, so when she decided to be a writer, she surprised no one. *Family Guardian*, her first book, won the National Readers Choice Award for Best Regency in 2007. Since then, she has sold over a dozen books and novellas, six of them set in the Regency era, to publishers such as Revell, Zondervan, Barbour, and Harlequin Love Inspired.

Eight of her books have been picked up by Thorndike Press for large-print publication, and *Lady in the Mist*, her first book with Revell, was chosen for hardcover publication by Crossings Book Club.

Laurie Alice teaches online writing courses and enjoys a speaking ministry that takes her from the Gulf Coast to the East Coast. She has recently relocated to Houston, Texas, with her husband and pets and is learning how to live in a big city again.

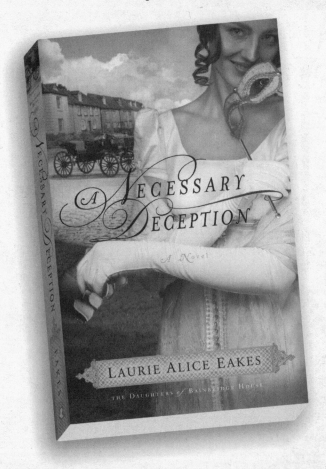

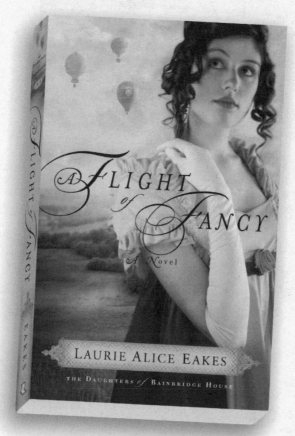

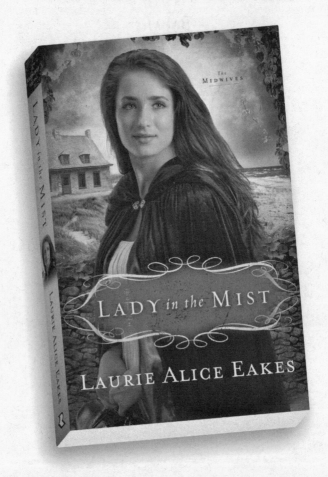

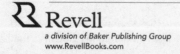

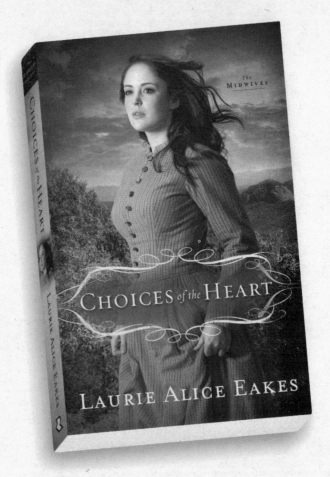